✓

COPY 2

Penzler, Otto   ed.
  Whodunit. Houdini. 13 tales of
magic, murder, mystery. Harper,
c1976.
  283p. 10.95

OCT   6 1976
FEB 1 7 1978

WHODUNIT? HOUDINI?

A JOAN KAHN BOOK

WHODUNIT? HOUDINI?

Thirteen Tales of Magic, Murder, Mystery

Edited by OTTO PENZLER

HARPER & ROW, PUBLISHERS

NEW YORK, HAGERSTOWN, SAN FRANCISCO

LONDON

Grateful acknowledgement is made for permission to reprint the following:

"From Another World" by Clayton Rawson. First published in *Ellery Queen's Mystery Magazine*. Copyright 1948 by Davis Publications, Inc. Reprinted by permission of Curtis Brown, Ltd.

"Rope Enough" from *Fancies and Goodnights* by John Collier. Reprinted by permission of A. D. Peters & Co. Ltd.

"The New Invisible Man" from *The Department of Queer Complaints* by Carter Dickson (John Dickson Carr). Copyright, 1940, William Morrow & Company, Inc.

"The Lord of Time" by Rafael Sabatini. First published in *Turbulent Tales*. Reprinted by permission of Brandt & Brandt.

(continued on following page)

FIRST EDITION

Designed by Sidney Feinberg

Library of Congress Cataloging in Publication Data
Main entry under title:

Whodunit? Houdini?
   CONTENTS: Rawson, C. From another world.—Kipling, R.
In the house of Suddhoo—Collier, J. Rope enough.
[etc.]
   1. Detective and mystery stories, English.
2. Detective and mystery stories, American.
I. Penzler, Otto.
PZ1.W608 [PR1309.D4]   823'.0872   76–6866
ISBN 0–06–013336–8

---

76 77 78 79 10 9 8 7 6 5 4 3 2 1

Contents

Introduction

Persian magi, from whom the word magician derives, were best known for their wisdom, for their ability to understand what baffled others. Most English Bibles translate magi to mean wise men, but the New English Bible more accurately translates it to mean astrologers.

Magic is a beautiful word. It encompasses everything from the delights of enchantment to the terrors of the black arts, from sorcery to legerdemain, from prestidigitation to fakirism, from trickery to necromancy. The feats of wizards, astrologers, conjurors, illusionists, witches and sorcerers have enthralled audiences from the beginning of human history. A vague connotation of evil surrounds all magicians. After all, they know and understand more than their audiences, and it is customary to distrust, and to fear, the things we don't understand.

Although a conjuror's trick may be nothing more than a carefully timed and practiced feat of sleight-of-hand, it *looks* like magic, so perhaps—just perhaps—there are forces at work about which we are better off not knowing. Today, it is easier for us to simply enjoy the art of the illusionist. He is usually on a stage, or on television, and his aim is clearly to entertain us. When we are amazed at the apparently impossible feats he performs, we can simply smile and murmur our stupefaction to the person next to us, and wonder how it was accomplished. We know that true magic has not been performed, merely the illusion of it.

In past centuries, these advantages were not provided to the magician's audience. The sudden appearance and disappearance of extremely concrete objects confused onlookers. They did not know how the white rabbit came to be in the magician's hat. Their only explanation for the apparent miracle came from the magician himself—and he said it was magic. If the illusionist was too adept, and his audience genuinely believed they had actually witnessed a magical act, he risked being burned as a minion of the devil.

We don't burn witches and warlocks and magicians today; we simply enjoy their performances. We don't believe their illusions are miracles; we know they are tricks. We don't believe conjurors have magical powers that were acquired form Dark Forces; we know they are merely well-rehearsed feats of legerdemain that we could probably learn ourselves if we took the time to do it.

And yet, do we really know these things, or do we just think we know them? Can we honestly be sure that no one has the ability to see the future, or communicate with the dead, or be guided by the juxtaposition of stars and planets, or cause inanimate objects to take the properties of animate ones? Many people claim to be able to do one or more of these magical acts, and still more believe those claims. Are Uri Geller and Jeanne Dixon simply entertainers, or are they the real magicians of today—the gifted who know things unknown to the rest of us?

The magicians in this book take many forms. In addition to such great stage illusionists as Norgil and the Great Merlini, there are those who practice chilling Black Magic, fakirs, and an actual historical figure believed by his contemporaries to have genuine powers that transcended those of ordinary mortals. There are even a few nonmagicians who use the tricks of the trade, if you'll pardon the expression, to help them solve crimes—or commit them.

Here, some of the world's greatest writers have entered the many worlds of magic: the bright, happy world of exciting stage shows, the darker world of crime and murder, and the velvet black world of unrelenting terror. Some of these thirteen tales deal with the question of whodunit. But, as with all magicians and magic acts, the deeper question is howdunit. Sometimes, the answer seems impossible. But don't look too hard. You might not want to know.

Otto Penzler

New York
February 1976

WHODUNIT? HOUDINI?

FROM ANOTHER WORLD

Clayton Rawson

Speak of the outstanding magicians in detective fiction and you must begin with the Great Merlini. Born around the turn of the century in a Barnum and Bailey circus car, he was obviously cut out for the performer's life. After four years as a carnival sideshow and circus magician, he established his own act and toured the world, retiring from the stage in 1939 to open a magic shop on Times Square. When the New York City Police Department was baffled by apparently impossible murders, Merlini often demonstrated that the illusionary techniques of stage magicians were used to commit crimes.

Clayton Rawson, the author of the Merlini stories, was one of America's foremost conjurors and a member of the Society of American Magicians.

For several years a friendly rivalry existed between Rawson and John Dickson Carr, each of whom was regarded as a master of solving "locked room" murders. Rawson concocted a situation in which a crime was committed under a set of circumstances that absolutely defied explanation and challenged Carr to invent a solution. Carr offered similar mental challenges to Rawson. These tours de force are chronicled in the pages of Ellery Queen's Mystery Magazine.

Rawson presented the problem in "From Another World" to Carr, who solved it and recorded his solution in a novel, He Wouldn't Kill Patience. *Rawson's solution is entirely different.*

"From Another World," the first short story ever written about the Great Merlini (there were four novels), was first published in the June 1948 issue of Ellery Queen's Mystery Magazine.

It was undoubtedly one of the world's strangest rooms. The old-fashioned rolltop desk, the battered typewriter, and the steel filing cabinet indicated that it was an office. There was even a calendar memo pad, a pen and pencil set, and an overflowing ashtray on the desk, but any resemblance to any other office stopped right there.

The desk top also held a pair of handcuffs, half a dozen billiard balls, a shiny nickel-plated revolver, one celluloid egg, several decks of playing cards, a bright green silk handkerchief, and a stack of unopened mail. In one corner of the room stood a large, galvanized-iron milk can with a strait jacket lying on its top. A feathered devil mask from the upper Congo leered down from the wall and the entire opposite wall was papered with a Ringling Bros. and Barnum & Bailey twenty-four sheet poster.

A loose-jointed dummy figure of a small boy with popeyes and violently red hair lay on the filing cabinet together with a skull and a fishbowl filled with paper flowers. And in the cabinet's bottom drawer, which was partly open and lined with paper, there was one half-eaten carrot and a twinkly-nosed, live white rabbit.

A pile of magazines, topped by a French journal, *l'Illusioniste,* was stacked precariously on a chair, and a large bookcase tried vainly to hold an even larger flood of books that overflowed and formed dusty stalagmites growing up from the floor—books whose authors would have been startled at the company they kept. Shaw's *Saint Joan* was sandwiched between Rowan's *Story of the Secret Service* and the *Memoirs of Robert Houdin.* Arthur Machen, Dr. Hans Gross, William Blake, Sir James Jeans, Rebecca West, Robert Louis Stevenson, and Ernest Hemingway were bounded on either side by Devol's *Forty Years a Gambler on the Mississippi* and Reginald Scot's *Discoverie of Witchcraft.*

The merchandise in the shop beyond the office had a similar surrealist quality, but the inscription on the glass of the outer door, although equally strange, did manage to supply an explanation. It read: *Miracles For Sale*—THE MAGIC SHOP, *A. Merlini, Prop.*

And that gentleman, naturally, was just as unusual as his place of business. For one thing, he hadn't put a foot in it, to my knowledge, in at least a week. When he finally did reappear, I found him at the desk sleepily and somewhat glumly eying the unopened mail.

He greeted me as though he hadn't seen another human being in at least a month, and the swivel chair creaked as he settled back in it, put his long legs up on the desk, and yawned. Then he indicated the card bearing his business slogan—NOTHING IS IM-POSSIBLE—which was tacked on the wall.

"I may have to take that sign down," he said lazily. "I've just met a theatrical producer, a scene designer, and a playwright all of whom are quite impossible. They came in here a week before opening night and asked me to supply several small items mentioned in the script. In one scene a character said 'Begone!' and the stage directions read: 'The genie and his six dancing girl slaves vanish instantly.' Later an elephant, complete with howdah and princess, disappeared the same way. I had to figure out how to manage all that and cook up a few assorted miracles for the big scene in heaven, too. Then I spent thirty-six hours in bed. And I'm still half asleep." He grinned wryly and added, "Ross, if you want anything that is not a stock item, you can whistle for it."

"I don't want a miracle," I said. "Just an interview. What do you know about ESP and PK?"

"Too much," he said. "You're doing another magazine article?"

"Yes. And I've spent the last week with a queer assortment of characters, too—half a dozen psychologists, some professional gamblers, a nuclear physicist, the secretary of the Psychical Research Society, and a neurologist. I've got an appointment in half an hour with a millionaire, and after that I want to hear what you think of it."

"You interviewed Dr. Rhine at Duke University, of course?"

I nodded. "Sure. He started it all. He says he's proved conclusively that there really are such things as telepathy, mind reading, clairvoyance, X-ray vision, and probably crystal gazing as well. He wraps it all up in one package and calls it ESP—meaning extrasensory perception."

"That," Merlini said, "is not the half of it. His psychokinesis, or PK for short, is positively miraculous—and frightening." The magician pulled several issues of the *Journal of Parapsychology* from the stack of magazines and upset the whole pile. "If the conclusions Rhine has published here are correct—if there really is a tangible mental force that can not only reach out and influence the movements of dice but exert its mysterious control over other physical objects as well—then he has completely upset the apple cart of modern psychology and punctured a whole library of general scientific theory as well."

"He's already upset me," I said. "I tried to use PK in a crap game Saturday night. I lost sixty-eight bucks."

My skepticism didn't disturb Merlini. He went right on, gloomier than ever. "If Rhine is right, his ESP and PK have reopened the Pandora's box in which science thought it had forever sealed voodoo and witchcraft and enough other practices of primitive magic to make your hair stand on end. And *you're* growling about losing a few dollars—"

Behind me a hearty, familiar voice said, "I haven't got anything to worry about except a homicidal maniac who has killed three people in the last two days and left absolutely no clues. But can I come in?"

Inspector Homer Gavigan of the New York City Police Department stood in the doorway, his blue eyes twinkling frostily.

Merlini, liking the Cassandra role he was playing, said, "Sure. I've been waiting for you. But don't think that PK won't give you a splitting headache, too. All a murderer would have to do to commit the perfect crime—and a locked room one at that—would be to exert his psychokinetic mental force from a distance against the gun trigger." He pointed at the revolver on the desk. "Like this—"

Gavigan and I both saw the trigger, with no finger on it, move. *Bang!*

The gun's report was like a thunderclap in the small room. I knew well enough that it was only a stage prop and the cartridge a blank, but I jumped a foot. So did Gavigan.

"Look, dammit!" the inspector exploded, "how did you—"

The Great Merlini grinned. He was fully awake now and enjoying himself hugely. "No," he said, "that wasn't PK, luckily. Just ordinary run-of-the-mill conjuring. The Rising Cards and the Talking Skull are both sometimes operated the same way. You can have the secret at the usual catalogue price of—"

Like most policemen Gavigan had a healthy respect for firearms and he was still jumpy. "I don't want to buy either of them," he growled. "Do we have a date for dinner—or don't we? I'm starved."

"We do," Merlini said, pulling his long, lean self up out of the chair and reaching for his coat. "Can you join us, Ross?"

I shook my head. "Not this time. I've got a date just now with Andrew Drake."

In the elevator Merlini gave me an odd look and asked, "Andrew Drake? What has he got to do with ESP and PK?"

"What doesn't he have something to do with?" I replied. "Six months ago it was the Drake Plan to Outlaw War; he tried to take over the U.N. single-handed. Two months ago he announced he was setting up a $15-million research foundation to find a cancer cure in six months. 'Polish it off like we did the atom bomb,' he says. 'Put in enough money, and you can accomplish anything.' Now he's head over heels in ESP with some Yoga mixed in. 'Unleash the power of the human mind and solve all our problems.' Just like that."

"So that's what he's up to," Merlini said as we came out on to Forty-second Street, a block from Times Square, to face a bitterly cold January wind. "I wondered."

Then, as he followed Gavigan into the official car that waited and left me shivering on the curb, he threw a last cryptic sentence over his shoulder.

"When Drake mentions Rosa Rhys," he said, "you might warn him that he's heading for trouble."

Merlini didn't know how right he was. If any of us had had any clairvoyant ability at all, I wouldn't have taken a cab up to Drake's; all three of us would have gone—in Gavigan's car and with the siren going full blast.

As it was, I stepped out all alone in front of the big Ninety-eighth Street house just off Riverside Drive. It was a sixty-year-old mansion built in the tortured style that had been the height of architectural fashion in the 1880's but was now a smoke-blackened monstrosity as coldly depressing as the weather.

I nearly froze both ears just getting across the pavement and up the steps, where I found a doctor with his finger glued—or frozen perhaps—to the bell push. A doctor? No, it wasn't ESP; a copy of the *AMA Journal* stuck out of his overcoat pocket, and his left hand carried the customary small black case. But he didn't have the medical man's usual clinical detachment. This doctor was jumpy as hell.

When I asked, "Anything wrong?" his head jerked around, and his pale blue eyes gave me a startled look. He was a thin, well-dressed man in his early forties.

"Yes," he said crisply. "I'm afraid so." He jabbed a long fore-finger at the bell again just as the door opened.

At first I didn't recognize the girl who looked out at us. When I had seen her by daylight earlier in the week, I had tagged her as in the brainy-but-a-bit-plain category, a judgment I revised somewhat now, considering what the Charles hair-do and Hattie Carnegie dress did for her.

"Oh, hello, doctor," she said. "Come in."

The doctor began talking even before he crossed the threshold. "Your father, Elinor—is he still in the study?"

"Yes, I think so. But what—"

She stopped because he was already gone, running down the hall toward a door at its end. He rattled the doorknob, then rapped loudly.

"Mr. Drake! Let me in!"

The girl looked puzzled, then frightened. Her dark eyes met mine for an instant, and then her high heels clicked on the pol-ished floor as she too ran down the hall. I didn't wait to be invited. I followed.

The doctor's knuckles rapped again on the door. "Miss Rhys!" he called. "It's Dr. Garrett. Unlock the door!"

There was no answer.

Garrett tried the doorknob once more, then threw his shoulder against the door. It didn't move.

"Elinor, do you have a key? We must get in there—quickly!"

She said, "No. Father has the only keys. Why don't they answer? What's wrong?"

"I don't know," Garrett said. "Your father phoned me just now. He was in pain. He said, *'Hurry! I need you. I'm'* "— the doctor hesitated, watching the girl; then he finished " '—*dying.'* After that—no answer." Garrett turned to me. "You've got more weight than I have. Think you can break this door in?"

I looked at it. The door seemed solid enough, but it was an old house and the wood around the screws that held the lock might give. "I don't know," I said. "I'll try."

Elinor Drake moved to one side and the doctor stepped behind me. I threw myself against the door twice and the second time felt it move a bit. Then I hit it hard. Just as the door gave way I heard the tearing sound of paper.

But before I could discover what caused that, my attention was held by more urgent matters. I found myself staring at a green-shaded desk lamp, the room's only source of light, at the over-turned phone on the desk top, and at the sprawled shape that lay on the floor in front of the desk. A coppery highlight glinted on a letter opener near the man's feet. Its blade was discolored with a dark wet stain.

Dr. Garrett said, "Elinor, you stay out," as he moved past me to the body and bent over it. One of his hands lifted Andrew Drake's right eyelid, the other felt his wrist.

I have never heard a ghost speak but the sound that came then was exactly what I would expect—a low, quivering moan shot with pain. I jerked around and saw a glimmer of white move in the darkness on my left.

Behind me, Elinor's whisper, a tense thread of sound, said, "Lights," as she clicked the switch by the door. The glow from the ceiling fixture overhead banished both the darkness and the specter—but what remained was almost as unlikely. A chair lay overturned on the carpet, next to a small table that stood in the center of the room. In a second chair, slumped forward with her head resting on the tabletop, was the body of a woman.

She was young, dark-haired, rather good-looking, and had an excellent figure. This latter fact was instantly apparent because— and I had to look twice before I could believe what I saw—she wore a brief, skin-tight, one-piece bathing suit. Nothing else.

Elinor's eyes were still on the sprawled shape on the floor. "Father. He's—dead?"

Garrett nodded slowly and stood up.

I heard the quick intake of her breath but she made no other sound. Then Garrett strode quickly across to the woman at the table.

"Unconscious," he said after a moment. "Apparently a blow on the head—but she's beginning to come out of it." He looked again at the knife on the floor. "We'll have to call the police."

I hardly heard him. I was wondering why the room was so bare. The hall outside and the living room that opened off it were furnished with the stiff, formal ostentation of the overly rich. But Drake's study, by contrast, was as sparsely furnished as a cell in a Trappist monastery. Except for the desk, the small table, the two chairs, and a three-leaf folding screen that stood in one corner, it contained no other furniture. There were no pictures on the walls, no papers, and although there were shelves for them, no books. There wasn't even a blotter or pen on the desk top. Nothing but the phone, desk lamp and, strangely enough, a roll of gummed paper tape.

But I only glanced at these things briefly. It was the large case-ment window in the wall behind the desk that held my attention —a dark rectangle beyond which, like a scattered handful of bright jewels, were the lights of New Jersey and, above them, frosty pinpoints of stars shining coldly in a black sky.

The odd thing was that the window's center line, where its two halves joined, was criss-crossed by two-foot strips of brown paper tape pasted to the glass. The window was, quite literally, sealed shut. It was then that I remembered the sound of tearing paper as the lock had given way and the door had come open.

I turned. Elinor still stood there—motionless. And on the inside of the door and on the jamb were more of the paper strips. Four were torn in half, two others had been pulled loose from the wall and hung curled from the door's edge.

At that moment a brisk, energetic voice came from the hall. "How come you leave the front door standing wide open on the coldest day in—"

Elinor turned to face a broad-shouldered young man with wavy hair, hand-painted tie, and a completely self-assured manner. She said, "Paul!" then took one stumbling step and was in his arms.

He blinked at her. "Hey! What's wrong?" Then he saw what lay on the floor by the desk. His self-confidence sagged.

Dr. Garrett moved to the door. "Kendrick," he said, "take Eli-nor out of here. I'll—"

"No!" It was Elinor's voice. She straightened up, turned sud-denly and started into the room.

But Paul caught her. "Where are you going?"

She tried to pull away from him. "I'm going to phone the police." Her eyes followed the trail of bloodstains that led from the body across the beige carpet to the overturned chair and the woman at the table. "She—killed him."

That was when I started for the phone myself. But I hadn't taken more than two steps when the woman in the bathing suit let out a hair-raising shriek.

She was gripping the table with both hands, her eyes fixed on Drake's body with the rigid unblinking stare of a figure carved from stone. Then, suddenly, her body trembled all over, and she opened her mouth again— But Garrett got there first.

He slapped her on the side of the face—hard.

It stopped the scream, but the horror still filled her round dark eyes and she still stared at the body as though it were some demon straight from hell.

"Hysteria," Garrett said. Then seeing me start again toward the phone, "Get an ambulance, too." And when he spoke to Paul Kendrick this time, it was an order. "And get Elinor out of here —quickly!"

Elinor Drake was looking at the girl in the bathing suit with wide, puzzled eyes. "She—she killed him. Why?"

Paul nodded. He turned Elinor around gently but swiftly and led her out.

The cops usually find too many fingerprints on a phone, none of them any good because they are superimposed on each other. But I handled the receiver carefully just the same, picking it up by one end. When headquarters answered, I gave the operator the facts fast, then asked him to locate Inspector Gavigan and have him call me back. I gave Drake's number.

As I talked I watched Dr. Garrett open his black case and take out a hypodermic syringe. He started to apply it to the woman's arm just as I hung up.

"What's that, doc?" I asked.

"Sedative. Otherwise she'll be screaming again in a minute."

The girl didn't seem to feel the needle as it went in.

Then, noticing two bright spots of color on the table, I went across to examine them closely and felt more than ever as though I had stepped straight into a surrealist painting. I was looking at two rounded conical shapes each about two inches in length. Both were striped like candy canes, one in maroon against a white background, the other in thinner brilliant red stripes against an opalescent amber.

"Did Drake," I asked, "collect seashells, too?"

"No." Garrett scowled in a worried way at the shells. "But I once did. These are mollusks, but not from the sea. *Cochlostyla*, a tree snail. Habitat: the Philippines." He turned his scowl from the shells to me. "By the way, just who are you?"

"The name is Ross Harte." I added that I had had an appointment to interview Drake for a magazine article and then asked, "Why is this room sealed as it is? Why is this girl dressed only in—"

Apparently, like many medical men, Garrett took a dim view of reporters. "I'll make my statement," he said a bit stiffly, "to the police."

They arrived a moment later. Two uniformed prowl-car cops first, then the precinct boys and after that, at intervals, the homicide squad, an ambulance intern, a fingerprint man and photographer, the medical examiner, an assistant D.A. and later, because a millionaire rates more attention than the victim of a Harlem stabbing, the D.A. himself, and an assistant chief inspector even looked in for a few minutes.

Of the earlier arrivals the only familiar face was that of the Homicide Squad's Lieutenant Doran—a hard-boiled, coldly efficient, no-nonsense cop who had so little use for reporters that I suspected he had once been bitten by one.

At Dr. Garrett's suggestion, which the intern seconded, the girl in the bathing suit was taken, under guard, to the nearest hospital. Then Garrett and I were put on ice, also under guard, in the living room. Another detective ushered Paul Kendrick into the room a moment later.

He scowled at Dr. Garrett. "We all thought Rosa Rhys was bad medicine. But I never expected anything like this. Why would *she* want to kill him? It doesn't make sense."

"Self-defense?" I suggested. "Could he have made a pass at her and—"

Kendrick shook his head emphatically. "Not that gal. She was making a fast play for the old man—and his money. A pass would have been just what she wanted." He turned to Garrett. "What were they doing in there—more ESP experiments?"

The doctor laid his overcoat neatly over the back of an ornate Spanish chair. His voice sounded tired and defeated. "No. They had gone beyond that. I told him that she was a fraud, but you know how Drake was—always so absolutely confident that he couldn't be wrong about anything. He said he'd put her through a test that would convince all of us."

"Of what?" I asked. "What was it she claimed she could do?"

The detective at the door moved forward. "My orders," he said, "are that you're not to talk about what happened until after the lieutenant has taken your statements. Make it easy for me, will you?"

That made it difficult for us. Any other conversational subject just then seemed pointless. We sat there silent and uncomfortable. But somehow the nervous tension that had been in our voices was still there—a foreboding, ghostly presence waiting with us for what was to happen next.

A half hour later, although it seemed many times that long, Garrett was taken out for questioning, then Kendrick. And later I got the nod. I saw Elinor Drake, a small, lonely figure in the big hall, moving slowly up the wide stairs. Doran and the police stenographer who waited for me in the stately dining room with its heavy crystal chandelier looked out of place. But the lieutenant didn't feel ill at ease; his questions were as coldly efficient as a surgeon's knife.

I tried to insert a query of my own now and then, but soon gave that up. Doran ignored all such attempts as completely as if they didn't exist. Then, just as he dismissed me, the phone rang. Doran answered, listened, scowled and then held the receiver out to me. "For you," he said.

I heard Merlini's voice. "My ESP isn't working so well today, Ross. Drake is dead. I get that much. But just what happened up there, anyway?"

"ESP my eye," I told him. "If you were a mind reader you'd have been up here long ago. It's a sealed room—in spades. The sealed room to end all sealed rooms."

I saw Doran start forward as if to object. "Merlini," I said quickly, "is Inspector Gavigan still with you?" I lifted the receiver from my ear and let Doran hear the "Yes" that came back.

Merlini's voice went on. "Did you say sealed room? The flash from headquarters didn't mention that. They said an arrest had already been made. It sounded like a routine case."

"Headquarters," I replied, "has no imagination. Or else Doran has been keeping things from them. It isn't even a routine sealed room. Listen. A woman comes to Drake's house on the coldest January day since 1812 dressed only in a bathing suit. She goes with him into his study. They seal the window and door on the inside with gummed paper tape. Then she stabs him with a paper knife. Before he dies, he knocks her out, then manages to get to the phone and send out an SOS.

"She's obviously crazy; she has to be to commit murder under those circumstances. But Drake wasn't crazy. A bit eccentric maybe, but not nuts. So why would he lock himself in so carefully with a homicidal maniac? If headquarters thinks that's routine I'll—" Then I interrupted myself. There was too much silence on the other end of the wire. "Merlini! Are you still there?"

"Yes," his voice said slowly, "I'm still here. Headquarters was much too brief. They didn't tell us her name. But I know it now."

Then, abruptly, I felt as if I had stepped off into some fourth-dimensional hole in space and had dropped on to some other nightmare planet.

Merlini's voice, completely serious, was saying, "Ross, did the police find a silver denarius from the time of the Caesars in that room? Or a freshly picked rose, a string of Buddhist prayer beads, perhaps a bit of damp seaweed?"

I didn't say anything. I couldn't.

After a moment, Merlini added, "So—they did. What was it?"

"Shells," I said dazedly, still quite unconvinced that any conversation could sound like this. "Philippine tree snail shells. Why, in the name of—"

Merlini cut in hastily. "Tell Doran that Gavigan and I will be there in ten minutes. Sit tight and keep your eyes open."

"Merlini!" I objected frantically; "if you hang up without—"

"The shells explain the bathing suit, Ross, and make it clear why the room was sealed. But they also introduce an element that

Gavigan and Doran and the D.A. and the commissioner are not going to like at all. I don't like it myself. It's even more frightening as a murder method than PK."

He hesitated a moment, then let me have both barrels.

"Those shells suggest that Drake's death might have been caused by even stranger forces—evil and evanescent ones—from another world!"

My acquaintance with a police inspector cut no ice with Doran; he ordered me right back into the living room.

I heard a siren announce the arrival of Gavigan's car shortly after, but it was a long hour later before Doran came in and said, "The inspector wants to see all of you—in the study."

As I moved with the others out into the hall I saw Merlini waiting for me.

"It's about time," I growled at him. "Another ten minutes and you'd have found me DOA, too—from suspense."

"Sorry you had to cool your heels," he said, "but Gavigan is being difficult. As predicted, he doesn't like the earful Doran has been giving him. Neither do I." The dryly ironic good humor that was almost always in his voice was absent. He was unusually sober.

"Don't build it up," I said. "I've had all the mystery I can stand. Just give me answers. First, why did you tell me to warn Drake about Rosa Rhys?"

"I didn't expect murder, if that's what you're thinking," he replied. "Drake was elaborating on some of Rhine's original experiments aimed at discovering whether ESP operates more efficiently when the subject is in a trance state. Rosa is a medium."

"Oh, so that's it. She and Drake were holding a séance?"

Merlini nodded. "Yes. The Psychical Research Society is extremely interested in ESP and PK. It's given them a new lease on life. And I knew they had recommended Rosa, whom they had previously investigated, to Drake."

"And what about the Roman coins, roses, Buddhist prayer beads —and snail shells? Why the bathing suit and how does that explain why the room was sealed?"

But Doran, holding the study door open, interrupted before he could reply.

"Hurry it up!" he ordered.

Going into that room now was like walking on to a brightly lighted stage. A powerful electric bulb of almost floodlight brilliance had been inserted in the ceiling fixture and its harsh white glare made the room more barren and cell-like than ever. Even Inspector Gavigan seemed to have taken on a menacing air. Perhaps it was the black mask of shadow that his hat brim threw down across the upper part of his face; or it may have been the carefully intent way he watched us as we came in.

Doran did the introductions. "Miss Drake, Miss Potter, Paul Kendrick, Dr. Walter Garrett."

I looked at the middle-aged woman whose gayly frilled, altogether feminine hat contrasted oddly with her angular figure, her prim determined mouth, and the chilly glance of complete disapproval with which she regarded Gavigan.

"How," I whispered to Merlini, "did Isabelle Potter, the secretary of the Psychical Research Society, get here?"

"She came with Rosa," he answered. "The police found her upstairs reading a copy of Tyrrell's *Study of Apparitions.*" Merlini smiled faintly. "She and Doran don't get along."

"They wouldn't," I said. "They talk different languages. When I interviewed her, I got a travelogue on the other world—complete with lantern slides."

Inspector Gavigan wasted no time. "Miss Drake," he began, "I understand the medical foundation for cancer research your father thought of endowing was originally your idea."

The girl glanced once at the stains on the carpet, then kept her dark eyes steadily on Gavigan. "Yes," she said slowly, "it was."

"Are you interested in psychical research?"

Elinor frowned. "No."

"Did you object when your father began holding séances with Miss Rhys?"

She shook her head. "That would only have made him more determined."

Gavigan turned to Kendrick. "Did you?"

"Me?" Paul lifted his brows. "I didn't know him well enough for that. Don't think he liked me much, anyway. But why a man like Drake would waste his time—"

"And you, doctor?"

"Did I object?" Garrett seemed surprised. "Naturally. No one but a neurotic middle-aged woman would take a séance seriously."

Miss Potter resented that one. "Dr. Garrett," she said icily, "Sir Oliver Lodge was not a neurotic woman, nor Sir William Crookes, nor Professor Zoëllner, nor—"

"But they were all senile," Garrett replied just as icily. "And as for ESP, no neurologist of any standing admits any such possibility. They leave such things to you and your society, Miss Potter—and to the Sunday supplements."

She gave the doctor a look that would have split an atom, and Gavigan, seeing the danger of a chain reaction if this sort of dialogue were allowed to continue, broke in quickly.

"Miss Potter. You introduced Miss Rhys to Mr. Drake and he was conducting ESP experiments with her. Is that correct?"

Miss Potter's voice was still dangerously radioactive. "It is. And their results were most gratifying and important. Of course, neither you nor Dr. Garrett would understand—"

"And then," Garrett cut in, "they both led him on into an investigation of Miss Rhys's psychic specialty—apports." He pronounced the last word with extreme distaste.

Inspector Gavigan scowled, glanced at Merlini, and the latter promptly produced a definition. "An apport," he said, "from the French *apporter,* to bring, is any physical object supernormally brought into a séance room—from nowhere usually or from some impossible distance. Miss Rhys on previous occasions, according to the Psychical Society's *Journal,* has apported such objects as Roman coins, roses, beads, and seaweed."

"She is the greatest apport medium," Miss Potter declared somewhat belligerently, "since Charles Bailey."

"Then she's good," Merlini said. "Bailey was an apport medium whom Conan Doyle considered bona fide. He produced birds, Oriental plants, small animals, and on one occasion a young shark eighteen inches long which he claimed his spirit guide had whisked instantly via the astral plane from the Indian Ocean and projected, still damp and very much alive, into the séance room."

"So," I said, "that's why this room was sealed. To make absolutely certain that no one could open the door or window in the dark and help Rosa by introducing—"

"Of course," Garrett added. "Obviously there could be no apports if adequate precautions were taken. Drake also moved a lot of his things out of the study and inventoried every object that remained. He also suggested, since I was so skeptical, that I be the one to make certain that Miss Rhys carried nothing into the room on her person. I gave her a most complete physical examination —in a bedroom upstairs. Then she put on one of Miss Drake's bathing suits."

"Did you come down to the study with her and Drake?" Gavigan asked.

The doctor frowned. "No. I had objected to Miss Potter's presence at the séance and Miss Rhys countered by objecting to mine."

"She was quite right," Miss Potter said. "The presence of an unbeliever like yourself would prevent even the strongest psychic forces from making themselves manifest."

"I have no doubt of that," Garrett replied stiffly. "It's the usual excuse, as I told Drake. He tried to get her to let me attend but she refused flatly. So I went back to my office down the street. Drake's phone call came a half hour or so later."

"And yet"—Gavigan eyed the two brightly colored shells on the table—"in spite of all your precautions she produced two of these."

Garrett nodded. "Yes, I know. But the answer is fairly obvious now. She hid them somewhere in the hall outside on her arrival and then secretly picked them up again on her way in here."

Elinor frowned. "I'm afraid not, doctor. Father thought of that and asked me to go down with them to the study. He held one of her hands and I held the other."

Gavigan scowled. Miss Potter beamed.

"Did you go in with them?" Merlini asked.

She shook her head. "No. Only as far as the door. They went in and I heard it lock behind them. I stood there for a moment or two and heard Father begin pasting the tape on the door. Then I went back to my room to dress. I was expecting Paul."

Inspector Gavigan turned to Miss Potter. "You remained upstairs?"

"Yes," she replied in a tone that dared him to deny it. "I did."

Gavigan looked at Elinor. "Paul said a moment ago that your father didn't like him. Why not?"

"Paul exaggerates," the girl said quickly. "Father didn't dislike him. He was just—well, a bit difficult where my men friends were concerned."

"He thought they were all after his money," Kendrick added. "But at the rate he was endowing medical foundations and psychic societies—"

Miss Potter objected. "Mr. Drake did *not* endow the Psychical Society."

"But he was seriously considering it," Garrett said. "Miss Rhys —and Miss Potter—were selling him on the theory that illness is only a mental state due to a psychic imbalance, whatever that is."

"They won't sell me on that," Elinor said, and then turned suddenly on Miss Potter, her voice trembling. "If it weren't for you and your idiotic foolishness Father wouldn't have been—killed." Then to Gavigan, "We've told all this before, to the lieutenant. Is it quite necessary—"

The inspector glanced at Merlini, then said, "I think that will be all for now. Okay, Doran, take them back. But none of them are to leave yet."

When they had gone, he turned to Merlini. "Well, I asked the questions you wanted me to, but I still think it was a waste of time. Rosa Rhys killed Drake. Anything else is impossible."

"What about Kendrick's cabdriver?" Merlini asked. "Did your men locate him yet?"

Gavigan's scowl, practically standard operating procedure by now, grew darker. "Yes. Kendrick's definitely out. He entered the cab on the other side of town at just about the time Drake was sealing this room and he was apparently still in it, crossing Central Park, at the time Drake was killed."

"So," I commented, "he's the only one with an alibi."

Gavigan lifted his eyebrows. "The only one? Except for Rosa Rhys they *all* have alibis. The sealed room takes care of that."

"Yes," Merlini said quietly, "but the people with alibis also have motives while the one person who could have killed Drake has none."

"She did it," the inspector answered. "So she's got a motive, and we'll find it."

"I wish I were as confident of that as you are," Merlini said. "Under the circumstances you'll be able to get a conviction without showing motive, but if you don't find one, it will always bother you."

"Maybe," Gavigan admitted, "but that won't be as bad as trying to believe what she says happened in this room."

That was news to me. "You've talked to Rosa?" I asked.

"One of the boys did," Gavigan said sourly. "At the hospital. She's already preparing an insanity defense."

"But why," Merlini asked, "is she still hysterical with fright? Could it be that she's scared because she really believes her story —because something like that really did happen in here?"

"Look," I said impatiently, "is it top secret or will somebody tell me what she says happened?"

Gavigan glowered at Merlini. "Are you going to stand there and tell me that you think Rosa Rhys actually believes—"

It was my question that Merlini answered. He walked to the table in the center of the room. "She says that after Drake sealed the window and door, the lights were turned off and she and Drake sat opposite each other at this table. His back was toward the desk, hers toward that screen in the corner. Drake held her hands. They waited. Finally she felt the psychic forces gathering around her—and then, out of nowhere, the two shells dropped onto the table one after the other. Drake got up, turned on the desk light, and came back to the table. A moment later it happened."

The magician paused for a moment, regarding the bare, empty room with a frown. "Drake," he continued, "was examining the shells, quite excited and pleased about their appearance when suddenly, Rosa says, she heard a movement behind her. She saw Drake look up and then stare incredulously over her shoulder." Merlini spread his hands. "And that's all she remembers. Something hit her. When she came to, she found herself staring at the blood on the floor and at Drake's body."

Gavigan was apparently remembering Merlini's demonstration with the gun in his office. "If you," he warned acidly, "so much as try to hint that one of the people outside this room projected some mental force that knocked Rosa out and then caused the knife to stab Drake—"

"You know," Merlini said, "I half expected Miss Potter would suggest that. But her theory is even more disturbing." He looked at me. "She says that the benign spirits which Rosa usually evoked were overcome by some malign and evil entity whose astral substance materialized momentarily, killed Drake, then returned to the other world from which it came."

"She's a mental case, too," Gavigan said disgustedly. "They have to be crazy if they expect anyone to believe any such—"

"That," Merlini said quietly, "may be another reason Rosa is scared to death. Perhaps she believes it but knows you won't. In her shoes, I'd be scared, too." He frowned. "The difficulty is the knife."

Gavigan blinked. "The knife? What's difficult about that?"

"If I killed Drake," Merlini replied, "and wanted appearances to suggest that psychic forces were responsible, you wouldn't have found a weapon in this room that made it look as if I were guilty. I would have done a little de-apporting and made it disappear. As it is now, even if the knife was propelled supernaturally, Rosa takes the rap."

"And how," Gavigan demanded, "would you make the knife disappear if you were dressed, as she was, in practically nothing?" Then, with sudden suspicion, he added, "Are you suggesting that there's a way she could have done that—and that you think she's not guilty because she didn't?"

Merlini lifted one of the shells from the table and placed it in the center of his left palm. His right hand covered it for a brief moment, then moved away. The shell was no longer there; it had vanished as silently and as easily as a ghost. Merlini turned both hands palms outward; both were unmistakably empty.

"Yes," he said, "she could have made the knife disappear, if she had wanted to. The same way she produced the two shells." He made a reaching gesture with his right hand and the missing shell reappeared suddenly at his fingertips.

Gavigan looked annoyed and relieved at the same time. "So," he said, "you do know how she got those shells in here. I want to hear it. Right now."

But Gavigan had to wait.

At that moment a torpedo hit the water-tight circumstantial case against Rosa Rhys and detonated with a roar.

Doran, who had answered the phone a moment before, was swearing profusely. He was staring at the receiver he held as though it were a live cobra he had picked up by mistake.

"It—it's Doc Hess," he said in a dazed tone. "He just started the autopsy and thought we'd like to know that the point of the murder knife struck a rib and broke off. He just dug out a triangular pointed piece of—steel."

For several seconds after that there wasn't a sound. Then Merlini spoke.

"Gentlemen of the jury. Exhibit A, the paper knife with which my esteemed opponent, the district attorney, claims Rosa Rhys stabbed Andrew Drake, is a copper alloy—and its point, as you can see, is quite intact. The defense rests."

Doran swore again. "Drake's inventory lists that letter opener, but that's all. There is no other knife in this room. I'm positive of that."

Gavigan jabbed a thick forefinger at me. "Ross, Dr. Garrett was in here before the police arrived. And Miss Drake and Kendrick."

I shook my head. "Sorry. There was no knife near the door and neither Elinor nor Paul came more than a foot into the room. Dr. Garrett examined Drake and Rosa, but I was watching him, and I'll testify that unless he's as expert at sleight of hand as Merlini, he didn't pick up a thing."

Doran was not convinced. "Look, buddy. Unless Doc Hess has gone crazy too, there was a knife and it's not here now. So somebody took it out." He turned to the detective who stood at the door. "Tom," he said, "have the boys frisk all those people. Get a policewoman for Miss Drake and Potter and search the bedroom where they've been waiting. The living room, too."

Then I had a brainstorm. "You know," I said, "if Elinor is covering up for someone—if three people came in here for the séance instead of two as she says—the third could have killed Drake and then gone out, with the knife. And the paper tape could have been —" I stopped.

"—pasted on the door *after* the murderer left?" Merlini finished. "By Rosa? That would mean she framed herself."

"Besides," Gavigan growled, "the boys fumed all those paper strips. There are fingerprints all over them. All Drake's."

Merlini said, "Doran, I suggest that you phone the hospital and have Rosa searched, too."

The lieutenant blinked. "But she was practically naked. How in blazes could she carry a knife out of here unnoticed?"

Gavigan faced Merlini, scowling. "What did you mean when you said a moment ago that she could have got rid of the knife the same way she produced those shells?"

"If it was a clasp knife," Merlini explained, "she could have used the same method other apport mediums have employed to conceal small objects under test conditions."

"But dammit!" Doran exploded. "The only place Garrett didn't look was in her stomach!"

Merlini grinned. "I know. That was his error. Rosa is a regurgitating medium, like Helen Duncan, in whose stomach the English investigator, Harry Price, found a hidden ghost—a balled-up length of cheesecloth fastened with a safety pin which showed up when he X-rayed her. X-rays of Rosa seem indicated, too. And search her hospital room and the ambulance that took her over."

"Okay, Doran," Gavigan ordered. "Do it."

I saw an objection. "Now *you've* got Rosa framing herself, too," I said. "If she swallowed the murder knife, why should she put blood on the letter opener? That makes no sense at all."

"None of this does," Gavigan complained.

"I know," Merlini answered. "One knife was bad. Two are much worse. And although X-rays of Rosa before the séance would have shown shells, I predict they won't show a knife. If they do, then Rosa needs a psychiatric examination as well."

"Don't worry," Gavigan said gloomily. "She'll get one. Her attorney will see to that. And they'll prove she's crazier than a bedbug without half trying. But if that knife isn't in her—" His voice died.

"Then you'll never convict her," Merlini finished.

"If that happens," the inspector said ominously, "you're going to have to explain where that knife came from, how it really disappeared, and where it is now."

Merlini's view was even gloomier. "It'll be much worse than that. We'll also have an appearing and vanishing murderer to explain: someone who entered a sealed room, killed Drake, put blood on the paper knife to incriminate Rosa, then vanished just as neatly as any of Miss Potter's ghosts—into thin air."

And Merlini's prediction came true.

The X-ray plates didn't show the slightest trace of a knife. And it wasn't in Rosa's hospital room or in the ambulance. Nor on Garrett, Paul, Elinor Drake, Isabelle Potter, nor, as Doran discovered, on myself. The Drake house was a mess by the time the boys got through taking it apart—but no knife with a broken point was found anywhere. And it was shown beyond doubt that there were no trapdoors or sliding panels in the study; the door and window were the only exits.

Inspector Gavigan glowered every time the phone rang. The commissioner had already phoned twice and without mincing words expressed his dissatisfaction with the way things were going.

And Merlini, stretched out in Drake's chair, his heels up on the desk top, his eyes closed, seemed to have gone into a trance.

"Blast it!" Gavigan said. "Rosa Rhys got that knife out of here somehow. She had to! Merlini, are you going to admit that she knows a trick or two you don't?"

The magician didn't answer for a moment. Then he opened one eye. "No," he said slowly, "not just yet." He took his feet off the desk and sat up straight. "You know," he said, "if we don't accept the theory of the murderer from beyond, then Ross must be right after all. Elinor Drake's statement to the contrary, there must have been a third person in this room when that séance began."

"Okay," Gavigan said, "we'll forget Miss Drake's testimony for the moment. At least that gets him into the room. Then what?"

"I don't know," Merlini said. He took the roll of gummed paper tape from the desk, tore off a two-foot length, crossed the room, and pasted it across the door and jamb, sealing us in. "Suppose I'm the killer," he said. "I knock Rosa out first, then stab Drake—"

He paused.

Gavigan was not enthusiastic. "You put the murder knife in your pocket, not noticing that the point is broken. You put blood on the paper knife to incriminate Rosa. And then—" He waited. "Well, go on."

"Then," Merlini said, "I get out of here." He scowled at the sealed door and at the window. "I've escaped from handcuffs, strait jackets, milk cans filled with water, packing cases that have been nailed shut. I know the methods Houdini used to break out of safes and jail cells. But I feel like he did when a shrewd old turnkey shut him in a cell in Scotland one time and the lock—a type he'd overcome many times before—failed to budge. No matter how he tried or what he did, the bolt wouldn't move. He was sweating blood because he knew that if he failed, his laboriously built-up reputation as the escape king would be blown to bits. And then—" Merlini blinked. "And then—" This time he came to a full stop, staring at the door.

Suddenly he blinked. "Shades of Hermann, Kellar, Thurston— and Houdini! So that's it!"

Grinning broadly, he turned to Gavigan. "We will now pass a miracle and chase all the ghosts back into their tombs. If you'll get those people in here—"

"You know how the vanishing man vanished?" I asked.

"Yes. It's someone who has been just as canny as that Scotch jailer, and I know who."

Gavigan said, "It's about time." Then he walked across the room and pulled the door open, tearing the paper strip in half as he did so.

Merlini, watching him, grinned again. "The method by which magicians let their audiences fool themselves—the simplest and yet most effective principle of deception in the whole book—and it nearly took me in!"

Elinor Drake's eyes still avoided the stains on the floor. Paul, beside her, puffed nervously on a cigarette, and Dr. Garrett looked drawn and tired. But not the irrepressible Potter. She seemed fresh as a daisy.

"This room," she said to no one in particular, "will become more famous in psychic annals than the home of the Fox sisters at Lily-dale."

Quickly, before she could elaborate on that, Merlini cut in. "Miss Potter doesn't believe that Rosa Rhys killed Drake. Neither do I. But the psychic force she says is responsible didn't emanate from another world. It was conjured up out of nothing by someone who was—who had to be—here in this room when Drake died. Someone whom Drake himself asked to be here."

He moved into the center of the room as he spoke and faced them.

"Drake would never have convinced anyone that Rosa could do what she claimed without a witness. So he gave someone a key—someone who came into this room *before* Drake and Rosa and Elinor came downstairs."

The four people watched him without moving—almost, I thought, without breathing.

"That person hid behind that screen and then, after Rosa produced the apports, knocked her out, killed Drake, and left Rosa to face the music."

"All we have to do," Merlini went on, "is show who it was that Drake selected as a witness." He pointed a lean forefinger at Isabelle Potter. "If Drake discovered how Rosa produced the shells and realized she was a fraud, you might have killed him to prevent an exposure and save face for yourself and the society; and you might have then framed Rosa in revenge for having deceived you. But Drake would never have chosen you. Your testimony wouldn't have convinced any of the others. No. Drake would have picked one of the skeptics—someone he was certain could never be accused of assisting the medium."

He faced Elinor. "You said that you accompanied Rosa and your father to the study door and saw them go in alone. We haven't asked Miss Rhys yet, but I think she'll confirm it. You couldn't expect to lie about that and make it stick as long as Rosa could and would contradict you."

I saw Doran move forward silently, closing in.

"And Paul Kendrick," Merlini went on, "is the only one of you who has an alibi that does not depend on the sealed room. That leaves the most skeptical one of the three—the man whose testimony would by far carry the greatest weight.

"It leaves you, Dr. Garrett. The man who is so certain that there are no ghosts is the man who conjured one up!"

Merlini played the scene down; he knew that the content of what he said was dramatic enough. But Garrett's voice was even calmer. He shook his head slowly.

"I am afraid that I can't agree. You have no reason to assume

that it must be one of us and no one else. But I would like to hear
how you think I or anyone else could have walked out of this room
leaving it sealed as it was found."

"That," Merlini said, "is the simplest answer of all. You walked
out, but you didn't leave the room sealed. You see, *it was not
found that way!*"

I felt as if I were suddenly floating in space.

"But look—" I began.

Merlini ignored me. "The vanishing murderer was a trick. But
magic is not, as most people believe, only a matter of gimmicks
and trapdoors and mirrors. Its real secret lies deeper than a mere
deception of the senses; the magician uses a far more important,
more basic weapon—the psychological deception of the mind.
Don't believe everything you see is excellent advice; but there's a
better rule: don't believe everything you *think.*"

"Are you trying to tell me," I said incredulously, "that this room
wasn't sealed at all? That I just thought it was?"

Merlini kept watching Garrett. "Yes. It's as simple as that. And
there was no visual deception at all. It was, like PK, entirely mental. You saw things exactly as they were, but you didn't realize that
the visual appearance could be interpreted two ways. Let me ask
you a question. When you break into a room the door of which has
been sealed with paper tape on the inside, do you find yourself still
in a sealed room?"

"No," I said, "of course not. The paper has been torn."

"And if you break into a room that had been sealed but from
which someone has *already gone out*, tearing the seals—what
then?"

"The paper," I said, "is still torn. The appearance is—"

"—*exactly the same!*" Merlini finished.

He let that soak in a moment, then continued. "When you saw
the taped window, and then the torn paper on the door, you made
a false assumption—you jumped naturally, but much too quickly,
to a wrong conclusion. We all did. We assumed that it was you who
had torn the paper when you broke in. Actually, it was Dr. Garrett
who tore the paper—when he went out!"

Garrett's voice was a shade less steady now. "You forget that
Andrew Drake phoned me—"

Merlini shook his head. "I'm afraid we only have your own

statement for that. You overturned the phone and placed Drake's body near it. Then you walked out, returned to your office where you got rid of the knife—probably a surgical instrument which you couldn't leave behind because it might have been traced to you."

Doran, hearing this, whispered a rapid order to the detective stationed at the door.

"Then," Merlini continued, "you came back immediately to ring the front-door bell. You said Drake had called you, partly because it was good misdirection; it made it appear that you were elsewhere when he died. But equally important, it gave you the excuse you needed to break in and find the body without delay— *before Rosa Rhys should regain consciousness and see that the room was no longer sealed!*"

I hated to do it. Merlini was so pleased with the neat way he was tying up all the loose ends. But I had to.

"Merlini," I said. "I'm afraid there is one little thing you don't know. When I smashed the door open, I heard the paper tape tear!"

I have seldom seen the Great Merlini surprised, but that did it. He couldn't have looked more astonished if lightning had struck him.

"You—you *what?*"

Elinor Drake said, "I heard it, too."

Garrett added, "And I."

It stopped Merlini cold for a moment, but only a moment.

"Then that's more misdirection. It has to be." He hesitated, then suddenly looked at Doran. "Lieutenant, get the doctor's overcoat, will you?"

Garrett spoke to the inspector. "This is nonsense. What possible reason could I have for—"

"Your motive was a curious one, doctor," Merlini said. "One that few murderers—"

Merlini stopped as he took the overcoat Doran brought in and removed from its pocket the copy of the AMA *Journal* I had noticed there earlier. He started to open it, then lifted an eyebrow at something he saw on the contents listing.

"I see," he said, and then read: "*A Survey of the Uses of Radioactive Tracers in Cancer Research* by Walter M. Garrett, M.D. So that's your special interest?" The magician turned to Elinor Drake. "Who was to head the $15-million foundation for cancer research, Miss Drake?"

The girl didn't need to reply. The answer was in her eyes as she stared at Garrett.

Merlini went on. "You were hidden behind the screen in the corner, doctor. And Rosa Rhys, in spite of all the precautions, successfully produced the apports. You saw the effect that had on Drake, knew Rosa had won, and that Drake was thoroughly hooked. And the thought of seeing all that money wasted on psychical research when it could be put to so much better use in really important medical research made you boil. Any medical man would hate to see that happen, and most of the rest of us, too.

"But we don't all have the coldly rational, scientific attitude you do, and we wouldn't all have realized so quickly that there was one very simple but drastic way to prevent it—murder. You are much too rational. You believe that one man's life is less important than the good his death might bring, and you believed that sufficiently to act upon it. The knife was there, all too handy, in your little black case. And so—Drake died. Am I right, doctor?"

Doran didn't like this as a motive. "He's still a killer," he objected. "And he tried to frame Rosa, didn't he?"

Merlini said, "Do you want to answer that, doctor?"

Garrett hesitated, then glanced at the magazine Merlini still held. His voice was tired. "You are also much too rational." He turned to Doran. "Rosa Rhys was a cheap fraud who capitalized on superstition. The world would be a much better place without such people."

"And what about your getting that job as the head of the medical foundation?" Doran was still unconvinced. "I don't suppose that had anything to do with your reasons for killing Drake?"

The doctor made no answer. And I couldn't tell if it was because Doran was right or because he knew that Doran would not believe him.

He turned to Merlini instead. "The fact still remains that the cancer foundation has been made possible. The only difference is that now two men rather than one pay with their lives."

"A completely rational attitude," Merlini said, "does have its advantages if it allows you to contemplate your own death with so little emotion."

Gavigan wasn't as cynical about Garrett's motives as Doran, but his police training objected. "He took the law into his own hands. If everyone did that, we'd all have to go armed for self-protection. Merlini, why did Ross think he heard paper tearing when he opened that door?"

"He did hear it," Merlini said. Then he turned to me. "Dr. Garrett stood behind you and Miss Drake when you broke in the door, didn't he?"

I nodded. "Yes."

Merlini opened the medical journal and riffled through it. Half a dozen loose pages, their serrated edges showing where they had been torn in half, fluttered to the floor.

Merlini said, "You would have made an excellent magician, doctor. Your deception was not visual, it was auditory."

"That," Gavigan said, "tears it."

Later I had one further question to ask Merlini.

"You didn't explain how Houdini got out of that Scottish jail, nor how it helped you solve the enigma of the unsealed door."

Merlini lifted an empty hand, plucked a lighted cigarette from thin air and puffed at it, grinning.

"Houdini made the same false assumption. When he leaned exhaustedly against the cell door, completely baffled by his failure to overcome the lock, the door suddenly swung open and he fell into the corridor. The old Scot, you see, hadn't locked it at all!"

IN THE HOUSE OF SUDDHOO

Rudyard Kipling

Magicians can perform wonderful tricks on stage, fooling an audience with illusions, making them believe something is true when it is not true. Offstage, a skillful illusionist can still fool an audience. It is then that trouble may arise. Confidence men, liars, cheats, and charlatans all try to make their audiences believe that something is true when it is not true. And they all know that it is easiest to fool people when you tell them exactly what they want to hear.

Rudyard Kipling, England's most popular writer for many years, knew this basic tenet of the conjuring arts. He also knew people. "In the House of Suddhoo" is the oldest story in this book, but it could have been written yesterday. Just as the population of the world has increased since the story was written, so has the number of tricksters and charlatans. And it is surprising how little their methods have changed. The tricks that worked then still work today. Superstitions seem immutable. Just see how many people still wear charms and amulets around their necks to ward off "evil spirits" or "bad luck."

"In the House of Suddhoo" was first published in The Civil and Military Gazette *for April 30, 1886, under the title "Section 420, I.P.C." for the section of the Indian Penal Code which prohibited obtaining money under false pretenses. Its first book publication was in* Plain Tales from the Hills *(1888).*

> A stone's throw out on either hand
> From that well-ordered road we tread,
>   And all the world is wild and strange;
> *Churel* and ghoul and *Djinn* and sprite
> Shall bear us company tonight,
>   For we have reached the Oldest Land
> Wherein the Powers of Darkness range.
>   —*From the Dusk to the Dawn.*

The house of Suddhoo, near the Taksali Gate, is two-storied, with four carved windows of old brown wood, and a flat roof. You may recognize it by five red handprints arranged like the Five of Diamonds on the whitewash between the upper windows. Bhagwan Dass, the *bunnia,* and a man who says he gets his living by seal cutting live in the lower story with a troop of wives, servants, friends, and retainers. The two upper rooms used to be occupied by Janoo and Azizun and a little black-and-tan terrier that was stolen from an Englishman's house and given to Janoo by a soldier. Today, only Janoo lives in the upper rooms. Suddhoo sleeps on the roof generally, except when he sleeps in the street. He used to go to Peshawar in the cold weather to visit his son, who sells curiosities near the Edwardes' Gate, and then he slept under a real mud roof. Suddhoo is a great friend of mine, because his cousin had a son who secured, thanks to my recommendation, the post of head messenger to a big firm in the station. Suddhoo says that God will make me a lieutenant-governor one of these days. I daresay his prophecy will come true. He is very, very old, with white hair and no teeth worth showing, and he has outlived his wits—outlived nearly everything except his fondness for his son at Peshawar. Janoo and Azizun are Kashmiris, Ladies of the City, and theirs was an ancient and more or less honorable profession; but Azizun has since married a medical student from the northwest and has settled down to a most respectable life somewhere near Bareilly. Bhagwan Dass is an extortionate and an adulterator. He is very rich. The man who is supposed to get his living by seal cutting pretends to be very poor. This lets you know as much as is necessary of the four principal tenants in the house of Suddhoo. Then there is me, of course; but I am only the chorus that comes in at the end to explain things. So I do not count.

Suddhoo was not clever. The man who pretended to cut seals was the cleverest of them all—Bhagwan Dass only knew how to lie—except Janoo. She was also beautiful, but that was her own affair.

Suddhoo's son at Peshawar was attacked by pleurisy, and old Suddhoo was troubled. The seal-cutter man heard of Suddhoo's anxiety and made capital out of it. He was abreast of the times. He got a friend in Peshawar to telegraph daily accounts of the son's health. And here the story begins.

Suddhoo's cousin's son told me, one evening, that Suddhoo wanted to see me; that he was too old and feeble to come personally, and that I should be conferring an everlasting honor on the house of Suddhoo if I went to him. I went; but I think, seeing how well off Suddhoo was then, that he might have sent something better than an *ekka*, which jolted fearfully, to haul out a future lieutenant-governor to the city on a muggy April evening. The *ekka* did not run quickly. It was full dark when we pulled up opposite the door of Ranjit Singh's tomb near the main gate of the fort. Here was Suddhoo and he said that by reason of my condescension, it was absolutely certain that I should become a lieutenant-governor while my hair was yet black. Then we talked about the weather and the state of my health, and the wheat crops, for fifteen minutes, in the Huzuri Bagh, under the stars.

Suddhoo came to the point at last. He said that Janoo had told him that there was an order of the *Sirkar* against magic, because it was feared that magic might one day kill the empress of India. I didn't know anything about the state of the law; but I fancied that something interesting was going to happen. I said that so far from magic being discouraged by the government it was highly commended. The greatest officials of the state practiced it themselves. (If the financial statement isn't magic, I don't know what is.) Then, to encourage him further, I said that, if there was any *jadoo* afoot, I had not the least objection to giving it my countenance and sanction, and to seeing that it was clean *jadoo*—white magic, as distinguished from the unclean *jadoo* which kills folk. It took a long time before Suddhoo admitted that this was just what he had asked me to come for. Then he told me, in jerks and quavers, that the man who said he cut seals was a sorcerer of the cleanest kind; that every day he gave Suddhoo news of his sick son in Peshawar more quickly than the lightning could fly, and that this news was always corroborated by the letters. Further, that he had told Suddhoo how a great danger was threatening his son, which could be removed by clean *jadoo;* and, of course, heavy payment. I began to see exactly how the land lay, and told Suddhoo that *I* also understood a little *jadoo* in the western line, and would go to his house to see that everything was done decently and in order. We set off together; and on the way Suddhoo told me that he had paid the seal cutter between one hundred and two hundred rupees already; and the *jadoo* of that night would cost two hundred more. Which was cheap, he said, considering the greatness of his son's danger; but I do not think he meant it.

The lights were all cloaked in the front of the house when we arrived. I could hear awful noises from behind the seal-cutter's shop front, as if someone were groaning his soul out. Suddhoo shook all over, and while we groped our way upstairs told me that the *jadoo* had begun. Janoo and Azizun met us at the stair head, and told us that the *jadoo* work was coming off in their rooms, because there was more space there. Janoo is a lady of a freethinking turn of mind. She whispered that the *jadoo* was an invention to get money out of Suddhoo, and that the seal cutter would go to a hot place when he died. Suddhoo was nearly crying with fear and old age. He kept walking up and down the room in the half light, repeating his son's name over and over again, and asking Azizun if the seal cutter ought not to make a reduction in the case of his own landlord. Janoo pulled me over to the shadow in the recess of the carved bow windows. The boards were up, and the rooms were lit only by one tiny oil lamp. There was no chance of my being seen if I stayed still.

Presently, the groans below ceased, and we heard steps on the staircase. That was the seal cutter. He stopped outside the door as the terrier barked and Azizun fumbled at the chain, and he told Suddhoo to blow out the lamp. This left the place in jet darkness, except for the red glow from the two *huqas* that belonged to Janoo and Azizun. The seal cutter came in, and I heard Suddhoo throw himself down on the floor and groan. Azizun caught her breath, and Janoo backed on to one of the beds with a shudder. There was a clink of something metallic, and then shot up a pale blue-green flame near the ground. The light was just enough to show Azizun, pressed against one corner of the room with the terrier between her knees; Janoo, with her hands clasped, leaning forward as she sat on the bed; Suddhoo, face down, quivering, and the seal cutter.

I hope I may never see another man like that seal cutter. He was stripped to the waist, with a wreath of white jasmine as thick as my wrist round his forehead, a salmon-colored loincloth round his middle, and a steel bangle on each ankle. This was not awe-inspiring. It was the face of the man that turned me cold. It was blue-gray in the first place. In the second, the eyes were rolled back till you could see only the whites of them; and, in the third, the face was the face of a demon—a ghoul—anything you please except of the sleek, oily old ruffian who sat in the daytime over his turning-lathe downstairs. He was lying on his stomach with his arms turned and crossed behind him, as if he had been thrown down pinioned. His head and neck were the only parts of him off the floor. They were nearly at right angles to the body, like the head of a cobra at spring. It was ghastly. In the center of the room, on the bare earth floor, stood a big, deep, brass basin, with a pale blue-green light floating in the center like a nightlight. Round that basin the man on the floor wriggled himself three times. How he did it I do not know. I could see the muscles ripple along his spine and fall smooth again; but I could not see any other motion. The head seemed the only thing alive about him, except that slow curl and uncurl of the laboring back muscles. Janoo from the bed was breathing seventy to the minute; Azizun held her hands before her eyes; and old Suddhoo, fingering at the dirt that had got into his white beard, was crying to himself. The horror of it was that the creeping, crawly thing made no sound—only crawled. And, remember, this lasted for ten minutes, while the terrier whined, and Azizun shuddered, and Janoo gasped and Suddhoo cried.

I felt the hair lift at the back of my head, and my heart thump like a thermantidote paddle. Luckily, the seal cutter betrayed himself by his most impressive trick and made me calm again. After he had finished that unspeakable crawl, he stretched his head away from the floor as high as he could, and sent out a jet of fire from his nostrils. Now I knew how fire-spouting is done—I can do it myself—so I felt at ease. The business was a fraud. If he had only kept to that crawl without trying to raise the effect, goodness knows what I might not have thought. Both the girls shrieked at the jet of fire, and the head dropped, chin down on the floor, with a thud; the whole body lying then like a corpse with its arms trussed. There was a pause of five full minutes after this, and the blue-green flame died down. Janoo stooped to settle one of her anklets, while Azizun turned her face to the wall and took the terrier in her arms. Suddhoo put out an arm mechanically to Janoo's *huqa,* and she slid it across the floor with her foot. Directly above the body and on the wall were a couple of flaming portraits, in stamped paper frames, of the Queen and the Prince of Wales. They looked down on the performance, and, to my thinking, seemed to heighten the grotesqueness of it all.

Just when the silence was getting unendurable, the body turned over and rolled away from the basin to the side of the room, where it lay stomach up. There was a faint "plop" from the basin—exactly like the noise a fish makes when it takes a fly—and the green light in the center revived.

I looked at the basin, and saw, bobbing in the water the dried, shriveled, black head of a native baby—open eyes, open mouth and shaved scalp. It was worse, being so very sudden, than the crawling exhibition. We had no time to say anything before it began to speak.

Read Poe's account of the voice that came from the mesmerized dying man, and you will realize less than one half of the horror of that head's voice.

There was an interval of a second or two between each word, and a sort of "ring, ring, ring," in the note of the voice like the timbre of a bell. It pealed slowly, as if talking to itself, for several minutes before I got rid of my cold sweat. Then the blessed solution struck me. I looked at the body lying near the doorway, and saw, just where the hollow of the throat joins on the shoulders, a muscle that had nothing to do with any man's regular breathing, twitching away steadily. The whole thing was a careful reproduction of the Egyptian teraphim that one reads about sometimes; and the voice was as clever and as appalling a piece of ventriloquism as one could wish to hear. All this time the head was "lip-lip-lapping" against the side of the basin, and speaking. It told Suddhoo, on his face again whining, of his son's illness and of the state of the illness up to the evening of that very night. I always shall respect the seal cutter for keeping so faithfully to the time of the Peshawar telegrams. It went on to say that skilled doctors were night and day watching over the man's life; and that he would eventually recover if the fee to the potent sorcerer, whose servant was the head in the basin, were doubled.

Here the mistake from the artistic point of view came in. To ask for twice your stipulated fee in a voice that Lazarus might have used when he rose from the dead, is absurd. Janoo, who is really a woman of masculine intellect, saw this as quickly as I did. I heard her say *"Ash nahin! Farcib!"* scornfully under her breath; and just as she said so, the light in the basin died out, the head stopped talking, and we heard the room door creak on its hinges. Then Janoo struck a match, lit the lamp, and we saw that head, basin, and seal cutter were gone. Suddhoo was wringing his hands and explaining to anyone who cared to listen that, if his chances of eternal salvation depended on it, he could not raise another two hundred rupees. Azizun was nearly in hysterics in the corner; while Janoo sat down composedly on one of the beds to discuss the probabilities of the whole thing being a *bunao,* or "make-up."

I explained as much as I knew of the seal cutter's way of *jadoo;* but her argument was much more simple: "The magic that is always demanding gifts is no true magic," said she. "My mother told me that the only potent love spells are those which are told you for love. This seal-cutter man is a liar and a devil. I dare not tell, do anything, or get anything done, because I am in debt to Bhagwan Dass, the *bunnia,* for two gold rings and a heavy anklet. I must get my food from his shop. The seal cutter is the friend of Bhagwan Dass, and he would poison my food. A fool's *jadoo* has been going on for ten days, and has cost Suddhoo many rupees each night. The seal cutter used black hens and lemons and *mantras* before. He never showed us anything like this till tonight. Azizun is a fool, and will be a *pur dahnashin* soon. Suddhoo has lost his strength and his wits. See now! I had hoped to get from Suddhoo many rupees while he lived, and many more after his death; and behold, he is spending everything on that offspring of a devil and a she-ass, the seal cutter!"

Here I said, "But what induced Suddhoo to drag me into the business? Of course I can speak to the seal cutter, and he shall refund. The whole thing is child's talk—shame—and senseless."

"Suddhoo *is* an old child," said Janoo. "He has lived on the roofs these seventy years and is as senseless as a milch goat. He brought you here to assure himself that he was not breaking any law of the *Sirkar,* whose salt he ate many years ago. He worships the dust off the feet of the seal cutter, and that cow devourer has forbidden him to go and see his son. What does Suddhoo know of your laws or the lightning post? I have to watch his money going day by day to that lying beast below."

Janoo stamped her foot on the floor and nearly cried with vexation; while Suddhoo was whimpering under a blanket in the corner and Azizun was trying to guide the pipe-stem to Suddhoo's foolish old mouth.

Now the case stands thus. Unthinkingly, I have laid myself open to the charge of aiding and abetting the seal cutter in obtaining money under false pretenses, which is forbidden by section 420 of the Indian Penal Code. I am helpless in the matter for these reasons, I cannot inform the police. What witnesses would support my statements? Janoo refuses flatly, and Azizun is a veiled woman somewhere near Bareilly—lost in this big India of ours. I dare not again take the law into my own hands, and speak to the seal cutter; for certain am I that, not only would Suddhoo disbelieve me, but this step would end in the poisoning of Janoo, who is bound hand and foot by her debt to the *bunnia.* Suddhoo is an old dotard; and whenever we meet mumbles my idiotic joke that the *Sirkar* rather patronizes the Black Art than otherwise. His son is well now; but Suddhoo is completely under the influence of the seal cutter, by whose advice he regulates the affairs of his life. Janoo watches daily the money that she hoped to wheedle out of Suddhoo taken by the seal cutter, and becomes daily more furious and sullen.

She will never tell, because she dare not; but, unless something happens to prevent her, I am afraid that the seal cutter will die of cholera—the white arsenic kind—about the middle of May. And thus I shall have to be privy to a murder in the house of Suddhoo.

ROPE ENOUGH

John Collier

Fakirs, once a Muslim term but now encompassing Indian Hindus as well, are generally regarded as holy men possessed of magical powers. Their feats of resting on a bed of nails and walking barefoot on hot coals have astonished and puzzled westerners—and more than a few Orientals—for centuries. But perhaps the most famous illusion performed in all of Asia is the Indian rope trick.

In this familiar trick, an apparently ordinary rope rises vertically in the air and remains in that position. In "Rope Enough," the reader will discover what is beyond the top end of the rope.

John Collier writes grotesque fairy tales with a pervading—and perverse—humor that causes the reader to smile. The smile is not induced by joy, but rather is accompanied by a nervous shudder and a quick glance over the shoulder. His bizarre stories often deal with macabre murders. The finest collection of Collier's chillers is Fancies and Goodnights *(1951). "Rope Enough" was first published in book form in* Presenting Moonshine *(1941).*

Henry Fraser, well assured that almost everything is done by mirrors, was given a job in India. No sooner had he set foot on shore than he burst into a horselaugh. Those who were meeting him asked in some alarm the cause of this merriment. He replied he was laughing at the mere idea of the Indian rope trick.

He emitted similar startling sounds, and gave the same explanation, at a *tiffin* where he was officially made welcome; likewise on the Maidan, over *chota peg,* in rickshaws, in bazaars, in the club, and on the polo ground. Soon he was known from Bombay to Calcutta as the man who laughed at the Indian rope trick, and he gloried in the well-deserved publicity.

There came a day, however, when he was sitting in his bungalow, bored to death. His boy entered, and, with suitable *salaams,* announced that a mountebank was outside, who craved the honor of entertaining the sahib with a performance of the Indian rope trick. Laughing heartily, Henry consented, and moved out to his chair upon the veranda.

Below, in the dusty compound, stood a native who was emaciated to a degree, and who had with him a spry youngster, a huge mat basket, and a monstrous great sword. Out of the basket he dragged some thirty feet of stout rope, made a pass or two, and slung it up into the air. It stayed there. Henry chuckled.

The boy then, with a caper, sprang at the rope, clutched it, and went up hand over hand, like a monkey. When he reached the top he vanished into thin air. Henry guffawed.

Soon the man, looking upward with an anxious expression, began to hoot and holler after the boy. He called him down, he ordered him down, he begged him down, he began to swear and curse horribly. The boy, it seemed, took no notice at all. Henry roared.

Now the black, clapping his abominable great scimitar between his teeth, took hold of the rope himself, and went up it like a sailor. He, also, disappeared at the top. Henry's mirth increased.

Pretty soon some yelps and squeals were heard coming out of the empty air, and then a blood-curdling scream. Down came a leg, thump onto the ground, then an arm, a thigh, a head and other joints, and finally (no ladies being present) a bare backside, which struck the earth like a bomb. Henry went into fits.

Then the black came sliding down, holding on with one hand, fairly gibbering with excitement. He presented to Henry, with a *salaam,* his reeking blade for inspection. Henry rocked in his chair.

The black, seemingly overwhelmed with remorse, gathered up the fragments of his little stooge, lavishing a hundred lamentations and endearments upon each grisly member, and he stowed them all in the giant basket.

At that moment Henry, feeling the time had come for a show-down, and willing to bet a thousand to one they'd planted the whole compound full of mirrors before calling him out there, pulled out his revolver, and blazed away all six chambers in different directions, in the expectation of splintering at least one of those deceiving glasses.

Nothing of that sort happened, but the black, doing a quick pirouette in alarm, looked down in the dust at his feet, and held up a villainous little snake, no thicker than a lead pencil, which had been killed by one of Henry's stray bullets. He gave a gasp of relief, touched his turban very civilly, turned round again, and made a pass or two over the basket. At once, with a wriggle and a frisk, the boy sprang out, whole, alive, smiling, full of health and wicked-ness.

The black hastily hauled down the rope, and came cringing up to Henry, overflowing with gratitude for having been saved from that villainous little snake, which was nothing more nor less than a krait—one nip and a man goes round and round like a Catherine wheel for eleven seconds; then he is as dead as mutton.

"But for the Heavenborn," said the black, "I should have been a goner, and my wicked little boy here, who is my pride and delight, must have lain dismembered in the basket till the sahib's servants condescended to throw him to the crocodiles. Our worth-less lives, our scanty goods, are all at the sahib's disposal."

"That's all right," said Henry. "All I ask is, show me how the trick is worked, or the laugh will be on me from now on."

"Would not the sahib," said the black diffidently, "prefer the secret of a superb hair-restorer?"

"No. No," said Henry. "Nothing but the trick."

"I have," said the black, "the secret of a very peculiar tonic, which the sahib (not now, of course, but in later life) might find—"

"The trick," said Henry, "and without further delay."

"Very well," said the black. "Nothing in the world could be more simple. You make a pass, like that—"

"Wait a minute," said Henry. "Like that?"

"Exactly," said the black. "You then throw up the rope—so. You see? It sticks."

"So it does," said Henry.

"Any boy can climb," said the black. "Up boy! Show the sahib."

The boy, smiling, climbed up and disappeared.

"Now," said the black, "if the sahib will excuse me, I shall be back immediately." And with that he climbed up himself, threw down the boy in sections, and speedily rejoined Henry on the ground.

"All that," said he, scooping up legs and arms as he spoke, "all that can be done by anyone. There is a little knack, however, to the pass I make at this juncture. If the sahib will deign to observe closely—like that."

"Like that?" said Henry.

"You have it to perfection," said the black.

"Very interesting," said Henry. "Tell me, what's up there at the top of the rope?"

"Ah, sahib," said the black with a smile, "that is something truly delightful."

With that he *salaamed* and departed, taking with him his rope, his giant basket, his tremendous great scimitar, and his wicked little boy. Henry was left feeling rather morose: he was known from the Deccan to the Khyber Pass as the man who laughed at the Indian rope trick, and now he could laugh no more.

He decided to keep very quiet about it, but this unfortunately was not enough. At *tiffin*, at *chota peg*, at the club, on the Maidan, in the bazaar, and at polo, he was expected to laugh like a horse, and in India one has to do what is expected of one. Henry became extremely unpopular, cabals were formed against him, and soon he was hoofed out of the service.

This was the more distressing as in the meantime he had married a wife, strong-featured, upstanding, well groomed, straight-eyed, a little peremptory in manner, and as jealous as a demon, but in all respects a memsahib of the highest type, who knew very well what was due to her. She told Henry he had better go to America and make a fortune. He agreed, they packed up, and off they went to America.

"I hope," said Henry, as they stood looking at the skyline of New York, "I hope I shall make that fortune."

"Of course," said she. "You must insist upon it."

"Very well, my dear," said he.

On landing, however, he discovered that all the fortunes had already been made, a discovery that very generally awaits those who visit America on this errand, and after some weeks of drifting about from place to place, he was prepared to cut his demand down to a mere job, then to a lesser job, and finally to the price of a meal and a bed for the night.

They reached this extremity in a certain small town in the Middle West. "There is nothing for it, my dear," said Henry. "We shall have to do the Indian rope trick."

His wife cried out very bitterly at the idea of a memsahib performing this native feat in a Middle Western town, before a Middle Western audience. She reproached him with the loss of his job, the poor quality of his manhood, with the time he let her little dog get run over on the bund, and with a glance he had cast at a Parsee maiden at Bombay. Nevertheless, reason and hunger prevailed; they pawned her last trinket and invested in a rope, a roomy grip, and a monstrous old rusty scimitar they discovered in a junk shop.

When she saw this last, Henry's wife flatly refused to go on, unless she was given the star part and Henry took that of the stooge. "But," said Henry, drawing an apprehensive thumb down the notched and jagged edge of the grim and rusty bilbo, "but," said he, "you don't know how to make the passes."

"You shall teach me," she said, "and if anything goes wrong you will have only yourself to blame."

So Henry showed her. You may be sure he was very thorough in his instructions. In the end she mastered them perfectly, and there was nothing left to do but to stain themselves with coffee. Henry improvised a turban and loincloth; she wore a sari and a pair of ashtrays borrowed from the hotel. They sought out a convenient waste lot, a large crowd collected, and the show began.

Up went the rope. Sure enough, it stuck. The crowd, with a multiple snigger, whispered that everything was done by mirrors. Henry, not without a good deal of puffing, went up hand over hand. When he got to the top, he forgot the crowd, the act, his wife, and even himself, so surprised and delighted was he by the sight that met his eyes.

He found himself crawling out of something like a well, on to what seemed to be solid ground. The landscape about him was not at all like that below; it was like an Indian paradise, full of dells, bowers, scarlet ibises, and heaven knows what all. However, his surprise and delight came less from these features of the background than from the presence of a young female in the nearest of these bowers or arbors, which happened to be all wreathed, canopied, overgrown, and intertwined with passion flowers. This delightful creature, who was a positive houri, and very lightly attired, seemed to be expecting Henry, and greeted him with rapture.

Henry, who had a sufficiently affectionate nature, flung his arms round her neck and gazed deeply into her eyes. These were surprisingly eloquent. They seemed to say, "Why not make hey hey while the sun shines?"

He found the notion entirely agreeable, and planted a lingering kiss on her lips, noting only with a dim and careless annoyance that his wife was hooting and hollering from below. "What person of any tact or delicacy," thought he, "could hoot and holler at such a moment?" and he dismissed her from his mind.

You may imagine his mortification when his delicious damsel suddenly repulsed him from her arms. He looked over his shoulder, and there was his wife, clambering over the edge, terribly red in the face, with the fury of a demon in her eye, and the mighty scimitar gripped firmly between her teeth.

Henry tried to rise, but she was beforehand with him, and while yet he had but his left foot on the ground, she caught him one across the loins with the huge and jagged bilbo, which effectually hamstrung him, so that he fell groveling at her feet. "For heaven's sake!" he cried. "It's all a trick. Part of the act. It means nothing. Remember our public. The show must go on."

"It shall," said she, striking at his arms and legs.

"Oh, those notches!" cried he. "To oblige me, my dear, please sharpen it a little upon a stone."

"It is good enough for you, you viper," said she, hacking away all the time. Pretty soon Henry was a limbless trunk.

"For the love of God," said he, "I hope you remember the passes. I can explain everything."

"To hell with the passes!" said she, and with a last swipe she sent his head rolling like a football.

She was not long in picking up the scattered fragments of poor Henry, and flinging them down to earth, amid the applause and laughter of the crowd, who were more than ever convinced it was all done by mirrors.

Then, gripping her scimitar, she was about to swarm down after him, not from any soft-hearted intention of reassembling her unfortunate spouse, but rather to have another hack or two at some of the larger joints. At that moment she became aware of someone behind her and, looking round, there was a divine young man, with the appearance of a maharaja of the highest caste, an absolute Valentino, in whose eyes she seemed to read the words, "It is better to burn upon the Bed of Passion than in the Chair of Electricity."

This idea presented itself with an overwhelming appeal. She paused only to thrust her head through the aperture, and cry, "That's what happens to a pig of a man who betrays his wife with a beastly native," before hauling up the rope and entering into conversation with her charmer.

The police soon appeared upon the scene. There was nothing but a cooing sound above, as if invisible turtle doves were circling in amorous flight. Below, the various portions of Henry were scattered in the dust, and the bluebottle flies were already settling upon them.

The crowd explained it was nothing but a trick, done with mirrors.

"It looks to me," said the sergeant, "as if the biggest one must have splintered right on top of him."

THE NEW INVISIBLE MAN

Carter Dickson

*Successful mystery writers share a quality with successful magicians—
they succeed in their attempts to baffle an audience. And, just as a perfect
illusion appears to the observer to be impossible, so does the perfect crime.*

*No author has committed more "impossible" fictional crimes than
Carter Dickson (who is even more famous under his real name John
Dickson Carr). The master of the macabre has slain a veritable regiment
in sealed rooms and other impregnable locales. His best-known detectives,
Gideon Fell and Sir Henry Merrivale, have never failed to unmask the
culprits in these classic crimes.*

*In "The New Invisible Man," Colonel March, the head of Scotland
Yard's aptly-named Department of Queer Complaints, calmly hears an
account of a murder committed by a pistol fired by a glove—an empty
glove unattached to an arm in an otherwise unoccupied room. Because of
his knowledge of "The Sphinx" and other conjuror's arts, however, March
remains unwilling to believe in miracles—or in the impossible.*

"The New Invisible Man" was first published in book form in The
Department of Queer Complaints *(1940).*

A taxi brought him to the Derby Street entrance of New Scotland Yard. He was a well-dressed man with somewhat protuberant
eyes, an inquiring nose, and a frantic seriousness of manner. And
he was so excited that the constable on duty at the entrance could
hardly make out a word he was saying.

"Murdered him right in front of me!" gabbled the newcomer, holding on to his bowler hat as though it might blow off. "Might have murdered me too, and very nearly did, because the next bullet hit the lampshade beside me, and—"

"Now, sir!" urged the law soothingly. "Who did all this?"

"A pair of gloves did," said the newcomer.

"A what?"

"A pair of gloves. Only they hadn't got any hands inside them. Or any arms or body either, for that matter. The fellow was invisible. And mark my words, he'll kill that girl next!"

The constable stood back and studied him. This man did not look demented. His eyes were watery, and he gulped out steamy breaths on the raw air.

"Yes, sir," said the constable. "Straight on; first turning; third door on the left."

He spoke a formula. The door he indicated bore only the words, D-3, COLONEL MARCH, but many stories lay behind it. It is, in fact, the home of queer tales, and exists solely for the purpose of receiving them. To the Metropolitan Police come strangers with complaints which do not seem to bear the light of day or reason. But, unless the complainant is an obvious lunatic, such matters have to be investigated; and Department D-3 is their clearinghouse.

D-3 has its own staff, notably Inspector (ex-Captain) Roberts, who served under Colonel March in different days. It is not governed by the routine organization, and deals direct with the commissioner's office. Some maintain that Colonel March was put in charge of it because nothing on earth could possibly surprise him. He is also well served by his vast fund of good-for-nothing information, and his absorption in any kind of puzzle from a jigsaw up. Those who get past Inspector Roberts find in the inner office a large, amiable man (weight seventeen stone) with a speckled face, an interested blue eye, and a very short pipe projecting from under a cropped mustache which might be sandy or gray.

On this particular morning, the agitated man in the bowler hat did get past the outer office. Business, as Colonel March pointed out to Inspector Roberts, was bad; and they might as well hear what the man had to say.

"I am aware," said the newcomer, with a certain dignity, "that

you must think me mad. Very well. Say that I *am* mad—" His
native caution checked him. "Er—no, don't say that; perhaps I am
a little upset. But surely my name and standing should be sufficient
guarantee that I am telling the truth? My name is Rodman, Horace
Rodman. I am the senior partner of Rodman and Hughes, Chart-
ered Accountants and Income Tax Consultants. I have lived for
sixteen years at Number 24 St. Nicholas Row, Hampstead. Sir, I
saw a murder done; and, heaven help me, nobody will believe it."

His voice had acquired an asthmatic and passionate note.

"It's quite all right," March assured him. "I knew a fellow once
who had the same trouble. Just fire away."

"I'm not sure I know how," said Rodman abruptly, after a pause.
He reflected. "It concerns a new block of flats which has just gone
up opposite my house in St. Nicholas Row." He reflected again. "A
number of houses were torn down to make room for the flats. My
friend Mrs. Atchison, of Number 18, told me she was not sorry to
see Number 23 go, because it certainly had an unpleasant reputation in her grandfather's time."

"You mean it was supposed to be haunted?" asked March, with
still greater interest.

"No, no, no!" cried the other. "I did not say so," he added. "And
I cannot imagine any—er—'haunt' transferring itself to the mod-
ernistic building across the way. I must tell you about the architec-
ture; it has a great deal of bearing on what I saw. You have probably noticed these new Spanish-style buildings, in yellow stucco
with green facings: where every corner is rounded, and every
room has one long window stretching entirely across it, like the
glass door of a bookcase? Eh? Yes. That was how I could see so
clearly.

"You see, the flats are not yet quite finished. Although there are
a number of 'let' signs in the windows, only three or four families
have moved in. I am interested in my fellow man, sir," said Mr.
Rodman, rather defiantly. "I am a student of human nature, and
I don't care who knows it. Well, I *had* noticed the couple occupying the four-room flat which is directly opposite the second-floor
windows of my house. They are (or profess to be) a Mr. and Mrs.
James Hartley. The husband is a nondescript young man, who
drives a 1936 Hillman coupé, and has an office in the City. The
wife is a really beautiful and, I believe, refined girl."

His sudden lyricism embarrassed him.

"I had several times noticed the young lady going in and out; and once I met her in the street. I have also seen her, with a dustcloth round her head, cleaning the windows opposite. Mrs. Atchison thought this unbecoming in her. So did Mr. and Miss Paulus, at Number 20. I can only say," declared Mr. Rodman emphatically, "that I don't agree. She has hair the color of ripe— well, such is the case. This much I can tell you: she is in very terrible fear of something. For God's sake do not think I am imagining things for one reason or another. If you had seen her face, as I did, after it happened—

"It happened, you see, only last night, February twelfth, when I was going up to bed. My bedroom is on the second-floor front. I usually retire punctually at eleven; but I was a little later than usual, because I had been fidgety all evening. I don't know why.

"Before turning on the light in my bedroom, I went across to draw the curtains. That was how I came to be looking straight across, not forty feet away, into the dark window opposite. No curtains have been put up there. It is not Mr. and Mrs. Hartley's bedroom or sitting room. As a matter of fact, it is not yet furnished, except for carpets that have been fitted throughout, and one or two odds and ends packed away there. I had seen it by daylight, and knew it for a room hardly more than ten feet square, raw enough, with cream-painted walls, cream-varnished doors, and gray carpeting.

"It was a quiet night, and very cold. In front of the flats there is a double street lamp, which threw a faint kind of glow up over the yellow-and-green building and high up through the window. Someone, bent low, was moving quickly and stealthily round that room. It might be nothing? Quite. Quite! But the man was carrying an automatic pistol, and wore a big pair of dirty, white cotton gloves—I saw one of them flatten out against the window like a starfish."

Rodman paused. Colonel March's big sandy-haired head was bent forward with concentration. He glanced sideways at Inspector Roberts, who was now not quite so sure of the visitor's lack of mental balance.

"You could see all this," said March, "from across the street?"

"I fetched a pair of field glasses," said Rodman, with sudden loftiness. "Kindly do not interrupt me. The man took off his gloves, and put them down with the pistol on a round table in the middle of the room. Then he came toward the window and turned on the light. It was a dusty electric bulb, hanging from an unshaded socket in the ceiling near the window. But it gave a passable light; and I had a good look at the man's face. It was not James Hartley, or any man I had seen in those flats. I tell you I knew he was an old sinner, from the very turn of his neck and hands. He was a wicked-faced old man with a drooping mustache and thick-lensed spectacles which gave him an intensity of stare rather like the pictures of Dr. Crippen. His overcoat had a fur collar, too. And he began to run his hands along the window ledge, as though he were searching for something.

"Please remember the bareness of that room. I could see all of it. There was nobody else there. It had three cream-painted doors —one in the rear wall, in line with the window, and one in each of the two side walls. I should have noticed if any door had moved an inch. Not one did. The only articles of furniture were an ordinary kitchen chair, near the window; and the bare table in the center, on which the man had put down his pistol and gloves. A box with three doors and a window. There wasn't a crevice where anyone could have hidden.

"The man began groping along the window ledge. Finally he opened one big pane of the window and put out his bald head; I remember his shadow from the street lamp climbing up the yellow stucco wall. He uttered a peculiar kind of whistle, which sounded very loud in the quiet street. Then he drew in his head and turned back to the door at the rear of the room as he was in the act of locking the window.

"If that whistle was a signal, he got an answer. Two shots were fired at him point blank.

"They were fired, I tell you, from the other side of that table in the middle of the room, between the table and the rear door. They were fired from the heavy automatic which had been lying on the table. I saw them fired. The first bullet struck him in the chest and kicked him back against the window ledge, where he fell. The second bullet missed him, drilled through his window, smashed my window, and broke the glass shade of the lamp not a foot from my head. I saw the hand that fired the pistol; but there was no other person in that room."

Rodman nodded his head twice.

"I have the bullet, you know," he added with ghoulish hopefulness. "I dug it out of the wall in my bedroom and brought it along."

Colonel March was refreshed. His large face wore a quizzical look which was not disbelief at all; he tapped his fingers on the desk separating him from Rodman, as though he were about to make a move in a game of draughts.

"Just a moment," he interposed, "while I make sure I understand you. You *saw* this pistol fire the shots?"

"I did."

"Where was the pistol, exactly?"

Rodman changed color. "Held by one of the big gloves, at the back of the room."

"Was it on the table?"

"No; above the table."

"I see. You were actually looking through the place where the murderer must have been standing?"

"I was."

"Excellent! . . . Any comments, Roberts?"

Inspector Roberts smiled. "Well, sir, it's interesting enough; but where's the corpse? People usually complain in the case of a murder, you know. Mr. Rodman says this occurred last night. That would be F Division. I was talking to the divisional-inspector only this morning, and he said nothing about it."

"Oh, yes. I am aware of that," snapped Rodman, still a curious color. "You see, I haven't told you the worst of it yet. Shall I go on? Thank you.

"I was alarmed. I'm not ashamed to admit that. For a few seconds I quite literally couldn't move. I knew I had to go over there: duty. Besides, I was curious. But I had to find a policeman first. I hurried downstairs, got my hat and coat, and tumbled out. There was no difficulty about finding a policeman; the man on the beat had heard the shots too, and was coming to investigate. The window in the flat was now dark. I told the policeman what I had seen, though I daresay he didn't take it all in, for one reason or another. We entered the flats together.

"There were two lifts, but they didn't work; there was a porter, but we couldn't find him. We were in a great concrete shell of a building, rasping to every echo, and with a few frosted-glass lights. But I knew (Mrs. Atchison had found out) the number of the Hartleys' flat. We went upstairs and knocked. After a minute or two Mrs. Hartley opened the door. Er—her first name is Elizabeth, or Betty. She was wearing a pink dressing gown, and looked as though she had been roused out of bed. But she was frightened; I could tell that. The trouble was—"

"Well?" prompted Colonel March.

"She swore there was absolutely nothing wrong in the flat; that she had been in bed, and had heard no shots. The constable said quite sensibly, 'Well, ma'am, there were shots, because I heard them myself; and this gentleman says one of them nearly killed him.' She said that the inner walls of the flat were soundproof. It is only fair to admit that this is true.

"We demanded to be shown the unfurnished room. She made no difficulty about this. It opened off the central hall, where odds and ends of lumber were stacked in confusion: a sewing machine, a big box full of framed photographs, sheets of printed paper, a folding Japanese screen through which the constable unfortunately put his foot. We cleared this away, and went in. That was when I began to have a queer sensation that something spongy had got into my head where the brain ought to be.

"For the old man I had seen, alive or dead, was not in the room. And there was no bullet hole in the window."

"There was no bullet hole in the window," he repeated.

"Gentlemen, I think that bewildered me more than the absence of the victim. There might have been time for a victim to have been carried away or hidden before we arrived. I say there *might*. But a solid .38-caliber bullet (I have it here) had gone through the glass of this window before it went through the glass of mine; and there was not a scratch here to show where it had passed. Gloves and pistol were also missing.

"The policeman, I admit, looked at me oddly. I went round that room like—I had almost said, like a terrier sniffing. I don't care! Let me assure you that there was no possibility of having been mistaken about the room, or got the wrong room. There is only one place on a direct line with my bedroom; you must test it as I did then.

"I saw the gray carpeting, the cream walls. Here was the kitchen chair. Here was the table. Here were the three equidistant doors: the rear one opened into the hall, the right-hand one opened into the sitting room, and the left-hand one into an empty linen closet. The only thing I had been unable to see from my bedroom was a radiator under the window. The only mark of any kind in the room was a long triangular indentation in the pile of the carpet where, Mrs. Hartley explained, the folding Japanese screen had stood before they cleared this room of lumber.

"Now, Mrs. Hartley was terrified of something. That I'll swear. She has very expressive hazel eyes, and she did not even seem to hear what I was saying. She stood there with her face flushed, hugging her dressing gown round her in the cold, but she seemed as much puzzled as terrified. I warned her, for her own good, that if she was having anything to do with thieves and killers she would regret it."

He moved his neck.

"The worst of it occurred when her husband came bursting in, tying on *his* dressing gown, and alleging that *he* had been roused by our voices 'yelling' in his flat in the middle of the night. I was not yelling. But he was in a vile temper. His hair, which was rumpled, stuck straight out in front like the peak of a cap; and his face, which I should have described as nondescript and rather unpleasant, now looked concretely sinister.

"By this time the constable had grown apologetic, but I would have none of this. 'Never apologize, never explain' is my motto; an aristocratic motto, if I may say so. Hartley, I am afraid, was angry. He denied that he had ever seen or heard of the old man.

" 'So,' he said, 'you saw a pair of gloves pick up a gun and shoot somebody who doesn't exist? Blast my ears with lightning! Did you wake me up in the middle of the night just to tell me that? You didn't see a line of cigars hanging in the air and smoking themselves, did you? Look at this flat. It's an ordinary flat, or at least I thought it was. Look at this door. It's a practical door, and no invisible man walked through it. If you want to search the place, go ahead. And then get out.'

"But this did not last. When we went into the sitting room, where it was warm, something occurred that struck the anger off his face. Up to that time I was at my wits' end. Perhaps I talked sharply, and turned things out of drawers; but I am accustomed to being obeyed unquestioningly, as any clerk of mine will tell you. Then I knew I was right, for I saw it: a photograph, in an old-fashioned frame, brightly lighted by a table lamp. There was no mistaking those staring spectacled eyes; it was a photograph of the old man who had disappeared.

"Hartley knew that I had seen it, and his expression altered. The whole atmosphere of the room changed, too. He made a quick movement to get in front of the picture, or snatch it away, but I was there ahead of him. His forward movement was so violent that he slipped on the smooth pile of the carpet; he must have twisted his ankle, for he went down with a crash that turned him muddy pale. Mrs. Hartley ran to him, screaming his first name. When she lifted up his shoulders I was rather appalled by the look she gave me; for what had I done?

"A few minutes later I was out in the street, advised by the constable to go home. They showed me proofs of the truth. I could not doubt the truth, and you will sympathize with me when I say I had the horrors all night. But I'm a taxpayer, and a decent citizen, and I insist on knowing the meaning of it. That photograph was a picture of Hartley's grandfather, who died before the war."

At this point, quietly, a constable came into the room with an official form filled up. There was a rattle as Inspector Roberts put coal on the fire. The echo of Rodman's shrill voice still seemed to linger; firelight grew brighter in the big room while Roberts used the poker. And the constable said, "A Mr. and Mrs. Hartley to see you, sir."

"Ask Mr. and Mrs. Hartley to wait a moment," said Colonel March blandly.

He got up and went over to stand with his back to the fire. He had the military trick of standing as though bent a little forward from the waist, his arms slightly curved at his sides; but this stiffness contrasted with the amusement of his speckled face. A bland blue eye surveyed them, and his short pipe seemed in danger of scorching his nose as he sniffed amusedly at it.

"We must discuss the matter first," he explained. "Mr. Rodman,

I rather envy you. Your adventure is what a younger generation would describe as hot stuff."

"If," said Rodman, freezing up, "you prefer to make fun of—"

"Not at all," the other assured him. "I believe every word you say."

Inspector Roberts, though youngish, was well trained. He did not actually drop the poker with which he was stirring the fire, though he looked as if it had been a near thing.

"You think," cried Rodman, "I saw a—?"

"Ghost? Oh, no." Colonel March added, as though consolingly, "Not this time, anyhow."

"Then it was a real crime after all? A real man was shot with a real bullet in that room? Is that what you think?"

"I am quite sure of it."

Rodman seemed as taken aback as though he had never believed this. "But how? I ask you, *how?* There was nobody in the room; there was no corpse, as your friend says; there was no bullet hole in the window; there was—"

"Wait a bit," urged March. "Never mind your notebook for the moment, Roberts. Before we consider any course of action, I should like to dig a few more gems out of our friend's admirable narrative style. Mr. Rodman, how long have the Hartleys lived in that flat?"

"Two weeks last Monday, I think."

"Previous to last night, had you ever been inside the room where the man was shot?"

"Never."

"That little table in the room, now. You said it was a round table. Was it also a three-legged table?"

"Didn't I tell you it was? But please listen to me," begged Rodman, as though he had not been able to get a word in edgeways. "If a man was killed there, who was he? I've questioned people till I'm blue in the face, and nobody ever saw him or heard of him. Where's his body? And how was it done? And did Hartley kill him? I ask you, as a public servant, to answer relevant questions, if you can think of any answer. What difference does it make whether the table had three legs or four legs? Or whether the room had one door or two doors or six doors, for that matter?"

"On the contrary," said Colonel March, "the number of doors

is very important. If there had been only one door in the room, the criminal would not have been able to act."

"But I tell you nobody went in or out by any of the doors!"

"Oh, that," said Colonel March. "I quite agree with you."

"Then—"

"No, you don't," said the other, with ferocious geniality. He pointed his finger. "You're enjoying yourself immensely. You never got such a thrill in your life as you've had out of this. You came here with the particular purpose of mystifying me, to spread the glad tidings of terror to a wider audience than Mrs. Atchison; and now you're damned well going over the same jumps you set for me. Ask Mr. and Mrs. Hartley to come in."

It might be wondered how Rodman's description of this couple coincided with the facts. It is possible that his account of Mrs. Hartley, at least, was colored by a romantic imagination. Betty Hartley did not seem ethereal or spiritual. She was a good-looking, healthy-looking girl whose grave hazel eyes were redeemed by dimples at the corners of the mouth; a brown velour hat was tilted over her thick yellow hair. Her husband, peering over her shoulder, had rather a strong face with a trace of irony in it. They both stopped dead on the threshold when they saw Rodman.

"Oh, bother!" said the girl explosively.

"Come in," said Colonel March, teetering before the fire. "Come in and sit down. This is Inspector Roberts. The other one I think you know. Mr. Rodman had been telling us a very interesting story—"

"I don't doubt it," observed Hartley with an air of gloom. "Well, what do you think?"

"I think," said Colonel March, "that you were very foolish to come here."

Rodman had been right about one thing, at least: Betty Hartley was afraid.

"He insisted on coming," she said. "I told him not to come. I begged him not to, though not for the reason you may be thinking. We came here to give our version of what happened the other night. But since Mr. Rodman has been good enough to—"

"My dear young lady," said Rodman, as though he were beginning a letter. He tried to soften this. "Please see, try to see, that I am acting in your own interests. Look at you; you're trembling. I have always made my own decisions in this life, and—"

Betty Hartley spoke fretfully. She said, "Oh, dry up!"

"As for me," remarked Hartley with a cheerful air, "I hold by the *corpus delicti*. I wouldn't like to swear how the thing works, but I know it gives a devil of a lot of trouble in detective stories. You can't hang me until you can produce the victim's teeth or whiskers. And I hope, conversely, that I'm not to blame if a ghost walks on the premises." His tone changed, and he looked up. "Why was I foolish to come here?"

Colonel March's voice became sharp.

"Because, if I know your symptoms at all, you ought to be at home in bed," March answered. "You must have a nasty bullet wound in your shoulder where your wife shot you last night."

There was a silence of such bursting quality that they even became aware of dim outer noises in the building: the passing of footsteps and the closing of a door. It took a little time for the words to sink in. Mr. Horace Rodman got to his feet, and sat down again. He has since described (to Mrs. Atchison) that he has seldom been so taken aback in his life—especially at the scared face of Betty Hartley. But he was just as taken aback by the subsequent amusement. Hartley had sat down, looking less ill. And both Hartley and Colonel March were chuckling.

"So you spotted it," said Hartley. "Well, thank the Lord for that."

"Furthermore," insisted the colonel, with an expression of great pleasure nevertheless, "if you don't put your arm back in that sling again, you'll get into serious trouble with the doctor. Mrs. Hartley, I beg your pardon. I know the shooting wasn't a part of the game, but I hardly think you'll get into any difficulty over—"

"I don't see how you can stand there and laugh," cried the girl. "It was horrible. And you don't understand! I—"

"I hope I understand," said the colonel. He turned to Hartley. "You're a theatrical producer, aren't you?"

"And doing well," agreed the other with decision. "Two fairly good runs in two years. Not West End, maybe. But wait! So you'd heard of me, eh? Which one did you see, *The Riddle in Red* or *Dead Voices?*"

Colonel March was apologetic.

"As a matter of fact, neither. Mr. Rodman's painstaking account of your talk made it seem likely, and *you* said, 'Look at this door. It's a practical door.' The choice of term was distinctive. A *practical* door or window, meaning a real one, is a word used exclusively in stage terminology. The big box of framed photographs suggested the theater, as the sheets of printed paper suggested playbills. But when I heard about the long triangular indentation in the pile of the carpet, just as used by your famous predecessor, I felt sure you were trying out a variation of the original illusion. D'you mind telling me what you were up to?"

"Stage version of *The Invisible Man,*" replied Hartley with enthusiasm. "Never been done. And I can do it. Look! If I take—" He broke off. "You know the basis of the trick?"

"It deserves to be mentioned with reverence," said March, in equal enthusiasm. "It is a variation of the first really revolutionary stage-illusion of modern times. The magician and illusionist, Colonel Stodare, presented it first as 'The Sphinx' in 1865. On the same principle the great Maskelyne built his Disappearing Cabinet, and it has been the foundation of nearly every ghost-illusion since.

"This is how 'The Sphinx' was presented. In the middle of three sides of a black-draped stage stood a circular table with three legs. On this table appeared a severed head without a body. It talked, answered questions and so on; yet the audience could see over, under, and through the table to assure themselves there was no person there. Ah, you remember it? Now imagine a square, which is the stage. In the center of the square imagine a triangle, formed by the three legs of the table, with its apex or point toward the audience. In each of the two long sides of the triangle—toward the audience—is set a looking glass. You think you are seeing under the table to the back wall. What you actually see is the reflection of the two side walls and floor, similar black curtains and carpeting, coming together to form a perfect whole. The invisible body, of course, is hidden by the two sheets of looking glass.

"You, Mr. Hartley, made an ingenious improvement on it. Your room had three white-painted doors, exactly the same on three sides. Your Sphinx-table stood in the middle. One of the looking glasses would reflect half of the under part of the door on the right; the other would reflect half of the under part of the door on the left. The walls were the same; carpet was fitted up to the base-boards. A watcher opposite would apparently see under the table —to the rear wall, carpet, and rear door: which door was really the fitted-together reflection of the doors on either side.

"In your sinister Crippen roll, evilly mustached, you had to take certain precautions. You had to wait until you were in the room, until you had put down gloves and pistol on the table and moved to the window, before you could turn on the light. Otherwise you would have been seen smack in the looking glass. Afterward a pair of gloves, ably played by your wife and helpmeet, could be made to appear above the table and perform what antics they liked. The invisible man!"

Hartley made a gesture of silent applause. Betty Hartley was almost in tears. But by this time Mr. Horace Rodman had reached a point of hysteria.

"Illusion!" he howled. "Don't tell me I saw an illusion. I won't believe it. I won't have it. A real bullet broke my window. It nearly killed me. But it went through their window without—"

"You play this one," Hartley said politely to Colonel March.

"Thank you," said the colonel. "Correct me if I am wrong: that was an error; that was not intended, any more than you were intended to be shot." He turned to Rodman. "I rather think that part of it is clear, from your own recital. When you went bursting into their flat that night, it was very cold in the little room. You particularly commented to me on how cold it was. But there was a radiator in that room, and the flat was centrally heated through-out. In the next breath you explained how you went into the sitting room, where it was quite warm. Am I being deeply subtle if I suggest that it was cold because the window—or one pane of it— had been open for some little time? You pointed out that several panes of those long windows opened out like little doors. The terrible mustached figure opened one pane, stuck his head out, and whistled to attract your attention in case he hadn't already done so. He left it a few inches open, and didn't think to lock it again until you broke in with the policeman some time afterward. I rather think that is how the bullet crept out."

Hartley was nursing his arm and musing.

"My dear old grandpop," he said, "the most villainous-looking old coot who ever carried a collection plate in church. I have impersonated him, under the stimulus of his picture, in several repertory productions where some seedy thug is—"

"I think I must be going mad," Rodman interrupted, staring at Colonel March. "What did I hear you say? 'Whistled to attract my attention?' Attract *my* attention? Why?"

Hartley looked politely at his wife.

"And *you* play this one," he said.

"I will," said Betty, seeming to bristle up inside. She turned on Rodman. "Do you know what you are?"

"My dear young lady—"

The dear young lady rose in a glory of rage.

"Do you know what you've been doing, you and your precious Mrs. Atchison? Do you deny you've been snooping and spying on us, just as you do on everyone else you can, only worse, ever since we've moved into that flat? You've tried to find out everything about us you can. You've stood up there with a pair of field glasses and followed me from room to room, making life a perfect misery to me. I'll bet—"

("Better see that the door is closed," Colonel March said to Hartley.)

"—and, since we were going to test the mirror illusion anyway, I thought we'd just teach you a jolly good lesson, and scare your hair off. I suppose it's all my fault, really. I thought that was a property gun, loaded with blanks. Only it wasn't. And I'm glad I broke your beastly old window, anyway. But when we saw what an awful row we'd caused with real shots, we had to pretend it didn't happen, or you'd have had us in the police court for shooting at you. Jim would have had to explain what he was about, and ruined the play—"

"Light of my life—" began her husband pacifically.

"And of course, Jim would go on. I had to hold you off while he got rid of the grandfather make-up and slid the mirrors out from the grooves in the table and hid them, and closed the window. Oh, I don't mind anything else; but I can't forgive you for being so virtuous and triumphant when you grabbed that photograph, and saw Jim slip and land with his full weight on the carpet just after he'd g-got a bullet—"

"You'll have to say it another time, Mrs. Hartley," said Inspector Roberts, looking out of the open door. "Mr. Rodman seems to have left us in a hurry."

She grew calmer, and grinned impishly. "That's off my chest, anyhow. I'm terribly sorry, though. Can he prosecute us?"

"Somehow," said Hartley, "I don't think he will. When this story begins to circulate—no, I don't think he will. With regard to his future conduct, too; when the butcher and the candlestick-maker hear their version of his heroic conduct, he will be—"

Colonel March nodded magnificently, like an emperor.

"Exactly," he said. "The real invisible man."

BLIND MAN'S BUFF

Frederick Irving Anderson

The greatest thief in English literature is A. J. Raffles, the gentleman jewel thief whose adventures were originally written by E. W. Hornung and are now made public by Barry Perowne. The American counterpart of the consummate criminal is the Infallible Godahl, created for The Saturday Evening Post *by one of America's greatest short story writers, the almost forgotten Frederick Irving Anderson.*

Godahl is such a brilliant thief that he has never even been suspected of a crime. The intellectual superior of any potential adversary on the side of the law, his nefarious endeavors are inevitably successful. They cannot fail, because Godahl's massive brain has foreseen every possibility, anticipated every difficulty, and discovered a solution to every problem.

The only man aware of Godahl's infallibility is Oliver Armiston, an author who recorded some of his achievements. The crimes were so perfectly conceived and flawlessly executed that other criminals patterned their own crimes, successfully, on Armiston's stories. The police finally had to pay Armiston substantial amounts not *to write stories.*

Godahl's only fear is of the afflicted. He believes that the loss of sight, of hearing, or other infirmities causes a heightening of sensitivity of the senses that remain, giving the "afflicted" person an advantage over a "normal" one.

Six tales about the ultimate criminal, including "Blind Man's Buff," were published in Adventures of the Infallible Godahl *(1914).*

"Godahl, attend!" said that adept in smart crime to himself as he paused at the curb. "You think you are clever; but there goes your better."

He had to step into the street to make way for the crowd that overflowed the pavement—men and women, newsboys, even un-horsed actors leaving their pillars for the time for the passing sensation, the beginning of the homing matinée crowds—all elbowing for a place about a tall, slender man in black who, as he advanced, gently tapped a cane point before him. What attracted the vortex, however, was not so much the man himself as the fact that he wore a black mask. The mask was impenetrable. People said he had no eyes. It was Malvino the Magician, born to eternal darkness. From a child, so the story went, his fingers had been schooled with the same cruel science they ply in Russia to educate the toes of their ballet dancers—until his fingers saw for him.

Head erect, shoulders squared, body poised with the precision of a skater—his handsome, clear-cut features, almost ghastly in contrast to the band of silk ribbon that covered the sockets where sight should have been—he advanced with military step in the cleared circle that ever revolved about him, his slender cane shooting out now and again with the flash of a rapier to tap-tap-tap on the flags. Why pay for an orchestra chair to witness his feats of legerdemain? Peopling silk hats with fecund families of rabbits, or even discovering a hogshead of boiling water in an innocent by-stander's vest pocket, was as nothing to this theatric negotiation of Broadway in the rush hour of late Saturday afternoon. Malvino the Magician seemed oblivious to everything save the subtle impulses of that wand of a cane.

He stopped, suddenly alert to some immediate impression. The vague features relaxed; the teeth shone.

"Ah! Godahl, my friend!" he cried. He turned and advanced deliberately through the crowd that opened a path in front of him. Those wonderful hands reached out and touched Godahl on the arm, without hesitation as to direction.

Godahl could not repress a smile. Such a trick was worth a thousand dollars a week to the front of the house; and nobody knew better than the Great Malvino the value of advertising. That was why he walked Broadway unattended twice a day.

When he spoke it was in French. "I am sickened of them all," he said, sweeping his cane in a circle to indicate the gaping crowd straining to catch his words. "See! We have at hand a public chauffeur with nothing better to do than to follow in the wake of the Great Malvino. Godahl, my friend, you are at leisure? Then we will enter."

And Godahl, playing his cards with enjoyment and admiration as well, permitted the blind man to open the door and help him —Godahl, possessing five senses—into the cab; pleased doubly, indeed, to note that the magician had managed to steal his wallet in the brief contact. "To the park!" ordered Malvino, showing his teeth to the crowd as he shut the door.

Godahl had known Malvino first in Rome. The great of the earth gravitate toward each other. No one knew how great Godahl was except himself. He knew that he had never failed. No one knew how great Malvino was except Godahl. Once he had attempted to imitate Malvino and had almost failed. The functions of the third finger of his left hand lacked the wonderful coordination possessed by the magician. Malvino knew Godahl as an entertaining cosmopolitan, of which the world possesses far too few.

"I would exercise my Eng-lish," said the mask, "if you will be so good, my friend. Tell me—you know the lake shore in that city of Chicago?"

"As a book," said Godahl. "You are about to parade there—eh?"

"I am about to parade there," replied Malvino, imitating the accents of the other. "Therefore I would know it—as a book. Read it to me—slowly—page by page, my friend. I walk there shortly."

Godahl possessed, first of all, a marvelous faculty of visualizing. It was most necessary, almost as much so in fact for him in his profession as for Malvino in his—Malvino without eyes. In a matter-of-fact manner, like a mariner charting some dangerous channel, he plotted the great thoroughfare from the boulevard entrance to the auditorium. The other listened attentively, recording every word. He had made use of Godahl in this way before and knew the value of that man's observations. Then suddenly, impatiently, "One moment; there is another thing—of immediate need. The Pegasus Club? We are passing it at this moment—eh? You are one of the—what is it they say?—ah, yes, the fifty little millionaires—ha-ha!—yes?"

Godahl looked out of the window. Indeed, they were passing the club now. They had been proceeding slowly, turning this way and that, halted now and again or hurried on by traffic policemen, until they were merely a helpless unit in the faltering tide of Fifth Avenue; it was past five in the evening and all uptown New York was on the move, afoot and awheel.

It was said of Malvino that he would suffer himself to be whirled round twenty times on being set down in some remote neighborhood of a strange city, and with the aid of his cane find his way back to his hotel with the surety of a pigeon. But even that faculty did not explain how he knew they were passing a certain building, the Pegasus Club, at this moment. Unless, thought Godahl—who was better pleased to study the other's methods than to ask questions—unless the sly fox had it recorded in his strange brain map that carriage wheels rattled over cart tracks a hundred yards below this point. Godahl smiled. It was simple after all.

"I perform for your club Tuesday night. One thousand dollars they will pay me—the monkey who sees without eyes! My friend, it is good to be a monkey, even for such as these, who—but—" He paused and laid his hand on his companion's arm. "If I could but see the color that is called blue once! They tell me it is cool. They cannot make me feel how cool it is. You will go to sea with me next summer and tell me about it—eh? Will you not, my friend? But three of these—what you call the fifty little millionaires—you will tell me why they are called that, three of these came to me in my hotel and would grasp my hand. And why not? I would grasp the hand of the devil himself if he but offered it. They are surprised. They would blindfold my poor eyes—my poor eyes, Godahl!—blindfold them again, and again offer me their hands, thinking Malvino a charlatan. Ha-ha! Again I must shake hands with them! One wears a ring, with a great greasy stone. See! I have it here with me. It is bottleglass. Yet would this barbarian wear it until I in pity took it from him."

Godahl burst into a laugh. So this was the thief! Colwell, one of the so-called fifty little millionaires who gave the Pegasus Club its savor—who exhibited their silk hats and ample bootsoles in the plate-glass windows every Sunday afternoon—had been crying over the loss of a ring stone: a garish green affair for which he had paid hugely abroad.

"I am a marvelous man, eh, friend Godahl?"

"Indeed yes!" agreed the other, smiling.

"Malvino the Magician sought Godahl, his friend, this afternoon. Petroff, my manager, he walks ten steps behind me, in the crowd. He taps three times with his stick. Three steps to the right. Ha! There is Godahl! The *canaille* applaud; even Godahl must smile. My friend, Tuesday night Petroff is too clumsy. You will be my manager; but you must be somewhere else."

"Indeed not!" cried Godahl warmly; and to himself, "What does he drive at?"

"Indeed yes!" said the blind man, laying his hand again on the other's arm. "I ask it of you. You will be in other places. If you but say yes you will take me to sea in June and tell me what is the color blue. Listen! First, Malvino will play the monkey. Then I am to be locked in a room for five minutes. At the end of five minutes, if I am gone, that which I have is mine—even to their wallets—fat wallets like this one of yours, which I now return intact."

Godahl accepted the return of his wallet absent-mindedly.

"It is what Mr. Colwell calls a sporting proposition. See! I have it in writing. It is in addition to the $1,000. That I already possess. Now these fifty little millionaires, friend Godahl—are they all like the three who came to me in my hotel? The one with the slippery stone in his ring—the stone that I have—that one had $8,000— forty thousand francs—in one wallet in $1,000-notes. Does the American nation make new money especially for such as these? The notes were new, the imprint still crisp, like the face of my watch. Forty thousand francs in one wallet! I know, because I had the wallet as he talked. No, my friend. I have it not now. I put it back. Ha-ha! What? And there are fifty of them like that. I am to carry away what I can find! Godahl, it is told that the very servants of the club own rows of brick houses and buy consols at correct times. But fifty little millionaires! And Malvino is to be locked in a room, alone! I have it in writing."

A passing street lamp looked in and caught Godahl in the act of blinking.

"Godahl, my friend, if you will tell me what I must know, then I will teach you what you wish to know. You wish to know many things, eh? I can tell, for I always feel your eyes when you are by.

Tell me now, every inch of the way. Play it is the lake front in that city of Chicago."

Godahl chuckled. He did not love the fifty little millionaires. Those marvelous fingers! Malvino was playing with them in the air now in his earnestness. They could rob a poor box! Godahl, smiling grimly, began to draw the map his friend desired. Three steps up from the street, then the first glass door. Inside, two vestibules. Past them, on the right, the smoking room and lounge, a log fire at each end. On the left the street parlor, a great table in the center, and heavy chairs, all upholstered—none far from the walls. Between the rooms, on the left wall, the electric-switch panel. Would he play with light and darkness? It would be as well to hold the secret of this panel. On the floors, deep carpets—

"Deep carpets!" repeated the magician. "It is well I know. I do not like deep carpets. And this room, where I shall be left alone behind locked doors—"

"It would have to be the cloakroom, on the left of the main entrance," said Godahl. Yes, that would be the only available room for such a test. No other rooms off the street parlor could be locked, as there were no doors. In this cloakroom there were two doors: one on the main corridor and one on the first vestibule. There was a small window, but it was not to be thought of for one of Malvino's girth. The doors were massive, of oak; and the locks —Godahl remembered the locks well, having had need to examine them on a recent occasion—were tumbler locks. It would be rare business to see a man, even a magician, leave the cloakroom without help. And that, too, was in the bond—this sporting proposition.

"The locks have five tumblers," laughed Godahl, more and more amused.

"Let there be fifty!" whispered the other contemptuously. "Tell me, my observing friend, who counts the tumblers of a lock from the outside, do these doors open in or out?"

"In," said Godahl—and the long fingers closed on his wrist in a twinkling.

"In, you say?"

"In!" repeated Godahl; and he made a mental note to study the peculiar characteristics of doors that open in.

Malvino buried himself in his furs. The car sped on through the winding thoroughfares of the park, and Godahl fell to counting the revolving flashes of the gas lamps as they rushed by.

"This is the one place in your great city where I find joy," said the blind man at length. "There are no staring crowds; I can pick my thoughts; and the pavements are glass. Outside of these walls your city is a rack that would torture me. Tell me, why is blue so cool? June will be too late for the Mediterranean. We will start before. If you will but tell me, friend Godahl, so that I can feel it, I will give you the half—no! I will not. What is money to you? Are you quite sure about the doors opening in? Yes? That is good. Godahl, if I could see I think I would be like you—looking on and laughing. Let me tell you something of doors that open in—what! We are traveling at an unlawful speed! Mr. Officier—indeed, yes, the Great Malvino! Pity his poor eyes! Here is money falling from your hair! You are not a frugal man—so careless!"

The park policeman who had stopped them to warn them against speed stood staring at the crisp bill the blind man had plucked from his hair, as the taxicab sped forward again. Malvino directed the driver to his hotel through the speaking tube, and a few minutes later they were set down there. Godahl declined dinner with his queer friend.

"I have here your wallet once more, friend Godahl!" laughed the blind magician. "The fifty little millionaires! Ha-ha! You promise? You will not be there when I am there?"

"You have my stickpin," said Godahl. "I believe you are collecting bogus stones. That one is bogus, but it was thought to be a fine gift by a friend who is now dead."

The other, with evident disappointment, returned the pilfered stickpin. "You promise! You will not be there when I am there, my friend?"

Godahl held the blue-white hand in his own for a moment as they parted. "No, I promise you," he said; and he watched his queer friend walk away—Malvino erect, smiling, unfaltering in his fine stride, conscious to the last dregs of the interest he excited on all sides. He shunned the elevator and started up the broad marble stairs, his slender cane tap-tap-tapping, lighting the way for his confident tread.

Godahl dined at his club—looking on and laughing, as Malvino had said with a directness that rather startled the easy rogue into wakefulness. Godahl's career had defied innuendo; his was not an art, but a science, precise, infallible. But several times that afternoon in the somber shadows of their cab he had felt, with a strange thrill, that black inpenetrable mask turn on him as though an inner vision lighted those darkened orbs.

Frankly, he avoided afflicted persons in the pursuit of his trade, not because of compunction, which troubled him not at all, but because a person lacking in any of the five senses was apt to be uncannily alert in some one of the remaining four. He was intensely a materialist, a gambler who pinned his faith to marked cards, never to superstition. He believed intuition largely a foolish fetish, except as actuated by the purely physical cravings; yet he recognized a strange clarity in the mental outlook of the afficted that seemed unexplainable by any other means.

Malvino, too, played with marked cards. After all, magic is but the clever arrangement of properties. But why had Malvino picked him? Why had Malvino confided in him at all? There were a dozen other members of the Pegasus Club who would have served as well, so far as furnishing the business of the affair; who would have entered the game as a huge joke. To hold up the fifty little millionaires in their upholstered wallow would surely set the whole town by the ears. Something of the sort was needed to bring the ribald crew back to earth. But, thought Godahl, if the task were to be done he would much prefer to do it himself, not look on as a supernumerary.

Malvino, of course, was a thief. The only reason he did not practice his profession was that he found the business of playing the monkey paid better. Then, too, as a thief he must bury his talents; and there is nothing so sweet to the Latin as applause. Malvino could not keep his fingers quiet. Godahl had permitted himself to be stripped in their ride through sheer enjoyment of observation. There is nothing too small to be learned and learned well. Nevertheless, it had irritated him to think that this master had whispered in his ear familiarly. It smacked too much of kinship. Godahl knew no kin!

As he swept the magnificent dining room with his eyes, however, he could not repress a chuckle of sheer delight. It would be a hundred-day jest. They all conformed pretty well to type—a type against which the finer sensibilities of Godahl revolted. In the beginning the Pegasus had been the coming together of a few kindred souls—modest, comfortable, homelike; a meeting place of intellectual men who took their chiefest pleasure in the friction of ideas. In this way the organization had come to have a name, even among the many clubs of the city.

Godahl had adopted it as his home, and—he cynically paraphrased it—he might be without honor in his own country, but never in his own home. He had always been pleased to think that when he entered here he left the undesirable something outside, like the dust of his shoes on the doormat. Not that he lacked the lust of the game or a conscious pride in that slick infallibility which had made him a prince for whom other men went poor. There are times and places for all things. And this had been home.

Until, one by one, this tribe had crept in, overturned traditions, substituted the brass of vulgar display for the gold of the fine communion they did not profess to understand, much less to practice. A newspaper wag had finally dubbed them the Club of the Fifty Little Millionaires, and the name had stuck. It happened that a handful of them had been brooded in the same coop, that of a copper king who had begun at the slagpile and ended in philanthropy. As the newcomers gained ascendency the old sect of friends gradually drifted away. The pace was too fast for them.

There was truth in what Malvino had said of the servants; and there is nothing quite so unappetizing as the contempt of those who serve one meat and drink. But Godahl, looking on and laughing, still preserved the habit of picking his meals here with discriminating taste—though now he was less particular about wiping his feet on the doormat than formerly. He even indulged in play occasionally, and while he played he listened to the talk about things worth knowing.

Tonight the talk was all Malvino at the particular rubber where he chose to play. It was to be a rare occasion. True, they were to pay the magician roundly for the séance and had offered him, besides, a sporting proposition in the shape of written permission to carry off all his fingers could lift, but they chose to interpret sport according to their own lights. Two centuries ago it was sport in merry England to tie a gamecock to a stump and shy brickbats at it. The game was conducted according to rules carefully worked out, and was popular with all concerned—except the gamecock.

Godahl, at length getting his fill, rose in disgust and passed out. At the corner the street lamp winked at him in its knowing way, and Godahl, forgetting the gorge that had risen in him, returned the wink, smiling.

Colwell, the master of ceremonies, was venturing to a chosen few that a certain faker would be ineligible for dates on a kerosene circuit in Arkansas before the evening was over, when the telephone boy brought him a message from the Victoria. Malvino had started, and was driving to avoid the inevitable crowd that dogged his steps.

The committee was giving a last touch to its properties—a camera and flashlight apparatus arranged behind a screen—when there came the familiar tap-tap-tapping of the cane on the marble steps. If the lilt of his gait were any criterion the mask was in fine fettle.

"So," he was whispering, "three steps up from the street—two vestibules—and deep carpets. Deep carpets are bad!"

As he passed through the first vestibule this strange, impassive figure in dead black ran his fingers along the wall. There was the door, indeed, by which he would escape.

"Malvino the Magician!" cried a flunkey in gold lace as the inner doors swung open. Colwell was there, with extended hand. The hand of the other closed on it without hesitation, holding it for a moment.

"You speak no French? No? It is—most unfortunate. I speak things—and I am most awkward in your tongue. Is there the color blue here? I would touch it before I play."

He waved his cane toward the entrance. "The corridor? It is empty—yes? It is so in the bond. Thus," he cried, his teeth glowing at the circle of faces before him, "thus am I to take away that which is mine—is it not?"

Colwell elevated a knowing eyebrow at his companions. Colwell had not been a plumber's assistant for nothing in the days of his youth. He had plugged the key slots with molten lead. Once closed it would require the aid of a carpenter, not a locksmith—not even a magical locksmith—to negotiate the doors of the cloakroom. Colwell did not begrudge his walletful of small change at auction bridge, but he was decidedly averse to letting it fall into the hands of this blind beggar.

They helped him out of his coat. "My cane, too!" he said as he handed the cane to Colwell. It was of ebony, as thin as a baton and without ornament of any kind, save a platinum top. "It is—my faithful Achates! It is—a little brother to my poor senses. It is wonderful—" He swayed slightly and put out a hand to steady himself against Colwell. "But tonight, gentlemen, in your honor Malvino disarms himself, for the—how is it?—the fifty little millionaires—ha-ha!—who are so good as to receive me.

"Am I," he continued, "to have the honor of shaking the hands of the gentlemen? I do not know." He paused as though embarrassed, shrugged his shoulders deprecatingly, and then, smiling: "Myself, as a person, is not present if you so desire—only my talents, which you buy and pay for. Ah, I am awkward in your tongue. Sometimes, gentlemen, I am the guest, sometimes I am only the monkey, with his tricks. You understand? I thank you, sir. Saunders, of Texas Union? Ah, of the landed gentry of this great country! I am indeed pleasured."

A smile went the rounds. Saunders, of Texas Union, who was shaking the hand of the mask with one hand and discreetly feeling the muscles under the black-sleeved arm with the other, had been a puddler at Homestead until his talents for ragtime rescued him from oblivion and gave him Texas Union as a pocket piece. He brought forward Jones, of Pacific Cascade; Welton, of Tonopah Magnet; Smithers, of Excelsior Common; Jamieson, of Alleghany Western—and so on down the line. The guest, in his naïveté, seemed under the impression that the handles to the names referred to ancestral acres. These men had been named in the daily papers so often in connection with their pet manipulations in the market that they themselves had come to accept the nomenclature, using it much as an Englishman would say Kitchener of Khartoum or Marlborough of Blenheim.

So the mask was passed round the room. He was well worth

seeing at close range. He accepted each hand with a steely grip; concentrated the vague blackness of his mask on each face, and spoke briefly and in halting phrases. In laying aside his cane he seemed to have lost something of the poise that distinguished the Great Malvino on the street or on the stage; and he leaned heavily on a shoulder here, on an arm there, as he was passed from one to another. There was a tremor of excitement in the room. A diversion had been promised; but what it was to be the honorable gentlemen of the committee had kept to themselves and their confederates. Colwell, Saunders, and Mason—of Independent Guano—whispered together for a moment; and when the circle of introductions was complete the guest was led to the center of the room. He took his place at the head of the big table, exploring it nervously with his fingers while he waited for the company to be seated.

What followed was somewhat tame, and they expressed themselves to that effect occasionally behind their hands. They had seen the same thing before; a two-dollar bill gave the veriest street loafer the same privilege every afternoon and evening at the Victoria, except for a few parlor pieces the magician reserved for private entertainments. But even the makings of these were to be had for a few pennies in any one of the numerous shops on Sixth Avenue devoted to the properties of magic. It was merely quickness of hand against slowness of eye. It is said that the persistency of vision amounts to one-hundredth of a second. These fingers found ample room to work in that slit of time. Yet the circle looked on languidly, like an audience at a championship fistfight tolerating the preliminaries.

The performer had borrowed a pack of cards bearing the unbroken seal of the club, and was playing a solitary game of whist, cards faced—a trick of Malvino's, by the way, which has never been satisfactorily explained—when suddenly the barons of Tonopah, Alleghany, and so forth, sat up with a thrill of anticipation. It was evident to all, except perhaps the performer himself, that the apex of the evening was at hand. Mason softly opened the electric-switch cabinet; Colwell and Saunders moved carelessly toward the table, taking up positions on each hand of the mask, as though for a better view of the game.

Then came blank, overwhelming darkness! There was the scuffle of feet; the snapping impact of body against body; a gasp; a half-uttered cry of pain; then: "Confound him!" It was the voice of Colwell, breathing hard. "He's like a bull—Gad! Can't you—"

Then another voice—that of Saunders: "Steady, I've got him! Ready?"

The unseen struggle ceased suddenly. There were several in that thrilled circle that grew sick. It seemed evident that the honorable gentlemen of the committee had overpowered the magician, were about to strip him of his mask, to show him up as the charlatan who had too long duped a city. They wanted their money's worth. Colwell was laughing, short, sharp; he had the mask now—they could hear the silken ribbon rip as it came away.

"Now! Mason, let him have it!"

The words ended in a roar of mingled rage and pain; there came a sharp snap-snap—as of bones coming away from their sockets; and simultaneously the muffled explosion and the blinding glare of the camera flashlight. And in the one-hundredth of a second of incandescence there was indelibly imprinted on the vision of the audience the figure of the magician holding two men at arm's length, each by the wrist, their features hideously contorted. Then dead darkness fell, in the midst of which hung the imprinted scene in silhouette against a phosphorescent pall.

Someone thought of the lights. It was the magician himself. This curious circumstance was not noted until later. The switch clicked and the chandeliers sprang into being again. Colwell held the torn mask in his hand. Every eye, still straining for sight after the shock of the flashlight, sought the blind face of the performer. It was horribly blind now, stripped of its silk ribbon. Covering the eye-sockets he stumbled across the room, almost fell against the table. His uncertain hand sought Colwell's arm, traveled down its length, and took from the fingers the torn mask and replaced it. The master of ceremonies gazed at the cadaverous face, fascinated. The room was deathly silent. The magician flashed his teeth in a poor attempt at a smile. His voice, when he spoke, was in whispers as crisp as leaves.

"Ah—my poor eyes! I do not sell—gentlemen, I am clumsy with your words. Let me not offend those who are my friends among you when I say I do not sell you my private self—it is only the monkey in me you can buy."

Colwell and Saunders were making efforts to soothe their arms, which were suffering exquisitely. Several men pushed forward, ashamed, to bridge the embarrassment with their apologies to the magician, who stared at them imperturbably with the mask. Things gradually came to rights, except for the honorable gentlemen of the committee, who took the first chance to retire with their troubles. The hands of the mask were like steel and when he wrenched the bones in their sockets he had not dealt lightly.

"We proceed," said the magician with a deprecating wave of his hand. "The room! I am to be your prisoner. It is so written."

The few members who knew of Colwell's precautions of plugging the key slots with lead thought wryly of the fact now. If this thing went any further the Pegasus Club would be the butt of the town!

"We will forget that," said Welton, of Tonopah Magnet, assuming leadership in a movement to make amends. "Besides," he added with a laugh, "we haven't given you a chance to go through our pockets yet. You would have to escape empty-handed."

"Your pardon!" said the mask with a grand bow. "I have already taken the opportunity."

So saying he displayed the contents of his capacious pockets. He had at least a score of wallets and several rolls of banknotes. The room exploded in a cry of amazement. Then the truth flashed upon them. When they passed the guest from hand to hand his nimble fingers had been busy substituting wads of paper for wallets.

"The hour is late," he continued, feeling the face of his watch. "I must be gone in five minutes. The room—if you will."

Welton, of Tonopah Magnet, roaring with laughter, took the magician—they admitted now he was at least that—and led him to the door of the cloakroom.

"One favor!" said the mask at the threshold. "My coat—my hat —my faithful cane. Ah! I thank you. I bid you good night!"

The naïveté of the words was masterly. Welton, of Tonopah Magnet, drew the door shut with a slam and the lock clicked. He faced the others and turned his trousers pockets inside out comically. He was not worrying about the safety of his cash, but he did admire the deftness of those fingers.

"I am glad to say he left my watch," he said, and he put his watch on the table. It was lacking five minutes of midnight. "What gets me," he continued, turning toward the closed door, "is how we are going to get the poor devil out without a battering ram! Colwell has most certainly earned everlasting fame by his brilliant entertainment this evening."

The keys were useless now that the spring locks had snapped shut on the prisoner. Someone suggested sending for the engineer, but one and all agreed that the game must be played out in common decency. They all retired to the lounging room to give the blind beggar five minutes to find out the trick that had been played on him.

At the end of five minutes they sent for the engineer, and that grimy individual appeared, loaded down with tools; he expressed it as his reverend opinion that a damned fine door was about to be turned into scrap. There was one chance—that a gasoline torch might blow the lead from the keyslot. But, no—the molten metal only completed the upsetting of the fine mechanism. There was nothing to do but to cut around the lock with a compass saw.

"Cheer up, Malvino!" said Welton through the door. "We will be with you in another minute."

Just then Godahl ran in from the street. He threw his hat and coat to an attendant.

"Ha! The devil to pay—eh?" he cried excitedly. "I just this minute heard of it; and I rushed here."

"What?" said a number of voices at once.

The usually exquisite Godahl was somewhat disheveled and his eyes were red.

"Malvino!" cried he, staring at them as though perplexed at their blandness. "Do you mean to say you don't know why he didn't show up this evening?"

"Didn't show up! What do you mean?"

"You really don't know?" cried Godahl, his eyes blazing.

"No! What? Tell us the answer!" said someone with a laugh.

"The police found him bound and gagged in a deserted cab in Central Park. They've got him in Bellevue Hospital now, raving. By Gad! If I—"

The room laughed. Even the grimy engineer boring a hole to start his compass saw looked over his shoulder and grinned at Godahl.

"Don't excite yourself, Godahl," said Welton, of Tonopah Magnet. "Somebody's been stringing you. We've got Malvino here now. Gad, I wish we didn't have him! You're just in time to help us out of a devil of a mess. That humorist Colwell has plugged the locks with lead; and we can't get the blind beggar out without sawing the door down. He's sweating blood in there now."

"In there?" cried Godahl, pushing his way through the ring round the engineer.

"In there!" repeated Welton. "The kleptomaniac has got a cool ten thousand of mine."

"No!"

"Yes!" said Welton, mimicking Godahl's tone. "You didn't know there was that much money in the world, eh?"

"Let me get this straight," said Godahl, laying a hand on the engineer's arm to stop his work. "You think you have Malvino locked in there with your wallets? I tell you Malvino hasn't been within a mile of this place tonight!"

"I'll lay you a thousand on it!" cried Welton.

"Tut! tut! Believe me, you are betting on the wrong card." Godahl's eyes danced.

"I lay you a thousand on it!" reiterated the Tonopah magnate. "We'll have to let Malvino hold my stake until we get him out. Gad, he went through me so clean I couldn't swear at this minute that I've got on socks!"

"You are betting on a sure thing?"

"I'm taking candy from a child," retorted Welton.

"I take you!" cried Godahl, his eyes twinkling. "Anybody else want any candy? I warn you!"

There were several. It wasn't every day in the week that they could get Godahl on the hip.

"I warn you again," said Godahl as he accepted the markers, "that Malvino is not in that room. If anybody is there, it is an impostor. You can prove it in a minute by telephoning Bellevue."

The biting saw completed its half circle about the lock; the door swung open. The room was empty!

Several volunteers ran to the rear door. Their sharp chorus of amazement started the crowd tumbling after them. The rear door was off its hinges! It stood propped against the jamb. A child could see what had happened. The prisoner, laden with the cash of the fifty little millionaires, had simply drawn the bolts of the two hinges and lifted the door out of its frame. On the floor was a wad of handbills like those the rogue had left in his dupes' pockets in place of their wallets. They read: "Malvino! He Has No Eyes! Watch His Fingers!"

The fifty little millionaires gazed at each other dumbfounded, feeling their pockets the while. The Infallible Godahl fell into a chair, roaring with laughter. He threw back his head, kicked out his heels, buried his hands wrist deep in the crisp bills that lined his pockets—all in cold, hard cash! On the whole, he had never spent a more profitable evening.

As for Malvino the Magician, that charlatan could be mighty thankful that it was not he whom the honorable gentlemen of the committee had subjected to manhandling. For Malvino had the eyes of a hawk. So much Godahl had ascertained earlier in the evening when he, in the guise of a murderous cabby, was subjecting the Italian to the indignity of a gag.

THE LORD OF TIME

Rafael Sabatini

"The Lord of Time" is a fictional adventure of an actual historical character, the charlatan Count Alessandro Cagliostro. Born in Palermo, Italy, in 1743, Cagliostro was a great favorite of French society during Marie Antoinette's reign. Claiming to be two thousand years old and reputed to possess magical powers, he conducted séances and practiced hypnotism for important royal personages.

Unjustly accused of a swindle involving a priceless diamond necklace, he was banished from France by Louis XVI. Cagliostro and his beautiful wife, Serafina, took refuge in Rome, where she denounced him to the Holy Inquisition as a heretic, magician, and conjuror of demons. Condemned to life imprisonment, he died in the fortress of San Leo in 1795.

"The Lord of Time" is a story about Cagliostro, who was a master magician. Or was he? It is surely a crime story, because a brutal murder is committed. Or is it? At least a clever con job is pulled off. Or is it? This puzzling tale was first published between hard covers in Turbulent Tales *(1946), one of the least-remembered books by Rafael Sabatini, who is better known for such adventure novels as* The Sea Hawk *(1915),* Scaramouche *(1921), and* Captain Blood *(1922).*

It was Cagliostro's queer arresting gesture before the crucifix in the great square that supplied the decisive spur to the wishes of the Cardinal-Prince Louis de Rohan.

From the moment of his entrance into Strasbourg, in his gilded rococo coach, drawn by six cream-colored ponies, Count Cagliostro had been the focus of attention in the town, even before he had afforded evidence of his miraculous powers.

Without fee or guerdon he cured diseases which ordinary doctors had pronounced beyond human relief. As a result, and very soon, the house in which he lodged was besieged from early morning to late evening by the crowds that thronged to implore his aid or to gratify in some degree the extraordinary curiosity he excited. The fame of him ran, like a ripple over water, through Alsace. His power to expel disease was accounted superhuman and was almost the least of the superhuman attributes discovered in him. He was credited with possessing the secret of the fixation of mercury and the transmutation of metals; precious stones composed themselves under his hands from the commonest elements; he could restore youth to the aged, and he was actually master of an elixir of life itself; he possessed gifts of prophecy and clairvoyance, and he could read thoughts as easily as another might detect the signs of emotion on a countenance; to such extraordinary lengths did he carry the art with which Mesmer had lately astonished the world that he was said to have the power of controlling the very souls of men, and that he rendered manifest how far was Mesmer from understanding the application of those forces upon the wills of which he had more or less accidentally blundered. In short, this Count Cagliostro, coming no man knew whence, was being pronounced divine.

That great aristocrat, that nobel Maecenas, the Cardinal-Prince de Rohan, who was more royal than the king—for in his veins ran the blood of every house that had ever given kings to France—heard of these marvels, and was moved to desire a nearer acquaintance with them. All his life a passionate student of alchemy, botany, astrology, and the occult in general, the cardinal brought to the study of the supernatural the open-mindedness of a credulous person. It seemed to him that if Cagliostro were indeed sincere, and not merely a charlatan, like so many in France just then, he might bring to real fruition pursuits which His Eminence had hitherto found vexatiously elusive in results. And then came the report of those queer words in the square to quicken his desire.

Count Cagliostro had gone forth one evening to take the air, followed at a respectful distance by his servant, the slight, dark, pallid fellow who bore the curious name of Abdon. The count's appearance was that of a man in the prime of life, between thirty and forty. Of middle height, his frame was thick-set and vigorous, and he carried his big, coarsely handsome head with an air of majesty on his powerful neck. He was dressed with an ostentation that in itself took the eye. His blue silk coat was laced in gold along the seams, with the sword worn through the pocket; his red-heeled shoes were fastened with buckles of precious stones; brilliants flashed in the billows of lace at his throat; rubies attached his solitaire and glowed in the buckle that held the white plumes in his hat *à la mousquetaire.* It has been testified by practically all who knew him, and who have left records, that few could support the direct gaze of his full, bold, dark, uncanny eyes.

As he walked, men turned to observe and to follow him, until an inquisitive crowd had formed at a respectful distance in his wake. This was customary. Just as it was customary for him, aloof and absorbed, to appear unconscious of the attention he was attracting.

And then at last he came to pause before the crucifix in its open shrine. Leaning upon the jeweled head of his ebony cane, he stood for some moments in thoughtful, wistful contemplation.

"Strange, Abdon," he said at last, over his shoulder, to his servant, "that one who can never have seen Him should so faithfully reproduce His lineaments." There was an implication here that sent a thrill of awe through the attendant, but respectfully silent, crowd. Then, after a long pause, Cagliostro sighed and spoke again. "Do you remember that evening in Jerusalem when they crucified Him?"

The spectators caught their breath, then held it so as not to miss the answer. Abdon, bowing low with something of the Orient in his manner, replied quietly but distinctly, "You forget, master, that I have been with you only fifteen hundred years."

"Ah, true," said the count. "I was forgetting. But with so many centuries to remember—" He left the sentence there, shrugged, and sauntered on.

A report of this left the cardinal-prince wondering whether this man of marvels was indeed divine or merely the most impudent charlatan that had ever walked the earth. His Eminence, considering it incumbent upon him to resolve the question, sent a gentleman of his following, the Baron de Planta, to command Cagliostro to wait upon him at the Château de Saverne, where His Eminence had his seat.

Cagliostro's reception of the command reflected his lofty disdain of the mighty of this world.

"If the cardinal is ill let him come to me, and I will cure him. If he is well he has no need of me, nor I of him."

That anyone should send such a message to the cardinal-prince implied to the Baron de Planta that the end of the world was at hand. And this was confirmed by the manner in which the matchlessly urbane and gracious cardinal received it.

"Sublime reply, whatever the man may be," was the liberal opinion he expressed.

Louis de Rohan was approaching fifty at the time, but his tall figure still preserved the grace of youth as did his countenance, which, reflecting his mind, was handsome in a rather infantile way; it was so smooth of contours, and so free of lines, that his ashen hair seemed prematurely faded.

Accustomed from earliest youth to sycophancy, the proud independence of Count Cagliostro drew this great prince, temporal and spiritual, to seek the man of marvels at his lodging in Strasbourg, like the humblest suitor. There, attended only by de Planta, he waited without resentment in the thronged antechamber to take his turn, as was imposed by one who made a parade of awarding no precedence to rank.

What reservations the cardinal's ingenuous mind still harbored on the subject of Count Cagliostro's claims were dispelled almost as soon as he came to stand in the count's presence. Under the hypnotic gaze of the man's singular eyes, dark and lustrous and of a penetration that seemed unearthly, His Eminence experienced such a sense of awe that his own glance fell abashed. But when he had accepted the proffered chair a mild resentment stirred in him that he, who had borne as an equal the gaze of kings, should have suffered himself so easily to be stared down. Determinedly he raised his eyes again, and compelled himself to meet and hold the other's glance. Soon, however, whilst Cagliostro, who remained standing before him, talked in a deep vibrant voice and in a language that was only just perceptibly French, the cardinal became aware that it was not himself but the count who was exercising this compulsion: that it was his own glance that was being held, and that he was powerless to withdraw it from those glittering orbs that seemed presently to wax and wane as he watched them in a helpless fascination. Rohan began to be pervaded by a sense of his own unreality; it was as if all power of will and of self-assertion had gone out of him. His senses were being further lulled into subjection by the rise and fall in rhythmical hypnotic cadences of the voice addressing him in that curious Italianate-French.

"Now that I behold you I perceive the source of your persistence, monseigneur. We have met before."

To this the bewildered cardinal, after a faltering search in his memory, made answer: "I don't remember."

"How should you? Between this and that stand for you the walls of a dozen deaths, a dozen rebirths. The soul-memory deep within you is choked and smothered by the ponderous strata of all the flesh it has since worn, with the lusts, the passions, the sins, and aspirations that belong to each. It was sixteen centuries ago in Antioch. You were a Roman proconsul, and I was, *mutatis mutandis,* much as I am now, a wanderer upon the face of the earth, a traveler down the ages."

Even in the befogged state of his senses this was more than His Eminence could be expected to digest. Indeed, indignation at the impudent affront to his intelligence aroused combativeness.

"You will have evidence of this?" he said, in quiet mockery.

"Evidence!" boomed the sonorous voice. "What is evidence? The thing seen. And what shall be seen of the eternal verities by poor human vision, as narrowly restricted to the immediate environment as is that of the blind earthworm to the soil in which it burrows? Can the earthworm see the stars? How, then, help him if he asks for evidence of their existence? And how help man if he asks for evidence of what lies beyond them?"

Despite himself the cardinal must admit that there was theological authority for these implications.

"And yet," the mystagogue continued, "since you ask for it, some evidence I shall hope to give you before all is said. So condescend to hear me out.

"You were drawn to me in those far-off days as you are drawn now, which is to say that you were inquisitive about me; inquisitive and mistrustful. Then your Roman arrogance, your Roman skepticism, obfuscated your understanding. You supposed me an impostor, a vain seducer, even as remains of arrogance and skepticism, heritage of those Roman days—a heritage which has cursed and warped your every incarnation—still afflict you now. It is so, monsiegneur. Do not interrupt me.

"In those days I was your friend. I realized the greatness latent in your soul, a soul so closely in tune with mine; and I sought to deliver it from its dull chrysalis of carnal pride, to set it free to soar in the empyrean, and from those calm altitudes to survey eternity. I would have made you lord of life and time, you who then, as now, were but the ephemeral lord of a fleshly envelope. I would have spread before you the fruits of the Tree of Life and rendered you everlasting as myself. But stubborn and obstinate in your puny pride you mocked; and so I left you to your poor carnal limitations, and went my ways."

And here the cardinal, deathly pallid, and with eyes that still stared but were now dull and vacant, contrived at last to interrupt him.

It required a supreme effort to break through the web that was being spun about his wits, to conquer a difficulty of articulation such as will trammel a man in dreams. But he conceived that he had received illumination, and at all costs he must voice it.

"I know you now," he cried. "You are the Wandering Jew, the accursed cobbler of Jerusalem who spat upon Our Lord, and is doomed to walk the earth until He comes again."

A smile swept like a shadow across the olympian calm of Cagliostro's countenance. Sorrowfully the great, compelling eyes considered the prelate.

"How history repeats itself! So you said then, sixteen hundred years ago. When your wits were baffled by proof of my unaccountable longevity, they took refuge from the intolerable truth in the only explanation legend offered you. But you are wrong now as you were wrong then. I am not the Wandering Jew. I am older than Cartaphilus, older than Jerusalem, where I was with Solomon at the building of the Temple. And I shall survive them both. For I have eaten of the Tree of Life. My *elixir vitae* is distilled from its fruits. To me, existence is not as a string of beads—a succession of brief moments of consciousness in eternity; fleeting, uncomprehended glimpses of the world. To me, existence is a continuous stream, visible from its source to the limitless ocean of eternity into which it flows. For me, this illusion men call time has no reality. For I am He Who Is."

On those last five words his vibrant, metallic voice had swelled to a trumpet note. Thence it fell again at once to its quieter level.

"Yet that you tell me again, as you told me sixteen centuries ago in Antioch, that I am Cartaphilus, proves that I have touched in you at least a chord of that soul-memory which survives deep down in each of us. What you have remembered is what you called me once before. Let me now help your poor human weakness. Look into this mirror and endeavor to see what once you were when last I was beside you."

Leaning his elbow on the table beside the cardinal, Cagliostro extended his left hand, which was gloved in black velvet. Cupped in the palm of it he displayed a crystal sphere something less in circumference than a tennis ball.

So dominated by now that, in obeying, he experienced no sense of derogating, Rohan directed his gaze as he was bidden. For some moments he stared into the empty depths of the crystal. Suddenly he moved and caught his breath. He leaned forward, peering.

"I see. I see," he murmured thickly. "I see men; a multitude; an arena; a pillared marble tribune."

"Center your gaze upon that tribune," Cagliostro commanded. "What do you find there?"

"A man of medium height and powerful frame, boldly featured, with eyes that burn their way into one's brain. He is in white; a snowy chlamys edged with gold. I know his face. Ah! It is yourself."

"And the man in the chair? Look at him: the man who sits elbow on knee and chin on fist, with a proud sad face that is wreathed in weariness and disdain? Can you name him?"

The cardinal bent closer still; he hesitated; he was breathing heavily. "Can it be myself?"

The gloved hand closed upon the crystal and was swiftly withdrawn. Cagliostro drew himself erect, and his voice rang hard. "Yourself. Marcus Vinicius, as you then were named."

The abruptness of movement and tone seemed to shatter a spell. Rohan sat up, restored to a normal alertness. The color crept back into his cheeks. He passed a hand, long and slim, and delicate as a woman's, across eyes and brow.

"You are master of strange secrets, sir," he said slowly and gravely. Then he added a complaint. "My senses are a little dazed, I think."

"That will pass." Cagliostro spoke harshly, and waved a hand contemptuously. "No man may look down the ages and hope to escape vertigo. It will pass. What I have discovered for you, however, remains. So that you have faith, you may now prevail where you failed before. To help you I am here; for your soul is now of a strength to bear the secrets I could impart to you, to employ the power which must never be bestowed unworthily. I am at your service, Prince Louis. And my coming is timely, if only so that I may restore your fortune so sadly sapped by the Prince de Gué-menée."

The cardinal was startled. "You know that?"

Again Cagliostro waved a hand. He was prodigal of gesture. "Does not all the world know it?" he asked, like a man scorning to make a mystery of the possession of knowledge reached by ordinary channels.

It was, indeed, common knowledge how much of his fortune Louis de Rohan had sacrificed to buttress the honor of his family which had been so sadly imperiled by the bankruptcy of his nephew the Prince de Guémenée. Vast though his wealth might be, it could scarcely bear the strain of some thirty millions which that bankruptcy was imposing upon it. With deeply rooted habits of prodigal expenditure in the maintenance of his more than princely establishment, without knowledge of economy, a knowledge which his munificent spirit scorned to acquire, the cardinal-prince was sweeping toward the edge of financial difficulties.

He was not, however, at present concerned with this. His thoughts were consumed in the endeavor to extricate the present startling experience from the fog, as of a dream, that seemed to enshroud it.

"It is all strange," he murmured. "So very strange! Incredible! And yet something within me seems to compel belief."

"Now God be thanked that you are at last given grace to conquer the obstinacy of material skepticism. You yield at last to the instinctive knowledge of reincarnation deep in each of us: the oldest and strongest of human beliefs, persistent in spite of temporary occlusions; a belief that is at war with no creed that ever was."

"Yes, yes, that is true," the cardinal agreed, with the eagerness of one who persuades himself. "There is no heresy in that belief. It can be reconciled. No heresy that I can perceive."

"There is none," said Cagliostro, as one speaking with full authority. "We will return to that. Meanwhile, there are Your Eminence's pressing needs." His tone blended condescension with command.

"Ah, yes." The cardinal's will—never, it must be admitted, of the strongest—continued in suspension, a thing that veered as Cagliostro blew upon it. He smiled wanly. "My nephew's affairs are absorbing millions."

Cagliostro, erect, dominant, his great head thrown back, made a wide gesture of effacement. "Dismiss your anxieties. I have been stigmatized a magician, and persecuted as a warlock, by the ignorance of men. But, as you will come to perceive, I practice no magic that is not the natural magic of knowledge, the application of the hidden forces of nature, the fruits of study, and of long centuries of experience. Among the secrets I have mastered, building upon what I learned in ancient Egypt from the priests of Isis, who already had glimmerings of these sciences, three are preeminent: the elixir of life, the philosopher's stone with its power of transmuting metals, and the gift of healing all ills to which the flesh is subject. The last I hold at the disposal of suffering mankind; the second I place at the service of those whom I can trust not to abuse the power that gold bestows; the first I guard most jealously from all save the few—the very few—who, under the most rigorous tests, give proof that the indefinite prolongation of their lives will be for the benefit of humanity.

"When I shall have relieved your most urgent need, as I so easily can, and when, thereby, I shall have increased your faith in me, we may, if you so incline, turn our attention to matters of real and abiding weight."

There was much more of the same kind before they parted on

that fateful day. It followed from it that Count Cagliostro presently transferred himself from his Strasbourg lodging to be an honored guest at the cardinal-prince's imposing Château de Saverne. There, by the orders of a bemused prelate at once attracted and repelled, who knew not what to believe, a laboratory was prepared for him. And there, one day, a month later, he set a crown to the empire he was obtaining over Louis de Rohan by demonstrating that his claim to transmute base metal into gold was no mountebank's boast. From the crucible set up in that laboratory he withdrew an ingot of pure gold of the value of five thousand livres, which under the cardinal's eyes he had transmuted out of lead. He presented it to his noble host, as a mere earnest of all that was to come, with as light and casual a manner as if he were handing him a leaf plucked from a tree in passing.

For the manufacture of more, however, there were certain ingredients that Cagliostro lacked, and so as to come within reach of these he proposed to his noble patron that they should transfer themselves to Paris, to the Hôtel de Rohan.

Meanwhile, pending this removal, his apartments at the Château de Saverne were daily becoming more and more thronged by all that was noble, wealthy, and fashionable in Alsace, attracted by his fame as a healer and a man of marvels, a fame which rippled thence in ever-widening circles over the face of France, and set Paris itself agog in expectation of his advent.

Arrogant, domineering, impatient even, he would move through the press of distinguished suitors, his great head thrown back, his terrible, uncanny eyes at once dazzling and awing those upon whom he fixed them. Waving his short, powerful, jeweled hands in fantastic gestures, he chattered constantly in that queer, inflated jargon of his that was compounded of Italian, Italianate-French, and scraps of Spanish, a sort of *lingua franca* that would have been more or less understood in any country where a Romance language was spoken. He was abrupt and harsh of speech and manner, observing few of the amenities that obtained in the polite world which now paid court to him. But as a healer his success was manifest; and not only with malingerers and hypochondriacs, but also with the genuinely afflicted. Sometimes he would display his powers of reading the secrets of a man's soul, and sometimes he would even foretell a future event.

Very soon the respect commanded for him by the aegis of the cardinal-prince was converted by the clear magnitude of his own arts into reverence and even worship. No enemy troubled the serenity of his days until suddenly the Prince de Guémenée, the man whose dishonest extravagances had rendered Cagliostro's services so timely to the cardinal, came gliding like a malevolent snake into this Eden.

Monsieur de Guémenée was a hard-bitten man of the world, regarding the hereafter with a good deal of mistrust, and of the present accepting no more than those material parts of whose reality his senses enabled him to test the evidences. The charlatanism and quackery which in that disjointed period of transition were rampant in France moved him to contempt. That his uncle, the uncle upon whom he was depending for his existence, should be falling a prey to one of these empirics—for that was Monsieur de Guémenée's view of Count Cagliostro—aroused in him the remorseless anger that is born of selfish fear.

He descended suddenly upon the Château de Saverne with intent to disillusion the cardinal and send the warlock packing. Armed with something besides indignation and commonsense, he never doubted that he should accomplish his object. He arrived in the dusk of a September day and, being bidden to supper so soon as he had changed from his traveling clothes, he must curb until afterward his agnostic impatience.

It was not necessary that Cagliostro should be pointed out to him among the considerable company at the open table kept by the munificent cardinal. The man's dominant air and magnetic personality made him sufficiently conspicuous. Although overdressed —his black satin coat was excessively gold-laced, and he wore with it a red waistcoat—and overjeweled, and although his table manners left much to be desired, yet he escaped being ridiculous or even vulgar by the majestic assurance of his demeanor.

Observing the spell which the man appeared to cast upon those about him, meeting once or twice and finding himself unable to support the glance of those singularly uncanny eyes, Monsieur de Guémenée began to apprehend that the battle ahead might sternly test his strength. Nevertheless, he engaged it intrepidly with his uncle in the magnificent pillared library whither the cardinal conducted him after supper.

His Eminence took a seat at his ormolu-encrusted writing table, while his nephew faced him from a tall armchair upholstered in red velvet on which was embroidered an *R* surmounted by a coronet.

Monsieur de Guémenée was approaching thirty. Like his uncle he was tall and slender, and he bore also in his countenance a strong resemblance to the cardinal, but lacked the cardinal's gentle candid air. He sat back, crossed his legs, and plunged straight into the matter.

"I have come, monseigneur, to talk to you about this man who calls himself Count Cagliostro."

His Eminence, of imperturbable urbanity, looked mildly at his nephew.

"How should you prefer to call him, Charles?"

"An impudent imposter," was the downright answer. "A common swindler; a quacksalver whose proper place is on the Pont Neuf; a charlatan who makes a victim of Your Eminence. What his real name may be I have not yet ascertained."

The handsome cardinal betrayed no annoyance. But there was some sorrow in his glance. "I could bear with a good grace to be such a victim as Count Cagliostro makes me. I can bear it thankfully even; and so, my dear Charles, should you, considering how much we are likely to owe him."

"Ah! And how much is he likely to owe to you by the time he has invaded Paris, as I hear is the intention, under your exalted sponsorship; by the time you have presented him at court and set him on the way to swindle all the people of our world?"

"You are vulgar and commonplace in your views, Charles. God commiserate me that I should discover it in a man of my own blood."

Monsieur de Guémenée leaned forward. "Monseigneur. I have been looking into this man's history."

"In that case, my dear Charles, perhaps I can add something to the information you already possess. Look at this ring." He held out a fine white hand on the middle finger of which gleamed a magnificent brilliant carved with the Rohan arms. "That is a gift from Count Cagliostro. And not only a gift, an evidence of his powers. It is a creation of his own. In the laboratory abovestairs I, myself, saw it taken from the crucible in which it was fused by him."

"Jugglery!" scoffed Monsieur de Guémenée. "Common jugglery. If he can do that, what need to live upon you?"

"He does not live upon me. Here it is he, not I, who is the benefactor. And what of the cures he daily makes upon all-comers, sometimes of maladies accounted mortal? Is that jugglery? And all is done freely, without recompense, for the love of humanity. Is that the way of an impostor, a quacksalver? And then the alms he distributes, the gold he makes. Jugglery? A stupidity of the malicious. For if he is indeed a juggler, he must be the richest juggler that ever lived. Whence does he derive his wealth, Charles?"

His Eminence set the question with the air of a man delivering checkmate. But Monsieur de Guémenée had an answer ready.

"I can enlighten Your Eminence upon that, for I have been at pains to inform myself. He derives it from the lodges of so-called Egyptian freemasonry which he has been founding in France and elsewhere; he derives it from the sensation-seeking gulls whom he initiates into these claptrap mysteries and from whom the Grand-Copht, as he calls himself, demands rich fees for his impostures."

The cardinal stiffened and sat bolt upright, unable, despite his deep-seated amiability, to restrain resentment. "If you come to me merely as a retailer of vulgar scandal, of almost blasphemous calumny, I will not listen to you further."

"A moment's patience, monseigneur. There is something else; something you may easily investigate for yourself, and not so easily dismiss. If you will condescend to hear me, I will—"

And then the double doors were thrown open by a lackey, who entered, ranged himself aside, and announced: "His Excellency Count Cagliostro."

Monsieur de Guémenée sank back into his chair with a movement of petulance as the man of marvels came into view. He made a deliberate entrance, grave and masterful, from the carriage of his head to the manner in which he set his feet, and his eyes, the while, were steadily upon the Prince de Guémenée. He had seen the hasty movement and observed now the sullenness which the young man was not concerned to conceal.

As the door closed, he halted and, maintaining that steady regard under which Monsieur de Guémenée, to his profound annoyance, began to feel uncomfortable, he spoke, subduing his resonant voice.

"If I seem to be inopportune, Monsieur de Guémenée, if I interrupt the criticisms you were about to offer, you have in this more matter for thankfulness than you may suspect."

The cardinal smiled his satisfaction at this immediate evidence of Cagliostro's supernatural gifts of omniscience. But Monsieur de Guémenée did not choose to be impressed.

"An easy guess, sir. I trust, for the sake of the wits of those you delude, that you have more convincing tricks of clairvoyance."

His Eminence flushed with pain at this coarse insult. He would have spoken, but the mystagogue raised a hand in a gesture that imperiously commanded that the answer be left to him. He had remained standing on wide-planted feet within a yard or so of Monsieur de Guémenée, and his uncanny eyes never left the young man's face. He spoke quietly.

"There is no ground for resentment. Monsieur de Guémenée but makes himself the mouthpiece of the vulgar and of the base calumny in which the vulgar deal. Men will ever sneer at what they do not understand. That is why they remain fast in the slime of their brutish ignorance. Kindliness dictates that I deliver Your Eminence's nephew from the fog that envelops him to his own hurt. If Your Eminence will give me leave alone with him for a few moments I shall hope to accomplish it."

Rohan smiled. "That will be yet another miracle." He rose at once. "By all means, since you are so generously disposed, enlighten this maladroit young man. I shall be at hand, in my closet."

He moved, tall and stately, with a silken swish of his scarlet robes, to a little door that led to a small adjoining chamber which he frequently used for his studies. Monsieur de Guémenée sprang to his feet, at first purely out of deference to his uncle. But as the little door closed upon His Eminence he betrayed yet another reason for that sudden rising.

"Monsieur Cagliostro, I have no wish to hear you. I will not remain to be annoyed by your impertinences."

The count, who had deferentially been facing the door through which His Eminence had passed, turned slowly to confront him.

"Are you afraid, Monsieur de Guémenée?"

"Afraid?"

"Of being convinced against your preconceptions, of seeing your prejudices destroyed. Look at me. Look in my face, in my eyes, sir."

The prince looked up to meet that burning intent glance, then lowered his eyes again, his manner sullen. "Why should I do that?" he asked contemptuously.

"To conquer the difficulty that you experience in doing it."

"Difficulty? You want to laugh, I think." And in defiance, so as to prove how easily he could support those awful eyes, he stared boldly into them.

"Sit down, Monsieur de Guémenée," the count commanded, and with a shrug Monsieur de Guémenée sank again into the tall red chair.

"Why, here's to humor you, then. But I warn you not to strain my patience." He was conscious even as he spoke that he was using jactancy as a cloak for a vague discomfort, for an irritating sense that he was being dominated.

Count Cagliostro began to talk, in a low, crooning voice. "I remember once, nearly two thousand years ago, as I was walking one evening on the shore of Lake Tiberias, I met a man whose mind was as obstinately delimited as is your own to the things that may be apprehended through the bodily senses."

After that, partly because what the mystagogue said seemed gibberish, partly because of the jargon in which he delivered himself, the prince could understand but little of what he was being told. But as he listened, consciousness vaguely grew that something was happening to him, something which inspired him with an increasing dread, yet from which he could no longer escape. The glare of the eyes into which he was staring had become intolerable, yet he found himself powerless to seek relief by averting his gaze. His own eyes were held as irresistibly, as inexplicably, as his very will to avert them was caught in some impalpable tentacle against which it seemed useless to struggle. The eyes into which he gazed grew in size to the dimensions of the eyes of an ox; they continued to dilate until they were great twin pools gradually merging into a single glowing pool in which he felt that presently he must plunge and drown himself. And all the while that droning voice growing more and more distant was pursuing with its unintelligible narrative, adding something to the utter subjugation of his senses. Gradually at first, then with increasing swiftness, his consciousness diminished until it was totally blotted out.

For what ensued we must follow Monsieur de Guémenée's own account as set down by him in a letter some years thereafter. He was awakened from that singular slumber into which he had lapsed by the booming of a great bell, like that of Nôtre Dame, which resolved itself as consciousness cleared into the tinkling note of the Sèvres clock on the tall overmantel. It was striking the hour of ten.

From this he knew that his lapse could only have been momentary, and as he recovered he found that the queer spell to which he had been succumbing was shattered, and he was once more entirely himself. He was still seated in the tall red chair, but Cagliostro no longer stood before him. The man of mystery had moved over to the fireplace, and was planted there now beside the clock, his shoulders to the overmantel.

Monsieur de Guémenée's first and dominant emotion was indignation, the more bitter because he could not understand the nature of the trick that had been played upon him. It was from anxiety to show that this trick, whatever it might be, had failed that he sprang to his feet and gave expression to his wrath in terms that took no account of Cagliostro's feeling.

"Miserable buffoon, do you dream that you can constrain me to remain here to listen to your lying explanations? If you do, you are as mistaken as when you suppose that I could be deceived by them. I have nothing to say to you, nothing to hear from you. My affair is with your silly dupe, His Eminence, my uncle."

Cagliostro remained impassive. "So be it, sir. I'll not detain you. I merely ask that you remark the time. You will have noted that it has just struck ten."

"Go to the devil," said de Guémenée, and strode tempestuously across the room, to pass into the closet to which the cardinal had withdrawn. He was conscious of being swept along by a tide of ungovernable anger, and this was swollen by the mildness with which the ever urbane cardinal-prince received him.

His Eminence stood reading by a bookcase on the far side of the little room. Between him and his nephew there was a writing table, on which some documents were pinned down by a paperweight in the shape of a miniature, but fairly solid, silver battle-ax. At his nephew's gusty entrance he closed the book upon his forefinger and looked up.

"Well, Charles? Has his excellency satisfied you?"

Recklessly out of his towering passion the young man answered, "Do you suppose me as besotted as yourself that I could condescend to listen to that charlatan's impostures?"

"Charles!" His Eminence raised his brows, his eyes grew round in horror. "I think you are wanting in respect."

"What respect do you inspire, you, a prince of the house of Rohan, lending yourself to the swindling plans of this scoundrel, this jail bird?"

His Eminence stiffened where he stood. His voice was cold and stern.

"Monsieur, you go too far. You will leave my house at once, and you will never enter it again until you have sued for and obtained pardon, both from me and from Monsieur de Cagliostro, for your insulting words."

"Sue pardon from this mountebank! I?"

"On your knees, monsieur."

"Why, you fool," stormed Monsieur de Guémenée, lost in his rage to reason and decency alike, "do you know what he is? Do you know, for example, that in England he was jailed for swindling and for debt? I have proofs of it, and—"

"I care not what you have, monsieur. You will leave my house at once. I do not permit myself to be addressed in such terms as those which you have employed. You have gone too far. You have forgotten the respect due, not only to my person, but to my office. In all my life this has never happened to me before. You say that this man has been jailed for debt. Whether it is true or not, that fate is one that is very likely to overtake you in the near future, for from this moment you cease to interest me; you may wrestle with your own difficulties, and yourself satisfy the creditors you have abused, as you have abused my patience and my good nature. Not another penny of mine shall stand between you and the fate you have invited."

"My God!" cried Monsieur de Guémenée. But even now there was more anger than dismay in his soul.

"With that knowledge take your departure, sir, and do not venture to return. You are an ingrate whom I never wish to see again."

Trembling with fury, Monsieur de Guémenée steadied himself with a hand upon the writing table. He controlled himself to ask in a voice that was steady, dangerously steady, considering his condition: "Is that your last word, monseigneur."

With a great dignity the cardinal replied: "My last word, monsieur."

"Then your last word it shall be," said his frenzied nephew and, snatching up the silver battle-ax, he hurled it straight and true at his uncle's august head. He saw it strike him full upon the brow before His Eminence could so much as put up a hand to avert the unexpected missile; he saw the blood gush forth; saw the tall scarlet figure sway an instant where it stood, the fine hands clawing the air as if seeking a support; then, with a sound as of a rush of wings, the cardinal-prince sank together, crumpled and fell, to lie inert.

Terror-stricken by his deed, his blind rage driven forth by panic, Monsieur de Guémenée leaned forward over the table, clawing its sides with nerveless hands. "Monseigneur! Monseigneur!" he cried, in a choking wail, then sprang past the table and went to kneel beside the fallen man. Horror came up like a great tide about him at sight of the gaping vertical wound in the brow, where the ax, hard-driven at close quarters, had split the skull. His Eminence was quite dead.

Then, as he knelt there, paralyzed in body and in spirit, he heard the door open softly behind him. He looked up and round, to behold Cagliostro, stern and grim, upon the threshold.

"Wretched man, what have you done?" asked the vibrant voice.

The prince leapt to his feet. There was blood on his hands and on the ruffles at his wrists. "It is your act," he raved. "Yours. Behold the havoc you have wrought. It is you who are responsible for this."

Cagliostro preserved a terrible calm. "Tell that to your judges if you think it will save you from being broken on the wheel, from being disemboweled alive for this hideous parricide. Ah, you quail!

But that is the least of the punishment in store for you. You will have earned the execration of all upright men for this horrible murder of your uncle and benefactor. Your name will hereafter become a byword."

"Cease! In God's name, cease!" cried Monsieur de Guémenée. "Do you think I do not realize it?" And then his tone changed to a piteous whine. "Sir, sir, you are reported to possess more than human powers. Of your pity, help me in this my dreadful need."

"Ah! You believe in me now. It is true that I possess more than ordinary human powers; but the power to raise the dead is not within them."

"Is it not? Is it not?" Monsieur de Guémenée reverted abruptly to his earlier frenzy. He was leering now with wicked cunning. "So much the worse for you. Since yours is the blame, you shall bear the punishment. I will rouse the house, and declare that it was you who did this thing. What then, my friend? What then? Will your word weigh against mine, do you suppose?"

Cagliostro smiled. "Ingenious. Unfortunately there is a witness. Look behind you, Monsieur."

Startled, Monsieur de Guémenée looked round. Dimly in the shadows of a farther doorway, a doorway of whose existence he had been in ignorance, he discerned the figure of a man. Looking more closely his straining eyes recognized the Baron de Planta. "How long have you been there, monsieur?" he asked.

Cold and stern the Baron answered him, "From the moment that you threw the ax."

The courage went out of Monsieur de Guémenée, taking all fury with it. He raised his blood-stained hands in a gesture of impotence. "What shall I do? Mon Dieu, what shall I do?"

"What are you prepared to do if I can save you?" asked Cagliostro.

Monsieur de Guémenée faced him; advanced toward him.

"Save me, do you say? Do you mock my distress? What help can you, what help can any, give? You have said that you cannot raise the dead."

"True. But I can undo what is done. Even that is possible to such as I, for I am He Who Is. Listen, my prince, and seek to understand. This deed of yours is something done in time. Time, sir, is not a reality, not one of the fundamental verities. It is an illusion, a human convention for the measuring of actions concerned with our little moment of existence, this heartbeat in eternity which we call life. To such as I who stand untrammeled by the bonds of time, the past and the future are as they are in eternity; that is to say they are not at all; for in eternity there is always and only the present. If I were to turn time back for you, Monsieur de Guémenée, if I were to turn it back to the moment at which you rose to go in quest of your uncle, so that all that now lies in the past would lie once more in the future and would be inevitable, if I were to do this, what would you do for me?"

"For you?" Monsieur de Guémenée could only stare and stare. Nevertheless, he answered the fantastic question, passionately sobbing, "God knows there is nothing that I would not do."

Cagliostro approached him, smiling gently. "I ask a little thing of you in return for so much. You have procured from England evidence that I was in prison there. You have been at great pains to do this simply so that you might destroy my credit with your uncle, and raise a barrier to my accompanying him to Paris. I am not the first great prophet who has suffered imprisonment. Some have even been put to death by the vicious ignorance of men. For myself I fear nothing from that revelation. But others whom I am concerned to help and serve must suffer if, yielding to prejudice, they should turn from me.

"What I offer you now is this: If you will swear to me on your honor as a gentleman to destroy this evidence which you have wasted such pains in obtaining and never to mention this matter to a living soul, I on my side will so put back the clock for you, that what has been will be still to come and may therefore be avoided. Do you swear, monsieur?"

There was such firm authority in the voice that even the Sadducean mind of Monsieur de Guémenée was more than half conquered by it. Feebly the other half still battled with reason.

"What you are proposing is impossible."

"Will you make the experiment? Will you swear as I require? It is your only hope."

Desperately came the answer, "I swear! I swear!" and in pursuit of it the oath was circumstantially given in the terms Cagliostro dictated.

As Monsieur de Guémenée uttered the last formidable word of it, his senses swam. He had a moment of faintness, which even as it overtook him he attributed to the strain of what he had endured. Then his senses cleared, and as sight, momentarily occluded, was restored to him, he found himself in the library, seated once more in the tall red chair, his legs composedly crossed.

For a moment he could not understand how he had come there, or, indeed, anything. His wits were in chaos. Then, out of it, emerged a sharp pellucid perception of the thing he had done and of the horrible situation in which he found himself. Wild-eyed he looked around, and saw Cagliostro standing as before by the over-mantel in such a position that his shoulders eclipsed the face of the Sèvres clock. He stood with wide-planted feet, his countenance as enigmatically calm as that of Amhitaba upon his nenuphar.

"Well, sir? Well?" The sight of him thus stirred Monsieur de Guémenée to distraction. "You know what is to do."

The booming voice answered him. "It is done."

"Done? It is done?"

Cagliostro shrugged in weariness. "The stupidity of human nature can be unfathomable. Did you expect to witness some visible, material operation? What is done is an effort to the spirit, of the will, sir. Look at your hands."

The prince obeyed. He turned his hands about as he stared at them. They were white and clean; there was no faintest trace of blood upon them or upon his ruffles. Vacantly, foolishly, he looked again at Cagliostro, and Cagliostro answered the agonized question in those wide eyes.

"I have accomplished no less than I promised, Monsieur de Guémenée. We have stepped back in time." He moved aside, disclosing the face of the blue-and-gold Sèvres clock and, as he moved, it began to strike the hour of ten, just as it had struck in the moment before de Guémenée had risen to go to his uncle.

A sense of awe encompassed him, of a quite different order from the last. His heart was beating in his throat; he had a sensation of stifling. He was in the presence of forces that he could not understand. Then, with reviving skepticism, another dread arose. He was the dupe of some imposture. Hands could be wiped, clocks could be turned back; but the dead could not be restored to life. In that room beyond the little door his uncle lay with a split skull.

As if answering his thought, Count Cagliostro crossed the room to the closet door, opened it, and spoke.

"I think Your Eminence will now find Monsieur de Guémenée persuaded of the error with which he did me injustice."

From within the closet he was answered by a movement made manifest by the rustle of silken robes and, as Monsieur de Guémenée sat forward, wild-eyed, clutching the arms of his chair, the tall, handsome figure of the cardinal came into view and paused under the lintel. His Eminence, smooth of brow and calm of eye, composed and urbane as ever, was quietly smiling his satisfaction.

"I knew he would find it easy to convince you, Charles, and I rejoice in it. Men of the same blood must hold together in all important things." His elegant hand was placed affectionately upon Cagliostro's shoulder. "You will find His Excellency, Charles, the arch-enemy of all fraud and error. Trust him as I do, and you cannot fail to profit by it."

"I think he holds the proof of that," said Cagliostro quietly.

Monsieur de Guémenée, breathing with difficulty, answered nothing. He asked himself had he merely dreamt, was he still dreaming, or had some unfathomable miracle been wrought? Then, as his uncle advanced into the room, he remembered the deference due to that august personage, and staggered like a drunkard to his feet.

Many years later, in his prison in the fortress of San Leo, when his thaumaturgy had brought him into the clutches of the Holy Office, Cagliostro told this story to a young Dominican who had been charged to show him the error of his ways.

"When we reflect," he ended, "that all this that the Prince de Guémenée had seen and heard and felt and done had no existence save in my mind and will, may we not ask ourselves what, after all, is objective truth?"

PAPA BENJAMIN

William Irish

Because it is so elusive, so indefinite, magic takes many forms. So does terror. You can't touch it, but you can feel it. You don't know exactly where it begins or when it ends, but you always know of its existence. It is irrational but, in its way, sensible. It is primitive, yes, but also as modern as the next tick of the clock.

Black magic is one of the oldest forms of magic, of apparently supernatural force. It is easy to ridicule it, to disbelieve it, to laugh at it (if you dare). Yet whole nations have believed in its power for centuries. Why?

When he began his career, Cornell Woolrich produced several romantic novels that caught the attention of critics. A favorable comparison with F. Scott Fitzgerald was made and all seemed rosy for the brilliant young writer. Then he made a mistake and forever lost stature with the intellectual taste-makers. He wrote novels and stories of crime, murder, and suspense. Anyone writing in this genre could have only limited talent, they agreed, so Woolrich was dumped on the slag heap of "popular" writers and ignored by "serious" critics ever since.

Cornell George Hopley-Woolrich also wrote as William Irish and George Hopley. Under any name, he was able to produce a sense of terror unmatched by any writer of this century—"serious" or "popular."

"Papa Benjamin" was originally published in Dime Mystery *magazine in July 1935 under the title "Dark Melody of Madness"; its first book appearance was in* I Wouldn't Be in Your Shoes *(1943).*

At four in the morning, a scarecrow of a man staggers dazedly into the New Orleans police headquarters building. Behind him at the curb a lacquered Bugatti purrs like a drowsy cat, the finest car that ever stood out there. He weaves his way through the anteroom, deserted at that early hour, and goes in through the open doorway beyond. The sleepy desk sergeant looks up; an idle detective scanning yesterday's *Times-Picayune* on the two hind legs of a chair tipped back against the wall raises his head; and as the funnel of light from the cone-shaped reflector overhead plays up their visitor like flashlight-powder, their mouths drop open and their eyes bat a couple of times. The two front legs of the detective's chair come down with a thump. The sergeant braces himself, eager, friendly, with the heels of both hands on his desk top and his elbows up in the air. A patrolman comes in from the back room, wiping a drink of water from his mouth. His jaw also hangs when he sees who's there. He sidles nearer the detective and says behind the back of his hand, "That's Eddie Bloch, ain't it?"

The detective doesn't take the trouble to answer. It's like telling him what his own name is. The three stare at the figure under the light, interested, respectful, almost admiring. There is nothing professional in their scrutiny, they are not the police studying a suspect; they are nobodies looking at a celebrity. They take in the rumpled tuxedo, the twig of gardenia that has shed its petals, the tie hanging open in two loose ends. His topcoat was slung across his arm originally; now it trails along the dusty station-house floor behind him. He gives his hat the final, tortured push that dislodges it. It drops and rolls away behind him. The policeman picks it up and brushes it off—he never was a bootlicker in his life, but this man is Eddie Bloch.

Still it's his face, more than who he is or how he's dressed, that would draw stares anywhere. It's the face of a dead man—the face of a dead man on a living body. The shadowy shape of the skull seems to peer through the transparent skin; you can make out its bone structure as though an X-ray were outlining it. The eyes are stunned, shocked, haunted gleams, set in a vast purple hollow that bisects the face like a mask. No amount of drink or dissipation could do this to anyone, only long illness and the foreknowledge of death. You see faces like that looking up at you from hospital cots when all hope has been abandoned—when the grave is already waiting.

Yet, strangely enough, they knew who he was just now. Instant recognition of who he was came first—realization of the shape he's in comes after that, more slowly. Possibly it's because all three of them have been called on to identify corpses in the morgue in their day. Their minds are trained along those lines. And this man's face is known to hundreds of people. Not that he has ever broken or even fractured the most trivial law, but he has spread happiness around him, set a million feet to dancing in his time.

The desk sergeant's expression changes. The patrolman mutters under his breath to the detective, "Looks like he just came out of a bad smash-up with his car." "More like a drinking bout, to me," answers the detective. They are simple men, capable within their limitations, but those are the only explanations they can find for what they now see before them.

The desk sergeant speaks. "Mr. Eddie Bloch, am I right?" He extends his hand across the desk in greeting.

The man can hardly stand up. He nods, he doesn't take the hand.

"Is there anything wrong, Mr. Bloch? Is there anything we can do for you?" The detective and the patrolman come over closer. "Run in and get him a drink of water, Latour," the sergeant says anxiously. "Have an accident, Mr. Bloch? Been held up?"

The man steadies himself with one arm against the edge of the sergeant's desk. The detective extends an arm behind him, in case he should fall backward. He keeps fumbling, continually fumbling in his clothes. The tuxedo jacket swims on him as his movements shift it around. He is down to about a hundred pounds in weight, they notice. Out comes a gun, and he doesn't even have the strength to lift it up. He pushes it and it skids across the desk top, then spins around and points back at him.

He speaks, and if the unburied dead ever spoke, this is the voice they'd use. "I've killed a man. Just now. A little while ago. At half-past three."

They're completely floored. They almost don't know how to handle the situation for a minute. They deal with killers every day, but killers have to be gone out after and dragged in. And when fame and wealth enter into it, as they do once in a great while, fancy lawyers and protective barriers spring up to hedge the killers in on all sides. This man is one of the ten idols of America, or was until just lately. People like him don't kill people. They don't come in out of nowhere at four in the morning and stand before a simple desk sergeant and a simple detective, stripped to their naked souls, shorn of all resemblance to humanity, almost.

There's silence in the room for a minute, a silence you could cut with a knife. Then he speaks again, in agony. "I tell you I've killed a man! Don't stand there looking at me like that! I've killed a man!"

The sergeant speaks, gently, sympathetically. "What's the matter, Mr. Bloch, been working too hard?" He comes out from behind the desk. "Come on inside with us. You stay here, Latour, and look after the telephone."

And when they've accompanied him into the back room: "Get him a chair, Humphries. Here, drink some of this water, Mr. Bloch. Now what's it all about?" The sergeant has brought the gun along with him. He passes it before his nose, then breaks it open. He looks at the detective. "He's used it all right."

"Was it an accident, Mr. Bloch?" the detective suggests respectfully. The man in the chair shakes his head. He's started to shiver all over, although the New Orleans night is warm and mellow. "Who'd you do it to? Who was it?" the sergeant puts in.

"I don't know his name," Bloch mumbles. "I never have. They call him Papa Benjamin."

His two interrogators exchange a puzzled look. "Sounds like—" The detective doesn't finish it. Instead he turns to the seated figure and asks almost perfunctorily: "He was a white man, of course?"

"He was colored," is the unexpected answer.

The thing gets more crazy, more inexplicable, at every step. How should a man like Eddie Bloch, one of the country's best-known band leaders, who used to earn a thousand dollars every week for playing at Maxim's, come to kill a nameless colored man —and then be put into this condition by it? These two men have never seen anything like it in their time; they have subjected suspects to forty-eight-hour grillings and yet compared to him now those suspects were fresh as daisies when they got through with them.

He has said it was no accident and he has said it was no hold-up. They shower questions at him, not to confuse him but rather to try to help him pull himself together. "What did he do, forget his place? Talk back to you? Become insolent?" This is the South, remember.

The man's head goes from side to side like a pendulum.

"Did you go out of your mind for a minute? Is that how it was?" Again a nodded no.

The man's condition has suggested one explanation to the detective's mind. He looks around to make sure the patrolman outside isn't listening. Then very discreetly: "Are you a needle-user, Mr. Bloch? Was he your source?"

The man looks up at them. "I've never touched a thing I shouldn't. A doctor will tell you that in a minute."

"Did he have something on you? Was it blackmail?"

Bloch fumbles some more in his clothes; again they dance around on his skeletonized frame. Suddenly he takes out a cube of money, as thick as it is wide, more money than these two men have ever seen before in their lives. "There's three thousand dollars there," he says simply and tosses it down like he did the gun. "I took it with me tonight, tried to give it to him. He could have had twice as much, three times as much, if he'd said the word, if he'd only let up on me. He wouldn't take it. That was when I had to kill him. That was all there was left for me to do."

"What was he doing to you?" They both say it together.

"He was killing me." He holds out his arm and shoots his cuff. The wristbone is about the size of the sergeant's own thumb joint. The expensive platinum wristwatch that encircles it has been pulled in to the last possible notch and yet it still hangs almost like a bracelet. "See? I'm down to 102. When my shirt's off, my heart's so close to the surface you can see the skin right over it move like a pulse with each beat."

They draw back a little, almost they wish he hadn't come in here. That he had headed for some other precinct instead. From the very beginning they have sensed something here that is over their heads, that isn't to be found in any of the instruction books. Now they come out with it. "How?" Humphries asks. "How was he killing you?"

There's a flare of torment from the man. "Don't you suppose I would have told you long ago, if I could? Don't you suppose I would have come in here weeks ago, months ago, and demanded protection, asked to be saved—if I could have told you what it was? If you would have believed me?"

"We'll believe you, Mr. Bloch," the sergeant says soothingly. "We'll believe anything. Just tell us—"

But Bloch in turn shoots a question at them, for the first time since he has come in. "Answer me! Do you believe in anything you can't see, can't hear, can't touch—?"

"Radio," the sergeant suggests not very brightly, but Humphries answers more frankly, "No."

The man slumps down again in his chair, shrugs apathetically. "If you don't, how can I expect you to believe me? I've been to the biggest doctors, biggest scientists in the world—they wouldn't believe me. How can I expect you to? You'll simply say I'm cracked, and let it go at that. I don't want to spend the rest of my life in an asylum—" He breaks off and sobs. "And yet it's true, it's true!"

They've gotten into such a maze that Humphries decides it's about time to snap out of it. He asks the one simple question that should have been asked long ago, and the hell with all this mumbo-jumbo. "Are you sure you killed him?" The man is broken physically and he's about ready to crack mentally too. The whole thing may be a hallucination.

"I know I did. I'm sure of it," the man answers calmly. "I'm already beginning to feel a little better. I felt it the minute he was gone."

If he is, he doesn't show it. The sergeant catches Humphries' eye and meaningfully taps his forehead in a sly gesture.

"Suppose you take us there and show us," Humphries suggests. "Can you do that? Where'd it happen, at Maxim's?"

"I told you he was colored," Bloch answers reproachfully. Maxim's is tony. "It was in the Vieux Carré. I can show you where, but I can't drive any more. It was all I could do to get down here with my car."

"I'll put Desjardins on it with you," the sergeant says and calls through the door to the patrolman, "Ring Dij and tell him to meet Humphries at the corner of Canal and Royal right away!" He turns and looks at the huddle on the chair. "Buy him a bracer on the way. It don't look like he'll last till he gets there."

The man flushes a little—it would be a blush if he had any blood left in him. "I can't touch alcohol any more. I'm on my last legs. It goes right through me like—" He hangs his head, then raises it again. "But I'll get better now, little by little, now that he's—"

The sergeant takes Humphries out of earshot. "Pushover for a padded cell. If it's on the up-and-up, and not just a pipe dream, call me right back. I'll get the commissioner on the wire."

"At this hour of the night?"

The sergeant motions toward the chair with his head. "He's Eddie Bloch, isn't he?"

Humphries takes him under the elbow, pries him up from the chair. Not roughly, but just briskly, energetically. Now that things are at last getting under way, he knows where he's at; he can handle them. He'll still be considerate, but he's businesslike now; he's into his routine. "All right, come on Mr. Bloch, let's get up there."

"Not a scratch goes down on the blotter until I'm sure what I'm doing," the sergeant calls after Humphries. "I don't want this whole town down on my neck tomorrow morning."

Humphries almost has to hold him up on the way out and into the car. "This it?" he says. "Wow!" He just touches it with his nail and they're off like velvet. "How'd you ever get this into the Vieux Carré without knocking over the houses?"

Two gleams deep in the skull jogging against the upholstery, dimmer than the dashboard lights, are the only sign that there's life beside him. "Used to park it blocks away—go on foot."

"Oh, you went there more than once?"

"Wouldn't you—to beg for your life?"

More of that screwy stuff, Humphries thinks disgustedly. Why should a man like Eddie Bloch, star of the mike and the dance floor, go to some colored man in the slums and beg for his life?

Royal Street comes whistling along. He swerves in toward the curb, shoves the door out, sees Desjardins land on the running board with one foot. Then he veers out into the middle again without even having stopped. Desjardins moves in on the other side of Bloch, finishes dressing by knotting his necktie and buttoning his vest. "Where'd you get the Aquitania?" he wants to know, and then, with a look beside him, "Holy Kreisler, Eddie Bloch! We used to hear you every night on my Emerson—"

"Matter?" Humphries squelches. "Got a talking jag?"

"Turn," says a hollow sound between them and three wheels take the Bugatti around into North Rampart Street. "Have to leave it here," he says a little later, and they get out. "Congo Square," the old stamping ground of the slaves.

"Help him," Humphries tells his mate tersely, and they each brace him by an elbow.

Staggering between them with the uneven gait of a punch-drunk pug, quick and then slow by turns, he leads them down a ways, and then suddenly cuts left into an alley that isn't there at all until you're smack in front of it. It's just a crack between two houses, noisome as a sewer. They have to break into Indian file to get through at all. But Bloch can't fall down; the walls almost scrape both his shoulders at once. One's in front, one behind him.

"You packed?" Humphries calls over his head to Desjardins, up front.

"Catch cold without it," the other's voice comes back out of the gloom.

A slit of orange shows up suddenly from under a window sill and a shapely coffee-colored elbow scrapes the ribs of the three as they squirm by. "This far 'nough, honey," a liquid voice murmurs.

"Bad girl, wash y'mouth out with soap," the unromantic Humphries warns over his shoulder without even looking around. The sliver of light vanishes as quickly as it came.

The passage widens out in places into moldering courtyards dating back to French or Spanish colonial days, and once it goes under an archway and becomes a tunnel for a short distance. Desjardins cracks his head and swears with talent and abandon.

"Y'left out—" the rearguard remarks dryly.

"Here," pants Bloch weakly, and stops suddenly at a patch of blackness in the wall. Humphries washes it with his torch and crumbling mildewed stone steps show up inside it. Then he motions Bloch in, but the man hangs back, slips a notch or two lower down against the opposite wall that supports him. "Let me stay down here! Don't make me go up there again," he pleads. "I don't think I can make it any more. I'm afraid to go back in there."

"Oh, no!" Humphries says with quiet determination. "You're showing us," and scoops him away from the wall with his arm. Again, as before, he isn't rough about it, just businesslike. Dij keeps the lead, watering the place with his own torch. Humphries trains his on the band leader's $40 custom-made patent-leather shoes jerking frightenedly upward before him. The stone steps turn to wood ones splintered with usage. They have to step over a huddled black drunk, empty bottle cradled in his arms. "Don't light a match," Dij warns, pinching his nose, "or there'll be an explosion."

"Grow up," snaps Humphries. The Cajun's a good dick, but can't he realize the man in the middle is roasting in hell-fire? This is no time—

"In here is where I did it. I closed the door again after me." Bloch's skull face is all silver with his life sweat as one of their torches flicks past it.

Humphries shoves open the sagging mahogany panel that was first hung up when a Louis was still king of France and owned this town. The light of a lamp far across a still, dim room flares up and dances crazily in the draft. They come in and look.

There's an old broken-down bed, filthy with rags. Across it there's a motionless figure, head hanging down toward the floor. Dij cups his hand under it and lifts it. It comes up limply toward him, like a small basketball. It bounces down again when he lets it go—even seems to bob slightly for a second or two after. It's an old, old colored man, up in his eighties, even beyond. There's a dark spot, darker than the weazened skin, just under one bleared eye and another in the thin fringe of white wool that circles the back of the skull.

Humphries doesn't wait to see any more. He turns, flips out and down, and all the way back to wherever the nearest telephone can be found, to let headquarters know that it's true after all and they can rouse the police commissioner. "Keep him there with you, Dij," his voice trails back from the inky stairwell, "and no quizzing. Pull in your horns till we get our orders!" The scarecrow with them tries to stumble after him and get out of the place, groaning, "Don't leave me here! Don't make me stay here—!"

"I wouldn't quiz you on my own, Mr. Bloch," Dij tries to reassure him, nonchalantly sitting down on the edge of the bed next to the corpse and retying his shoelace. "I'll never forget it was your playing 'Love in Bloom' on the air one night in Baton Rouge two years ago gave me the courage to propose to my wife—"

But the commissioner would, and does, in his office a couple hours later. He's anything but eager about it, too. They've tried to shunt him, Bloch, off their hands in every possible legal way open to them. No go. He sticks to them like flypaper. The old colored man *didn't* try to attack him, or rob him, or blackmail him, or kidnap him, or anything else. The gun didn't go off accidentally, and he didn't fire it on the spur of the moment either, without thinking twice, or in a flare of anger. The commissioner almost beats his own head against the desk in his exasperation as he reiterates over and over: "But why? Why? Why?" And for the steenth time, he gets the same indigestible answer, "Because he was killing me."

"Then you admit he did lay hands on you?" The first time the poor commissioner asked this, he said it with a spark of hope. But this is the tenth or twelfth and the spark died out long ago.

"He never once came near me. I was the one looked him up each time to plead with him. Commissioner Oliver, tonight I went down on my knees to that old man and dragged myself around the floor of that dirty room after him, on my *bended knees,* like a sick cat—begging, crawling to him, offering him three thousand, ten, any amount, finally offering him my own gun, asking him to shoot me with it, to get it over with quickly, to be kind to me, not to drag it out by inches any longer! No, not even that little bit of mercy! Then I shot—and now I'm going to get better, now I'm going to live—"

He's too weak to cry; crying takes strength. The commissioner's hair is about ready to stand on end. "Stop it, Mr. Bloch, stop it!" he shouts, and he steps over and grabs him by the shoulder in defense of his own nerves, and can almost feel the shoulder bone cutting his hand. He takes his hand away again in a hurry. "I'm going to have you examined by an alienist!"

The bundle of bones rears from the chair. "You can't do that! You can't take my mind from me! Send to my hotel—I've got a trunkful of reports on my condition! I've been to the biggest minds in Europe! Can you produce anyone that would dare go against

the findings of Buckholtz in Vienna, Reynolds in London? They
had me under observation for months at a time! I'm not even on
the borderline of insanity, not even a genius or musically talented.
I don't even write my own numbers, I'm mediocre, uninspired—
in other words completely normal. I'm saner than you are at this
minute, Mr. Oliver. My body's gone, my soul's gone, and all I've
got left is my mind, but you can't take that from me!"

The commissioner's face is beet-red. He's about ready for a
stroke, but he speaks softly, persuasively. "An eighty-odd-year-old
colored man who is so feeble he can't even go upstairs half the
time, who has to have his food pulleyed up to him through the
window in a basket, is killing—whom? A white stumblebum his
own age? No-o-o, Mr. Eddie Bloch, the premier bandsman of
America, who can name his own price in any town, who's heard
every night in all our homes, who has about everything a man can
want—that's who!"

He peers close, until their eyes are on a level. His voice is just
a silky whisper. "Tell me just one thing, Mr. Bloch." Then like the
explosion of a giant firecracker, "How?" He roars it out, booms it
out.

There's a long-drawn intake of breath from Eddie Bloch. "By
thinking thought-waves of death that reach me through the air."

The poor commissioner practically goes all to pieces on his own
rug. "And you don't need a medical exam!" he wheezes weakly.

There's a flutter, the popping of buttons, and Eddie Bloch's coat,
his vest, his shirt, undershirt, land one after another on the floor
around his chair. He turns. "Look at my back! You can count every
vertebra through the skin!" He turns back again. "Look at my ribs.
Look at the pulsing where there's not enough skin left to cover my
heart!"

Oliver shuts his eyes and turns toward the window. He's in a
particularly unpleasant spot. New Orleans, out there, is stirring,
and when it hears about this, he's going to be the most unpopular
man in town. On the other hand, if he doesn't see the thing
through now that it's gone this far he's guilty of a dereliction of
duty, malfeasance in office.

Bloch, slowly dressing, knows what he's thinking. "You want to
get rid of me, don't you? You're trying to think of a way of covering

this thing up. You're afraid to bring me up before the grand jury on account of your own reputation, aren't you?" His voice rises to a scream of panic. "Well, I want protection! I don't want to go out there again—to my death! I won't accept bail! If you turn me loose now, even on my own cognizance, you may be as guilty of my death as he is. How do I know my bullet stopped the thing? How does any of us know what becomes of the mind after death? Maybe his thoughts will still reach me, still try to get me. I tell you I want to be locked up, I want people around me day and night, I want to be where I'm safe—!"

"Shh, for God's sake, Mr. Bloch! They'll think I'm beating you up—" The commissioner drops his arms to his sides and heaves a gigantic sigh. "That settles it! I'll book you all right. You want that and you're going to get it! I'll book you for the murder of one Papa Benjamin, even if they laugh me out of office for it!"

For the first time since the whole thing has started, he casts a look of real anger, ill-will, at Eddie Bloch. He seizes a chair, swirls it around, and bangs it down in front of the man. He puts his foot on it and pokes his finger almost in Bloch's eye. "I'm not two-faced. I'm not going to lock you up nice and cozy and then soft-pedal the whole thing. If it's coming out at all, then all of it's coming out. Now start in! Tell me everything I want to know, and what I want to know is—everything!"

The strains of "Good Night Ladies" die away; the dancers leave the floor, the lights start going out, and Eddie Bloch throws down his baton and mops the back of his neck with a handkerchief. He weighs about two hundred pounds, is in the pink, and is a good-looking brute. But his face is sour right now, dissatisfied. His outfit starts to case its instruments right and left, and Judy Jarvis steps up on the platform, in her street clothes, ready to go home. She's Eddie's torch singer, and also his wife. "Coming, Eddie? Let's get out of here." She looks a little disgusted herself. "I didn't get a hand tonight, not even after my rumba number. Must be staling. If I wasn't your wife, I'd be out of a job I guess."

Eddie pats her shoulder. "It isn't you, honey. It's us, we're beginning to stink. Notice how the attendance has been dropping the past few weeks? There were more waiters than customers tonight.

I'll be hearing from the owner any minute now. He has the right to cancel my contract if the intake drops below five grand."

A waiter comes up to the edge of the platform. "Mr. Graham'd like to see you in his office before you go home, Mr. Bloch."

Eddie and Judy look at each other. "This is it now, Judy. You go back to the hotel. Don't wait for me. G'night, boys." Eddie Bloch calls for his hat and knocks at the manager's office.

Graham rustles a lot of accounts together. "We took in forty-five hundred this week, Eddie. They can get the same ginger ale and sandwiches any place, but they'll go where the band has something to give 'em. I notice the few that do come in don't even get up from the table any more when you tap your baton. Now, what's wrong?"

Eddie punches his hat a couple of times. "Don't ask me. I'm getting the latest orchestrations from Broadway sent to me hot off the griddle. We sweat our bald heads off rehearsing—"

Graham swivels his cigar. "Don't forget that jazz originated here in the South, you can't show this town anything. They want something new."

"When do I scram?" Eddie asks, smiling with the southwest corner of his mouth.

"Finish the week out. See if you can do something about it by Monday. If not, I'll have to wire St. Louis to get Kruger's crew. I'm sorry, Eddie."

"That's all right," broad-minded Eddie says. "You're not running a charity bazaar."

Eddie goes out into the dark dance room. His crew has gone. The tables are stacked. A couple of old colored crones are down on hands and knees slopping water around on the parquet. Eddie steps up on the platform a minute to get some orchestrations he left on the piano. He feels something crunch under his shoe, reaches down, picks up a severed chicken's claw lying there with a strip of red-tag tied around it. How the hell did it get up there? If it had been under one of the tables, he'd have thought some diner had dropped it. He flushes a little. D'ye mean to say he and the boys were so rotten tonight that somebody deliberately threw it at them while they were playing?

One of the scrubwomen looks up. The next moment, she and

her mate are on their feet, edging nearer, eyes big as saucers, until they get close enough to see what it is he's holding. Then there's a double yowl of animal fright, a tin pail goes rolling across the floor, and no two stout people, white or colored, ever got out of a place in such a hurry before. The door nearly comes off its hinges, and Eddie can hear their cackling all the way down the quiet street outside until it fades away into the night. "For gosh sake!" thinks the bewildered Eddie, "they must be using the wrong brand of gin." He tosses the object out onto the floor and goes back to the piano for his music scores. A sheet or two has slipped down behind it and he squats to collect them. That way the piano hides him.

The door opens again and he sees Johnny Staats (traps and percussion) come in in quite a hurry. He thought Staats was home in bed by now. Staats is feeling himself all over like he was rehearsing the shim-sham and he's scanning the ground as he goes along. Then suddenly he pounces—and it's on the very scrap of garbage Eddie just now threw away! And as he straightens up with it, his breath comes out in such a sign of relief that Eddie can hear it all the way across the still room. All this keeps him from hailing Staats as he was going to a minute ago and suggesting a cup of java. But, "Superstitious," thinks broad-minded Eddie. "It's his good-luck charm, that's all, like some people carry a rabbit's foot. I'm a little that way myself, never walk under a ladder—"

Then again, why should those two mammies go into hysterics when they lamp the same object? And Eddie recalls now that some of the boys have always suspected Staats has colored blood, and tried to tell him so years ago when Staats first came in with them, but he wouldn't listen to them.

Staats slinks out again as noiselessly as he came in, and Eddie decides he'll catch up with him and kid him about his chicken claw on their way home together. (They all roost in the same hotel.) So he takes his music sheets, some of which are blank, and he leaves. Staats is way down the street—in the *wrong direction,* away from the hotel! Eddie hesitates for just a minute, and then he starts after Staats on a vague impulse, just to see where he's going, just to see what he's up to. Maybe the fright of the scrubwomen and the way Staats pounced on that chicken claw just now have built up to this, without Eddie's really knowing it.

And how many times afterward he's going to pray to his God that he'd never turned down that other way this night—away from his hotel, his Judy, his boys—away from the sunlight and the white man's world. Such a little thing to decide to do, and afterward no turning back—ever.

He keeps Staats in sight, and they hit the Vieux Carré. That's all right. There are a lot of quaint places here a guy might like to drop in. Or maybe he has some Creole sweetie tucked away, and Eddie thinks, I'm lower than a ditch to spy like this. But then suddenly right before his eyes, half way up the narrow lane he's turned into —there isn't any Staats any more! And no door opened and closed again either. Then when Eddie gets up to where it was, he sees the crevice between the old houses, hidden by an angle in the walls. So that's where he went! Eddie almost has a peeve on by now at all this hocus-pocus. He slips in himself and feels his way along. He stops every once in a while and can hear Staat's quiet footfall somewhere way up in front. Then he goes on again. Once or twice the passage spreads out a little and lets a little green-blue moonlight partway down the walls. Then later, there's a little flare of orange light from under a window and an elbow jogs him in the appendix. "You'd be happier here. Doan go the rest of the way," a soft voice breathes. A prophecy if he only knew it!

But hardboiled Eddie just says, "G'wan to bed, y' dirty stay-up!" out of the corner of his mouth, and the light vanishes. Next a tunnel and he bangs the top of his head and his eyes water. But at the other end of it, Staats has finally come to a halt in a patch of clear light and seems to be looking up at a window or something, so Eddie stays where he is, inside the tunnel, and folds the lapels of his black jacket up over his white shirt front so it won't show.

Staats just stands there for a spell, with Eddie holding his breath inside the tunnel, and then finally he gives a peculiar, dismal whistle. There's nothing carefree or casual about it. It's a hollow swampland sound, not easy to get without practice. Then he just stands there waiting, until without warning another figure joins him in the gloom. Eddie strains his eyes. A gorilla-like, Negro roustabout. Something passes from Staat's hand to his—the chicken claw possibly—then they go in, into the house Staats has been facing. Eddie can hear the soft shuffle of feet going upstairs on the inside, and the groaning, squeaking of an old decayed door —and then silence.

He edges forward to the mouth of the tunnel and peers up. No light shows from any window, the house appears to be untenanted, deserted.

Eddie hangs onto his coat collar with one hand and strokes his chin with the other. He doesn't know just what to do. The vague impulse that has brought him this far after Staats begins to peter out now. Staats has some funny associates—something funny is going on in this out-of-the-way place at this unearthly hour of the morning—but after all, a man's private life is his own. He wonders what made him do this; he wouldn't want anyone to know he did it. He'll turn around and go back to his hotel now and get some shut-eye; he's got to think up some novelty for his routine at Maxim's between now and Monday or he'll be out on his ear.

Then just as one heel is off the ground to take the turn that will start him back, a vague, muffled wailing starts from somewhere inside that house. It's toned down to a mere echo. It has to go through thick doors and wide, empty rooms and down a deep, hollow stairwell before it gets to him. Oh, some sort of a revival meeting, is it? So Staats has got religion, has he? But what a place to come and get it in!

A throbbing like a faraway engine in a machine shop under-scores the wailing, and every once in a while a *boom* like distant thunder across the bayou tops the whole works. It goes *boom-putta-putta-boom-putta-putta-boom!* And the wailing, way up high at the moon: *Eeyah-eeyah-eeyah—!*

Eddie's professional instincts suddenly come alive. He tries it out, beats time to it with his arm as if he were holding a baton. His fingers snap like a whip. "My God, that's grand! That's gorgeous! Just what I need! I gotta get up there!" So a chicken foot does it, eh?

He turns and runs back, through the tunnel, through the court-yards, all the way back where he came from, stooping here, stoop-ing there, lighting matches recklessly and throwing them away as he goes. Out in the Vieux Carré again, the refuse hasn't been collected. He spots a can at the corner of two lanes, topples it over. The smell rises to heaven, but he wades into it ankle-deep like any levee-rat, digs into the stuff with both forearms, scattering it right and left. He's lucky, finds a verminous carcass, tears off a claw, wipes it on some newspaper. Then he starts back. Wait a minute! The red rag, red strip around it! He feels himself all over, digs into all his pockets. Nothing that color. Have to do without it, but maybe it won't work without it. He turns and hurries back through the slit between the old houses, doesn't care how much noise he makes. The flash of light from Old Faithful, the jogging elbow. Eddie stoops, he suddenly snatches in at the red kimono sleeve, his hand comes away with a strip of it. Bad language, words that even Eddie doesn't know. A five-spot stops it on the syllable, and Eddie's already way down the passage. If only they haven't quit until he can get back there!

They haven't. It was vague, smothered when he went away; it's louder, more persistent, more frenzied now. He doesn't bother about giving the whistle, probably couldn't imitate it exactly anyhow. He dives into the black smudge that is the entrance to the house, feels greasy stone steps under him, takes one or two and then suddenly his collar is four sizes too small for him, gripped by a big ham of a hand at the back. A sharp something that might be anything from a pocket-knife blade to the business edge of a razor is creasing his throat just below the apple and drawing a preliminary drop or two of blood.

"Here it is, I've got it here!" gasps Eddie. What kind of religion is this, anyway? The sharp thing stays, but the hand lets go his collar and feels for the chicken claw. Then the sharp thing goes away too, but probably not very far away.

"Whyfor you didn't give the signal?"

Eddie's windpipe gives him the answer. "Sick here, couldn't."

"Light up, lemme see yo' face." Eddie strikes a match and holds it. "Yo' face has never been here before."

Eddie gestures upward. "My friend—up there—he'll tell you!"

"Mr. Johnny yo' friend? He ax you to come?"

Eddie thinks quickly. The chicken claw might carry more weight than Staats. "That told me to come."

"Papa Benjamin sen' you that?"

"Certainly," says Eddie stoutly. Probably their deacon, but it's a hell of a way to—The match stings his fingers and he whips it out.

Blackness and a moment's uncertainty that might end either way. But a lot of *savoir-faire,* a thousand years of civilization, are backing Eddie up. "You'll make me late, Papa Benjamin wouldn't like that!"

He gropes his way on up in the pitch blackness, thinking any minute he'll feel his back slashed to ribbons. But it's better than standing still and having it happen, and to back out now would bring it on twice as quickly. However, it works, nothing happens.

"Fust thing y'know, all N'yorleans be comin' by," growls the African watchdog sulkily, and flounders down on the staircase with a sound like a tired seal. There is some other crack about "darkies lookin' lak pinks," and then a long period of scratching.

But Eddie's already up on the landing above and so close to the *boom-putta-boom* now it drowns out every other sound. The whole framework of the decrepit house seems to shake with it. The door's closed but the thread of orange that outlines it shows it up to him. Behind there. He leans against it, shoves a little. It gives. The squealings and the grindings it emits are lost in the torrent of noise that comes rushing out. He sees plenty, and what he sees only makes him want to see all the more. Something tells him the best thing to do is slip in quietly and close it behind him before he's noticed, rather than stay there peeping in from the outside. Little Snowdrop might always come upstairs in back of him and catch him there. So he widens it just a little more, oozes in, and kicks it shut behind him with his heel—and immediately gets as far away from it as he can. Evidently no one has seen him.

Now, it's a big shadowy room and it's choked with people. It's lit by a single oil lamp and a hell of a whole lot of candles, which may have shone out brightly against the darkness outside but are pretty dim once you get inside with them. The long flickering shadows thrown on all the walls by those cavorting in the center are almost as much of a protection to Eddie, as he crouches back amidst them, as the darkness outside would be. He's been around, and a single look is enough to tell him that whatever else it is, it's no revival meeting. At first, he takes it for just a gin or rent party with the lid off, but it isn't that either. There's no gin there, and there's no pairing off of couples in the dancing—rather it's a roomful of devils lifted bodily up out of hell. Plenty of them have passed out cold on the floor all around him and the others keep stepping over them as they prance back and forth, only they don't always step over but sometimes *on*—on prostrate faces and chests and outstretched arms and hands. Then there are others who have gone off into a sort of still trance, seated on the floor with their backs to the wall, some of them rocking back and forth, some just staring glassy-eyed, foam drooling from their mouths. Eddie quickly slips down among them on his haunches and gets busy. He too starts rocking back and forth and pounding the floor beside him with his knuckles, but he's not in any trance, he's getting a swell new number for his repertoire at Maxim's. A sheet of blank score paper is partly hidden under his body, and he keeps dropping one hand down to it every minute jotting down musical notes with the stub of pencil in his fingers. "Key of A," he guesses. "I can decide that when I instrument it. Mi-re-do, mi-re-do. Then over again. Hope I didn't miss any of it."

Boom-putta-putta-boom! Young and old, black and tawny, fat and thin, naked and clothed, they pass from right to left, from left to right, in two concentric circles, while the candle flames dance crazily and the shadows leap up and down on the walls. The hub of it all, within the innermost circle of dancers, is an old, old man, black skin and bones, only glimpsed now and then in a space between the packed bodies that surround him. An animal pelt is banded about his middle; he wears a horrible juju mask over his face—a death's head. On one side of him, a squatting woman clacks two gourds together endlessly, that's the "putta" of Eddie's rhythm; on the other, another beats a drum, that's the "boom." In one upraised hand he holds a squalling fowl, wings beating the air; in the other a sharp-bladed knife. Something flashes in the air, but the dancers mercifully get between Eddie and the sight of it. Next glimpse he has, the fowl isn't flapping any more. It's hanging limply down and veins of blood are trickling down the old man's shriveled forearm.

"That part don't go into my show," Eddie thinks facetiously. The horrible old man has dropped the knife; he squeezes the life blood from the dead bird with both hands now, still holding it in mid-air. He sprinkles the drops on those that cavort around him, flexing and unflexing his bony fingers in a nauseating travesty of the ceremony of baptism.

Drops spatter here and there about the room, on the walls. One lands near Eddie and he edges back. Revolting things go on all around him. He sees some of the crazed dancers drop to their hands and knees and bend low over these red polka dots, licking them up from the floor with their tongues. Then they go about the room on all fours like animals, looking for others.

"Think I'll go," Eddie says to himself, tasting last night's supper all over again. "They ought to have the cops on them."

He maneuvers the score sheet, filled now, out from under him and into his side pocket; then he starts drawing his feet in toward him preparatory to standing up and slipping out of this hell hole. Meanwhile a second fowl, black this time (the first was white), a squeaking suckling pig, and a puppy dog have gone the way of the first fowl. Nor do the carcasses go to waste when the old man has dropped them. Eddie sees things happening on the floor, in between the stomping feet of the dancers, and he guesses enough not to look twice.

Then suddenly, already reared a half-inch above the floor on his way up, he wonders where the wailing went. And the clacking of the gourds and the boom of the drum and the shuffling of the feet. He blinks, and everything has frozen still in the room around him. Not a move, not a sound. Straight out from the old man's gnarled shoulder stretches a bony arm, the end dipped in red, pointing like an arrow at Eddie. Eddie sinks down again that half-inch. He couldn't hold that position very long, and something tells him he's not leaving right away after all.

"White man," says a bated breath, and they all start moving in on him. A gesture of the old man sweeps them into motionlessness again.

A cracked voice comes through the grinning mouth of the juju mask, rimmed with canine teeth. "Whut you do here?"

Eddie taps his pockets mentally. He has about fifty on him. Will that be enough to buy his way out? He has an uneasy feeling, however, that none of this lot is as interested in money as they should be—at least not right now. Before he has a chance to try it out, another voice speaks up. "I know this man, *papaloi.* Let me find out."

Johnny Staats came in here tuxedoed, hair slicked back, a cog in New Orleans' nightlife. Now he's barefooted, coatless, shirtless —a tousled scarecrow. A drop of blood has caught him squarely on the forehead and been traced, by his own finger or someone else's, into a red line from temple to temple. A chicken feather or two clings to his upper lip. Eddie saw him dancing with the rest, groveling on the floor. His scalp crawls with repugnance as the man comes over and squats down before him. The rest of them hold back, tense, poised, ready to pounce.

The two men talk in low, hoarse voices. "It's your only way, Eddie. I can't save you—"

"Why, I'm in the very heart of New Orleans! They wouldn't dare!" But sweat oozes out on Eddie's face just the same. He's no fool. Sure the police will come and sure they'll mop this place up. But what will they find? His own remains along with that of the fowls, the pig, and the dog.

"You'd better hurry up, Eddie. I can't hold them back much longer. Unless you do, you'll never get out of this place alive and you may as well know it! If I tried to stop them, I'd go too. You know what this is, don't you? This is voodoo!"

"I knew that five minutes after I was in the room." And Eddie thinks to himself, "You son-of-a-so-and-so! You better ask Mombo-jombo to get you a new job starting in tomorrow night!" Then he grins internally and, clown to the very end, says with a straight face, "Sure I'll join. What d'ye suppose I came here for anyway?"

Knowing what he knows now, Staats is the last one he'd tell about the glorious new number he's going to get out of this, the notes for which are nestled in his inside pocket right now. And he might even get more dope out of the initiation ceremonies if he pretends to go through with them. A song or dance for Judy to do with maybe a green spot focused on her. Lastly, there's no use denying there *are* too many razors, knives, and the like, in the room to hope to get out and all the way back where he started from without a scratch.

Staats's face is grave, though. "Now don't kid about this thing. If you knew what I know about it, there's a lot more to it than there seems to be. If you're sincere, honest about it, all right. If not, it might be better to get cut to pieces right now than to tamper with it."

"Never more serious in my life," says Eddie. And deep down inside he's braying like a jackass.

Staats turns to the old man. "His spirit wishes to join our spirits."

The *papaloi* burns some feathers and entrails at one of the candle flames. Not a sound in the room. The majority of them squat down all at once. "It came out all right," Staats breathes. "He reads them. The spirits are willing."

"So far so good," Eddie thinks. "I've fooled the guts and feathers."

The *papaloi* is pointing at him now. "Let him go now and be silent," the voice behind the mask cackles. Then a second time he says it, and a third, with a long pause between.

Eddie looks hopefully at Staats. "Then I can go after all, as long as I don't tell anyone what I've seen?"

Staats shakes his head grimly. "Just part of the ritual. If you went now, you'd eat something that disagreed with you tomorrow and be dead before the day was over."

More sacrificial slaughtering, and the drum and gourds and wailing start over again, but very low and subdued now as at the beginning. A bowl of blood is prepared and Eddie is raised to his feet and led forward, Staats on one side of him, an anonymous colored man on the other. The *papaloi* dips his already caked hand into the bowl and traces a mark on Eddie's forehead. The chanting and wailing grow louder behind him. The dancing begins again. He's in the middle of all of them. He's an island of sanity in a sea of jungle frenzy. The bowl is being held up before his face. He tries to draw back, his sponsors grip him firmly by the arms. "Drink!" whispers Staats. "Drink—or they'll kill you where you stand!"

Even at this stage of the game, there's still a wisecrack left in Eddie, though he keeps it to himself. He takes a deep breath. "Here's where I get my vitamin A for today!"

Staats shows up at orchestra rehearsal next A.M. to find somebody else at drums and percussion. He doesn't say much when Eddie shoves a two-week check at him, spits on the floor at his feet and growls: "Beat it, you filthy—"

Staats only murmurs, "So you're crossing them? I wouldn't want to be in your shoes for all the fame and money in this world, guy!"

"If you mean that bad dream the other night," says Eddie, "I haven't told anybody and I don't intend to. Why, I'd be laughed at. I'm only remembering what I can use of it. I'm a white man, see? The jungle is just trees to me; the Congo just a river; the nighttime just a time for electric lights." He whips out a couple of C's. "Hand 'em these for me, will ya, and tell 'em I've paid up my dues from now until doomsday and I don't want any receipt. And if they try putting rough-on-rats in my orange juice, they'll find themselves stomping in a chain-gang!"

The C's fall where Eddie spat. "You're one of us. You think you're pink? Blood tells. You wouldn't have gone there—you couldn't have stood that induction—if you were. Look at your fingernails sometime, look in a mirror at the whites of your eyes. Good-bye, dead man."

Eddie says good-bye to him, too. He knocks out three of his teeth, breaks the bridge of his nose, and rolls all over the floor on top of him. But he can't wipe out that wise, knowing smile that shows even through the gush of blood.

They pull Eddie off, pull him up, pull him together. Staats staggers away, smiling at what he knows. Eddie, heaving like a bellows, turns to his crew. "All right, boys. All together now!" *Boom-putta-putta-boom-putta-putta-boom!*

Graham shoots five C's on promotion and all New Orleans jams its way into Maxim's that Saturday night. They're standing on each other's shoulders and hanging from the chandeliers to get a look. "First time in America, the original VOODOO CHANT," yowl the three-sheets on every billboard in town. And when Eddie taps his baton, the lights go down and a nasty green flood lights the platform from below and you can hear a pin drop. "Good evening, folks. This is Eddie Bloch and his Five Chips, playing to you from Maxim's. You're about to hear for the first time on the air the Voodoo Chant, the age-old ceremonial rhythm no white man has ever been permitted to listen to before. I can assure you this is an accurate transcription, not a note has been changed." Then very softly and faraway it begins: *Boom-putta-putta-boom!*

Judy's going to dance and wail to it, she's standing there on the steps leading up to the platform, waiting to go on. She's powdered orange, dressed in feathers, and has a small artificial bird fastened to one wrist and a thin knife in her other hand. She catches his eye, he looks over at her, and he sees she wants to tell him something. Still waving his baton he edges sideways until he's within earshot.

"Eddie, don't! Stop them! Call it off, will you? I'm worried about you!"

"Too late now," he answers under cover of the music. "We've started already. What're you scared of?"

She passes him a crumpled piece of paper. "I found this under your dressing-room door when I came out just now. It sounds like a warning. There's somebody doesn't want you to play that number!"

Still swinging with his right hand, Eddie unrolls the thing under his left thumb and reads it:

You can summon the spirits but can you dismiss them again? Think well.

He crumples it up and tosses it away. "Staats trying to scare me because I canned him."

"It was tied to a little bunch of black feathers," she tries to tell him. "I wouldn't have paid any attention, but my maid pleaded with me not to dance this when she saw it. Then she ran out on me—"

"We're on the air," he reminds her between his teeth. "Are you with me or aren't you?" And he eases back center again. Louder and louder the beat grows, just like it did two nights ago. Judy swirls on in a green spot and begins the unearthly wail Eddie's coached her to do.

A waiter drops a tray of drinks in the silence of the room out there, and when the headwaiter goes to bawl him out he's nowhere to be found. He has quit cold and a whole row of tables has been left without their orders. "Well, I'll be—!" says the captain and scratches his head.

Eddie's facing the crew, his back to Judy, and as he vibrates to the rhythm, some pin or other that he's forgotten to take out of his shirt suddenly catches him and strikes into him. It's a little below the collar, just between the shoulder blades. He jumps a little, but doesn't feel it any more after that.

Judy squalls, tears her tonsils out, screeches words that neither he nor she know the meaning of but that he managed to set down on paper phonetically the other night. Her little body goes through all the contortions, tamed down of course, that that brownskin she-devil greased with lard and wearing only earrings performed that night. She stabs the bird with her fake knife and sprinkles imaginary blood in the air. Nothing like this has ever been seen before. And in the silence that suddenly lands when it's through, you can count twenty. That's how it's gotten under everyone's skin.

Then the noise begins. It goes over like an avalanche. But just the same, more people are ordering strong drinks all at once than has ever happened before in the place, and the matron in the women's restroom has her hands full of hysterical sob-sisters.

"Try to get away from me, just try!" Graham tells Eddie at curfew time. "I'll have a new contract, gilt-edged, ready for you in the morning. We've already got six-grand worth of reservations on our hands for the coming week—one of 'em by telegram all the way from Shreveport!"

Success! Eddie and Judy taxi back to their rooms at the hotel, tired but happy. "It'll be good for years. We can use it for our signature on the air, like Whiteman does the Rhapsody."

She goes into the bedroom first, snaps on the lights, calls to him a minute later: "Come here and look at this—the cutest little souvenir!" He finds her holding a wax doll, finger high, in her hands. "Why, it's you, Eddie, look! Small as it is it has your features! Well isn't that the clev—!"

He takes it away from her and squints at it. It's himself all right. It's rigged out in two tiny patches of black cloth for a tuxedo, and the eyes and hair and features are inked onto the wax.

"Where'd you find it?"

"It was in your bed, up against the pillow."

He's fixing to grin about it, until he happens to turn it over. In the back, just a little below the collar, between the shoulderblades, a short but venomous-looking black pin is sticking.

He goes a little white for a minute. He knows who it's from now and what it's trying to tell him. But that isn't what makes him change color. He's just remembered something. He throws off his coat, yanks at his collar, turns his back to her. "Judy, look down there, will you? I felt a pin stick me while we were doing that number. Put your hand down. Feel anything?"

"No, there's nothing there," she tells him.

"Musta dropped out."

"It couldn't have," she says. "Your belt line's so tight it almost cuts into you. There couldn't have been anything there or it'd still be there now. You must have imagined it."

"Listen, I know a pin when I feel one. Any mark on my back, any scratch between the shoulders?"

"Not a thing."

"Tired, I guess. Nervous." He goes over to the open window and pitches the little doll out into the night with all his strength. Damn coincidence, that's all it was. To think otherwise would be to give them their inning. But he wonders what makes him feel so tired just the same—Judy did all the exercising, not he—yet he's felt all in ever since that number tonight.

Out go the lights and she drops off to sleep right with them. He lies very quiet for a while. A little later he gets up, goes into the bathroom where the lights are whitest of all, and stands there looking at himself close to the glass. "Look at your fingernails sometime; look at the whites of your eyes," Staats had said. Eddie does. There's a bluish, purplish tinge to his nails that he never noticed before. The whites of his eyes are faintly yellow.

It's warm in New Orleans that night but he shivers a little as he stands there. He doesn't sleep any more that night. . . .

In the morning, his back aches as if he were sixty. But he knows that's from not closing his eyes all night, and not from any magic pins.

"Oh, my God!" Judy says, from the other side of the bed; "look what you've done to him!" She shows him the second page of the *Picayune*. "John Staats, until recently a member of Eddie Bloch's orchestra, committed suicide late yesterday afternoon in full view of dozens of people by rowing himself out into Lake Pontchartrain and jumping overboard. He was alone in the boat at the time. The body was recovered half an hour later."

"I didn't do that," says Eddie grimly. "I've got a rough idea what did, though." Late yesterday afternoon. The night was coming on, and he couldn't face what was coming to him for sponsoring Eddie, for giving them all away. Late yesterday afternoon—that meant *he* hadn't left that warning at the dressing room or left that death sentence on the bed. He'd been dead himself by then—not white, not black, just yellow.

Eddie waits until Judy's in her shower, then he phones the morgue. "About Johnny Staats. He worked for me until yesterday, so if nobody's claimed the body send it to a funeral parlor at my exp—"

"Somebody's already claimed the remains, Mr. Bloch. First thing this morning. Just waited until the examiner had established suicide beyond a doubt. Some colored organization, old friends of his it seems—"

Judy comes in and remarks: "You look all green in the face."

Eddie thinks: "I wouldn't care if he was my worst enemy, I can't let that happen to him! What horrors are going to take place tonight somewhere under the moon?" He wouldn't even put cannibalism beyond them. The phone's right at his fingertips, and yet he can't denounce them to the police without involving himself, admitting that he was there, took part at least once. Once that comes out, bang! goes his reputation. He'll never be able to live it down—especially now that he's played the Voodoo Chant and identified himself with it in the minds of the public.

So instead, alone in the room again, he calls the best-known private agency in New Orleans. "I want a bodyguard. Just for tonight. Have him meet me at closing-time at Maxim's. Armed, of course."

It's Sunday and the banks are closed, but his credit's good anywhere. He raises a G in cash. He arranges with a reliable crematorium for a body to be taken charge of late tonight or early in the morning. He'll notify them just where to call for it. Yes, of course! He'll produce the proper authorization from the police. Poor Johnny Staats couldn't get away from "them" in life, but he's going to get away from them in death, all right. That's the least anyone could do for him.

Graham slaps a sawbuck-cover on that night, more to give the waiters room to move around in than anything else, and still the place is choked to the roof. This Voodoo number is a natural, a wow.

But Eddie's back is ready to cave in, while he stands there jogging with his stick. It's all he can do to hold himself straight.

When the racket and the shuffling are over for the night, the private dick is there waiting for him. "Lee is the name."

"Okay, Lee, come with me." They go outside and get in Eddie's

Bugatti. They whizz down to the Vieux, scrounge to a stop in the middle of Congo Square, which will still be Congo Square when its official name of Beauregard is forgotten.

"This way," says Eddie, and his bodyguard squirms through the alley after him.

" 'Lo, suga' pie," says the elbow-pusher, and for once, to her own surprise as much as anyone else's, gets a tumble.

" 'Lo, Eglantine," Eddie's bodyguard remarks in passing, "So you moved?"

They stop in front of the house on the other side of the tunnel. "Now here's what," says Eddie. "We're going to be stopped half-way up these stairs in here by a big orangutan. Your job is to clean him, tap him if you want, I don't care. I'm going into a room up there, you're going to wait for me at the door. You're here to see that I get out of that room again. We may have to carry the body of a friend of mine down to the street between us. I don't know. It depends on whether it's in the house or not. Got it?"

"Got it."

"Light up. Keep your torch trained over my shoulder."

A big, lowering figure looms over them, blocking the narrow stairs, apelike arms and legs spread-eagled in a gesture of malignant embrace, receding skull, teeth showing, flashing steel in hand. Lee jams Eddie roughly to one side and shoves up past him. "Drop that, boy!" Lee says with slurring indifference, but then he doesn't wait to see if the order's carried out or not. After all, a weapon was raised to two white men. He fires three times, from two feet away and considerably below the obstacle, hits where he aimed to. The bullets shatter both kneecaps and the elbow joint of the arm holding the knife.

"Be a cripple for life now," he remarks with quiet satisfaction. "I'll put him out of his pain." So he crashes the butt of gun down on the skull of the writhing colossus, in a long arc like the overhand pitch of a baseball. The noise of the shots goes booming up the narrow stairwell to the roof, to mushroom out there in a vast rolling echo.

"Come on, hurry up," says Eddie, "before they have a chance to do away with—"

He lopes on up past the prostrate form, Lee at his heels. "Stand there. Better reload while you're waiting. If I call your name, for Pete's sake don't count ten before you come in to me!"

There's a scurrying back and forth and an excited but subdued jabbering going on on the other side of the door. Eddie swings it wide and crashes it closed behind him, leaving Lee on the outside. They all stand rooted to the spot when they see him. The *papaloi* is there and about six others, not so many as on the night of Eddie's initiation. Probably the rest are waiting outside the city somewhere, in some secret spot, wherever the actual burial, or burning, or—feasting—is to take place.

Papa Benjamin has no juju mask on this time, no animal pelt. There are no gourds in the room, no drum, no transfixed figures ranged against the wall. They were about to move on elsewhere, he just got here in time. Maybe they were waiting for the dark of the moon. The ordinary kitchen chairs on which the *papaloi* was to be carried on their shoulders stands prepared, padded with rags. A row of baskets covered with sacking are ranged along the back wall.

"Where is the body of John Staats?" raps out Eddie. "You claimed it, took it away from the morgue this morning." His eyes are on those baskets, on the bleared razor he catches sight of lying on the floor near them.

"Better far," cackles the old man, "that you had followed him. The mark of doom is on yo' even now—" A growl goes up all around.

"Lee," grates Eddie, "in here!" Lee stands next to him, gun in hand. "Cover me while I take a look around."

"All of you over in that corner there," growls Lee, and kicks viciously at one who is too slow in moving. They huddle there, cower there, glaring, spitting like a band of apes. Eddie makes straight for those baskets, whips the covering off the first one. Charcoal. The next. Coffee beans. The next. Rice. And so on.

Just small baskets that Negro women balance on their heads to sell at the marketplace. He looks at Papa Benjamin, takes out the wad of money he's brought with him. "Where've you got him? Where's he buried? Take us there, show us where it is."

Not a sound, just burning, shriveling hate in waves that you can almost feel. He looks at that razor blade lying there, bleared, not bloody, just matted, dulled, with shreds and threads of something clinging to it. Kicks it away with his foot. "Not here, I guess," he mutters to Lee and moves toward the door.

"What do we do now, boss?" his henchman wants to know.

"Get the hell out of here I guess, where we can breathe some air," Eddie says, and moves on out to the stairs.

Lee is the sort of man who will get what he can out of any situation, no matter what it is. Before he follows Eddie out, he goes over to one of the baskets, stuffs an orange in each coat pocket, and then prods and pries among them to select a particularly nice one for eating on the spot. There's a thud and the orange goes rolling across the floor like a volley-ball. "Mr. Bloch!" he shouts hoarsely, "I've found—him!" And he looks pretty sick.

A deep breath goes up from the corner where the Negroes are. Eddie just stands and stares, and leans back weakly for a minute against the doorpost. From out of the layers of oranges in the basket, the five fingers of a hand thrust upward, a hand that ends abruptly, cleanly at the wrist.

"His signet," says Eddie weakly, "there on the little finger—I know it."

"Say the word! Should I shoot?" Lee wants to know.

Eddie shakes his head. "They didn't—he committed suicide. Let's do what we have to—and get out of here!"

Lee turns over one basket after the other. The stuff in them spills and sifts and rolls out upon the floor. But in each there's something else. Bloodless, pallid as fish flesh. That razor, those shreds clinging to it, Eddie knows now what it was used for. They take one basket, they line it with a verminous blanket from the bed. Then with their bare hands they fill it with what they have found, and close the ends of the blanket over the top of it, and carry it between them out of the room and down the pitch-black stairs, Lee going down backward with his gun in one hand to cover them from the rear. Lee's swearing like a fiend. Eddie's trying not to think what the purpose, the destination of all those baskets was. The watchdog is still out on the stairs, with a concussion.

Back through the lane they struggle and finally put their burden down in the before-dawn stillness of Congo Square. Eddie goes up against a wall and is heartily sick. Then he comes back again and says: "The head—did you notice—?"

"No, we didn't," Lee answers. "Stay here, I'll go back for it. I'm armed. I could stand anything now, after what I just been through."

Lee's gone about five minutes. When he comes back, he's in his shirt, coatless. His coat's rolled up under one arm in a bulky bulge. He bends over the basket, lifts the blanket, replaces it again, and when he straightens up, the bulge in his folded coat is gone. Then he throws the coat away, kicks it away on the ground. "Hidden away in a cupboard," he mutters. "Had to shoot one of 'em through the palm of the hand before they'd come clean. What were they up to?"

"Practice cannibalism maybe, I don't know. I'd rather not think."

"I brought your money back. It didn't seem to square you with them."

Eddie shoves it back at him. "Pay for your suit and your time."

"Aren't you going to tip off the squareheads?"

"I told you he jumped in the lake. I have a copy of the examiner's report in my pocket."

"I know, but isn't there some ordinance against dissecting a body without permission?"

"I can't afford to get mixed up with them, Lee. It would kill my career. We've got what we went there for. Now just forget everything you saw."

The hearse from the crematorium contacts them there in Congo Square. The covered basket's taken on, and what's left of Johnny Staats heads away for a better finish than was coming to him.

"G'night, boss," says Lee. "Any time you need any other little thing—"

"No," says Eddie, "I'm getting out of New Orleans." His hand is like ice when they shake.

He does. He hands Graham back his contract, and a split week later he's playing New York's newest, in the frantic Fifties. With a white valet. The Chant, of course, is still featured. He has to; it's his chief asset, his biggest draw. It introduces him and signs him off, and in between Judy always dances it for a high spot. But he can't get rid of that backache that started the night he first played it. First he goes and tries having his back baked for a couple of hours a day under a violet-ray lamp. No improvement.

Then he has himself examined by the biggest specialist in New York. "Nothing there," says the big shot. "Absolutely nothing the matter with you: liver, kidneys, blood—everything perfect. It must be all in your own mind."

"You're losing weight, Eddie," Judy says, "you look bad, darling." His bathroom scales tell him the same thing. Down five pounds a week, sometimes seven, never up an ounce. More experts. X-rays this time, blood analysis, gland treatments, everything from soup to nuts. Nothing doing. And the dull ache, the lassitude, spreads slowly, first to one arm, then to the other.

He takes specimens of everything he eats, not just one day, but every day for weeks, and has them chemically analyzed. Nothing. And he doesn't have to be told that anyway. He knows that even in New Orleans, way back in the beginning, nothing was ever put into his food. Judy ate from the same tray, drank from the same coffee pot he did. Nightly she dances herself into a lather, and yet she's the picture of health.

So that leaves nothing but his mind, just as they all say. "But I don't believe it!" he tells himself. "I don't believe that just sticking pins into a wax doll can hurt me—me or anyone!"

So it isn't his mind at all, but some other mind back there in New Orleans, some other mind *thinking,* wishing, ordering him dead, night and day.

"But it can't be done!" says Eddie. "There's no such thing!"

And yet it's being done; it's happening right under his own eyes. Which leaves only one answer. If going three thousand miles away on dry land didn't help, then going three thousand miles away across the ocean will do the trick. So London next, and the Kit-Kat Club. Down, down, down go the bathroom scales, a little bit each week. The pains spread downward into his thighs. His ribs start showing up here and there. He's dying on his feet. He finds it more comfortable now to walk with a stick—not to be swanky, not to be English—to rest as he goes along. His shoulders ache each night just from waving that lightweight baton at his crew. He has a music stand built for himself to lean on, keeps it in front of his body, out of sight of the audience while he's conducting, and droops over it. Sometimes he finishes up a number with his head lower than his shoulders, as though he had a rubber spine.

Finally he goes to Reynolds, famous the world over, the biggest

alienist in England. "I want to know whether I'm sane or insane."
He's under observation for weeks, months; they put him through
every known test, and plenty of unknown ones, mental, physical,
metabolic. They flash lights in front of his face and watch the
pupils of his eyes; they contract to pinheads. They touch the back
of his throat with sandpaper; he nearly chokes. They strap him to
a chair that goes around and around and does somersaults at so
many revolutions per minute, then ask him to walk across the
room; he staggers.

Reynolds takes plenty of pounds, hands him a report thick as a
telephone book, sums it up for him. "You are as normal, Mr. Bloch,
as anyone I have ever handled. You're so well-balanced you
haven't even got the extra little touch of imagination most actors
and musicians have." So it's not his own mind, it's coming from the
outside, is it?

The whole thing from beginning to end has taken eighteen
months. Trying to out-distance death, with death gaining on him
slowly but surely all the time. He's emaciated. There's only one
thing left to do now, while he's still able to crawl aboard a ship—
that's to get back to where the whole thing started. New York,
London, Paris, haven't been able to save him. His only salvation,
now, lies in the hands of a decrepit colored man skulking in the
Vieux Carré of New Orleans.

He drags himself there, to that same half-ruined house, without a bodyguard, not caring now whether they kill him or not,
almost wishing they would and get it over with. But that would
be too easy an out, it seems. The gorilla that Lee crippled that
night shuffles out to him between two sticks, recognizes him,
breathes undying hate into his face, but doesn't lift a finger to
harm him. The spirits are doing the job better than he could
ever hope to. Their mark is on this man, woe betide anyone who
comes between them and their hellish satisfaction. Eddie Bloch
totters up the stairs unopposed, his back as safe from a knife as if
he wore steel armor. Behind him the Negro sprawls upon the
stairs to lubricate his long-awaited hour of satisfaction with rum
—and oblivion.

He finds the old man alone there in the room. The Stone Age
and the twentieth century face each other, and the Stone Age has
won out.

"Take it off me," says Eddie brokenly. "Give me my life back—I'll do anything, anything you say!"

"What has been done cannot be undone. Do you think the spirits of the earth and of the air, of fire and water, know the meaning of forgiveness?"

"Intercede for me, then. You brought it about. Here's money, I'll give you twice as much, all I earn, all I ever hope to earn—"

"You have desecrated the *obiah*. Death has been on you from that night. All over the world and in the air above the earth you have mocked the spirits with the chant that summons them. Nightly your wife dances it. The only reason she has not shared your doom is because she does not know the meaning of what she does. You do. You were here among us."

Eddie goes down on his knees, scrapes along the floor after the old man, tries to tug at the garments he wears. "Kill me right now, then, and be done with it. I can't stand any more—" He bought the gun only that day, was going to do it himself at first, but found he couldn't. A minute ago he pleaded for his life, now he's pleading for death. "It's loaded, all you have to do is shoot. Look! I'll close my eyes—I'll write a note and sign it, that I did it myself—"

He tries to thrust it into the witch doctor's hand, tries to close the bony, shriveled fingers around it, tries to point it at himself. The old man throws it down, away from him. Cackles gleefully, "Death will come, but differently—slowly, oh, so slowly!"

Eddie just lies there flat on his face, sobbing dryly. The old man spits, kicks at him weakly. He pulls himself up somehow, stumbles toward the door. He isn't even strong enough to get it open at the first try. It's that little thing that brings it on. Something touches his foot, he looks, stoops for the gun, turns. Thought is quick but the old man's mind is even quicker. Almost before the thought is there, the old man knows what's coming. In a flash, scuttling like a crab, he has shifted around to the other side of the bed, to put something between them. Instantly the situation's reversed, the fear has left Eddie and is on the old man now. He's lost the aggression. For a minute only, but that minute is all Eddie needs. His mind beams out like a diamond, like a lighthouse through a fog. The gun roars, jolting his weakened body down to his shoes. The old man falls flat across the bed, his head too far over, dangling down over the side of it like an over-ripe pear. The bed-frame sways gently with his weight for a min-ute, and then it's over.

Eddie stands there, still off-balance from the kickback. So it was as easy as all that! Where's all his magic now? Strength, willpower flood back through him as if a faucet was suddenly turned on. The little smoke there was can't get out of the sealed-up room, it hangs there in thin layers. Suddenly he's shaking his fist at the dead thing on the bed. "I'm gonna live now! I'm gonna live, see?" He gets the door open, sways with it for a minute. Then he's feeling his way down the stairs, past the unconscious watchdog, mumbling it over and over but low, "Gonna live now, gonna live!"

The commissioner mops his face as if he were in the steam room of a Turkish bath. He exhales like an oxygen tank. "Judas, Joseph, and Mary, Mr. Bloch, what a story! Wish I hadn't asked you; I won't sleep tonight." Even after the accused has been led from the room, it takes him some time to get over it. The upper right-hand drawer of his desk helps some—just two fingers. So does opening the windows and letting in a lot of sunshine.

Finally he picks up the phone and gets down to business. "Who've you got out there that's absolutely without a nerve in his body? I mean a guy with so little feeling he could sit on a hatpin and turn it into a paper clip. Oh, yeah, that Cajun, Desjardins, I know him. He's the one goes around striking parlor matches off the soles of stiffs. Well, send him in here."

"No, stay outside," wheezes Papa Benjamin through the partly open door to his envoy. "I'se communin' with the *obiah* and yo' unclean, been drunk all last night and today. Deliver the sum-mons. Reach yo' hand in to me, once fo' every token, yo' knows how many to take."

The crippled Negro thrusts his huge paw through the aperture, and from behind the door the *papaloi* places a severed chicken claw in his upturned palm. A claw bound with a red rag. The messenger disposes of it about his tattered clothing, thrusts his hand in for another. Twenty times the act is repeated, then he lets his arm hang stiffly at his side. The door starts closing slowly.

"Papoloi," whines the figure on the outside of it, "why you hide yo' face from me, is the spirits angry?"

There's a flicker of suspicion in his yellow eyeballs in the dimness, however. Instantly the opening of the door widens. Papa Benjamin's familiar wrinkled face thrusts out at him, malignant eyes crackling like fuses. "Go!" shrills the old man, " 'liver my summons. Is you want me to bring a spirit down on you?" The messenger totters back. The door slams.

The sun goes down and it's nighttime in New Orleans. The moon rises, midnight chimes from St. Louis Cathedral, and hardly has the last note died away than a gruesome swampland whistle sounds outside the deathly still house. A fat Negress, basket on arm, comes trudging up the stairs a moment later, opens the door, goes in to the *papaloi,* closes it again, traces an invisible mark on it with her forefinger and kisses it. Then she turns and her eyes widen with surprise. Papa Benjamin is in bed, covered up to the neck with filthy rags. The familiar candles are all lit, the bowl for the blood, the sacrificial knife, the magic powders, all the paraphernalia of the ritual are laid out in readiness, but they are ranged about the bed instead of at the opposite end of the room as usual.

The old man's head, however, is held high above the encumbering rags, his beady eyes gaze back at her unflinchingly, the familiar semicircle of white wool rings his crown, his ceremonial mask is at his side. "I am a little tired, my daughter," he tells her. His eyes stray to the tiny wax image of Eddie Bloch under the candles, hairy with pins, and hers follow them. "A doomed one, nearing his end, came here last night thinking I could be killed like other men. He shot a bullet from a gun at me. I blew my breath at it, it stopped in the air, turned around, and went back in the gun again. But it tired me to blow so hard, strained my voice a little."

A revengeful gleam lights up the woman's broad face. "And he'll die soon, *papaloi?"*

"Soon," cackles the weazened figure in the bed. The woman gnashes her teeth and hugs herself delightedly. She opens the top of her basket and allows a black hen to escape and flutter about the room.

When all twenty have assembled, men and women, old and

young, the drum and the gourds begin to beat, the low wailing starts, the orgy gets under way. Slowly they dance around the three sides of the bed at first, then faster, faster, lashing themselves to a frenzy, tearing at their own and each other's clothes, drawing blood with knives and fingernails, eyes rolling in an ecstasy that colder races cannot know. The sacrifices, feathered and furred, that have been fastened to the two lower posts of the bed, squawk and flutter and fly vertically up and down in a barnyard panic. There is a small monkey among them tonight, clawing, biting, hiding his face in his hands like a frightened child. A bearded Negro, nude torso glistening like patent-leather, seizes one of the frantic fowls, yanks it loose from its moorings, and holds it out toward the witch doctor with both hands. "We'se thirsty, *papaloi*, we'se thirsty fo' the blood of ou' enemies."

The others take up the cry. "We'se hung'y, *papaloi*, fo' the bones of ou' enemies!"

Papa Benjamin nods his head in time to the rhythm.

"Sac'fice, *papaloi*, sac'fice!"

Papa Benjamin doesn't seem to hear them.

Then back go the rags in a gray wave and out comes the arm at last. Not the gnarled brown toothpick arm of Papa Benjamin, but a bulging arm thick as a piano leg, cuffed in serge, white at the wrist, ending in a regulation police revolver with the clip off. The erstwhile witch doctor's on his feet at a bound, standing erect atop the bed, back to the wall, slowly fanning his score of human devils with the mouth of his gun, left to right, then right to left again, evenly, unhurriedly. The resonant bellow of a bull comes from his weazened slit of a mouth instead of *papaloi's* cracked falsetto. "Back against that wall there, all of you! Throw down them knives and jiggers!"

But they're slow to react; the swift drop from ecstasy to stupefaction can't register right away. None of them are over bright anyway or they wouldn't be here. Mouths hang open, the wailing stops, the drums and gourds fall still, but they're still packed close about this sudden changeling in their midst, with the familiar shriveled face of Papa Benjamin and the thick-set body, business suit, of a white man—too close for comfort. Blood lust and religious mania don't know fear of a gun. It takes a cool head for that, and the only cool head in the room is the withered cocoanut atop the broad shoulders behind that gun. So he shoots twice, and a woman at one end of the semicircle, the drum beater, and a man at the other end, the one still holding the sacrificial fowl, drop in their tracks with a double moan. Those in the middle slowly draw back step by step across the room, all eyes on the figure reared up on the bed. An instant's carelessness, the wavering of an eye, and they'll be in on him in a body. He reaches up with his free hand and rips the dead witch-doctor's features from his face, to breathe better, see better. They dissolve into a crumpled rag before the blacks' terrified eyes, like a stocking cap coming off someone's head—a mixture of paraffin and fiber, called moulage—a death mask taken from the corpse's own face, reproducing even the fine lines of the skin and its natural color. Moulage. So the twentieth century has won out after all. And behind them is the grinning, slightly perspiring, lantern-jawed face of Detective Jacques Desjardins, who doesn't believe in spirits unless they're under a neat little label. And outside the house sounds the twenty-first whistle of the evening, but not a swampland sound this time; a long, cold, keen blast to bring figures out of the shadows and doorways that have waited there patiently all night.

Then the door bursts inward and the police are in the room. The prisoners, two of them dangerously wounded, are pushed and carried downstairs to join the crippled doorguard, who has been in custody for the past hour, and single file, tied together with ropes, they make their way through the long tortuous alley out into Congo Square.

In the early hours of that same morning, just a little more than twenty-four hours after Eddie Bloch first staggered into police headquarters with his strange story, the whole thing is cooked, washed, and bottled. The commissioner sits in his office listening attentively to Desjardins. And spread out on his desk as strange an array of amulets, wax images, bunches of feathers, balsam leaves, *ouangas* (charms of nail parings, hair clippings, dried blood, powdered roots), green mildewed coins dug up from coffins in graveyards, as that room has ever seen before. All this is state's evidence now, to be carefully labeled and docketed for the use of the prosecuting attorney when the proper time comes. "And this," explains

Desjardins, indicating a small dusty bottle, "is methylene blue, the chemist tells me. It's the only modern thing we got out of the place, found it lying forgotten with a lot of rubbish in a corner that looked like it hadn't been disturbed for years. What it was doing there or what they wanted with it I don't—"

"Wait a minute," interrupts the commissioner eagerly. "That fits in with something poor Bloch told me last night. He noticed a bluish color under his fingernails and a yellowness to his eyeballs, but *only* after he'd been initiated that first night. This stuff probably had something to do with it, an injection of it must have been given him that night in some way without his knowing it. Don't you get the idea? It floored him just the way they wanted it to. He mistook the signs of it for a giveaway that he had colored blood. It was the opening wedge. It broke down his disbelief, started his mental resistance to crumbling. That was all they needed, just to get a foothold in his mind. Mental suggestion did the rest, has been doing it ever since. If you ask me, they pulled the same stunt on Staats originally. I don't believe he had colored blood any more than Bloch has. And as a matter of fact the theory that it shows up in that way generations later is all the bunk anyway, they tell me."

"Well," says Dij, looking at his own grimy nails, "if you're just going to judge by appearances that way, I'm full-blooded Zulu."

His overlord just looks at him, and if he didn't have such a poker face, one might be tempted to read admiration or at least approval into the look. "Must have been a pretty tight spot for a minute with all of them around while you put on your act!"

"Nah, I didn't mind," answered Dij. "The only thing that bothered me was the smell."

Eddie Bloch, the murder charge against him quashed two months ago, and the population of the state penitentiary increased only this past week by the admission of twenty-three ex-voodoo-worshippers for terms varying from two to ten years, steps up on the platform at Maxim's for a return engagement. Eddie's pale and washed-out looking, but climbing slowly back up through the hundred-and-twenties again to his former weight. The ovation he gets ought to do anyone's heart good, the way they clap and stamp and stand up and cheer. And at that, his name was kept out of the recently concluded trial. Desjardins and his mates did all the states-witnessing necessary.

The theme he comes in on now is something sweet and harmless. Then a waiter comes up and hands him a request. Eddie shakes his head. "No, not in our repertoire any more." He goes on leading. Another request comes, and another. Suddenly someone shouts it out at him, and in a second the whole place has taken up the cry. "The Voodoo Chant! Give us the Voodoo Chant!"

His face gets whiter than it is already, but he turns and tries to smile at them and shake his head. They won't quit, the music can't be heard, and he has to tap a lay-off. From all over the place, like a cheering section at a football game, "We want the Voodoo Chant! We want—!"

Judy's at his side. "What's the matter with 'em anyway?" he asks. "Don't they know what that thing's done to me?"

"Play it, Eddie, don't be foolish," she urges. "Now's the time, break the spell once and for all, prove to yourself that it can't hurt you. If you don't do it now, you'll never get over the idea. It'll stay with you all your life. Go ahead. I'll dance it just like I am."

"Okay," he says.

He taps. It's been quite some time, but he can rely on his outfit. Slow and low like thunder far away, coming nearer. *Boom-putta-putta-boom!* Judy whirls out behind him, lets out the first preliminary screech, *Eeyaeeya!*

She hears a commotion in back of her, and stops as suddenly as she began. Eddie Bloch's fallen flat on his face and doesn't move again after that.

They all know, somehow. There's an inertness, a finality about it that tells them. The dancers wait a minute, mill about, then melt away in a hush. Judy Jarvis doesn't scream, doesn't cry, just stands there staring, wondering. That last thought—did it come from inside his own mind just now—or outside? Was it two months on its way, from the other side of the grave, looking for him, looking for him, until it found him tonight when he played the chant once more and laid his mind open to Africa? No policeman, no detective, no doctor, no scientist, will ever be able to tell her. Did it come from inside or from outside? All she says is, "Stand close to me, boys—real close to me, I'm afraid of the dark."

JULIET AND THE MAGICIAN

Manuel Peyrou

When the great writers of mystery and detective stories are discussed, the names that head the list of immortals are almost exclusively English and American, as if writers from other nations eschewed the genre. Well, to be truthful, both quantitatively and qualitatively, they lag far behind the English-language authors. Of course there are exceptions, but not enough to notice. Among writers in Spanish, no doubt the best-known author of crime stories is Jorge Luis Borges, the unmatched Argentinian teller of magical and complex fables. His close friend, Manuel Peyrou, is also from Argentina, where he made his reputation as a distinguished journalist.

Of his countryman, Borges once wrote, "I do not hesitate to declare that Manuel Peyrou is one of the first storytellers of Hispanic letters."

Peyrou's first published book was The Sleeping Sword *(1945), a collection of detective stories. "Juliet and the Magician" is his first story to be translated and published in English. Originally published in* The Night Repeated *(1953), its first appearance in English was in the August 1958 issue of* The Saint Detective Magazine.

The translator of "Juliet and the Magician" is Donald A. Yates, who also translated Thunder of the Roses *(1948), Peyrou's attempt at a pure detective story—a suspense thriller set in an unnamed totalitarian Latin American country (it was produced during the reign of Juan Perón). Yates is also responsible for bringing Borges to American readers by translating much of his work in the 1960s.*

The real name of the magician Fang was not Fang, but Pedro Ignacio Gómez. He was the son of General Ignacio Gómez and nephew and grandson, respectively, of the colonel and sergeant major of the same name. His uncle, General Carballido, was one of the seven casualties of the Battle of the Arsenal, and his cousin, the son of the former, had traveled for many years through Europe to cure himself of a *surmenage* acquired during the Campaign of the Sierra. It would be easy to deduce from this that the military figures, early and contemporary, constituted the singular pride of the Gómez family; it would indeed be easy, but incorrect, because the family also numbered priests in sufficient quantity to reinforce its vanity.

The life of the boy Pedro Ignacio was divided between the awe of marching military files and the practice of religion. He helped with mass in the parish of another of his uncles, Father Gómez, widely known for his generous and liberal nature.

This precocious liturgy was of undeniable importance in young Pedro's life. He was a lad; however, he believed not in symbols but rather in realities. With the passage of time he began to suspect that all these matters resembled magic, and he wanted to perform more conclusive experiments, with palpable results. It would serve only to lengthen this story (and there is no intent to do so) to recount the times he failed in his efforts to extract a hen's egg from the mouth of Father Gómez, amid the benevolent jesting of the latter; or to record the dramatic instant when he nearly suffocated through having suddenly forgotten the system—learned through a correspondence course—of escaping from a hermetically sealed trunk. It is much better to come forward to the day when, converted into Fang, he made his debut in his hometown before an astonished and enthusiastic public.

Pedro Ignacio had a somewhat yellowish skin, his eyes were slightly almond-shaped, and he had a small nose; a few elementary make-up touches and he was an acceptable Chinese.

On the death of Padre Gómez, he inherited the equivalent in pesos of a thousand dollars, deposited in a branch of the Banco de Santa Fe; with professional inspiration he converted a large sum into kimonos, backdrops, folding screens, and bamboo contrivances. When he disembarked in London, everyone assumed he was arriving from Shanghai. He worked for several years in the music halls of England and Scotland, and in 1930, with his tricks perfected, he appeared at the Palace, in Paris.

In Paris begins the drama that interests us. In a theater in Montmartre at that time was playing the Great Dupré, illusionist, with his assistant, La Belle Juliette.

La Belle Juliette went on her afternoon off to see Fang's performance, and the fate of the Great Dupré was sealed: all of his power as illusionist was of no avail in breaking the biological charm contrived by tiny glands which conspired to make the girl's fickle heart beat faster. One December day, Juliet said good-bye to her friend and embarked with Fang for South America.

The addition of a beautiful female improved the appearance and the general effect of the spectacle; but Juliet's passion was brief. When she discovered that Fang was not Chinese she suffered an attack of fury and of insane exaltation. The truth was that she gave not a hoot for his not being Chinese; she simply could not pardon him for being South American. But Fang realized that racial discrimination was only a pretext for Juliet. The real reason was that she had overestimated the earning power of a magician. Money was Juliet's sentimental patron. She was subjected to the last and most abject of all servilities, according to Chesterton's expression: that of wealth. She found mysterious qualities in financially powerful men, for the simple reason of their being powerful; money implied intelligence and sympathy, and, at times, even dissembled the physical aspect of men.

In 1937 appears the third character of our story. Through Juliet's intrigues, Fang's assistants had abandoned him. He placed ads in the dailies, turned to specialized employment agencies, explored infinite possibilities, but he failed to encounter the docile, quick-witted man he needed. One night in a café on Corrientes Street in Buenos Aires, he was approached by a small man. "I need work," he said. "I am humble and loyal." That unlikely declaration nevertheless reflected the truth. What is more, the little man later proved it with his death. He was working as a dishwasher in a restaurant on the corner of Lavalle y Montevideo. He was excited by, enchanted with magic; he had spent the twenty pesos he amassed by pawning a camera for the admission to see Fang's array of tricks. Besides, he was slightly jaundiced and short. With a few light touches of pencil and a thin film of ocher he would look like a Chinese. His name was Venancio Peralta. Fang made a pleasant joke: "You will go on being Venancio; it will seem like a common local nickname for a little Chinaman."

Juliet was cold, superficial, and clever. She considered that her marriage to Fang was the tragedy of her life and she was taking her revenge out on him in a thoroughly precise manner. Fang, on the other hand, found in Venancio devotion, and a practical and efficient assistant.

In December of 1940 Fang was closing out a booking at the Capital. It had been two weeks since the program was changed. Among the tricks he included was the very widely publicized one of escaping dramatically in a few seconds from a bag which had been closed and sealed by witnesses chosen at random from the audience. Fang stepped into a large blue silk bag, the mouth of which was tied up before wax seals were affixed to the loop and knot. At this point a showy circular curtain would descend around Fang, and when it raised the magician would appear completely freed, exhibiting the knot and the seals intact. The members of the audience who had assisted in the act would search the bag and verify the undisturbed state of the fastening.

That night three men, two of whom were with their wives in the orchestra pit and another who occupied a box, came up to the stage at the invitation of Juliet, who was wearing a very low-cut black gown. Fang took off his kimono and stood clothed in long pants and a blue shirt. The bag was shown to the public and the three men examined it at length; it had no false stitches or openings. Fang put his legs into it and the others helped him get the rest of his body inside. Venancio displayed a sash and then tied it around the top of the bag; one of the men poured wax over the knot and placed a seal on it. The arrangement of the persons who surrounded Fang was as follows: with their backs to the audience were the two spectators who had come up from the main floor; then came Venancio, after him the man who came from the box, and finally, Juliet. When they had finished placing the wax seal, Venancio said, "The bird has escaped." One instant later, he clutched his hand to his breast, moved a few steps along the stage and, saying, "Go ahead; let the curtain down," disappeared off-stage. Juliet followed him with a look of surprise, but went ahead and dropped the circular curtain around Fang. At the end of ten seconds she raised it to reveal Fang with the blue bag in his hand, bowing to his public.

At that moment a man came rushing out from the wings and shouted something that could not be understood. The curtains closed then and disorder broke out on the stage. Fang, Juliet and the three men from the audience, terrified, ran toward the wings and found Venancio on the floor. One of the men claimed he was a doctor and examined him. He had a dagger driven into his chest. His last words were, "Don't blame anyone; I killed myself."

The news was carried to the manager; the latter appeared, very harassed, before the audience and announced that the performance was suspended and asked the crowd to leave the theater in an orderly fashion. A stagehand ran out into the street and returned with a policeman, who wasted ten minutes writing down trifles in a notebook. Finally, a police officer arrived and put into effect official measures. The measures were almost exclusively telephone calls in which he requested orders.

One hour later Dr. Fabian Giménez, a court judge, arrived. Dr. Giménez was a man of fifty years with the signs of good living and good drinking upon him, peevish and resigned to the inconveniences of his profession. They had called him away from a meal at the Círculo de Armas and he was cursing with moderation the criminal who elected such an hour for his atrocity. He was accompanied by his secretary, García Garrido.

The three men who had come up on the stage at Juliet's invitation were Dr. Angel Cóppola, physician at a municipal hospital; Manuel Gómez Terry, an unregistered accountant; and Máximo Lilienfeld, a newspaperman.

Dr. Cóppola was a heavy man, with the stiff, elegant air of one who has just stepped out of his tailor's; he had white hair, but his face seemed young; he was carefully shaved. He gave a rapid exhibition of his scientific knowledge which devastated Gómez Terry who was familiar only with folios, go-betweens, distributions and deeds, in addition to soccer. During this conversation they were observed with a certain irony by Lilienfeld, who was short, slender, blond, with bleached eyebrows and was dressed in a suit of ready-made clothes. At the same time Dr. Cóppola was wondering how this little, insignificant-appearing man happened to be occupying such an honored seat *avant-scène;* he was unaware that Lilienfeld was a newspaperman.

Dr. Giménez took statements from everyone, which were summed up and written down by young García Garrido. The show, it seemed, had proceeded in a routine manner, save in two respects: the position of Venancio and Juliet at the moment the bag was sealed and the sentence the former uttered only a few seconds before being stabbed. According to one of the members of the company, in order to facilitate the execution of the trick, Venancio always occupied the same spot, toward the right side of the stage, and Juliet habitually took up a position opposite him, toward the left. If in the last performance they had occupied their customary spots, the order would have been the following: Cóppola and Gómez Terry, their backs to the audience; then, flanking Fang, Juliet, Lilienfeld and finally Venancio. However, the order was as previously indicated: first the doctor and the accountant; then to the left of both, Venancio, followed by Lilienfeld and Juliet, standing around Fang.

Fang had requested permission to retire to his dressing room, claiming to have been deeply affected by the death of his assistant and friend; it was there that Dr. Giménez went to see him, setting up amid silk flowered kimonos, swords without cutting edges, and strolling doves and chickens an improvised office. The death of Venancio had injected disorder into the entire company; however, Juliet occupied herself solely and unaffectedly with her gown and personal appearance.

Dr. Cóppola, with scientific pomposity, spoke first, saying, "I suggest, judge, that you take particular note of this detail of . . ."

He was one of those persons who repeatedly say, "I suggest" without using an appropriate tone of suggestion. The judge heard him out patiently and had his remarks recorded. Cóppola said that, according to his scientific knowledge, the only manner in which a dagger could have entered Venancio's chest at the angle observed was directly in a line from the blue bag, that is, from Fang.

Dr. Giménez conceded some credit to Cóppola's suggestion, then called Fang and initiated his questioning. The latter made clear his reticence before the questions relating to his profession, which was understandable, and he began to become nervous when he noted that a theory about the crime was floating in the atmosphere of the dressing room.

"I was inside a bag, closed and sealed with assistance from the audience," said Fang in emphatic Spanish, now completely void of Chinese flourishes.

Dr. Giménez requested the bag and a stagehand went to look for it. It was still knotted at the top with all the wax seals intact. These were broken by the judge, with the purpose of making an examination of the interior. The material was closely woven and there were no signs of its having been perforated. Dr. Cóppola intervened again.

"Ever since my childhood," he said, "I have been fascinated by magic. Even now, burdened with responsibilities, I frequently perform tricks for my nephews and the children in my neighborhood. If the judge will permit me saying so, it is completely useless to examine that bag."

The judge turned about and regarded him with surprise.

"We want to know if there are any marks inside. Why not examine it?"

"I said *that* bag," persisted the doctor with heavy irony.

"Why do you accentuate *that* bag?"

"Because there is another one."

Fang was glaring at the doctor as if he would have liked to decimate him.

"My dear judge, I myself have performed this trick many times. Today I came to the theater to study the execution of it and correct any of my own defects. The fact of the matter is, there are two bags. When Fang is put into the one which the public sees, he carries folded up in his pocket another one. Once completely inside the outer bag, and before his assistant has tied up the mouth of it, Fang takes out the second identical bag from his pocket and sticks out its upper edge so that it is this second one that is tied and sealed and not the first. In order to accomplish this the collaboration of a practiced assistant is required, someone who pretends to help the witnesses from the audience in carrying out their task but who actually performs, unobserved, this fundamental part of the trick. When the curtain comes down, Fang has nothing more to do than detach one bag from the other, pulling down the first which has been lightly attached to the top of the second, hop out of it, fold it up quickly and place it in his pocket. In this way he is able to display the second bag with the seal perfectly intact."

"Then this bag is the one Fang was initially hiding in his pocket?"

"That is right. You must find the other one."

In the face of the doctor's words, Fang's expression suddenly turned to that of a person caught cheating. He reached into his pocket and took out the missing bag, holding it out to the judge. The latter examined it at length, but it was as free of marks as the other.

"It could not be this one," the doctor said, "since generally these fellows have three or four extras."

The judge ordered a search begun to carry forth to the farthest corners of the theater. For a solid hour Fang's trunks were searched, the dressing rooms gone over from top to bottom as well as the stage sets which were piled up on the stage; but the outcome was fruitless.

Besides, the certainty that Fang used only the two bags for his trick was substantiated by the theater manager, the stagehands, and by Juliet.

At this point, the newspaperman Lilienfeld spoke for the first time.

"Why should Venancio have said, 'The bird has escaped'?"

Then he wrinkled his bleached eyebrows and looked steadily at Fang. The latter stepped forward to explain the motive.

"I didn't hear the sentence clearly," he said, "but generally Venancio said something when he was ready to receive the mouth of the bag from me and tie it up."

"Yes, but he said 'The bird has escaped' when the bag was already sealed. . . ."

The judge had remained silent, with his gaze lost somewhere on the ceiling of the dressing room. García Garrido knew that he was thinking about his meal back at the Círculo de Armas, but the rest believed that he was concentrating on the mysterious nature of the crime. Finally, he seemed to react to something:

"There is one important fact," the judge said. "Venancio Peralta cried out before dying, 'Don't blame anyone; I killed myself.' That is attested to by Cóppola, Gómez Terry, and Lilienfeld as well as by Fang's wife. Nothing can erase this fact. I am not unaware that a man has to be very deranged to stab himself to death in the middle of a stage. It is a spectacular act; it indicates an undisputable morbidity, whose exact character must be determined by a scientific judgment. For this reason, I don't believe we should detain ourselves any longer. I am requesting that each of you, on your word of honor, agree not to leave the capital until the judicial investigation is completed. I see no need to arrest anyone at this time."

Fang appeared effusively thankful for the doctor's words; and in the melancholy, slightly metallic eyes of Juliet shone a strange light, a sort of furtive glint. All present swore to keep themselves at the judge's disposition and the latter, excusing himself, left, followed by his secretary.

The police officer effected the removal of Venancio's body, in keeping with the judge's order, and initiated the last formal steps required for the preparation of the official summary.

At three o'clock in the morning, Dr. Cóppola, Gómez Terry, and Máximo Lilienfeld found themselves out on the street. The wives of the first two had waited for their husbands in the theater lobby and now rejoined them. Lilienfeld's stomach was empty and he suggested that they go for a drink. Dr. Cóppola observed the journalist with the air of one performing a scientific examination and hesitated for a few minutes. He believed that Lilienfeld was trying to get him to pay for a meal; besides, the idea of letting himself be seen in a public place with an individual of the newspaperman's appearance was vaguely distasteful to him. The encounter, a few steps farther on, of an alehouse removed that burden from his mind; there he could not possibly run into anyone.

Lilienfeld ordered a beer; Gómez Terry a cup of coffee, and the doctor a soda. The women had coffee. It appeared to be a contest of economy. Presently, Lilienfeld ordered another beer and a sandwich. Dr. Cóppola had an atrocious appetite, but he contained himself; he reasoned that if he ate, the newspaperman would take advantage of this move to pass the entire bill onto him.

"It'll be less of a mess if it is suicide," opened Gómez Terry, in order to have something to say.

Lilienfeld ordered another beer and another sandwich and, while he was avidly chewing to the accompaniment of his tirelessly wrinkling eyebrows, he exclaimed, "What nonsense! The one sure thing is that it wasn't suicide!"

"But he said, 'Don't blame anyone; I killed myself.' "

"That's exactly what I mean," Lilienfeld continued. "He said, 'I killed myself,' that is to say, I made a fatal mistake, I had this coming, it's my own fault or whatever other similar statement you wish. No one has sought a logical relation between the events of tonight and these words."

"Then you have a theory? Why didn't you speak up?" questioned the doctor reproachfully.

"You were talking all the time and didn't give me a chance; besides, the judge was regarding me with condescention," said Lilienfeld. He ordered another beer, to the doctor's alarm, and continued, "There are three unusual things which break the routine tonight: Venancio says, 'The bird has escaped,' and Fang lies about the moment at which he heard these words. The truth is that he didn't *understand* the sentence very well, since if he had, the tragedy would not have occurred. In the second place, the order of the persons who surrounded Fang was altered at the last moment and Juliet switches to Venancio's place. And thirdly, Venancio says, 'Don't blame me; I killed myself.'

"This is the solution: Fang was driven to desperation over Juliet (for reasons which we may suspect) and plotted to murder her. However, he could not commit a common crime; everyone knew of their quarrels, apparently, and he would have been immediately under suspicion. The only solution was a murder in full view of everyone, with an unbreakable alibi for himself. He needed an accomplice for the crime in the same way that he needed one for his tricks. Venancio was his ally, virtually his slave, we understand. He accepted his benefactor's idea with enthusiasm because his devotion for Fang had inspired him to imitate the latter in even his hates and sympathies. They agreed, then, that Venancio, *after*

Fang had been closed in the bag, would press a dagger into the magician's hand *from the outside,* a weapon that could be easily concealed in a fold of the material. For years they had practiced the trick and Juliet always had occupied the same spot. During the time that the bag was being sealed with wax, everyone was very close to Fang and remained so until the operation was over. Fang was able, therefore, to calculate exactly the height of Juliet's heart. The girl had perceived, perhaps by intuition, that something was being planned against her; it is not unlikely that Venancio demonstrated excessive nervousness. At the moment when they were about to tie the mouth of the bag, Juliet slipped away and occupied Venancio's position; the latter could do nothing but take the girl's spot. Confused and undecided, Venancio finally managed to communicate a warning to Fang by saying, 'The bird has escaped'; but the magician, nervous for the first time during a stunt, heard the voice but didn't understand the meaning. Poor Venancio paid for his loyalty with his life."

Dr. Cóppola and Gómez Terry regarded Lilienfeld for the first time with respect.

"We must advise the judge," Cóppola said.

"I would prefer that you didn't; I don't like to get mixed up in tangles with the law," replied Lilienfeld. "Besides, Fang is condemned. Juliet knows that he tried to kill her and she has him in her power. The poor fellow has no way out but suicide. Perhaps he'll invent a good trick for that one."

To the astonishment of Cóppola and Gómez Terry, Lilienfeld produced a brand new hundred peso note and called the waiter. He had drunk ten glasses of beer.

"Excuse me, please, but I have a matter to attend to," he said, paying the bill.

"Going home to sleep?" asked the doctor.

"No; I must go and have a few beers with a friend," he replied.

THE MAD MAGICIAN

Maxwell Grant

*"Who knows what evil lurks in the hearts of men? The Shadow knows!"
That is the opening of the radio program about the most famous pulp
magazine detective ever created. Maxwell Grant single-handedly wrote
283 novels about the Shadow from 1931 to 1949.*

The Shadow is not the only crime fighter about whom Grant wrote. For
Crime Busters, *a Street and Smith magazine first published in December
1937, he created Norgil the Magician. The suave, handsome, and mustached conjuror appeared in a series of stories that never approached the
success of the Shadow tales, but consistently ranked among the magazine's most popular features.*

"The Mad Magician" was first published in the July 1938 issue of
Crime Busters; *it has never before appeared in book form. Filled with
action and colloquial speech, it is typical of the Norgil stories and, in fact,
of most pulp fiction. Its background of magic is absolutely authentic,
which should come as no surprise. Maxwell Grant is a pseudonym of
Walter B. Gibson, one of the world's greatest real-life prestidigitators.*

A white rabbit poked its head from the silk hat, took a look at
the audience and twitched its whiskers.

The audience laughed. Norgil didn't. For that hat wasn't a borrowed one. It was Norgil's own, one he had just handed to Miriam
as he began his act. Producing rabbits was Norgil's specialty—but
the bunnies always came from borrowed hats, never from his own.

Moreover, the rabbit wasn't one of Norgil's. He had run out of white rabbits and had been trying to get some new ones ever since he reached town.

The magician's neatly mustached face was grim as he looked at Miriam. Worry showed in the expression of the trim brunette. She could read Norgil's thoughts. He was cursing himself for ever sending his valuable assistant, Fritz, on that mission tonight and letting Miriam take responsibility for preparing the act.

Yet she had done it before, and handled things well. But something was radically wrong now. Miriam was as much surprised as Norgil. Both were wondering how the rabbit had gotten into the hat, and where it had come from in the first place!

Misgivings became a nightmare. The rabbit merely prefaced other unexpected things that happened. Miriam came forward with a dove and paper bag. Norgil shoved the bird into the bag and gestured toward an empty cage held by another assistant. He then fired a revolver shot and exploded the paper bag.

The dove was gone. The trick had worked all right, provided the dove had reappeared in the cage. But the audience saw the cage before Norgil had a chance to look for it, and the spectators howled gleefully.

A bird had appeared in the cage, sure enough, but it wasn't a dove! Norgil saw the assistant gawking at a bantam rooster, which was wagging its beak in an effort to voice an indignant crow.

Muttering to himself, Norgil faked a smile in response to the laughter that rolled in from every cranny of the theater. If the crowd out front thought the comedy was intended, Norgil was ready to make the best of it. Unfortunately, other tricks weren't due for the same hilarious finish.

Assistants wheeled a trunk on the stage. Norgil showed the trunk to be empty, and the audience could see beneath the platform on which the trunk stood. Suavely, the magician asked the audience to choose one flag from those of several nations. The choice was "Holland." Norgil bowed, waiting while the other flags were carried off, then he turned toward the trunk.

The magician held his revolver. All he needed was Miriam's cue that she was ready; then, a blank shot would bring her from the trunk, clad in Dutch attire from winged hat to wooden shoes. It was lucky that Norgil waited for that cue. It didn't come.

Instead, there was Miriam's plaintive whisper as she poked the trunk lid a half inch upward, "I can't come out! I haven't any costume!"

Norgil beckoned savagely toward the wing. Curtains closed in, while the audience guffawed at the failure of the trunk trick. Close to the footlights, Norgil tried to fill the gap with some sure-fire card tricks, while an assistant reorganized the show. But the card tricks nearly wrecked the act entirely.

When Norgil yanked the pack from his pocket, and began to change the spots by passing his hand over the cards, he found that he had a deck of blanks. Only his own daze saved him, for when the spectators saw his stupefied look, they thought he was clowning more than ever.

Then the curtains parted. More tricks were ready, and someone had set them straight. Mechanically, Norgil moved into his routine and finished the show amid remnants of laughter. When the curtains finally closed, he shook off some helpers who were swearing that they didn't know why things had gone wrong.

It wasn't the time for alibis or apologies. Those could come later. For the present, Norgil wanted the seclusion of his dressing room.

He reached it, sliding his dress coat from his shoulders and ripping off his white tie and collar. He plopped into a chair before his dressing table and switched on bright lights around the mirror, preparatory to removing his make-up.

Planting his elbows on the dressing table, Norgil propped his chin in both hands, to steady his whirling thoughts. Then, swiftly, he was leaning forward, eyes intent.

There on the mirror before his gaze, letters had formed themselves. Dark, scrawly letters, and they made the three words:

READ THE CARD

Norgil tilted his head sideways and his smile returned. To another this final happening might have seemed a further link in a chain of inexplicable incidents. But not to Norgil. The message written on the mirror simply proved that someone had deliberately gummed the act, and had topped off the procedure with a very old stunt.

The message had been written in secret ink, but heat from the electric-light bulbs had again made the writing visible.

Instructions to "read the card" did not puzzle Norgil. He dug in his pocket, brought out the blank pack that someone had planted there. Among the fifty-odd blanks, the magician found one card with a message in green ink, as scribbly as the writing on the mirror. It read:

You will pardon my interference with your splendid act. I did it to acquaint you with the clever methods which I, a fellow magician, possess. I have many tricks that will interest you. Wait in your dressing room until you receive a call from me.

Professor Caradoc

Norgil had never heard of Professor Caradoc, but he was convinced that the mystery man must certainly have some clever methods.

At the bottom of the card, Professor Caradoc had added: P.S. Heat this card and learn more.

To Norgil, the postscript indicated that Professor Caradoc had written something else, using lemon juice, which would remain invisible until the card was heated. As though to humor the absent professor, Norgil gave a smile, struck a match and held it beneath the card.

Three seconds later, Norgil was convinced that Professor Caradoc was quite as clever as he claimed. No more writing appeared along with the greenish ink.

Instead, the card gave a sudden crackle and vanished in a sheet of instantaneous flame, from between Norgil's fingertips!

II

Norgil was dressed in street clothes when Miriam knocked on the dressing-room door. At the magician's instruction, she came in, tears in her lovely eyes. She started to say, "I'm sorry about the show. I—I can't understand—"

Norgil stepped quickly forward and patted the girl's arm. A smile was again on his face, as he said, "It was not your fault, Miriam. It was all a ruse played on me, something I've learned about since returning here to the dressing room. It's funny,

though, that I didn't see this person around before the performance—"

"There was someone!" Miriam interjected quickly. "An old fellow with whiskers, roaming around backstage. He looked harmless, and nobody chased him—"

Norgil's deft fingers snapped. "Then that could have been
Professor Caradoc!" he exclaimed. "He must have—" The magician broke off as his phone rang. It was a handset on a side table.

When he lifted the receiver, a wheezy voice spoke across the
wire, introducing the talker as Professor Caradoc. The mystery
man was profuse with apologies for the way he had first introduced
himself. But he trusted that Norgil would forgive him, and pay an
immediate visit to Caradoc's home.

"You must come alone"—the wheezy voice was almost fearful
—"otherwise I cannot admit you. I am mistrustful of strangers,
since most of them wish to steal the secrets of my marvelous
creations. But you are an important man, Mr. Norgil. I feel that I
can talk with you freely."

"All right, sir," agreed Norgil, glancing at Miriam. "I'll come.
Tell me the address and I'll be over right away."

Caradoc gave the address and Norgil hung up. He glanced at his
watch.

"That was the old fellow you mentioned, all right," he told the
girl. "He's harmless, so I'm going over to see him. I'll be back by
eight o'clock, in time for the evening show—"

Miriam looked suddenly worried. "You've forgotten about Jenrick," she reminded the magician. "He's coming to the hotel at
eight o'clock. You have an appointment with him."

The girl assistant was correct. Jenrick was a big money man from
Chicago, and Norgil had been talking about the man for the past
two weeks. Jenrick desired to form a partnership with the magician and start on a round-the-world tour. His promises had increased with every letter, until finally tonight's appointment had
been made.

Norgil pulled a thick stack of letters from the pocket of the suit
he had put on. "Here's Jenrick's correspondence," he told Miriam.
"I brought the letters over from the hotel. Take them with you,
and wait at the hotel until Jenrick arrives. I plan to be back there

before him, but if I should be a few minutes late, keep him there until I return."

"Perhaps you'd rather have Fritz attend to it?" asked the assistant.

Norgil shook his head. "I sent Fritz on an errand. He was to call me, and hasn't. You'll have to wait for Jenrick."

Miriam ventured a question as she took the letters. She had heard much of Norgil's talk about Jenrick, and had a woman's natural curiosity. "How much is Jenrick willing to put up, boss?"

"Fifty thousand dollars," replied Norgil. "Provided that I can get ten thousand of my own. I have that much stowed away in the bank account.

"That's one reason"—the magician added a wise smile—"why I'm going to visit the old duck who just phoned me. We'll need some new stage illusions, if we start the world tour, and I think the old fellow has them."

Miriam agreed that it would be a good selling point with Jenrick. Norgil handed the girl a checkbook to carry along with the letters. With another glance at his watch, he left the dressing room, after reminding Miriam to be at the hotel in time to meet Jenrick.

A taxi took the magician to Caradoc's address. It wasn't a long trip, but the driver had some trouble picking the right house. The street was bumpy. The house itself was a grimy brick structure that formed part of an old row.

Most of the other houses were empty, and there were no lights visible in Caradoc's place. Despite the dusk, Norgil made out drawn blinds and shuttered windows that indicated the place was occupied.

Evidently, Professor Caradoc was something of a recluse who had chosen this shabby neighborhood as one that offered sure seclusion. Calculating thus, Norgil dismissed the cab and mounted the stone steps of the two-story house.

The magician rang the bell three times during the next few minutes. Each time there was a faint clang in response. Finally, rusted bolts were drawn. A crack of light came from within when the door inched open. Norgil sensed the observation of peering eyes. The door swung inward.

Stepping into a tiny, lighted vestibule, Norgil saw no one for the moment. Then a figure popped into view from behind the door itself. Norgil saw a tall but stooped form, the back of a bald head, as the man shut the door. He watched scrawny fingers thrust the bolts shut.

The man turned around. Norgil met the gaze of tiny, brilliant eyes that formed the only life in a hollow-cheeked face which had saffron skin, drawn as tight as the surface of a snare drum. From dryish lips came a tone that was no longer wheezy, but harsh:

"I am Professor Caradoc."

When Norgil stared, Caradoc chuckled. The professor drew his long-nailed fingers over his smooth chin.

"You thought I had a beard," clucked Caradoc. "I did, this afternoon, but it was a false one. Remember"—his voice thinned to a whisper as his bony forefinger tapped Norgil's shoulder—"that I must always be cautious.

"The ideas in this brain"—the finger rose to tap Caradoc's bald forehead—"are valuable, very valuable. It is seldom that I choose to allow visitors here."

The whisper ended. There was a momentary pause; then Caradoc's voice was harsh again as he questioned: "How long can you stay?"

Norgil consulted his watch. It was quarter past seven. That eight o'clock appointment could wait fifteen minutes, even when a man as important as Stephen Jenrick was concerned. Norgil said, "One hour."

There was pleasure in Caradoc's withery smile. The old professor stepped through to the hallway, beckoning for Norgil to follow.

As he crossed that inner threshold, Norgil the magician embarked upon the strangest hour of his life.

III

To Norgil, the basement room where Professor Caradoc conducted him was quite as fabulous as Ali Baba's cave. It was not stocked with jewels; instead, it contained objects that Norgil regarded as far more priceless—magical apparatus and stage pieces that Norgil had read about, but believed were no longer in existence. All were housed in the one huge room which occupied the entire basement.

There, Norgil saw old-fashioned tables fitted with mechanical devices. He eyed a life-size devil's head that grimaced, and thrust playing cards from its mouth and horns when Caradoc made it operate.

In one corner, Caradoc had a miniature theater, where a curtain rose and a tiny, mechanical magician performed tricks that worked automatically, with other little dolls as its assistants.

Professor Caradoc was pleased at Norgil's interest in these curios from the past. As the visitor examined them, Caradoc recounted their history, stating the ridiculous prices at which he had purchased the various pieces of apparatus. For forty years, he declared, this collection had been his hobby. He had traveled abroad and had been fortunate enough to pick up many items that would otherwise have been junked as worthless by persons who had inherited them.

It wasn't long, however, before Caradoc tried to draw Norgil's attention to newer paraphernalia of the professor's own invention. It was a wrench for Norgil to drop his interest in the old tricks, but he finally managed it.

Caradoc took him to a square-topped table that had a toy sofa on it. He placed a small doll upon the couch, pressed a button in the table. Mechanism buzzed; the doll rose a few inches in the air and wavered there.

"A genuine levitation!" enthused Caradoc. "Done by electromagnetism! This is only the model. If it were built on a large scale" —he spread his arms with a long sweep—"a living woman could be floated in mid-air!"

Norgil shook his head.

"It won't work, professor," he declared. "You couldn't hoist a girl half a foot by that system. The lifting power of an electromagnet decreases too rapidly in proportion to distance."

Caradoc looked disappointed. He turned off the motor, beckoned Norgil to the back of the room. The magician viewed an oblong cabinet, set upright, and topped by the shoulders and head of a life-size figure that seemed to emerge from the box itself.

The shoulders were draped with a silken garment, the white

throat of the wax image girded by a jeweled necklace. Long, dark hair draped from head to shoulders, while the face itself was partly concealed by a thin, curtainlike veil.

"The Veiled Isis," explained Caradoc. "The figure smiles, moves its eyes, even speaks!"

He lifted the veil to show the waxwork face behind it. The features were exquisitely molded and had a lifelike appearance. Professor Caradoc was ready to start the automaton in operation, when Norgil halted him.

"Too much like the Golem," explained the magician, "an illusion that I used a few years ago and finally put in storage. Sorry, professor."

"But you can open the cabinet," persisted Caradoc, "and show it empty."

"I know," smiled Norgil. "You could do the same with the Golem illusion."

Caradoc opened the cabinet anyway. It wasn't empty as he claimed. Something black jumped out of it, as surprisingly as the white rabbit had popped from Norgil's hat. Norgil gave a quick recoil, then laughed.

The thing was a black cat that had been asleep in the Isis cabinet. It was a big cat, and playful, once it had been roused. It stood on its hind legs and began to claw at the velvet fringes of a table.

"Stop it, Gandhi!" snapped Caradoc. "You'll overturn things as you did before!"

Gandhi didn't stop until Norgil coaxed him by wiggling his fingers near the cat's nose. Thus attracted, Gandhi was lured to a telephone cord in the corner of the room, where he played unmolested.

Professor Caradoc was lifting the top of the Isis cabinet, bringing the veiled bust with it. Norgil stopped him.

"The trick doesn't interest me," he repeated. "Perhaps you have other new ideas—"

"I have!" put in Caradoc. "Back here in the rear of the room."

"But I have an appointment," reminded Norgil. "I'm afraid I shall have to visit you again, professor."

Norgil drew his watch from his pocket. It showed twenty-five minutes to eight; but it had stopped. Norgil suddenly realized the reason. He had been too close to the electromagnet. When he asked Caradoc what time it was, the professor didn't know. He said that he hardly ever bothered about time.

"Call the hotel," he suggested. "Find out what time it is and tell them you might be a little late. Because there is one trick you must see—my Japanese Box."

Norgil picked up the telephone and Caradoc obligingly opened a door and went up a stairway to the second floor, to give Norgil privacy with the call. Norgil dialed the hotel's number, asked for Fritz.

When told that Fritz had not yet come in, or called, he then asked for Miriam's room. But Norgil's pretty assistant did not answer. So he called the desk clerk, learned that the time was seven forty-five and left a message.

"Tell Mr. Jenrick I'll see him after I leave here," declared Norgil.

"But where are you now?" asked the clerk.

"At 529 Walden Street," returned Norgil. "But that doesn't matter. I don't want Mr. Jenrick to come here. Have him wait at the hotel."

The clerk seemed to have trouble getting the message straight, but finally said that he understood. Norgil hung up, set his watch, called upstairs to Caradoc. The professor hurried down, his tight face forming a crackling smile when he learned that Norgil could spare a few more minutes.

Caradoc led the way toward a smaller, stone-walled and dismal section near the rear of the cellar. Once Norgil almost stumbled over Gandhi, the cat. Turning on another light, the professor indicated a box shaped like a massive cube. It measured about four feet in each direction and was one of the oddest boxes that Norgil had ever seen.

Every surface of the box was inlaid with squares, like a chessboard, making a pattern of black and white. Each square measured about three inches across, and near the corners of the box were air holes. From that, Norgil deduced that the box was intended for an escape act.

"A very clever idea," asserted Caradoc, in preliminary praise of his own invention. "You are locked in the box, and then"—he paused to snap his scrawny fingers—"like that, you are out again!"

"It won't do," objected Norgil. "The box looks too tricky. People would say that it was nothing but one of those Japanese puzzle boxes built on a large scale."

Professor Caradoc looked sorrowful.

"That's about all it is," he admitted. "But I never realized it before. However, I'll show you how it operates."

He stepped to the box, picked the center square in the top, and gave it a sharp thump with his forefinger. The whole top of the box slid apart in jigsaw fashion.

"Clever," said Norgil. "Still, I can't use it."

"Try it just once," urged Caradoc, "from the inside. See how simply it operates."

The old man's tone was so pleading that Norgil decided to humor him. Caradoc fitted the top together like a big slab, while Norgil entered the box and doubled himself inside it. Caradoc settled the lid in place and clamped it tight.

"Ready!" he announced.

Norgil found the center square and pressed it. Nothing happened. His muffled voice came from inside the box, telling Professor Caradoc that the device didn't work.

Caradoc leaned close to an air hole; his tone was a chuckly snarl, as he replied, "Of course it doesn't work, unless the top is turned over, so that you can press it from within. But I was careful, Norgil —very careful—not to invert the top.

"So you don't like the Japanese Box?" Caradoc's gloat was harsh. "You'll like it less and less, Norgil, the longer you stay inside it— and you will be there for a long, long while."

Laughing with insane glee, Professor Caradoc hopped across the room and pressed the light switch. With a quick glance back into the darkened room, he stepped to the passage and slammed the door behind him.

Again his head tilted as his lips voiced their vicious laugh. Professor Caradoc had outtricked Norgil, the world's best trickster!

IV

It was stuffy inside the Japanese Box and Norgil didn't improve the atmosphere with the things he said. He tried strong-arm tactics, too, attempting to wedge the box open by a powerful leverage from his shoulders, a method that had sometimes worked in challenge escapes that he had performed on the stage.

The box top wouldn't budge. Those clamps made it like a rock. Norgil settled back as comfortable as he could and thought things over. Professor Caradoc certainly must be a crackpot if he was doing this just to get Jenrick's offer. Jenrick's interest was in Norgil and his name, not Caradoc or any other unknown magician. For the life of him Norgil could not see how the professor had gained this information. Unless—

Something that had happened at the theater suddenly became clear to the magician. He had to act fast now. Whatever Caradoc planned to do, Norgil could spoil it as neatly as the old professor had ruined the afternoon show—provided only that Norgil could get out of the box!

That proviso was a tough one. Norgil was at last satisfied that the only way to open the box was to press the center square on the top. When he poked his finger through one of the air holes, he realized that he had about two feet more to go.

Norgil shoved a pencil through, then gave up the idea. It wouldn't work. That special square required a healthy thump to spring it. Another idea occurred to the imprisoned magician and he started to work on it.

Pulling a large silk handkerchief from his pocket, Norgil pushed it through the air hole, working it along the top of the box. Then, slowly, he pulled in the handkerchief. No results came. Norgil tried an air hole at the side of the box.

This time the handkerchief seemed to catch as he drew it inward. He tried the top again without success, so went back to the side process. Maybe the idea was goofy, but Norgil had a hunch that his patient task would eventually be rewarded. He kept on with his alternate procedure.

Perhaps Professor Caradoc would have enjoyed another laugh had he supposed that Norgil was trying to open that tight-locked box with the aid of a silk handkerchief. But it happened, at that moment, that Caradoc was very busy with a task of his own.

The old wizard was upstairs in another curio room, pulling a box from beneath the telephone table. Inside the box was a phonograph record. Caradoc changed a needle and started the disc in motion. Hooked to a loudspeaker, the record repeated a recent conversation in Norgil's voice.

Norgil hadn't talked to the hotel clerk at all! His dialing of the number had simply started the recording device. The supposed clerk had been Professor Caradoc, replying from an extension phone upstairs. It had been Caradoc who had stated that neither Miriam nor Fritz was in their rooms!

Cocking his head, Caradoc listened intently to the words that came from the record. Near the finish, he stopped the disc at intervals, to make tiny chalk marks. That done, Caradoc pressed a switch that actually connected the telephone with an outside wire.

Caradoc dialed the hotel's number. A clerk answered. The record was already in motion, revolving on a slow ratio. Caradoc settled the needle in place and let Norgil's voice speak for itself.

The clerk heard the first part of the magician's conversation and made replies that Caradoc caught from the telephone receiver. Then came Norgil's later comments, but Caradoc altered them by deft lifts of the needle, that made quick jumps between the chalk marks.

"Tell Mr. Jenrick," announced Norgil's voice, "that I'll . . . see . . . him . . . here."

The clerk inquired where Norgil was. Again the record replied, controlled by Caradoc's maneuvers. It said: "At 529 Walden Street. . . . I . . . want Mr. Jenrick to come here . . ."

The needle was up, the record moving soundlessly. Caradoc heard the clerk say that he would give the message to Jenrick. The professor let the receiver drop on its hook.

Behind the hotel desk, the clerk was jotting down the message when he heard a girl's voice. It was Miriam and she asked about the message, for she had heard the clerk mention Norgil's name. The man let her see it.

"That's odd," remarked Norgil's pretty assistant. "Norgil told me to meet him here. He also said Fritz would be back here, too."

"It is odd, Miss Traymer," agreed the clerk. "Mr. Norgil hesitated when he spoke, as though he was not quite sure what he intended saying."

That was enough for Miriam. She knew that Norgil had gone to look over the old apparatus, and now her chief would need these papers which he had asked her to bring to the hotel. There would be no time to wait for Fritz.

Leaving a note for him, Miriam hurried out.

It was eight o'clock. Jenrick was due any minute, but before the promotor should go to see Norgil, Miriam wanted her boss to have the letters.

The girl took a cab outside the hotel and reached Caradoc's house within ten minutes. She told the driver to wait a short while at the next corner. Groping her way up the dark steps of the professor's home, she rang the doorbell.

She met with no delay. Caradoc was expecting Jenrick, so he opened the door promptly. For a moment, he looked surprised; then, recognizing Miriam as one of the magician's assistants, he invited her into the house. Bolting the door, Caradoc beckoned Miriam through the hallway.

"Mr. Norgil is downstairs," explained the professor in a kindly, disarming tone. "He is looking at some of my marvelous creations. Come—we shall join him."

They reached the cellar. Caradoc opened a door on the right and turned on the light. Miriam eyed a weird device that looked like a figment from some nightmare.

It was a mummy case with a glass top, set on the horizontal between two frames that held huge knives. The blades looked like mammoth chisels, their sharp edges pointing to slots in the mummy case.

On a table, farther back, stood a dial that looked like a clock face, marked for a five-minute period. It was wired to the frames that held the chisel blades.

"The mummy torture," explained Caradoc. "A girl rests in the mummy case and the dial is started. At the end of five minutes" —he paused, gave a clicking sound with his tongue—"the blades cleave through."

Miriam nodded. She had seen other torture tricks, but none so elaborate as this one. She found herself imbibing some of the enthusiasm that Norgil felt for new stage illusions. The stunt looked like a sensation. She hoped Norgil would buy it.

Caradoc was eying her keenly. Suppressing a smile, the professor approached the mummy case. It was fixed to a center pivot which enabled him to swing it upward from a head rest, so that the case stood upright. The glass front proved to be a door, which Caradoc opened.

"I'm afraid it's a trifle small," observed the professor. "Wait until I call Norgil here—or, better, if you wish to try it—"

Miriam was used to intricate stage illusions; she thought the contrivance was just another deceptive device. She stepped inside, to see if she could fit the mummy case. She did, with ample room to spare. She was smiling as she faced Professor Caradoc, never guessing the surprise move that the stoopy old man intended to produce.

With a quick thrust of his long arm, Caradoc slammed the glass door shut. It clamped automatically. Miriam pounded the glass without a result.

That glass door was unbreakable; the mummy case itself was soundproof!

Gleefully, Caradoc tilted the case to the horizontal, letting its weighted head settle upon the rest provided for it. From within the mummy case, Miriam saw him start the five-minute dial. Caradoc's expression, his eagerness of action were all that Miriam needed to tell her that the dilemma was a real one.

Those cleavers weren't harmless. This device was one that could furnish actual death!

Leaving the light on, so that Miriam's terrified eyes could watch the progress of the dial, Caradoc stepped from the room, pulling the door half shut behind him. He gave a glance across the passage to the other room where Norgil was a prisoner in the Japanese Box.

Rubbing his scrawny hands, Caradoc started upstairs, muttering his thoughts in a whispered chuckle that was a pleasure to his own ears. The theme that he expressed was a simple one.

Soon, Caradoc would deal with Jenrick. After the visitor was gone, Caradoc, too, would depart. Some day, perhaps, the starved body of Norgil would be found in the Japanese Box, and Miriam's remains would be discovered in the mummy case.

The world would think that Norgil had tried some new tricks

that didn't work. That, at least, was the conclusion that formed itself in Caradoc's twisted brain. For the present, however, the old professor was satisfied with his latest accomplishment.

V

Four minutes and fifty seconds.

Miriam couldn't watch the dial. Hopeless, she lifted her eyes toward the door of the room. As her gaze fixed, the door swung inward.

Her surge of hope finished with the desolate thought that Professor Caradoc had returned to witness her death. An instant later, Miriam was swept by a new wave of elation as she recognized the figure in the doorway. The arrival wasn't Caradoc.

It was Norgil!

Knowing nothing of the magician's imprisonment in the Japanese Box, Miriam could readily believe that he had actually arrived. It was impossible, from the tight-cramped space of the glass-topped mummy casse, for her to acquaint him with the fact that her death was but a few seconds away.

But Norgil saw that for himself.

Looking first at the mummy case, he spied the menace of the knives, and the glass top gave him a view of Miriam. Norgil saw also how the mummy case had been pivoted to the horizontal. But the vital discovery came when he spotted the moving pointer of the dial, upon the table by the wall.

A second ticked, bringing a jolt of the pointer. Only three more remained. In a flash, Norgil realized that time was insufficient to reach that distant table and break the connection. He picked a closer goal, risking everything on one chance.

Driving forward, Norgil launched himself for the foot of the mummy case and took it with a flying tackle. For an instant, he was between the threatening blades; then, the force of his surge carried him in a long, downward sweep, below their level.

His clutch on the mummy case pivoted it to the upright position, where it stood between the four sets of pointing knives. The case balanced when upright, but that was something that Norgil hadn't learned. He lay on the floor, clinging tightly to the thing during the second and a half that remained.

A click came from the dial. The cleavers released. Splicing the air, four sets of blades slashed together, finding space instead of the slots in the sides of the mummy case.

Releasing the clutch, Norgil crawled out from beneath the blades. From the mummy case, Miriam met his gaze with a trembling smile. Reaching across the blades, Norgil released the clamps. Miriam pushed the front open until a big blade stopped it. There was just space for her to squeeze out and crawl beneath the knives to join Norgil.

The girl was shaky when Norgil drew her to her feet. Finding her voice, she gave her story, including the detail that Stephen Jenrick was to arrive soon at this house.

"Don't worry about Jenrick," advised Norgil. "He's smart enough to take care of himself. Smarter, perhaps, than we were. Anyway, we'll be here to see what happens."

They started out through the passage. At the bottom of the stairs leading above, Norgil pointed to the door of the big room where he had been a captive. He told Miriam, "In there I found something that has Caradoc labeled. I know how he'll handle Jenrick. Come upstairs—quietly!"

Caradoc wasn't on the first floor when they arrived there. He had evidently gone up to the second floor. Norgil opened a closet door. Among the props that he saw there was a brace of old dueling pistols. Norgil had them loaded by the time Miriam completed other preparations, at his direction.

A discordant bell echoed through the old house. Footsteps responded from the floor above. Caradoc was going down the front stairs to admit another visitor.

Soon the professor arrived in another curio room on the first floor, conducting Stephen Jenrick. The visitor was a man with heavy-jowled face, lips that were straight like the line of his nose, eyes that were keen and persuasive. He looked about, surprised that he didn't see Norgil. Since the magician was not present, Jenrick let his appraising gaze rest upon the bare-shouldered figure similar to the Veiled Isis, which topped the closed oblong cabinet.

"Norgil has gone," stated Caradoc. "He wanted my advice regarding his proposed business deal with you."

There was a lifting motion of Jenrick's grayish eyebrows. Caradoc understood the silent query.

"You have brought securities valued at fifty thousand dollars," continued Caradoc, "and you expect Norgil to put up ten thousand in cash. At present, he is not in a position to do so. But I would like to buy your securities, allowing you a reasonable profit."

The proposition interested Jenrick. He produced a sheaf of bonds, spread them for Caradoc's inspection, remarking that all were negotiable. Caradoc made a price: "Sixty thousand dollars."

Jenrick agreed. The old professor went to a corner, lifted a board in the floor. Burrowing deep, he brought out bundles of currency. Taking the bonds, he handed the money to Jenrick—six packages each containing ten thousand dollars in bills of one-hundred-dollar denomination.

While Jenrick was counting the money, Caradoc heard a sound. He couldn't locate it, but he eyed the closet, suspecting that Gandhi had gone in there. When Caradoc pulled the door wide, his gaze went stiff. On the closet shelf was the waxwork bust of Isis —but its veil was missing!

Before Caradoc could swing around, there was a rattle from the oblong box at the end wall of the room. Its door shot open, showing a figure in the cabinet. A bare arm thrust forward, aiming a big dueling pistol. Miriam tossed her head, to throw aside the veil and her loosened hair, as she commanded, "Stand where you are! Both of you!"

Caradoc recognized both Miriam and the pistol. He knew that the gun contained only one bullet. He faked a cringe. Miriam's aim shifted to Jenrick. Thrusting the bonds in his pocket, Caradoc made a quick spring for the cabinet. His long, clawish hands were free to aim for Miriam's neck. But Caradoc never completed that murderous drive.

A door flew open across the room. Norgil was facing Caradoc from the hallway. The magician was aiming the other dueling pistol. Caradoc stopped short, as helpless as Jenrick.

Just then there was a pounding at the front door. While Miriam kept the men covered, Norgil hurried out and admitted husky-looking Fritz, accompanied by two alert, keen-eyed men who seemed to know the magician by sight. Norgil directed, "All right. I've got them inside."

A moment later handcuffs had been snapped upon both Caradoc and Stephen Jenrick. Norgil helped Miriam from the oblong cabinet. While the girl was slipping her arms into the lowered sleeves of her dress, Norgil indulged in comments.

"You worked your swindle game too long," he told the surprised Jenrick. "Showing that batch of bonds was a smart game to coax a sucker into handing over ten thousand dollars as his share of a phony partnership."

"But—" Jenrick started to protest.

Norgil waved a hand, continued with, "These secret service men"—he indicated the two leanly trim men with Fritz—"informed me of a fake bond racket being pulled on other magicians and show folks. When I started getting your letters, I suspected you were the one behind the racket. So I led you on—and now have your letters, which will send you up for a stretch."

One of the government men put in, "Thanks for leading Jenrick into the trap, Mr. Norgil. But we thought it would be at the hotel. Fritz, however, got your girl's message, telling him to come here." The Fed indicated Professor Caradoc. "I don't get the connection of this man and Jenrick—"

Norgil smiled suavely. "Neither did I—at first." Then he swung on Caradoc. "You had a scheme of your own, professor, and you started to approach me about it. But in my dressing room, you found those letters from Jenrick. So you saw a chance for a bigger clean-up, and got the idea of luring Jenrick here." Norgil shook his head sadly. "But those letters didn't mention that government agents would be on Jenrick's trail. All you knew was that Jenrick was bringing fifty thousand dollars in bonds that you thought could be unloaded.

"You wanted those bonds in order to get real cash, so that you could be far away when you began to pass the counterfeit money that you've been manufacturing here. You figured you'd be out of reach by the time Jenrick began to spend the queer dough that you just paid him for the bonds!"

For the first time, Miriam and the others realized the depth of the game; how Norgil had played crook against crook to trap a pair of criminal artists.

Miriam and Fritz saw the Feds haul thousands more of Caradoc's fake money from the cache that the girl pointed out in the corner of the room. She went with them when Norgil conducted the group below, the prisoners being dragged along.

There, in one corner of the basement, Norgil showed them Caradoc's printing plant—which he had discovered after his escape from the box and just before hearing the professor trapping the girl in the adjoining, smaller room. The press was the discovery that had given the magician a perfect cue to Caradoc's game.

But before they departed, Norgil remembered something.

"We'd better bring Gandhi," he remarked. "He deserves some reward for his help."

Amid puzzled looks from the others, Norgil led the way to the Japanese Box. The old contrivance was standing closed.

"Caradoc bundled me inside there," explained Norgil. "He thought I couldn't get out, because I couldn't reach the center square of the top, to tap it. But the professor forgot Gandhi and left him in the room when he closed the door.

"There was just enough light for Gandhi to see the silk handkerchief that I kept poking from the air hole. Gandhi is playful, and he took the bait. He finally found out that the handkerchief occasionally poked from an air hole in the top, so he jumped on the box —like this."

Compressing the thumb and fingers of one hand, Norgil tapped them along the top of the box, until suddenly they thumped the center square. With a snap, the trick top broke wide. Whipping out his handkerchief, Norgil dangled it in the box, then scooped his other hand inside and brought out the purring form of Gandhi, the black cat.

"I'll take good care of him, professor," promised Norgil, ignoring the fact that Caradoc's scowl was as black as Gandhi's fur. "Perhaps I can use him in the act—"

The magician paused, a smooth smile forming beneath his pointed mustache. Then: "Yes, I can use Gandhi," he added, "along with the white rabbit that you planted in the wrong man's hat!"

ONE NIGHT IN PARIS

Walter B. Gibson

When Walter B. Gibson was a young reporter on the Philadelphia Public Ledger, *he was fascinated by magic and often wrote articles on the subject. Written with unusual skill and expertise, they attracted the attention of Howard Thurston and Harry Houdini, the most famous magicians in the world. They engaged him to ghostwrite books and articles under their bylines. He learned illusions from them and from other magicians and was soon regarded as one of the country's foremost conjurors. Later, he was encouraged by Sir Arthur Conan Doyle to write mystery fiction.*

Although Gibson has written about thirty-five books and several hundred articles on magic and magicians, plus innumerable pieces on witchcraft, sorcery, occult subjects, psychic phenomena, and true crime, he was most prolific as a fiction writer.

Hired by Street and Smith to write for their pulp magazines, Gibson produced more than a million words a year for fifteen years. He wrote more than 300 novels, 283 about a single character—one of the most important heroes ever to stride majestically across the pages of a popular publication: The Shadow. The Maxwell Grant byline under which the stories appeared was a Street and Smith "house name" used by Gibson (and occasionally by a few other writers) during the 1930s and 1940s. The only other pulp hero created by Gibson (Grant) is Norgil the Magician, who appears in the previous story.

The Great Gerard fights crime in two stories. "One Night in Paris" was originally published in The Saint Detective Magazine *in the issue of November 1955. It has never before been collected in book form.*

The haze of an early spring dusk clung over the Gare de Lyon when the Great Gerard and his blonde assistant, Mimi, detrained at the end of a swift ten-hour ride from Marseilles. They had lunched in the *wagon restaurant* of the *train rapide* and now Mimi was casting an envious eye toward the *Buffet Gastronomique.*

"Imagine," commented Gerard Whitestone with a whimsical smile, "dining in a station restaurant upon arrival in Paris! Going away, yes, but not coming in, with a whole world of restaurants to choose from! I'll check our luggage, Mimi, while you list a few of your favorite eating spots. We have until midnight."

"Only until midnight?" said Mimi. "Why, our show doesn't open at the Olympia until next Tuesday, remember?" The blonde paused, puckered her forehead and followed with an understanding nod. "I should have known it! Cutting our vacation on the Riviera three days short, just because you had a sudden yearning for Paris in the springtime! So what's happening at midnight?"

"A press conference," said Gerard, "at the home of the Chevalier Pinetti in the Allée des Bijoux. I'll tell you about it while we ride there in a cab, after I direct the driver."

The cabby needed direction. Even Gerard's most fluent French could not convince him that there was a street in Paris called the Allée des Bijoux. So Gerard told him to swing across the Ponte d'Austerlitz and work northwestward from the Boulevard Marcel.

"Pinetti was a famous magician of the late eighteenth century," Gerard told Mimi as they rode along. "About twenty years ago, Pinetti's house and much of his magical paraphernalia were acquired and restored by a magician named Eugene Lebrun—"

"Why, he's a circus performer!" interrupted Mimi. "I saw Lebrun at Madison Square Garden, doing a juggling act on a tightrope."

"But magic is his great love," Gerard assured her. "Don't you remember him tossing a pack of playing cards in air, jabbing a sword among them and impaling three that had been chosen by the audience?"

Mimi nodded as Gerard imitated the thrust of an imaginary sword in mid-air.

"That's magic," said Gerard, "and Lebrun not only does it on a tightrope. He uses an ordinary sword, not the trick kind."

"But he's still a circus performer," argued Mimi, "so why didn't he give Pinetti's apparatus to the Ringling Museum?"

"Because he needed a reason to be in Paris," explained Gerard, "and particularly during the war. He couldn't move his priceless collection, so he stayed here with it. He was even accused of collaborating with the Nazis so they would let him keep his treasures."

"And was Lebrun a collaborator?"

"Ostensibly, yes. It helped him fulfill his real mission, which was working for the French underground. When he finally left Paris, under a Nazi safe conduct, he had his treasure room sheathed with steel, fitted with bulletproof glass and locked with a vault door, so that enraged Parisians could not take out their anger by destroying his collection of old-time magic."

Mimi noted Gerard's smile by the lights of the Boulevard Marcel and added a comment, "There must have been a catch to that."

"There was," said Gerard. "Actually, the attack-proof room served as headquarters for the underground during Lebrun's absence. Meanwhile, Lebrun was traveling in allied countries, posing as a refugee, talking endlessly about his wonderful collection and hoping that the Nazis hadn't destroyed or stolen it. But nobody particularly believed him. Like many undercover agents, he was labeled as a highly doubtful character."

The case intrigued Mimi. She wanted to hear more and Gerard told it, while he watched for landmarks along the streets that the cab was threading, now that it had left the boulevard.

"After the war," declared the magician, "Lebrun was given a clean bill of health and he went on tour with the circus. Between times, he worked for the French government, checking subversive activities. Those have become hotter and hotter, as you may know. Lebrun has become a very busy bee, visiting the dozens of Commie cells in the Parisian honeycomb alone."

"That can't be very healthy for Lebrun."

"Nor for anyone who knows him. Such people are under suspicion from all sides. And that is why I insisted on a quick and outright deal when Lebrun sold me his treasures at a bargain price."

"But suppose he should take a notion to drop into his old curio room and use it as an occasional headquarters during your absence?"

"He can't," replied Gerard. "You'll see why when we get there. I believe this is the street."

Gerard called for the taxi to stop in front of a cobblestoned cul-de-sac which he defined as the Allée des Bijoux. Gerard and Mimi alighted and entered the dead-end street by the light of a single ancient lamppost. The blind alley terminated in a grilled gate, where steps led up to a formidable front door of a very old and solid house.

As they ascended, Mimi gazed curiously down another flight of steps to a basement door which bore a huge padlock. Gerard's gaze, always quick to pick up a lead, followed the blonde's.

"That's where Leon the concierge lives," explained Gerard, "when he's around—which isn't often."

Gerard unlocked the front door with a big key, found a light switch and illuminated a long hallway flanked on the left by a solid dividing wall between this house and the next. On the right was a parlor where Gerard pressed another light switch, causing Mimi to cry out in admiration.

The front room was beautifully furnished and decorated in Louis Quinze style, a glitter of gilt and curlicues, resplendent beneath a huge crystal chandelier which had been converted from candle power to electricity. Mimi's gaze roved from chaise longue to mantel clock, then to an ornate console and a geegawed footstool beside it.

Finally, her eyes centered on the rich, tufted carpeting that floored the room from wall to wall, continuing beneath a pair of silken curtains hanging from a wide arch at the back of the room.

Slipping one stockingless foot from its pump, Mimi began testing the thick, seamless nap with her bare toes.

Gerard intoned in guidebook style: "You are now viewing the reception room of the famous conjuror Jean-Joseph Pinetti Willedal de Merci, Chevalier of the Order of St. Phillipe, and Professor of Mathematics and Physics at the Royal Academy of Sciences and Belles-Lettres of Bordeaux, Aeronaut, and Geographical Engineer."

Gerard took a deep breath and added, "This is where he received visitors to observe his philosophical recreations and demonstrations, as they called scientific gadgets in those days."

Mimi gasped in new amazement. "You mean Pinetti really gave performances here?"

"Probably," smiled Gerard, "if this house was built as early as 1785, when the Chevalier was all the rage of Paris. I'm taking Lebrun's word for it and I hope the Parisian press will do the same. At midnight, I shall reveal the antique apparatus used by Pinetti and demonstrate his famous opening trick, which I shall use in our own show at the Olympia, beginning next Tuesday."

"So that's the tie-in," nodded Mimi. "I wondered when we would be getting back to business. But since you're not meeting the reporters until midnight, why are we here so early?"

"For a rehearsal, Mimi. I have the trick all set up, but I want to make sure it works."

"And where is all this marvelous apparatus?"

"In the back room, beyond those curtains."

Mimi stalked across the lush carpeting and drew aside the portières to find a pair of sliding doors locked tight. She swung about with the query, "Do you have the key?"

"No key will do," said Gerard. "Those doors are permanently closed with a sheet of steel backing them."

Mimi glanced down at the tufted carpeting that seemed to spring up like grass whenever she moved her foot. "But the carpeting goes on through to the other room."

"Naturally," said Gerard. "It is at least fifty years old and as fine and elegant as when it was new. I know, because the old concierge told me. Lebrun simply closed the doors and re-enforced them with armor plate. You'll see from the other side."

Gerard conducted Mimi out into the hall and along it to a door to the rear room. This door gave with a metallic sound when Gerard tapped it. It was fitted with heavy hasp and staple, linked with a padlock that had five circular segments, each bearing all the letters of the alphabet.

"A French letter lock," said Gerard. "The very one that Houdini used on a pair of handcuffs when he challenged the German escape artist, Engleberto Kleppini in Dortmund on the night of June 18, 1902. Kleppini never did get out of them. He thought he had the right word, but Houdini switched it."

"You turn to the right letters," said Mimi, "and the lock opens. There must be millions of combinations."

"There are," said Gerard. "That's why I put it on the door after I bought the collection from Lebrun a few months ago. We can be positive of one thing. No one can possibly have entered this room since then. Now let's get on with the rehearsal. It's going to surprise you."

Gerard turned the letters to form the word LOTUS. The door opened smoothly and Mimi saw a bulky array of magical apparatus looming in the last rays of sunset that filtered in through the frosted panes of a huge rear window.

"Pinetti's greatest trick," said Gerard, "was lighting a hundred candles instantly, by a single gunshot!"

He plucked an old-fashioned pistol from inside the door, aimed it into the room and fired. From everywhere, tiny tongues of flames licked into life, all set in candelabra about the room.

Mimi gasped in surprise as Gerard turned and bowed, his face gaining a Mephisthophelean gleam in the medley of flickers and shadows.

Then, Mimi's astonishment changed to horror. She was looking to Gerard's left and as he followed her gaze, he saw a man's figure lying face up in front of a fourfold Chinese screen. He swayed and almost dropped the pistol as he recognized the long, thin features of Eugene Lebrun, the collector who had stocked this room with its magical curiosa.

From his pained expression, Lebrun must have regretted the time he had wasted learning to perform the card-catching trick with an ordinary sword. Driven through his body, halfway to its hilt, was his favorite blade, projecting from the blood-dyed front of his tuxedo shirt.

II

Gerard's face remained taut in the flickery light. With a quick spring, he reached the screen and swept it aside in one motion, wheeling about to level the antique pistol toward the space beyond. But there was no one crouching there, nor any hiding place. Nothing but the sheet of stainless steel that blocked the archway with the double doors.

The floor was covered with the same thick carpeting that continued beneath the steel barrier into the front reception room, without the slightest space showing in the unruffled surface of its tufted texture. Continuing his turnabout, Gerard covered the remainder of the room.

All about was an array of old-style magical paraphernalia which included a large crystal clock dial, a miniature orange tree, a transparent glass casket, small draped tables, odd-shaped vases and decanters, devil's heads and midget automatic figures, but nowhere was there space enough for an assassin to be hidden.

Gerard relaxed and beckoned Mimi into the room. He stepped over, closed the hallway door and pressed a light switch. As the electric glow drowned the candlelight, Gerard picked up two small metal cones and handed one to Mimi.

"Start snuffing the candles," he told the frozen blonde, "before they smoke the place out. I'll show you how to fix them for the midnight demonstration. It won't take long."

Mechanically, Mimi followed the instructions that Gerard gave. The magician, meanwhile, began moving apparatus from beside the wall, even taking down some of the framed playbills that almost covered it. He wanted to make sure the walls were as solid as the steel sheet that blocked the archway. They proved to be exactly that.

Gerard turned his attention to the rear of the curio room where the casement windows formed the only route by which Lebrun's murderer could have left. Again, Gerard drew a complete blank. The sections of the window were most formidable of all.

"Bulletproof glass," said Gerard, as he tapped the frosted panes, "and solid steel bars between."

From his pocket, Gerard drew a pair of thin white gloves which he wore during the unique coin manipulative act that he alone performed while gloved. He pulled them on his hands, so that his deft fingers could probe the panes for cracks without leaving prints. Finally, he tested the window clamps, which were connected to sliding bars. All were tightly screwed in place.

"Nobody used the window route," said Gerard. "This is a perfect sealed room mystery."

"But maybe Lebrun brought someone here," said Mimi. "Some-one who killed him and went out, then spun the letters on the lock."

"Except," said Gerard, "that the lock happens to be my own and Lebrun did not know the combination. How he got in is just as puzzling as how the other man left!"

"But what could anyone gain, setting up a scene like this?"

"Plenty. If I'd brought the press here at midnight, as I planned, it would have pinned the crime on me. In fact"—Gerard's expression went grim—"it still could pin the crime on me as the only person who could have entered this room, because I can't pass up that midnight meeting."

Gerard stooped beside Lebrun's body and ran through the dead man's pockets for some clue. He found nothing. The pockets had been emptied, even Lebrun's *pochettes* or secret pockets, which Gerard as a fellow magician knew exactly where to find.

During that last stage of the search, Mimi, wincing as Lebrun's body gave a lifelike sway under Gerard's slight lift, exclaimed hoarsely, "Wait—there's something underneath him!"

With a dart of her hand, Mimi brought out the object. It was a magical playbill, the sort that Lebrun, when alive, would have added to the hundreds that adorned the walls. But this particular program, printed in an antique type, took on a peculiarly macabre significance. It read:

CABARET DE LA MORT
Soirée Fantastique

Under that was a line in Latin that Gerard translated: "All hope abandon, ye who enter here." The program was decorated with ghosts, skeletons, tombstones, and other symbols of death.

"I've heard of this place," said Gerard. "A lot of others have imitated it. This is the old original, and its reputation has become legendary."

He paused; the paper had a fresh feel, the antique printing a phony look. He pointed to the bottom lines:

Ce programme pour Mardi, le Septième d'Avril. Les portes ouvrirent à neuf heures.

"This program for Tuesday, April seventh," translated Mimi. "Why, that's today!"

"Read further," said Gerard, "and you'll find that the doors open at nine o'clock. That won't be for another hour or more. This playbill isn't from the past, like all the others in this room. It's from the future!"

From her expression, Mimi accepted the thing as totally incredible but Gerard had a simpler explanation.

"A plant," he said. "Fixed for Lebrun's body to be found at midnight in a room that I alone could have entered. With a piece of evidence"—he gestured to the playbill—"to prove that the body must have been brought here after nine o'clock by somebody from the Cabaret de la Mort in the Montmartre. This is one sealed room mystery that makes sense—the wrong way."

"And what," asked Mimi, "will you do about it?"

For answer, Gerard slid the incriminating playbill back beneath Lebrun's body. Still wearing his gloves, he went to the window and loosened a casement clamp, very slightly. From a cabinet in the corner that was marked APPARAUX MODERNE, he brought a compact tool kit titled: HOUDINI—INSTRUMENTS AUTHENTIQUE. From these, Gerard selected a miniature jimmy, narrow-pointed, of finely tempered steel.

"The sort of thing," Gerard told Mimi, "that Houdini smuggled into boxes with him, to pry his way out."

Gerard ushered Mimi past Lebrun's body to the hallway. He turned out the light, closed the curio room door and spun the letters of the lock. Using a flashlight, he found the stairs to the basement, where he picked up a ladder and carried it along through the back door, which he locked behind him. Planting the ladder against a tiny balcony, Gerard climbed to the curio room window.

From below, Mimi watched him work at the twilight tinted panes. With the jimmy, Gerard pried a window inward, then worked it tightly shut again. He rejoined Mimi, took the ladder and slid it from sight beyond a next-door fence.

"Thanks to the loosened window clamp," said Gerard, "the jimmy job will look genuine enough."

"You should have pried a smaller casement," said Mimi. "You could have gone through this, but nobody your size could go through one of the smaller ones."

"Neither could Lebrun," said Gerard, "and I want to make it look as though he went through the window—whether he was dead or alive. Now let's clear this neighborhood, quietly and inconspicuously."

By the time they had covered half a mile on foot, the tangy air had restored Mimi's appetite and she brought up the restaurant question, to which Gerard nodded.

"We'll wangle over to the Boul Mich," the magician decided, "and take a cab to the Cabaret de la Mort. I want to see what goes on there. First we'll go to a little hotel I remember, the Stellaire. We'll phone the cabaret from the hotel."

Apparently the cabaret had not opened, for it took Gerard three tries at five-minute intervals to get a reply. Then, Mimi heard him purr in his smoothest French: "La Cabaret de la Mort? You are open? You have a reservation in my name—the Great Gerard? Yes, for myself alone. Ah, excellent. I shall be there."

Twilight was purpling into night as Gerard and Mimi sped northward in a cab across the Pont Neuf toward the Place Pigalle, near which the Cabaret de la Mort was located.

"The plot thickens," said Gerard. "A reservation in my name at the Cabaret de la Mort simply clinches the trail that already leads from there."

"Except that you might produce an alibi."

"For my first night back in Paris?" Gerard inserted a laugh. "You'd never expect me to give a precise account of my peregrinations, would you, Mimi?"

"Whatever those are," said Mimi, "I guess I wouldn't. You have a fantastic way of bobbing in and out, faster than I vanish or reappear from an illusion cabinet. But an alibi would still be a good idea."

"I'll remember that, Mimi."

III

The Cabaret de la Mort proved to be a typical Montmartre deadfall with some appropriate refinements if a motif based upon the gruesome could be so classified.

Over the entrance, six steps down, burned an eternal blue-flamed light that gave off an odor of brimstone. A bearded character robed as Father Time greeted the customers and guided them along a passage where sudden ruddy flickers promised a view of some hellish pit. A girl with painted smile and vampire costume met them and croaked a request for reservations.

Gerard shook his head and said that he had none. They were looking now into the cabaret itself, where chandeliers were formed from skulls and crossbones and the tables bore a striking similarity to morgue slabs. Sizing the place as he would a theater, Gerard spotted a table deep in a corner and decided it must be the one reserved in his name. He gestured in the other direction.

"A table over there will do, Lady Dracula," he said.

From their table, Gerard and Mimi gained a good view of the stage, which was decorated like the interior of a crypt, with a pair of hanging curtains that resembled shrouds.

"I'd like to go backstage," said Gerard, "and see what's behind those drops."

"Pull a sneak whenever you want," said Mimi, "and I'll promise not to tell if you'll only order me some dinner first. I'm hungry enough to eat a horse."

"Did you say horse?" Gerard beckoned to a skeleton-clad waiter. "Or hearse? You'll probably find both on the menu."

Mimi grimaced as she read the horrendous titles given to ordinary dishes on the bill-of-fare. Gerard, meanwhile, was asking the waiter about the evening's entertainment.

"You will find it all on the program, M'sieu," the living skeleton told him. "I think they have just arrived from the printer. Ah, *oui.*" He nodded as the vampire lady approached with a stack of printed sheets. "Here they are."

Gerard studied the program as though he'd never seen it before though its exact duplicate was lying under Lebrun's body in the curio room.

"La danse des squelettes," he read aloud. "The dance of the skeletons—about on a par with singing waiters. Next on the bill—ah, this is interesting!—is an invitation for anyone to visit the grave beyond the shrouded curtains and test their fate for themselves."

"Not me," said Mimi. "I'll be working on a big mutton chop by that time. That is, if I've guessed the menu right. It's listed as haunch of werewolf."

Her smile was somber.

They had finished their *potage* when the skeleton dance went on. Then, as Mimi's mutton chop was served, the shrouds parted and revealed an upright coffin standing in the center of the stage, flanked by heavy black curtains. Father Time strode on stage as master of ceremonies and, at his invitation, a dapper Frenchman came from the audience to try out the coffin.

The man was ushered around behind the curtain at the left and from there he stepped in through an open side of the coffin, to face the audience. As the bearded emcee intoned about ashes, dust, and the grave conquering all, the smiling Frenchman underwent a startling transformation under the glare of lights within the coffin. Gradually, his features became skull-like, his form turned to a skeleton from which his evening clothes hung in drifts of rags and shreds.

As the audience gasped, even Mimi forgot to eat her *côtelette de loup garou,* while she stared first at the coffin, then at Gerard and exclaimed: "Why, it's incredible. You've never carried anything like that with our show. Why not?"

"You can't travel with it," explained Gerard. "The coffin front has a sheet of plate glass slanted across it. As lights flick off behind the glass, others come on as alternates in front, turning the glass into a mirror.

"To the right, behind that black curtain, is a duplicate of the coffin interior, containing the skeleton. That's what you're seeing right now. Keep watching, the lights are being switched back."

Gradually, the skeleton was becoming the living man again. As Mimi stared transfixed, Gerard whispered softly, "There's a better show at the corner table reserved in my name. If the man there is doubling for me, I wonder who his girl friend is."

Mimi glared toward the corner where a man in tuxedo was barely visible in the gloom, as he leaned forward to chat with a girl in a pink lamé wrap, whose vivid red hair caught the dull light from the skull lamps and reflected it with the brilliance of polished copper. Gerard smiled and gestured to the mutton chop with its sprig of parsley and its paper frill.

"Finish that bit of wolf in sheep's clothing," said Gerard. "Something is due to happen, as part of the frame-up. When the excitement starts, spot whatever you can and break out of here fast."

Other patrons were going to the stage to take the skeleton test, but Gerard could tell from the persuasive way that the man at the table was gesturing toward the stage that the red-haired girl intended to follow. Gerard slipped Mimi a printed card that he had brought from the Hotel Stellaire.

"Check in there," he told Mimi. "I'll see that you get your luggage. Wait"—he tore a corner from the card—"if I send anybody, I'll have them bring this. Make sure it matches up."

"All right," agreed Mimi, "but don't switch corners. I've known that to happen!"

Another person was going through the coffin transformation as the redhead arose from the corner table and went up on the stage. Mimi gave a deprecating sniff. "If anything is a plant, she is. You can tell from the way she walks that she's a show girl, probably from some local nightspot. Anyone would know it—"

The audience, apparently, did know it. From the half-filled hall came applause and voices calling: "Mademoiselle Pompom!" Then, as the girl took a bow, Father Time helped her remove her lamé wrap. Beneath, she was attired in a costume that would have rated as scanty indeed, except that it was artfully augmented by a few dozen pompoms which bedecked the shapely girl from shoulders to ankles, with some provokingly placed at salient locations.

"Meet Mademoiselle Pompom," droned Father Time, "the living contrast to this chamber of horrors. But tonight, she, too, shall go the way of all flesh."

The girl shrugged a shoulder as though she did not care and a loosened pompom fell to the floor, where she pretended not to notice it. Another shrug, another pompom dropped, while Father Time continued: "Yes, she will enter the coffin and fade to a skeleton before your gaze."

"Why all the stall?" asked Mimi. "Why doesn't she just shake off a few more powder puffs and creep into the crypt?"

"They are changing the skeleton," explained Gerard, "putting in one with pompoms and allowing for those that are due to drop. There she goes now."

The girl was stepping through the side curtain and the audience rocked with laughter as Father Time plucked a souvenir pompom from her hip. Gerard missed that bit, for he was watching the corner table, where a glint of light made a sudden sweep. No tableware could have produced that flash. The glitter came from the rising barrel of a machine gun. Gerard rose from his chair and sidled to a door that he was sure led backstage. Moments later, he had skirted the black curtain and was viewing Mademoiselle Pompom in the coffin. The murmur from the audience told him that the transformation from girl to skeleton had been consummated.

Gerard bounded forward, shot out his hand, caught the girl's wrist and wrenched her bodily from the coffin.

They were halfway to the stage door when the girl broke loose and darted back toward the coffin, leaving a strew of pompoms behind her. Gerard overtook her and voiced the warning, "Don't go back into that coffin unless you want to stay—for keeps!" Then, as Gerard profited by her hesitation and held her in a momentary clinch, the wisdom of his words was proven.

Out front, Father Time was gesturing to the reflected skeleton, hung with a few pompoms, that the audience thought occupied the coffin. He was droning, "Her stay in the haunt of the dead is over, now she shall return to the domain of the living and bloom anew!"

Mimi, remembering Gerard's admonition to watch everything, had just turned toward the deep corner of the cabaret. She, too, recognized the steel glint that Gerard had noted earlier.

At that instant, the machine gun chattered, tonguing its flame straight toward the coffin on the stage. The audience shrieked as the crash of glass echoed from the upright casket. The skeleton vanished instantly, leaving only a lighted void, framed with jagged edges of glass.

The illusion was destroyed, but instead of a life being snuffed out with it, the man with the machine gun—like the rest of the audience—was confronted with a new riddle:

What had become of Mademoiselle Pompom?

IV

One man could have answered that: the Great Gerard. At the rattle of the machine gun and the crackle of the glass, the redhead had gone limp in the magician's arms. He'd shaken her back to action, then rushed her out through the stage door, which opened on to one of the steep streets so common in the Montmartre. There, Gerard placed her in one of the inevitable Parisian taxicabs that was waiting to pick up the show-break trade.

Gerard poured directions to the driver and they swung around by the front street, where customers were stumbling up from the Cabaret de la Mort. Among them, Gerard saw Mimi, but there was no need to snatch her from the terrified throng.

Mimi not only was losing herself nicely in the shuffle; she was spotting someone. So the cab kept on its way and Gerard turned his attention to Mademoiselle Pompom. Over her fright, the girl's shivers were due solely to her scarcity of costume, so Gerard obligingly closed the cab windows to prevent the evening breeze from raising havoc with the last few pompoms. Whitestone introduced himself to the girl who stammered in surprise, "You—you are the Great Gerard? But you can't be. He was the man I was talking with at the table."

"I suppose he told you that," said Gerard, "but from the way he acted later, you shouldn't trust anything he said."

The girl accepted that understatement with a nod that showed she trusted the real Gerard. Soon, she was pouring out to him her story. Her name was Georgette Bragance and she had played bit parts at the Moulin Rouge until she'd found an opening as Mademoiselle Pompom at a small nightspot. There, the management of the Cabaret de la Mort had made her a proposition to spice their show by working as a stooge in the coffin number.

"I stopped by between my other shows," explained Georgette, "and if people recognized me, so much the better. Henri Durand said it would make me more popular."

"Henri Durand?" The name struck a note with Gerard. "You mean the theatrical writer with *La Monde du Nuit?*"

"Yes," replied Georgette. "I met him with Eugene Lebrun, the juggler, at the Cabaret de la Mort."

"Lebrun was working there?"

"He was helping them arrange tricks like the skeleton coffin and Durand was much interested. But it was Lebrun who promised to introduce me to you. I expected to find him in his cellar workshop this afternoon, but Durand was there instead. He said Lebrun had gone away, leaving his helper to finish the props."

"You saw the helper?"

"Only his back." Georgette doubled forward in the cab seat and made a hammering motion. "He was nailing up a big box, a long box"—she spread her arms—"long, like a coffin. It was heavy, too, when Durand and the helper took it upstairs and put it on a truck. The helper was still hunched, like this—"

"Did Durand go with him on the truck?"

"No, he left later in a cab. When I said that Lebrun had promised to introduce me to you, Durand said that was all arranged; that you had reserved a table where I was to meet you. I thought"—Georgette beamed a smile—"that after you saw me in the coffin, you would want me with your show."

"I still might." Gerard's eyes went quizzical. "Tell me, did Durand write the program for the Cabaret de la Mort?"

"Yes. I heard him talk about it with Lebrun."

"And that," said Gerard, "covers everything."

Georgette didn't begin to understand. She gave the magician a puzzled stare, only to have her wide eyes dazzled by glaring lights as the cab pulled up before the Gare de Lyon.

"You can't be taking me on a train!" exclaimed the girl. "Why, they wouldn't let me through the gate with so few clothes."

"You're staying right here," said Gerard. "As for clothes"—he gave Georgette an appraising survey, even including such details as foot size—"I'll take care of that when I get back."

Soon, Gerard returned, bringing a pair of woman's suitcases which he handed in through the cab door.

"You'll find all you need in there," he said. "They belong to Mimi, my leading lady, and she's just your build. Take your pick while you're riding to the Hotel Stellaire, where you will find Mimi. Give her this and say you'll be hearing from me later."

Gerard passed Georgette the torn corner from the hotel card and she rewarded him with a gracious smile from the cab window. How that smile would take with Mimi, when the redhead showed up at the Stellaire in the blonde's own smart attire, Gerard did not try to guess. He had other things to think about.

From Georgette's testimony, it was obvious that Durand and an accomplice had murdered Lebrun in his workshop beneath the Cabaret de la Mort and were about to truck away the body when the girl came along. Since Durand prepared the program, he could easily have stopped at the printer's and picked up an advance copy to plant with the body, to make it appear that the trail to the curio room had been followed many hours later.

That same accomplice, whose face Georgette had not seen, had doubtless doubled back to the cabaret to pose as Gerard at the table reserved in the magician's name. The man, when Gerard had seen him reach for the machine gun, had hunched himself much in the way Georgette had described Lebrun's helper.

A neat trick, indeed, to get rid of Georgette, who had learned too much, by falsely pinning her murder on Gerard, who would later be charged with Lebrun's death as well, with the planted program forming the perfect link between the cabaret and Pinetti's.

But it still didn't solve the riddle of Lebrun's body in the sealed room, even though Gerard, who knew a few tricks himself, had taken the teeth out of that mystery. Gerard's only policy now was to play it straight, at midnight, and see what developed from that time on.

At midnight, Gerard found the representatives of the Parisian press awaiting him at Pinetti's, twenty strong. As their story was to deal with the Great Gerard as a collector of magical curiosa and memorabilia, as well as a theatrical figure, the group included writers from off-trail publications, among them Henri Durand, of *La Monde du Nuit,* or *Nightlife,* as its English edition was termed.

Leon, the concierge, was back and had admitted the group to the front reception room. Now, with one exception, they were clamoring to see the curio collection. The exception was Durand, a man of medium build and dapper, round face, with just enough twist to his pointed mustache to give it the illusion of a smile that never appeared on the lips beneath.

Gerard remembered Durand from previous meetings as a pusher, always mugging the spotlight. The fact that he was out of character, staying in the background, fitted with his part as instigator of a double murder plot that had only half succeeded. But to pin down Durand as the brain of a subversive Commie group that had done away with Lebrun was a problem in its own right.

Had Mimi been present, she would have admired the bland way Gerard delivered his spiel about Pinetti, the ease with which he opened the letter lock and finally, his dramatic firing of the pistol shot that lighted the hundred candles. Then, in the midst of a theatrical bow to his audience of journalists, Gerard seemingly caught the reflected horror from their staring, frozen faces.

The magician turned, did a double-take at sight of Lebrun's sword-pierced body. He swung toward the newsmen again, just as the face of Henri Durand pushed forward from the chalk-white group. In an accusing tone, Durand voiced the words that Gerard expected: "This is a case for the police!"

Within a quarter hour, a squad of French detectives was going through Pinetti's preserves with a painful thoroughness. They questioned both Gerard and Leon, even searching the concierge's quarters on the floor below, finding nothing but old furniture and a room stacked with empty boxes.

They studied the front reception room where the newsmen had been congregated when Gerard arrived; then, observing how the smooth carpet ran intact beneath the steel-backed double doors, they concentrated on the curio room itself.

Carefully, they removed Lebrun's body from the floor, drawing out the sword point which Gerard had purposely left in place. One detective found the program from the Cabaret de la Mort and said "Ah!" as he handed it to a deputy inspector, who nodded wisely and repeated, "Ah!"

From then on, the investigation moved.

The deputy inspector, who introduced himself as Pierre Viviani, produced some thin-paper report sheets and checked them against last-minute bulletins supplied by a detective.

"This evening," said Viviani, in a casual tone, "there was an affray at the Cabaret de la Mort. We find that you made a reservation there this afternoon, Monsieur Gerard."

"That would have been difficult even for a magician," said Gerard. "I was on the train coming in from Marseilles."

"Someone phoned later, confirming the reservation."

"People have a way of misusing my name for publicity purposes, Inspector. I wouldn't put it past the Cabaret de la Mort. Apparently no one has even heard of the place."

"May I see that program?" requested Durand. He studied it intently for a moment, then added, "Why, it's tonight's! Whoever brought it here, inspector, must have been at the Cabaret de la Mort, about the time of the trouble there."

"And how," demanded Viviani sharply, "would you know so much about it?"

"Because I have prepared these programs and they are never delivered until show time. Sometimes they are late even then. Someone must have come here directly after the shooting at the Cabaret, perhaps bringing Lebrun's body with him!"

Viviani's thin eyebrows arched an inquiry. Durand promptly explained: "You see, Inspector, Lebrun worked at the Cabaret de la Mort, building their illusions. Perhaps it was he who reserved a table in the name of Gerard."

The inspector pondered; then nodded. "Lebrun was mixed up in many things," Viviani declared, "so many, that there is reason to suspect anyone who was closely associated with him." He turned to Gerard. "You for one, M'sieu."

"But all I did," said Gerard, "was buy this collection and place my own lock on the door."

From the corner of his eye, Gerard saw an irrepressible twitch of triumph at the tips of Durand's mustache. But it wasn't Durand who supplied the interruption; it was Viviani.

"But tonight"—the inspector crinkled the report sheets—"an attempt was made upon the life of a girl named Georgette Bragance. She vanished from a cabinet at the Cabaret de la Mort, when a man fired a machine gun at her from the table reserved in your name, M'sieu Gerard!"

"When I make girls disappear," said Gerard, "I use a revolver with blanks, not a machine gun loaded with real bullets. What is more, I work my illusions on my own stage, not someone else's. I must admit I specialize in table magic too, but not the sort you have just described."

Durand chose that moment to insert the comment that Gerard was sure would soon be due.

"About this room, M'sieu Gerard," suggested Durand, blandly, "you have just confirmed the fact that you alone could unlock its one door. Am I correct?"

Gerard nodded and Durand's deadpan saddened as the journalist turned to Viviani. "Perhaps, *M'sieu l'Inspecteur,*" he said, "you should go over this room inch by inch and make sure there is no other means of entry. Then you will know whether Gerard brought the body here."

Viviani ordered the inspection. Durand's secret triumph grew while the detectives tapped the walls and ceiling of the curio room. Next they were examing the steel barrier that blocked off the front room, only to find it as solid as it looked.

Finally, they turned to the casement windows, which they had taken for granted must be properly latched and bolted. It was Gerard's turn to worry now, for fear they would overlook his preparations, something he could hardly call to their attention. But the meticulous way of these Parisian investigators proved the deciding factor.

Under one detective's pressure, a casement began inching open. Another man was quick to spot the jimmy marks. Those came under microscopic inspection; bulbs flashed as close-up photos were taken.

From the way the glow faded from Durand's features, Gerard recognized that he was chiding himself for having overlooked those windows, never suspecting that Gerard, himself, had nullified the sealed room trap.

Detectives took more pictures, then went out into the backyard to study the windows from the outside. They came across the ladder in the yard next door, and when they questioned Leon, the concierge decided that he must have left it outside, the last time he locked up the house.

Burglary had become the obvious answer. Perhaps, as one detective put it, Lebrun had decided to steal back some of his magical collection, only to quarrel with some crook who had been aiding him. But Deputy Inspector Viviani was not impressed by what he termed a "far-fetched theory" and Gerard could understand why.

Most certainly, Viviani must know that Lebrun had been a secret investigator for the French government and that subversive plotters were responsible for his death. How Georgette and others figured was a riddle which one man could answer, if only in part. That man was Gerard Whitestone.

Curiously, as matters now stood, the Great Gerard was still more baffled than anyone about how Lebrun could have entered the tight-locked curio room, dead or alive. He had no intention, however, of letting anyone suspect that he was puzzled, least of all the Paris police.

V

Gerard was still fumbling for an answer when Viviani invited him to headquarters, something which he could not very well refuse.

There, Gerard learned the hard way that he was still Suspect Number One. He was questioned until after dawn, in the office of Inspector Raoul Beaumont, at the Sûreté headquarters in the Rue des Saussaies.

The inspector was a patient, gray-haired man who sat behind a desk with his long chin resting on his interlaced fingers as he listened, eyes closed, to the story that Gerard had repeated for the twentieth time.

"Your story sounds very good, M'sieu," Beaumont declared, "particularly as the medical examiner reports that Lebrun must have been dead as early as five o'clock, which is before your train arrived in Paris. We have checked with Marseilles and have learned that you were there in the morning.

"But suppose"—Beaumont eyed Gerard above a report sheet—"suppose you had taken a plane instead of the train. You would have had time to look up Lebrun, murder him and leave that body in the room, before you supposedly reached Paris—unless someone can prove you were on that train.

Gerard saw his dilemma. He couldn't very well nominate Mimi to support his alibi. The blonde might let something slip regarding their early visit to Pinetti's.

Gerard tried another tack. "But your own detectives found the window jimmied."

"A very good job," complimented Beaumont, "except that it required your cooperation. That window never could have been jimmied had it been tightly clamped."

Gerard shrugged as though regretting an oversight.

"You would have known if that window happened to be loose," said Beaumont. "You or an accomplice who helped bring the body there."

"Bring it there!" said Gerard. "I thought Lebrun was killed on the premises by his own card sword!" He picked up a photo of the room, pointed to an empty spot above a row of framed playbills. "Look—that's where the sword always hung."

"Reports show that Lebrun was suffocated," said Beaumont. "The blood from the sword wound did not flow profusely. Since you know nothing of how he died"—there was an ironic touch to the inspector's tone—"perhaps you can tell me *why* he died."

"Whoever killed him," said Gerard slowly, "may have been after some secret documents that Lebrun once kept in that room."

"They were after a code," agreed Beaumont. "We have samples of Lebrun's correspondence when he worked for the underground. Enemies of France have such correspondence, too, and would like to crack it to learn the names of other secret agents who are serving us still, against subversive factions. But it is practically impossible."

From a desk drawer, Beaumont brought a sheet of paper studded with rows of numbers. The top line ran: 8–22, 19–9, 46–53, 12–4, 102–7.

"A book code," the inspector said; "8–22 would mean the twenty-second word on the eighth page, and so on. But unless one has the book, he cannot crack the code." He beamed as he put his first direct question. "You don't have the book, do you?"

"Not unless it's in the curio room," said Gerard. "There are a lot of old manuscripts filed there."

"You have a list of them?"

Gerard shook his head. He brought a little packet of color photo slides from his pocket, held one to the light.

"Lebrun carried hundreds of these," explained Gerard. "Photos of the apparatus and the playbills in his curio room—a collection in themselves. In fact, he sold sets of these pictures. He said he'd had them made in case his collection was destroyed in the war.

"The rumor got around that Lebrun had already sold his collection and carried the photos, hoping to find some dupe who would buy the originals and never get them. But when I met his price, he gave me the key to the room before I paid him anything. I went there and personally checked the playbills and apparatus by the photos Lebrun had already given me."

Beaumont arched his eyebrows quickly. "Those manuscripts you mentioned? Where did they figure?"

"As a bonus, I've been through them and I might be able to tell if any have been stolen. But the fact that I have no list of them probably adds to my guilt."

Beaumont nodded emphatically. "It does," he said.

"If I were really guilty," snapped Gerard, "I'd never have come to Pinetti's house at midnight. That's the trouble with your French law. You frame a man right from the start, by considering him guilty unless he can prove himself innocent. Now in America—"

The inspector was on his feet, furious, eyes blazing, his fist pounding the desk as his voice drowned Gerard's.

"In America!" stormed Beaumont. *"Pouf!* You follow the barbarous practice of calling a man innocent until proven guilty. So your police throw that innocent man into prison where he can never vindicate himself. Then they go out to find all the evidence against him, ignoring whatever might prove his innocence!

"If he claims he saw a bushy-haired man commit a murder for which he is blamed, do they look for such a man? You do not. They throw out the dragnet as they call it and who do they bring in? Every bald-headed crook in the city! And when they fail to find evidence against the man"—Beaumont gave his arms a sweeping, hopeless gesture—"what do they do? They reduce the charge so he will plead guilty although he is innocent.

"But here in France, it is different! If we call a man already guilty, what else is there to prove? Only his innocence! So that is what the police try to do! When the accused man can help us, *ah!"*
—he studied Gerard narrowly—"why should we not let him help? If he runs away, it will only prove what we already think, that he

is guilty. Here"—Beaumont began stacking report sheets and photos—"take these. They may help!"

"You mean"—Gerard was incredulous—"I am free?"

"Absolument. Besides"—a twinkle showed beneath Beaumont's half-drooped lids—"we could not hope to keep you here. Knowing Houdini's secrets as you do, you would break out of our eighty-year-old cells as easily as he once did. You are guilty, so go!"

The inspector followed Gerard to the door and gestured for a guard to let the magician pass. Blandly, Beaumont added, "Besides, you may lead us to the accomplice who figured in Lebrun's death. At least, we should hear from you by tonight."

VI

An hour or so later, after Gerard had crossed the Seine four times and switched in and out of three halfway disguises, he pulled into the Hotel Stellaire and breakfasted with Mimi, his accomplice in innocence, and Georgette, the lone material witness in the strange case of Eugene Lebrun.

They ate in the little suite which the two girls shared and apparently the tense situation had smothered any rivalry between blonde and redhead. Mimi, for one, gave an eager report.

"I followed the machine gunner last night. I spotted the cab he took and I trailed it in another, to a place called the Sahara Café."

"You know it?" Gerard asked Georgette. "La Sahara?"

"A very cosmopolitan place," nodded Georgette. "You find Algerians mixing with provincials—and American tourists."

"That's what they took me for," beamed Mimi, "a tourist. They never suspected I'd come from the Cabaret de la Mort. In no time, I found out who he was. They call him Rodolph de la Détente."

"The Trigger," translated Gerard. "Do you know him, Georgette?"

"I have heard of him. I would recognize the man who was at the table in the cabaret. I was close enough to see his face and he didn't expect me to live to remember it."

She spoke with assurance.

Gerard nodded; then summed things as they stood.

"The police know a lot more than they say," he said, "but there is still more they would like to know. We've got to link Durand with Rodolph and the only way is to bait the hook." He turned to Mimi. "Give me that batch of letters we were going to answer after we reached Paris."

Mimi produced the letters. From them, Gerard drew one that listed odd items stored in a Parisian warehouse.

"Leftovers from the Lebrun collection," said Gerard, "that were never shipped to the Pinetti house. I'm calling a press conference for one o'clock, Mimi, so meet me at the Gare de Lyon at three."

"And what," put in Georgette, "shall I do?"

"Stay right here," said Gerard, "and keep out of sight. We will need you for the big payoff."

It was half past one before Gerard had finally assembled a very feeble quota of Parisian journalists in a little restaurant just off the Avenue des Champs Elysées.

Henri Durand was spokesman for the group, as Gerard expected he would be. Suave, debonair as usual, Durand was the first to congratulate Gerard on clearing himself with the police.

"I had very little difficulty," said Gerard. "They decided it was a burglary and they released me."

"But the program from the Cabaret de la Mort?"

"Must have been delivered early for once. Lebrun probably went to his workshop during the evening and picked one up when he left. When he reached the curio room, he walked in on the burglars."

"You mean he had the combination to your letter lock?"

"Of course. I gave it to him, so he could send me items when I was on the road. But he'd never have told anyone, not even if they'd tried to torture the combination out of him."

Momentarily, the suave mask slipped from Durand's face. Gerard guessed that Durand—with Rodolph's aid—must have forced Lebrun to reveal his secret way into the curio room, instead of the letter combination which Lebrun never had known.

"I hardly knew Lebrun," cried Durand. "I regarded him as a magical technician, rather than a historian, which would have interested me much more."

"It would have?" Gerard's face lighted as though in recognition of a fellow enthusiast. "Then you have heard of the celebrated French *prestidigitateur*, Robert-Houdin—"

"Of course." Durand turned to the few reporters and swelled in the manner of a quasi-authority. "Houdin was the great Parisian magician of a century ago. He had his own theater here."

"And you also know," prompted Gerard, "that Houdini took his name from Houdin."

"Certainly." Durand gave his fingers an impetuous snap. "I am trying to recall now, the exact circumstance—"

"Like every great magician," put in Gerard, "Houdin wanted a successor, so he chose a capable young magician and gave him the name Houdini, meaning like Houdin."

"That was it," said Durand, "and of course, as you all know"— he was turning to the group—"Houdini became so world famous that most people have forgotten Houdin."

Gerard's lips flickered with a smile that he covered by spreading out his warehouse list. He had caught Durand's weakness, the man's way of trading on other people's ignorance to assert his own self-importance. Now, Gerard was ready to play on Durand's own lack of knowledge. Laying the list on the table, the magician pointed out an item.

"This will interest you, Durand. The famous writing desk of Robert-Houdin. Of course you realize its historic value."

Gerard paused, letting Durand begin a nod; then, in time with it, Gerard continued, "It is the desk on which Houdin signed the agreement naming Houdini his successor and handed it to him in person, at Saint Gervais, near Blois."

Durand's nods continued; his eyes had an eager gleam.

"In it," said Gerard, "Robert-Houdin kept his unpublished memoirs, more valuable than the desk itself. Today, I shall have it brought to the Pinetti house and placed in the front reception room, manuscript and all."

"This desk," queried Durand. "Lebrun prized it greatly?"

"Very greatly," said Gerard. "He often went to the warehouse to look at it. This desk originally belonged to Houdin's friend and patron, the Count de l'Escapolier. You have heard of him?"

Durand gave a shrug and a smile: "Who has not?" he said. "That is, among those who know their magical history."

"Tomorrow morning, then," Gerard told the group, "you may

meet me at the Pinetti house to hear the full story of Lebrun's collection, including the famous writing desk."

Gerard phoned the warehouse, arranged for the delivery of the desk. He met Mimi at the Gare de Lyon, to give any Sûreté spotters the impression that she had just arrived in Paris. Gerard and the blonde went directly to the Pinetti house and entered the curio room.

The windows had been locked by the police and Gerard still was the only man who had the combination to the letter lock. But when Gerard compared photos given him by Beaumont with his present view of the room itself, he noticed points of difference.

"These were taken just before the room was closed," Gerard told Mimi. "But the screen has been moved, there is a drawer partway open in the corner file. Somebody has been in here since last night."

"But who?" queried Mimi. "And how?"

"Who? Durand," said Gerard. "How? That's what we must find out. It may answer the whole mystery."

Meticulously, Gerard went through the file, time and again, but with no result until, as the sinking sun was glinting through the big locked window, he paused among papers under the letter "H."

"Durand had Houdini on his mind," said Gerard, "and though his ignorance of historical facts is stupendous, he may be informed on technical matters—the very point he was trying to cover up. Houdini's secrets"—Gerard was going through a file of them, in alphabetical arrangement—"they're all here, through to Vanishing Elephant. Wait though: V, W—"

Gerard paused and gestured to the file: "It's gone, the last secret of the lot. Durand had to come and take it, for fear we'd find it and guess the answer."

"But what secret," queried Mimi, "begins with the letter W?"

"Walking Through a Wall," said Gerard. "The famous stunt Houdini did at the New York Hippodrome in the early twenties. They used to build a brick wall on the stage edge, toward the audience, so Houdini could work the act."

Gerard turned, pointed dramatically to the front of the curio room, with its glistening sheet of stainless steel.

"Lebrun knew Houdini's trick of walking through a brick wall,"

Gerard said, "so all he had to do was apply it to the steel wall that he installed here! If I'm right, we can soon find out. Come along."

Gerard led the puzzled blonde from the curio room, spun the letter lock and conducted Mimi downstairs to the storeroom stacked with empty boxes, directly beneath the arched doorway with steel wall. Among the boxes, Gerard found a hidden switch and pressed it.

Silently, a trap door opened downward in two sections from the ceiling. Through the opening, Mimi saw the under surface of the thick carpeting that covered the floor of the upstairs rooms.

"That's the trick of walking through a wall," said Gerard. "They'd put a screen on each side of the wall and Houdini would go behind one screen and come out from the other. Nobody thought of a trap door, because the stage was carpeted, right underneath the wall itself.

"But when the trap dropped open, he could wiggle under the wall, because the rug would sag from the weight of his body. Afterward"—Gerard pressed the switch and the wide trap closed —"when the trap came up in place it pressed the rug smooth again and nothing could be detected. Lebrun rigged his curio room for the same trick, so he could enter or leave it by way of the front reception room, without anyone knowing it!"

"And Durand must have learned the secret."

"Right. Either by trailing Lebrun, winning his confidence, or forcing him to talk." Gerard halted, tilted his head to listen. "Here comes the truck from the warehouse," he said. "I'd better get upstairs."

As a final touch, Gerard pressed the switch, dropping the trap door again. "Leave it open," he told Mimi, "I may need it. But if I use it, shut it fast!" He pressed a stubby revolver into Mimi's hand. "And you may need this, in case somebody shows up down here—like Durand's pal, Rodolph."

VII

Upstairs, Gerard met the truckers at the front door and superintended the unloading of several crates, which were left in the front hallway. Only one was opened at Gerard's order. It contained the famous writing desk, an ornamental, well-decorated piece of furniture which rated as a fine antique, regardless of its historical significance.

It was placed in a front corner of the reception room and Gerard was already trying a key in the desk lid when the truckers left. One man, pausing in the hallway, was fishing in a pocket of his coveralls for a match to light his pipe, when the front door closed behind the others.

Instantly, the trucker unmasked. He flung off his wide-visored work cap, and lurched forward, shoving a gun that he had pulled from his pocket. The muzzle met Gerard's eyes as he turned and above it, he saw the broad face of Henri Durand, beaming in triumph.

"I shall unlock that desk," said Durand, gesturing Gerard back with the gun. "Perhaps this Houdin manuscript is the very thing I seek."

Gerard's stare was puzzled. "You mean for cracking Lebrun's code?"

"You think ahead of me," purred Durand, "but not far enough ahead." His finger wavered on the trigger. Then he added almost savagely, "At least I must let you live until I have checked the manuscript. I may still need you." He shrugged. "Who knows?"

With that, Durand turned the key and lifted the desk lid. From within, a gun roared and Durand reeled backward with a howl, letting his own revolver fly from his other hand. His wrist was bleeding and instinctively he found himself clutching it, but the wound had not come from the gun inside the desk.

A pointed lever, long, sharp like a cat's claw, had delivered a deep scratch to Durand's wrist. Gerard, equally quick, had timed a swoop of his own, following that of the mechanism. Hardly had Durand recovered from his surprise when he saw Gerard picking up the revolver from the floor. Toying with the gun, the magician idled its muzzle straight toward Durand.

Then, suavely, Gerard was telling the disconcerted crook how badly he had slipped.

"I spoke of Houdin picking Houdini as his successor," said Gerard, "just to learn if your ignorance of magical history was as colossal as I suspected it might be. I really expected you to take it as a joke, Durand. But when I saw that you accepted the statement seriously, your game was as good as up."

There was perplexity in Durand's glare. Though he still clutched his wrist, he'd forgotten the wound and was anxious to hear Gerard's explanation. The magician obliged.

"For your elucidation," Gerard told Durand, "Houdin died three years before Houdini was born, so they never could have even met. What was more, the name was never given to Houdini. He simply appropriated it, like everything else he ever wanted, and he was roundly denounced by Houdin's descendants.

"I baited you with that talk about Houdin's unpublished memoirs, too. The autobiography of Robert-Houdin is one of the classics of magical literature, which has appeared in dozens of editions. I even tested you when I mentioned the Count de l'Escapolier, the original owner of this writing desk. Everyone acquainted with magical lore knows of this desk, Durand."

Durand's ugly eyes became more puzzled than before.

"Houdin fixed this desk for the count," continued Gerard, "with a blank pistol actuating a cat's claw, to trap a thief among the count's retinue of servants. That was more than a hundred years ago and the desk has been preserved as a museum piece ever since. When I saw it on Lebrun's list, Durand, I decided to try it out on you the same way, provided your ignorance proved sufficient to make you eligible."

Gerard's eyes grew hard. "I've a pretty good idea what you were searching for, Durand, when you killed Lebrun. You knew that among his papers were records of your subversive activities—records which would have proved utterly damning to you personally—and to your fellow conspirators. Not just witnessed statements, I'm quite sure. It can be taken for granted that it was not evidence collected second hand, but microfilms and sealed instructions bearing your signature. You knew you had to recover them, or face execution as a traitor to France.

"Some of the material would be in code, and you may have wanted Lebrun's secret code for another reason—to translate documents which Lebrun collected during and immediately after the war, and which may have since passed into the hands of your fellow conspirators."

While he spoke, Gerard was studying Durand as he would a

member of an audience during the performance of a specially delicate sleight or illusion. From those eyes, Gerard caught a sudden glint, as vocal as a snake's rattle. But not for an instant did Gerard follow the new direction of Durand's gaze.

"And now," said Gerard, "we can both tell our full stories at the Sûreté—"

Instead of finishing his sentence, Gerard made a quick wheel away from the hallway door, toward which Durand's eyes had sparked a signal. A hunched man was launching himself into a long lunge, thrusting an Apache knife ahead of him, with Gerard as the target.

It was Rodolph and instead of trying to aim the gun at the fellow, Gerard simply give it a back-hand fling squarely into the man's face. Rodolph dropped, then came up snarling with the knife, while Durand, bounding from beside the writing desk, reclaimed his gun. Both were blocking Gerard from the hallway, but he did not hesitate.

Already, the magician was diving for the portières at the rear of the room. He hit the floor on his side, rolled against the bolted doors and was instantly swallowed from sight by the thick tufts of the sagging rug. Then, Gerard had twisted himself beneath the steel wall and was gone, safely on the other side, as Durand's shots began to singe the rug tufts.

Rodolph sprang for the archway hoping to squirm beneath the steel wall and follow Gerard. But the hunched man's shoulder hit solid flooring.

Mimi, down below, had played the perfect assistant as she always did. She had seen the rug sag, then ease as Gerard's weight left it. Without an instant's hesitation, Mimi had pressed the switch that closed the smooth, swift-acting trap.

Gerard could not use the regular door to leave the curio room as it was locked on the outside by the letter lock. Instead, he loosened a window, scrambled out to the balcony and dropped to the yard below. In by the back way, he reached the room beneath the trap door, grabbed the revolver from Mimi and started out to meet Gerard and Rodolph.

When he reached the stairway, Gerard smiled, pocketed his gun and bowed. He was face to face with Inspector Beaumont.

"I assume," said Gerard, "that some of the reporters who left the press conference informed you about the desk that was to be delivered here?"

"They did," said Beaumont, "exactly as you presumed they would and I moved in with a squad—as you expected—rather than disappoint you."

At the top of the stairs, Gerard saw Beaumont's men, half a dozen of them, marching Durand and Rodolph out to the Parisian equivalent of a paddy wagon. No felicitations were exchanged. Gerard merely matched Durand's glare with a restrained smile. It was Beaumont who bowed when he said to Gerard, "You must pardon me, M'sieu, but I am needed at the Sûreté to question two men regarding the death of Eugene Lebrun."

The next morning, Gerard arrived at Beaumont's office bringing Mimi and Georgette to supply their respective testimonies. Beaumont nodded when he heard their stories.

"Both Durand and Rodolph have told us all they know," Beaumont stated. "They murdered Lebrun, but failed to find his code. Durand fell for your game perfectly. He thought the nonexistent Houdin manuscript would contain the key to Lebrun's code and he revealed his hand in his effort to get it."

Beaumont paused, flourished a sheaf of Lebrun's coded correspondence. "What we need now," he said, "is the one thing Durand still does not know. Where is Lebrun's code? Show me a book that might be the right one and I can test it!" For answer, Gerard placed a square wooden box upon the table. From within, he drew color photo slides, depicting Lebrun's playbills. All were numbered for reference to the originals.

"There is the code," said Gerard. "Playbills instead of book pages. Lebrun left sets of slides with people during the war and some must have been members of Durand's ring of Soviet intelligence agents, not just magical collectors."

Eagerly, Beaumont began looking at the slides, as he asked, "How did you hit on this?"

"Simply enough," said Gerard. "Lebrun would have attracted suspicion carrying a set of slides around Paris, where he had the originals to show people. But that was why he needed a secret entrance to the collection room, so he could go in and out, no matter who owned the place, when he had a message to decode."

"You are right," said Beaumont, as he studied a slide in the light. "Anyone could have borrowed a key from the concierge, copied it and entered Pinetti's house. But the secret room was another matter! A veritable fortress, except for the steel wall that anyone could walk through, except that no one guessed how—until you came along, Gerard. Ah!"

The exclamation told that Beaumont had found a code word on one of the numbered slides. He began trying others, holding them to the sunlight that streamed through the window. That was Gerard's awaited cue.

"Come," Whitestone told Mimi and Georgette, as he bowed them to the door. "The inspector is very busy and it is a fine day out, full of sunshine and fleecy clouds. After all"—Gerard's smile dismissed such minor things as murder—"there is no place like Paris in the spring!"

THE SHADOW

Ben Hecht

The life of Ben Hecht is punctuated with powerful ironies. Although regarded as one of the leading writers of the "Chicago School" during the 1920s and 1930s, his greatest work was accomplished in Hollywood. While much of his work is autobiographical, and therefore personal and individualistic, his most enduring was produced at a prodigious rate with a collaborator, Charles MacArthur. And, if some stories, novels, plays, and films are notable for their bitter cynicism and acidic irony (such as The Front Page*), other films are just as unrelievedly sentimental (such as* Miracle in the Rain *and* Wuthering Heights*).*

Hecht's first screen story, Underworld *(1927), directed by Josef von Sternberg, was also the first gangster movie and opened the floodgates for Edward G. Robinson and James Cagney during the 1930s.*

*Although the films Hecht wrote or co-authored with MacArthur are considered classics today (*Gunga Din, Notorious, Spellbound, His Girl Friday, Kiss of Death*), his stories inexplicably lack the popularity of less talented writers of the same period.*

"The Shadow," a strange tale of retribution involving the Marvelous Sarastro, first appeared in The Champion from Far Away *in 1931.*

The Marvelous Sarastro came from Warsaw although he sometimes hinted at Tibet and the Mountains of the Moon.

He was a Pole and a vaudeville magician but, given a sympathetic ear, he would fall to darkening his origins and clothing himself in such mysteries of parentage, race, and geography as gave one an uneasy feeling.

Never have I known a man to lie, boast, pose so tirelessly and childishly. But Sarastro was the true charlatan and one forgave him this. One even demanded it of him.

Often, while listening to his Mother Goose mysticism, his Munchausen adventures, his garbled and pompous chatter of genii, sylphs, and undines, I have grown annoyed at my own skepticism. How much more marvelous was the Marvelous Sarastro if one believed him! How much more entertaining this Arabian Night in which he lived, could one accept it with the heart of a child rather than the dull incredulity of a modern author.

And often, while smiling a bit condescendingly at my friend Sarastro as he unfolded his Brobdingnagian doings, I have been suddenly impressed by the thought of what a genius he would once have seemed; what a great man another age would have considered him—a savant, Magus, and dangerous kin of Lucifer. At such moments Sarastro's somewhat humorous appearance would take on an air of distinction and authority. His small eyes appeared sinister. His thin lips seemed cruel. His plump womanish face became a symbol of enigma. His long thin nose acquired a papal dignity. His silken brown hair, falling in a Dutch bob almost to his neck, was transformed into a fascinating and medieval coiffure.

It was with the foregoing notions about Sarastro that I called on him in his dressing room backstage at the Palace Theater. I had sat through his turn, thrilled as always by his dexterity and pompousness. For Sarastro was no glib magician apologizing for his pretenses with aged jokes and comical patter. He performed his levitations and disappearances, his transmutations and feats of legerdemain with the profound, unsmiling mein of one truly at work on miracles. But I noticed, nevertheless, a change in his manner. He seemed nervous and preoccupied.

He greeted me coldly as I opened the door of his dressing room and continued to remove his make-up in silence. I offered compliments. He nodded and said nothing. I remarked on his new feat —a disappearing cage full of birds. This was, said I, a miracle which would have astounded the great Herman.

"I am glad you saw it," said Sarastro. He was drying his face. "It is the last time."

"What is the last time?" I asked.

"The last time I perform," said Sarastro. "I leave tonight for Paris. You will never see me again. No one will ever see me again. It is the last of Sarastro."

"Why are you going to Paris?" I asked.

"To murder a man," said Sarastro. "I arrive on the fifteenth. On the morning of the sixteenth there will be one fiend less in the world."

I made no remark at this and disguised my delight with a sympathetic frown.

"What time do you sail?" I asked, as he put on his street clothes.

"At midnight."

"Would you care to honor me as my guest for supper?" I asked.

"Yes," said Sarastro. "Part of me being still human, I must continue to eat."

Twenty minutes later we entered a quiet, almost deserted café. Sarastro ordered food wearily but profusely.

"There is no hurry," he said. "My things are all on the boat. Here is my passport. Here is my ticket."

He showed me these documents.

"This is rather a new ambition," I said, "murder."

"Oh, no," said Sarastro. "I have had this ambition for twenty years."

"The same man?"

"Yes."

"I have never suspected it."

"Hate," said Sarastro, "is not an emotion which one wears on one's sleeve. It is a soul. When it enters a man he may live on, he may laugh, work, and go about, and there will be no difference to those who are his friends; but his soul has only one color, his nights have only one dream. For twenty years I have dreamed only one thing—to kill a man."

I said nothing. We ate in silence for several minutes.

"His name is Rico Sansone," said Sarastro. "Have you ever heard of him?"

"No," I said.

"On the sixteenth," said Sarastro, "you will hear that he is dead."

"Why are you going kill him?" I asked.

The medieval face smiled. A dreamy look filled the small eyes.

"Because," said Sarastro, "he is the most evil man in the world. I have been waiting for twenty years for his name to appear. For as long as he chose to hide there was no hope. He is too clever. Yes, even for me. Far too clever. But I knew that his vanity would betray him and that some day I would read again the name Rico Sansone. I knew he would return to the stage."

"Is he a magician?" I asked.

"Yes," said Sarastro. "The greatest that ever lived. The most profound and evil. He has no soul."

I nodded.

"He is greater than I," said Sarastro and closed his eyes as if overcome by this statement. "He begins his performance in Paris on the fifteenth."

"I would like to hear the story," I said frankly.

"You will," said Sarastro. "But I must have your oath not to interfere."

"You have it," I said.

"Very well," said Sarastro. "The story begins twenty years ago. I was a young man. I traveled with a small carnival through the villages of southeastern Europe. We were a company of clowns, gypsies, acrobats, and conjurors. We traveled in gilded wagons and performed for peasants and herdsmen on the outskirts of their villages.

"My powers developed early. I was young, but I was able to cast horoscopes, foretell the future, reveal the past, and converse with the gnomes and salamanders. I wore black tights and a small black jacket that came only to my waist. There was always a sword at my side, for in dealing with the spirits that infest the darkness beyond life one must always be armed. I was known as the Black Seer, and it was not only the peasants who held me in awe. My comrades themselves feared and respected me.

"One night we came to a village in Malo-Russia. Our cymbals sounded, our music played, our torches flickered in the spring wind, and the villagers crowded around our tents and wagons. I had taken my place in the black box on the platform outside my tent. There were holes in the box through which I could watch the crowd while the barker made his announcements. He ran up and down the platform, ringing his bell and shouting 'The Black Seer, the Marvel of Marvels, Sarastro the Magician, who speaks with the dead and reads the secrets of life. . . .'

"I saw her for the first time at this moment. Her young and gentle face surprised me among so many peasants. I said to myself, 'What a strange girl! What a beautiful child!' In a short while I began my performance in the tent. But I was restless. I kept watching the entrance. At length an old peasant led her in, holding her by the hand. I saw at once that she was blind.

"The old man led her to my side and asked that I tell her fortune. He said she was his daughter, but it needed no knowledge of the stars to see that he lied. I questioned him and learned her simple history. She had been born blind and cast aside as an infant by a tyrant-noble of the vicinity and she had been found and raised by this old man and his wife.

"I studied her face as he talked. Pure as a seraph's, her large sightless eyes calm, resigned. She was eighteen and beautiful, pale, delicate, noble. But that does not describe her. It is in the eyes that the soul of a woman is usually to be seen. Anna's eyes were empty. She could neither see nor be seen by them. But the spirit which found these eyes closed lighted the rest of her face and body. A kindly, radiant child spoke from her lips. I held her white hands which she had offered me trustingly and I cast her horoscope. A dark mist passed over me and I listened to the voices which foretell the future. 'Sorrow, sorrow,' they breathed, 'pain and sorrow. Fly . . . run. . . .'

"But I smiled and my own voice was serene as I spoke.

" 'The spirits promise you happiness,' I told her, 'your hands will touch beautiful things. Love and delight await you.'

"I was rewarded for my lies by a smile such as one sees on a child's face when it is dreaming.

"That was the beginning. Her face haunted me that night and I could not sleep. I made inquiries the next morning and sought her out. We walked through the hills. She did not need my hand to guide her. She knew every stone, every turn of the paths we followed. She spoke of the trees around us. She had strange names for them. And she spoke of the flowers that were to come soon in these woods. I forgot that she was blind. I came again the next day —and the next. Her purity, her sweetness delighted me. But there was something else—a sense of disquiet. It had come to me first from the stars. I had heard a warning out of the dark mists in which the voices of the dead are hidden.

"But now more than before I felt it behind the child's smile of her lips. When her hands touched mine for the first time she shuddered and grew pale. I knew then that she was aware of her destiny. The stars had told me she would not live long and that agony and terror waited for her on the short journey.

"She was innocent, untouched as yet by life. But it is unnecessary to know the ways of the world to know how one's heart will break. Here, hidden away, she awaited her fate without too much knowledge or too much dread. Yet her soul knew it completely. Her hand, when it sought mine in the silent shadowed woods, sought the hands of a protector. In my supernatural talent, she fancied, lay a hope of escape. I understood this as I looked at her.

"We remained for two weeks in this village. When we left Anna came with me as my wife. More than her beauty and her gentleness, the sense of her ominous future had made the thought of leaving her impossible. Thus, in seeking to save her, I fulfilled the terrible message of the stars. For it was I—Sarastro—who was the instrument fate had selected for her ruin.

"She was happy. We rode together in the gilded wagon. Her pure, trusting face was always beside me. So that she might never be lonely I instructed her in a few of the elements of magic. In a little time she was able to take her place on the platform outside my tent. Dressed in the colorful robe I bought for her she sat blindfolded—for who would believe so perfect, so beautiful a creature was without sight?—and guessed numbers, told fortunes. Everything delighted her. Everything made her smile. She was happy.

"But I was not. From the moment that I embraced her as my wife I was haunted. How can I tell you of this dread, the continual dread of knowing something, of waiting for something that one knows, of waiting for life to despoil one?

"I tried to learn more. I sought for some clue that would enable me to anticipate the thing that menaced us and so, perhaps, overcome it. But my magic could tell me nothing more. It only repeated for me the words of dread, of horror.

"Then I knew, one night as I stood in the black box outside my tent, that I needed no further word from the mists of prophecy. It was there. It had come. He stood among the peasants before our tent—a graceful figure, smiling, leaning on his cane. A man of the world amusingly out of place in this faraway little village. I looked at him through the holes in my box. As I looked a glow of fear came to my heart.

"He had turned his face and I saw his remarkable eyes lighted by the flare of our torches. They were round, colorless eyes. They were proud and smiling and yet lifeless.

"I watched him and felt afraid. He was studying Anna. Never once did he stop looking at her. When we started to enter the tent for the performance he disappeared. I said nothing to Anna. What was there to say? That a man had looked at her. She would understand too much.

"I was waiting for him the next night. Yes, eagerly. You know the eagerness with which one waits for all certainties whether they are bright or dreadful. He came back. He stood once more leaning on his cane, graceful, smiling and sinister. His eyes were on her face.

"In the wagon that night she spoke to me.

" 'There is a man looking at me,' she said, as we lay side by side. Her hand crept into mine. There was nothing more to say. The same thing was in our minds.

"On the third night I decided to act. My temper was quick and fiery. I came up to him as he stood watching Anna. He followed me as if my enraged demand to speak to him were a gracious request. Ah, how subtle he was, how graceful! But that is the way of those whose souls are fashioned in hell.

"On the outskirts of the crowd I seized his arm and demanded to know what he meant by coming every night and staring at my wife. He removed my hand as if it were a child's. I can tell you there was something terrifying in his strength as I felt it for the first time. For I knew . . . but that comes later. He looked at me with his cold lifeless eyes and he spoke softly and apologized for having given offense. He explained that he was a student of the occult traveling about the world in search of knowledge. He praised Anna as a woman of remarkable psychic powers. He said he had hoped to be able to induce her to join him as an assistant, for he was planning soon to go on the stage. But now that he knew she was my wife. . . . He shrugged his shoulders and apologized again for his seeming forwardness. Then he looked at me with a curious smile and said softly, 'She is blind, is she not?' In this moment as he smiled, I understood that he knew. Like myself, he had seen the ominous, the dreadful shadow around her.

"Yet I could do nothing. Despite my travels I was a rustic, young, hot-blooded, untutored in the ways of society. I had no words with which to resist his charm. Yes, even at that moment when I most understood him I found myself listening with interest to his talk —pleased, disarmed, moved somehow by the loneliness that underlay his eager, friendly manner. I recognized him as a genius. And he walked back to our tent with me, talking already as if I were his dearest friend.

"It was thus Rico entered our lives. Little by little, during the days that followed, he attached himself to us. He confessed simply that he had nothing to do, that he had no friends, no kin. He said he had been wandering alone over Europe since he was a boy. And he talked. Ah, his talk! We listened, Anna and I, to his tales. Yes, he had been everywhere, seen everything. He brought the world into our gilded wagon. He wooed us both as a lonely, brilliant man woos the friendship of those he likes.

"In his presence I always felt elated and flattered. But when he left and I was alone again with Anna a disquiet came. I waited darkly for her first words. You know the dangerous words a woman speaks when she finds herself interested in a man. But they did not come. Instead she would take my hands, press them to her cheeks and whisper, 'I do not like him, Sari. I do not like the way he looks at me. I feel something strange in him.'

"Then how eager I was to defend him, to remind her of his gay talk and of how he had made us laugh and feel happy. Thus does a man move in the grip of his destiny, thus do we dig with our own hands the appointed grave for our happiness. I was a fool, yes. But I was to be even a greater fool.

"For the time came when Anna took my hands one night and told me that our friend had made love to her. My heart grew black. I listened as she spoke for some telltale note in her voice. But, no. Anna's soul was as transparent, as pure as a child's. She clung to me as she had clung that first time in her native woods. And she repeated her fear of him. She told me he had come to her while she was alone, had taken her hand gently in his and asked her if she loved me and how deeply she loved me. Then he asked her if she loved me more than happiness or life. She had withdrawn her hand and answered only as a pure and noble soul can answer such questions. She had said, 'I cannot talk of love to you, even of my love for my husband. Please leave me.' And he had gone, pausing to ask her in the doorway to forgive him and to say that he understood now.

"It was late at night as she told me these things. And when she had finished and I was holding her in my arms there was a knock on the door. I opened it. It was Rico standing on the steps of our wagon. He held a heap of wildflowers in his arms.

"He entered without any word and laid the flowers on our table and I knew that he had picked them in woods beyond the village. Then he spoke. 'She has told you,' he said, and as I continued to stare at him blackly, he went on, 'it was not that I desired to hurt her, my friend. I asked only if she were happy. Because she has grown dear to me. She is the first woman to whom my heart has turned. And I asked, because for a moment I grew weak. I knocked at a forbidden door as a lonely beggar might knock timidly and foolishly at the door of a great house within which he had caught a glimpse of feasting. Forget my weakness. Let me remain your friend. I am heartbroken to think I have brought a moment of unhappiness or alarm to either of you. . . .'

"I remember more of his words. But what are words compared to the emotion that kindles them? And I will perhaps seem like a greater fool than I was when I tell you that tears filled my eyes and that I seized his hand. For I had never before heard so deep, so melancholy a voice as his. A voice so resigned, so caressing. I poured wine for the three of us. We drank—Rico and I. But Anna did not touch her glass. She did not speak once during his visit. When he left she sat motionless for a long time. I came to her and she raised her gentle, brooding face, and her words, uttered softly, brought the dread back into my heart.

" 'I'm afraid of him,' she murmured. 'I'm afraid, Sari.'

"This was in the third month of our friendship. We were in Bavaria. Rico had come with us to Baumburg. Our carnival had planned to remain here for several weeks and Anna and I had moved into a pension. And gradually we saw less and less of Rico. He came occasionally to talk and sometimes the three of us took walks. But I began to feel it was my companionship he desired, not Anna's. He had undertaken to initiate me into the mysteries of magic and we spent long hours together—without Anna. He was learned. He knew things that are not known by many men. I was again flattered, lured, disarmed. Under his care my mind was expanding, my powers developing.

"Then one day I was sitting in my tent preparing for the afternoon performance when a curious sense overcame me. I felt a pressure on my heart as if a hand were closing around it. It was a warning. When one is close to the secrets of life and death one understands their voice, their inner voice.

"I left the tent quickly and hurried to the pension. Anna had remained behind as she frequently did in the afternoon. I tried to rid myself of the oppression as I approached our home. It would not do to frighten Anna. Yet I found myself running toward the door. I paused, waited till I had recovered my breath and then, smiling, opened the door quietly. I saw Rico standing with his arms around her, her face raised to his lips.

"Speechless, powerless, I looked at them. I heard her voice murmuring words of love. Her arms moved around his neck and she kissed him. My head grew black. In another instant I would have fallen as one falls under a heavy blow. Yes, death seemed to enter me. Then I heard his voice. He spoke her name. He caressed her with words. At their sound a horror seized me. It was my voice. It was Sarastro talking. It was a voice that seemed to come from my own throat. A horrible, familiar voice. And I understood what had happened.

"I sprang forward shouting his name . . . Rico! He turned and faced me. He pointed his finger at me as if he were an image in a mirror. 'Rico,' he echoed.

"I heard Anna scream. But murder was in my heart. I fought with this monster. I flew at him with a knife. We struggled across the room and he answered my cries with cries that echoed each note, each inflection of my voice. I saw him through my rage. His face was contorted like my own. His every feature had changed. He was Sarastro. There were two Sarastros screaming together, tumbling over each other.

"Then he held me in hands that were like steel fetters. Powerless I lay, mad with rage and terror, under him. I could not move or cry out. His hand was on my throat. I lay gasping and crazed, and it was Sarastro who was holding me. Then this horrible and familiar figure changed. It became Rico. It was Rico Sansone who spoke. The breath was leaving my body. I was strangling, dying, yet I could hear him—'Sarastro. God! You are killing me. Sari— Sari. Have mercy. I am dying!' His voice was faint. I felt in this moment the agonies of a hundred deaths, for as my eyes grew dark I saw with horror the thing he had in his mind. He was pretending it was I who was killing him. And thus he would kill me and go to her as Sarastro. It would be Rico Sansone who was buried. It would be Sarastro who remained.

"For a moment I caught a glimpse of his cold, lifeless eyes burning now over my face as he enacted his false death-groaning, pleading for mercy. And a strength drawn from the soul filled my lungs. I cried out the name Anna—once, twice, knowing that by this she would understand it was I—I who was dying. And darkness seized me.

"An hour had passed when I opened my eyes. My head was splitting. My throat was stiffened. I raised myself and looked. He was gone. I saw her. She was standing in a corner of the room, crouched against the wall, her hand against her teeth and staring —staring into the terrible dark around her.

" 'It is I,' I whispered, 'Anna!'

"She shrank from my voice. I dragged myself to her feet, calling her name, sobbing, pleading. But when I touched her she sank to the floor.

"It had come—the agonies and terror foretold by the stars. I lifted her to the bed. She recovered her senses, but the touch of my hand was enough to make her scream. I sat beside her through

the night. I talked quietly of the little things that had been between us, of secrets only a husband may share with a woman. I
recalled myself to her as one who has been away for years might
struggle vainly to prove who he was. She lay silent, her face drawn
with terror and listened. Finally at dawn she whispered my name.

"This was the beginning. Rico had disappeared. I had frustrated
his diabolical plan with my last cry. With his evil happiness a
moment away he had released me and fled. But I kept this part
of the horror a secret from her.

"We laid our plans. As soon as she was able to walk we abandoned the carnival and left Baumburg. We went to Munich. We
were inseparable. She could not bear to have me away even for
a moment. The darkness in which she had found peace and love
had become filled with terror for her. I understood everything in
her soul. Yes, even the trembling that would seize her sometimes
when I took her hand.

"It would be folly to engage an attendant, a third one to watch,
to guard. It was I alone he could not deceive. To everyone else he
could become Sarastro. Even to her whose senses had learned
every breath, every inflection of the man she loved, he had been
Sarastro.

"Yes, we made our plans. We invented codes of greeting and
secret hand-clasps and intimate caresses by which she might know
me. Ah, how curious and terrible were these first months! With
what foolish ruses, desperate childish ruses, we struggled to evade
the terror that had closed around us! She was brave. She grew to
smile again. The months passed. She whispered to me now as we
lay together that her spirit was recovered. She was not afraid any
more, she said. The thing she had feared had come and had passed.
It was ended now. We were free.

"I agreed with her. I feigned exuberance, carelessness. You understand how it was. It was her soul I must cure of its dread, for
in this dread alone she would go mad. When she insisted I return
to work I went. I begged her to accompany me so that we might
be together while we performed. But she answered strangely that
she no longer felt the power in her to perform. Something had
passed from her. And I understood this, too. But I would not let
her see. It would not do to alarm her. I went alone. I pretended
I was without fear. But it was a lie. I was still waiting. . . .

"I thought first of flying to another part of the world. But one does not escape terror by running. He would be there—wherever I was. I knew this, because it was given to me to know my fate. I remembered his genius. He had been made in hell. He was a shadow from which I could not hope to hide. So we remained in Munich. I secured employment in a cabaret. Eight months passed. The dread, although it never left me, grew vaguer. And our life had become again almost like a honeymoon. Almost, I say, for there were moments in which I caught a glimpse of Anna's inner soul. I would wake at night to find her fingers tracing the contours of my face and body. I would lie motionless listening to her moan out of the nightmare whose nature I knew only too well. In the morning she would waken, tired and nervous. On such days I pretended to be ill and remained at her side. We said nothing, but we knew the shadow in each other's mind.

"These occasions, however, grew rarer. Ah, this fool's peace in which we struggled to live, this empty and ominous security we built around our love. Yes, for he was waiting. This monster, this fiend was hovering near us and I had only to close my eyes to feel his shadow.

"I entered the cabaret where I performed one evening, feeling unusually disturbed. It was winter. The cold had numbed me during my walk to the place. I was removing my overcoat in the dressing room and it came again as I had known it would. The warning . . . the hand closing over my heart. Without a word to anyone I left the place. In the street I felt choked, dizzy. I hailed a carriage with difficulty and drove to within a block of our home. And during this ride I kept muttering to myself that my terror was only a folly of the nerves.

"I entered our cottage by a back door quietly like a thief. And I stood listening. The room was in darkness but in the room beyond a light burned. 'She has gone to bed early,' I thought, and then, through the half-opened door of her bedroom I heard her voice. She was talking softly, happily. She was saying, 'My darling, you are ill again. We will go to sleep and in the morning you will feel better.' And a voice answered her caressingly, adoringly. My own voice it was, as before, but tender and gentle. . . .

"One does not reason in the midst of nightmare. Yet terror can wake the mind to a clairvoyance, an understanding beyond thought. I stood motionless, silent, listening. The light was turned out. I heard her laugh like a child in the dark, and this sound killed me. Yes, one is dead forever when happiness is torn from the heart. I slipped from the house like a thief. I walked in the cold streets. My thought returned. I had acted out of one clear impulse. Through the terror and agony of those moments when I heard him take her in his arms there had remained the certainty that above everything else I must save her.

"Now I knew I had acted wisely. Had I rushed into the room, had I made a noise—she would have died. She would have known in that moment, as I knew listening to him, that he had been there before. That he had crept through our defenses as a shadow creeps. That despite our plans, despite everything, he had stolen into her soul.

"He lay beside her now embracing her, wooing her, and she with her arms holding him. I thought of this thing as I walked. And I thought again that I had only to rush back, to speak her name. Yes, and destroy her. No, I kept on moving in the cold night. I had slunk away in order to save her. And as I walked I began to understand him. Yes, we were dealing with a monster. He would manage to leave her before I was due to return from the cabaret. And if I sensed something wrong he would rely on my love for her to keep this sense a secret. He knew me well, well enough to take my place in her arms, well enough to take my place in her soul and to reason with my own thoughts. He understood I would allow my heart to be eaten away with grief and I would not make a sign lest I destroy her whom I loved more than myself. It was I who must be careful, not he. Yes, he knew me. He gambled on me.

"I returned. I undressed as he had directed I should undress, quietly. She lay with her lips parted and the faint odor of a drug was on her breath. This I understood, too, and was grateful—grateful to him. I stretched myself beside her, closed my eyes and waited. She awoke in the morning and I felt her hands caress me solicitously. She asked if I felt better and when I turned to her she started back in alarm. But I saw, thank God, it was only my cold fingers on her hand that had frightened her. I held my breath, however, waiting as one waits for death. I was ill, she cried. She must send for a doctor. Her lips covered my face with kisses and

I choked back the tears. I strangled the agony in my heart. I said nothing. I pretended to be weary and I distracted her attention by continuous and querulous demands. She nursed me through the day.

"And thus it began again. My illness lasted for two weeks. I thought during these days that I would die. But I realized I must recover. She would begin to fear that there was something wrong. I left the bed finally. I postponed returning to the cabaret. But this, too, had to be done. I decided, however, to leave Munich. I explained to her that the climate was better in Berlin. We went to Berlin.

"What followed is hard to tell you. Terror leaves no memory. Yes, I no longer lived. There was only one thing in my mind. Perhaps it drove me mad. It has seemed to me always that all this time in Berlin I was able to eat, work, even sleep, only because of my desire to save her. This desire was greater than myself.

"I had determined to kill him the first moment I saw him—alone. I knew he was near us. He had tasted of the fruit of heaven and he would not go away now. I must be careful. Then I began to think he would kill me as he had at first intended and that he would go on living with her as Sarastro. She would never know I was dead. She would continue to love me in his arms, to press her kisses upon my murderer, until . . . this was the thought that contained in it the fullest measure of horror. The thought of that moment when she saw him and not me. . . .

"With this in view I wrote a long letter, sealed it and deposited it with a lawyer with instructions that he open it if I failed to communicate with him a single day and act immediately on the information it contained. For the rest I managed, God knows how, to spare her. The months passed and she felt no moment of dread. This was my reward. I asked questions, vague, subtle, disarming questions, and waited for her answers as one waits for a reprieve or a doom. Gradually I noticed that she spoke of things that were strange to me. She would continue his conversations—with me. She would speak of endearments I had never bestowed, of foolish, tender things I had never uttered.

"Do you understand the grief of these months? Yes, it is fortunate I cannot remember it. I can remember only prowling the streets like a madman, crawling into corners to weep, waking at night with my agony echoing through dreams of horror. I was like a thing in a trap, while he came and went, stealing her love, stealing my soul from under my eyes. But it was I, not he, who was afraid. It was I who held her life in my hands.

"I will pass over these months. What use is there now to remember them? They came to an end. I returned home one night after my performance. I was no longer so careful about my own comings and goings. I trusted him, do you understand—that out of his evil he would spare her as I spared her out of love. But when I entered the bedroom this time, when I opened the door of her bedroom this night, I knew he had blundered. She was alone.

"At the sound of my voice she turned. She stood facing me for a moment. Then she screamed. It is this scream I remember, it is with this voice she comes back to me. This cry of horror is my memory of Anna. She seized her face with her hands as if she were tearing something—yes, the darkness. As I rushed to her she fell. She did not speak again. In the morning she died."

I have written the story as nearly in Sarastro's words as I can remember.

I went with him to the boat. We said good-bye. Three weeks later my friend Sarastro was dead. I stared at the dispatch in a theatrical weekly with sadness and confusion. Under a Paris date line it recounted the end of the Marvelous Sarastro. He had been killed in an automobile accident. While motoring through the country his automobile had stalled on a railroad track and been demolished by an oncoming train. Sarastro, read the dispatch, had been cut to pieces. A friend who had been driving with him had escaped with slight injuries. The friend's name was given. It was Enrico Sansone.

THE MOMENT OF DECISION

Stanley Ellin

In some ways, the ultimate detective story is the riddle story—the puzzle without a solution, the winding road that leads nowhere. In these tales of uncertain endings, there is only one detective who can offer an answer to the problem: you.

Riddle stories have always intrigued inventive minds. The most famous is undoubtedly Frank Stockton's "The Lady or the Tiger?" The best may well be Stanley Ellin's "The Moment of Decision."

Since the publication of his first crime story, "The Specialty of the House," in the May 1948 issue of Ellery Queen's Mystery Magazine, *Ellin has been recognized as the master of his specialty—the short story of crime, mystery, and detection. The most prestigious prize available to writers of new mystery stories was the one offered by* EQMM *in its annual contests. As preposterous as it seems, Ellin won a special prize for his first story and thereafter won a prize every year for the next seven contests, culminating in a first prize for this brilliant riddle story that is as unforgettable, as hauntingly terrifying, in its way, as "The Specialty of the House."*

In 1961, the U.S. Steel Hour *adapted "The Moment of Decision" for a sixty-minute television program. The leading actor was a fellow who got a break in his first dramatic role—a former song-and-dance-man by the name of Fred Astaire. The ending was softened a bit for TV audiences, hinting that all will work out to a happy, safe, ordinary conclusion. Maybe it will. Read this story. Then make* your *decision.*

Hugh Lozier was the exception to the rule that people who are completely sure of themselves cannot be likable. We have all met the sure ones, of course—those controlled but penetrating voices which cut through all others in a discussion, those hard forefingers jabbing home opinions on your chest, those living Final Words on all issues—and I imagine we all share the same amalgam of dislike and envy for them. Dislike, because no one likes to be shouted down or prodded in the chest, and envy, because everyone wishes he himself were so rich in self-assurance that he could do the shouting down and prodding.

For myself, since my work took me regularly to certain places in this atomic world where the only state was confusion and the only steady employment that of splitting political hairs, I found absolute judgments harder and harder to come by. Hugh once observed of this that it was a good thing my superiors in the department were not cut of the same cloth, because God knows what would happen to the country then. I didn't relish that, but —and there was my curse again—I had to grant him his right to say it.

Despite this, and despite the fact that Hugh was my brother-in-law—a curious relationship when you come to think of it—I liked him immensely, just as everyone else did who knew him. He was a big, good-looking man, with clear blue eyes in a ruddy face, and with a quick, outgoing nature eager to appreciate whatever you had to offer. He was overwhelmingly generous, and his generosity was of that rare and excellent kind which makes you feel as if you are doing the donor a favor by accepting it.

I wouldn't say he had any great sense of humor, but plain good humor can sometimes be an adequate substitute for that, and in Hugh's case it was. His stormy side was largely reserved for those times when he thought you might have needed his help in something and failed to call on him for it. Which meant that ten minutes after Hugh had met you and liked you, you were expected to ask him for anything he might be able to offer. A month or so after he married my sister Elizabeth she mentioned to him my avid interest in a fine Copley he had hanging in his gallery at Hilltop, and I can still vividly recall my horror when it suddenly arrived, heavily crated and with his gift card attached, at my barren room-

and-a-half. It took considerable effort, but I finally managed to return it to him by forgoing the argument that the picture was undoubtedly worth more than the entire building in which I lived and by complaining that it simply didn't show to advantage on my wall. I think he suspected I was lying, but being Hugh he would never dream of charging me with that in so many words.

Of course, Hilltop and the two hundred years of Lozier tradition that went into it did much to shape Hugh this way. The first Loziers had carved the estate from the heights overlooking the river, had worked hard and flourished exceedingly; its successive generations had invested their income so wisely that money and position eventually erected a towering wall between Hilltop and the world outside. Truth to tell, Hugh was very much a man of the eighteenth century who somehow found himself in the twentieth, and simply made the best of it.

Hilltop itself was almost a replica of the celebrated, but long untenanted, Dane house nearby, and was striking enough to open anybody's eyes at a glance. The house was weathered stone, graceful despite its bulk, and the vast lawns reaching to the river's edge were tended with such fanatic devotion over the years that they had become carpets of purest green which magically changed luster under any breeze. Gardens ranged from the other side of the house down to the groves which half hid the stables and outbuildings, and past the far side of the groves ran the narrow road which led to town. The road was a courtesy road, each estate holder along it maintaining his share, and I think it safe to say that for all the crushed rock he laid in it Hugh made less use of it by far than any of his neighbors.

Hugh's life was bound up in Hilltop; he could be made to leave it only by dire necessity; and if you did meet him away from it you were made acutely aware that he was counting off the minutes until he could return. And if you weren't wary you would more than likely find yourself going along with him when he did return, and totally unable to tear yourself away from the place while the precious weeks rolled by. I know. I believe I spent more time at Hilltop than at my own apartment after my sister brought Hugh into the family.

At one time I wondered how Elizabeth took to this marriage,

considering that before she met Hugh she had been as restless and flighty as she was pretty. When I put the question to her directly, she said, "It's wonderful, darling. Just as wonderful as I knew it would be when I first met him."

It turned out that their first meeting had taken place at an art exhibition, a showing of some ultramodern stuff, and she had been intently studying one of the more bewildering concoctions on display when she became aware of this tall, good-looking man staring at her. And, as she put it, she had been about to set him properly in his place when he said abruptly, "Are you admiring that?"

This was so unlike what she had expected that she was taken completely aback. "I don't know," she said weakly. "Am I supposed to?"

"No," said the stranger, "it's damned nonsense. Come along now, and I'll show you something which isn't a waste of time."

"And," Elizabeth said to me, "I came along like a pup at his heels, while he marched up and down and told me what was good and what was bad, and in a good loud voice, too, so that we collected quite a crowd along the way. Can you picture it, darling?"

"Yes," I said, "I can." By now I had shared similar occasions with Hugh, and learned at firsthand that nothing could dent his cast-iron assurance.

"Well," Elizabeth went on, "I must admit that at first I was a little put off, but then I began to see that he knew exactly what he was talking about, and that he was terribly sincere. Not a bit self-conscious about anything, but just eager for me to understand things the way he did. It's the same way with everything. Everybody else in the world is always fumbling and bumbling over deciding anything—what to order for dinner, or how to manage his job, or whom to vote for—but Hugh always *knows*. It's *not* knowing that makes for all those nerves and complexes and things you hear about, isn't that so? Well, I'll take Hugh, thank you, and leave everyone else to the psychiatrists."

So there it was. An Eden with flawless lawns and no awful nerves and complexes, and not even the glimmer of a serpent in the offing. That is, not a glimmer until the day Raymond made his entrance on the scene.

We were out on the terrace that day, Hugh and Elizabeth and I, slowly being melted into a sort of liquid torpor by the August sunshine, and all of us too far gone to make even a pretence at talk. I lay there with a linen cap over my face, listening to the summer noises around me and being perfectly happy.

There was the low, steady hiss of the breeze through the aspens nearby, the plash and drip of oars on the river below, and now and then the melancholy *tink-tunk* of a sheep bell from one of the flock on the lawn. The flock was a fancy of Hugh's. He swore that nothing was better for a lawn than a few sheep grazing on it, and every summer five or six fat and sleepy ewes were turned out on the grass to serve this purpose and to add a pleasantly pastoral note to the view.

My first warning of something amiss came from the sheep—from the sudden sound of their bells clanging wildly and then baa-ing which suggested an assault by a whole pack of wolves. I heard Hugh say "Damn!" loudly and angrily, and I opened my eyes to see something more incongruous than wolves. It was a large black poodle in the full glory of a clownish haircut, a bright-red collar, and an ecstasy of high spirits as he chased the frightened sheep around the lawn. It was clear the poodle had no intention of hurting them—he probably found them the most wonderful playmates imaginable—but it was just as clear that the panicky ewes didn't understand this, and would very likely end up in the river before the fun was over.

In the bare second it took me to see all this, Hugh had already leaped the low terrace wall and was among the sheep, herding them away from the water's edge, and shouting commands at the dog who had different ideas.

"Down, boy!" he yelled. "Down!" And then as he would to one of his own hounds, he sternly commanded, "Heel!"

He would have done better, I thought, to have picked up a stick or stone and made a threatening gesture, since the poodle paid no attention whatever to Hugh's words. Instead, continuing to bark happily, the poodle made for the sheep again, this time with Hugh in futile pursuit. An instant later the dog was frozen into immobility by a voice from among the aspens near the edge of the lawn.

"Assieds!" the voice called breathlessly. *"Assieds-toi!"*

Then the man appeared, a small, dapper figure trotting across the grass. Hugh stood waiting, his face darkening as we watched.

Elizabeth squeezed my arm. "Let's get down there," she whispered. "Hugh doesn't like being made a fool of."

We got there in time to hear Hugh open his big guns. "Any man," he was saying, "who doesn't know how to train an animal to its place shouldn't own one."

The man's face was all polite attention. It was a good face, thin and intelligent, and webbed with tiny lines at the corners of the eyes. There was also something behind those eyes that couldn't quite be masked. A gentle mockery. A glint of wry perception turned on the world like a camera lens. It was nothing anyone like Hugh would have noticed, but it was there all the same, and I found myself warming to it on the spot. There was also something tantalizingly familiar about the newcomer's face, his high forehead, and his thinning gray hair, but as much as I dug into my memory during Hugh's long and solemn lecture I couldn't come up with an answer. The lecture ended with a few remarks on the best methods of dog training, and by then it was clear that Hugh was working himself into a mood of forgiveness.

"As long as there's no harm done—" he said.

The man nodded soberly. "Still, to get off on the wrong foot with one's new neighbors—"

Hugh looked startled. "Neighbors?" he said almost rudely. "You mean that you live around here?"

The man waved toward the aspens. "On the other side of those woods."

"The *Dane* house?" The Dane house was almost as sacred to Hugh as Hilltop, and he had once explained to me that if he were ever offered a chance to buy the place he would snap it up. His tone now was not so much wounded as incredulous. "I don't believe it!" he exclaimed.

"Oh, yes," the man assured him, "the Dane house. I performed there at a party many years ago, and always hoped that someday I might own it."

It was the word *performed* that gave me my clue—that and the accent barely perceptible under the precise English. He had been born and raised in Marseilles—that would explain the accent—and long before my time he had already become a legend.

"You're Raymond, aren't you?" I said. "Charles Raymond."

"I prefer Raymond alone." He smiled in deprecation of his own small vanity. "And I am flattered that you recognize me."

I don't believe he really was. Raymond the Magician, Raymond the Great would, if anything, expect to be recognized wherever he went. As the master of sleight of hand who had paled Thurston's star, as the escape artist who had almost outshone Houdini, Raymond would not be inclined to underestimate himself.

He had started with the standard box of tricks which makes up the repertoire of most professional magicians; he had gone far beyond that to those feats of escape which, I suppose, are known to us all by now. The lead casket sealed under a foot of lake ice, the welded-steel strait jackets, the vaults of the Bank of England, the exquisite suicide knot which nooses throat and doubles legs together so that the motion of a leg draws the noose tighter around the throat—all these Raymond had known and escaped from. And then at the pinnacle of fame he had dropped from sight and his name had become relegated to the past.

When I asked him why, he shrugged.

"A man works for money or for the love of his work. If he has all the wealth he needs and has no more love for his work, why go on?"

"But to give up a great career—" I protested.

"It was enough to know that the house was waiting here."

"You mean," Elizabeth said, "that you never intended to live any place but here?"

"Never—not once in all these years." He laid a finger along his nose and winked broadly at us. "Of course, I made no secret of this to the Dane estate, and when the time came to sell I was the first and only one approached."

"You don't give up an idea easily," Hugh said in an edged voice.

Raymond laughed. "Idea? It became an obsession really. Over the years I traveled to many parts of the world, but no matter how fine the place, I knew it could not be as fine as that house on the edge of the woods there, with the river at its feet and the hills beyond. Someday, I would tell myself, when my travels are done I will come here, and, like Candide, cultivate my garden."

He ran his hand abstractedly over the poodle's head and looked around with an air of great satisfaction. "And now," he said, "here I am."

Here he was, indeed, and it quickly became clear that his arrival was working a change on Hilltop. Or, since Hilltop was so completely a reflection of Hugh, it was clear that a change was being worked on Hugh. He became irritable and restless, and more aggressively sure of himself than ever. The warmth and good nature were still there—they were as much part of him as his arrogance, but he now had to work a little harder at them. He reminded me of a man who is bothered by a speck in the eye, but can't find it, and must get along with it as best he can.

Raymond, of course, was the speck, and I got the impression at times that he rather enjoyed the role. It would have been easy enough for him to stay close to his own house and cultivate his garden, or paste up his album, or whatever retired performers do, but he evidently found that impossible. He had a way of drifting over to Hilltop at odd times, just as Hugh was led to find his way to the Dane house and spend long and troublesome sessions there.

Both of them must have known that they were so badly suited to each other that the easy and logical solution would have been to stay apart. But they had the affinity of negative and positive forces, and when they were in a room together the crackling of the antagonistic current between them was so strong you could almost see it in the air.

Any subject became a point of contention for them, and they would duel over it bitterly: Hugh armored and weaponed by his massive assurance, Raymond flicking away with a rapier, trying to find a chink in the armor. I think that what annoyed Raymond most was the discovery that there was no chink in the armor. As someone with an obvious passion for searching out all sides to all questions and for going deep into motives and causes, he was continually being outraged by Hugh's single-minded way of laying down the law.

He didn't hesitate to let Hugh know that. "You are positively medieval," he said. "And of all things men should have learned since that time, the biggest is that there are no easy answers, no solutions one can give with a snap of the fingers. I can only hope for you that someday you may be faced with the perfect dilemma, the unanswerable question. You would find that a revelation. You would learn more in that minute than you dreamed possible."

And Hugh did not make matters any better when he coldly answered, "And *I* say, that for any man with a brain and the courage to use it there is no such thing as a perfect dilemma."

It may be that this was the sort of episode that led to the trouble that followed, or it may be that Raymond acted out of the most innocent and aesthetic motives possible. But, whatever the motives, the results were inevitable and dangerous.

They grew from the project Raymond outlined for us in great detail one afternoon. Now that he was living in the Dane house he had discovered that it was too big, too overwhelming. "Like a museum," he explained. "I find myself wandering through it like a lost soul through endless galleries."

The grounds also needed landscaping. The ancient trees were handsome, but, as Raymond put it, there were just too many of them. "Literally," he said, "I cannot see the river for the trees, and I am one devoted to the sight of running water."

Altogether there would be drastic changes. Two wings of the house would come down, the trees would be cleared away to make a broad aisle to the water, the whole place would be enlivened. It would no longer be a museum, but the perfect home he had envisioned over the years.

At the start of this recitative Hugh was slouched comfortably in his chair. Then as Raymond drew the vivid picture of what was to be, Hugh sat up straighter and straighter until he was as rigid as a trooper in the saddle. His lips compressed. His face became blood-red. His hands clenched and unclenched in a slow deadly rhythm. Only a miracle was restraining him from an open outburst, and it was not the kind of miracle to last. I saw from Elizabeth's expression that she understood this, too, but was as helpless as I to do anything about it. And when Raymond, after painting the last glowing strokes of his description, said complacently, "Well, now, what do you think?" there was no holding Hugh.

He leaned forward with deliberation and said, "Do you really want to know what I think?"

"Now, Hugh," Elizabeth said in alarm. "Please, Hugh—"

He brushed that aside.

"Do you really want to know?" he demanded of Raymond.

Raymond frowned. "Of course."

"Then I'll tell you," Hugh said. He took a deep breath. "I think that nobody but a damned iconoclast could even conceive the atrocity you're proposing. I think you're one of those people who take pleasure in smashing apart anything that's stamped with tradition or stability. You'd kick the props from under the whole world if you could!"

"I beg your pardon," Raymond said. He was very pale and angry. "But I think you are confusing change with destruction. Surely, you must comprehend that I do not intend to destroy anything, but only wish to make some necessary changes."

"Necessary?" Hugh gibed. "Rooting up a fine stand of trees that's been there for centuries? Ripping apart a house that's as solid as a rock? *I* call it wanton destruction."

"I'm afraid I do not understand. To refresh a scene, to reshape it—"

"I have no intention of arguing," Hugh cut in. "I'm telling you straight out that you don't have the right to tamper with that property!"

They were on their feet now, facing each other truculently, and the only thing that kept me from being really frightened was the conviction that Hugh would not become violent, and that Raymond was far too level-headed to lose his temper. Then the threatening moment was magically past. Raymond's lips suddenly quirked in amusement, and he studied Hugh with courteous interest.

"I see," he said. "I was quite stupid not to have understood at once. This property, which, I remarked, was a little too much like a museum, is to remain that way, and I am to be its custodian. A caretaker of the past, one might say, a curator of its relics."

He shook his head smilingly. "But I am afraid I am not quite suited to that role. I lift my hat to the past, it is true, but I prefer to court the present. For that reason I will go ahead with my plans, and hope they do not make an obstacle to our friendship."

I remember thinking, when I left next day for the city and a long, hot week at my desk, that Raymond had carried off the affair very nicely, and that, thank God, it had gone no further than it did. So I was completely unprepared for Elizabeth's call at the end of the week.

It was awful, she said. It was the business of Hugh and Raymond and the Dane house, but worse than ever. She was counting on my coming down to Hilltop the next day; there couldn't be any question about that. She had planned a way of clearing up the whole thing, but I simply had to be there to back her up. After all, I was one of the few people Hugh would listen to, and she was depending on me.

"Depending on me for what?" I said. I didn't like the sound of it. "And as for Hugh listening to me, Elizabeth, isn't that stretching it a good deal? I can't see him wanting my advice on his personal affairs."

"If you're going to be touchy about it—"

"I'm *not* touchy about it," I retorted. "I just don't like getting mixed up in this thing. Hugh's quite capable of taking care of himself."

"Maybe too capable."

"And what does that mean?"

"Oh, I can't explain now," she wailed. "I'll tell you everything tomorrow. And, darling, if you have any brotherly feelings you'll be here on the morning train. Believe me, it's serious."

I arrived on the morning train in a bad state. My imagination is one of the overactive kind that can build a cosmic disaster out of very little material, and by the time I arrived at the house I was prepared for almost anything.

But, on the surface, at least, all was serene. Hugh greeted me warmly, Elizabeth was her cheerful self, and we had an amiable lunch and a long talk which never came near the subject of Raymond or the Dane house. I said nothing about Elizabeth's phone call, but thought of it with a steadily growing sense of outrage until I was alone with her.

"Now," I said, "I'd like an explanation of all this mystery. The Lord knows what I expected to find out here, but it certainly wasn't anything I've seen so far. And I'd like some accounting for the bad time you've given me since that call."

"All right," she said grimly, "and that's what you'll get. Come along."

She led the way on a long walk through the gardens and past the stables and outbuildings. Near the private road which lay beyond the last grove of trees she suddenly said, "When the car drove you up to the house didn't you notice anything strange about this road?"

"No, I didn't."

"I suppose not. The driveway to the house turns off too far away from here. But now you'll have a chance to see for yourself."

I did see for myself. A chair was set squarely in the middle of the road and on the chair sat a stout man placidly reading a magazine. I recognized the man at once: he was one of Hugh's stable hands, and he had the patient look of someone who has been sitting for a long time and expects to sit a good deal longer. It took me only a second to realize what he was there for, but Elizabeth wasn't leaving anything to my deductive powers. When we walked over to him, the man stood up and grinned at us.

"William," Elizabeth said, "would you mind telling my brother what instructions Mr. Lozier gave you?"

"Sure," the man said cheerfully. "Mr. Lozier told us there was always supposed to be one of us sitting right here, and any truck we saw that might be carrying construction stuff or suchlike for the Dane house was to be stopped and turned back. All we had to do was tell them it's private property and they were trespassing. If they laid a finger on us we just call in the police. That's the whole thing."

"Have you turned back any trucks?" Elizabeth asked for my benefit.

The man looked surprised. "Why, you know that, Mrs. Lozier," he said. "There was a couple of them the first day we were out here, and that was all. There wasn't any fuss either," he explained to me. "None of those drivers wants to monkey with trespass."

When we were away from the road again I clapped my hand to my forehead. "It's incredible!" I said. "Hugh must know he can't get away with this. That road is the only one to the Dane place, and it's been in public use so long that it isn't even a private thoroughfare anymore!"

Elizabeth nodded. "And that's exactly what Raymond told

Hugh a few days back. He came over here in a fury, and they had quite an argument about it. And when Raymond said something about hauling Hugh off to court, Hugh answered that he'd be glad to spend the rest of his life in litigation over this business. But that wasn't the worst of it. The last thing Raymond said was that Hugh ought to know that force only invites force, and ever since then I've been expecting a war to break out here any minute. Don't you see? That man blocking the road is a constant provocation, and it scares me."

I could understand that. And the more I considered the matter, the more dangerous it looked.

"But I have a plan," Elizabeth said eagerly, "and that's why I wanted you here. I'm having a dinner party tonight, a very small, informal dinner party. It's to be a sort of peace conference. You'll be there, and Dr. Wynant—Hugh likes you both a great deal— and," she hesitated, "Raymond."

"No!" I said. "You mean he's actually coming?"

"I went over to see him yesterday and we had a long talk. I explained everything to him—about neighbors being able to sit down and come to an understanding, and about brotherly love and—oh, it must have sounded dreadfully inspirational and sticky, but it worked. He said he would be there."

I had a foreboding. "Does Hugh know about this?"

"About the dinner? Yes."

"I mean, about Raymond's being here."

"No, he doesn't." And then when she saw me looking hard at her, she burst out defiantly with, "Well, *something* had to be done, and I did it, that's all! Isn't it better than just sitting and waiting for God knows what?"

Until we were all seated around the dining room table that evening I might have conceded the point. Hugh had been visibly shocked by Raymond's arrival, but then, apart from a sidelong glance at Elizabeth which had volumes written in it, he managed to conceal his feelings well enough. He had made the introductions gracefully, kept up his end of the conversation and, all in all, did a creditable job of playing host.

Ironically, it was the presence of Dr. Wynant which made even this much of a triumph possible for Elizabeth, and which then turned it into disaster. The doctor was an eminent surgeon, stocky and gray-haired, with an abrupt, positive way about him. Despite his own position in the world he seemed pleased as a schoolboy to meet Raymond, and in no time at all they were as thick as thieves.

It was when Hugh discovered during dinner that nearly all attention was fixed on Raymond and very little on himself that the mantle of good host started to slip, and the fatal flaws in Elizabeth's plan showed through. There are people who enjoy entertaining lions and who take pleasure in reflected glory, but Hugh was not one of them. Besides, he regarded the doctor as one of his closest friends, and I have noticed that it is the most assured of men who can be the most jealous of their friendships. And when a prized friendship is being impinged on by the man one loathes more than anything else in the world—! All in all, by simply imagining myself in Hugh's place and looking across the table at Raymond who was gaily and unconcernedly holding forth, I was prepared for the worst.

The opportunity for it came to Hugh when Raymond was deep in a discussion of the devices used in affecting escapes. They were innumerable, he said. Almost anything one could seize on would serve as such a device. A wire, a scrap of metal, even a bit of paper —at one time or another he had used them all.

"But of them all," he said with a sudden solemnity, "there is only one I would stake my life on. Strange, it is one you cannot see, cannot hold in your hand—in fact, for many people it does not even exist. Yet it is the one I have used most often and which has never failed me."

The doctor leaned forward, his eyes bright with interest. "And it is—?"

"It is a knowledge of people, my friend. Or, as it may be put, a knowledge of human nature. To me it is as vital an instrument as the scalpel is to you."

"Oh?" said Hugh, and his voice was so sharp that all eyes were instantly turned on him. "You make sleight of hand sound like a department of psychology."

"Perhaps," Raymond said, and I saw he was watching Hugh now, gauging him. "You see there is no great mystery in the matter. My profession—my art, as I like to think of it—is no more than the art of misdirection, and I am but one of its many practitioners."

"I wouldn't say there were many escape artists around nowadays," the doctor remarked.

"True," Raymond said, "but you will observe I referred to the art of misdirection. The escape artist, the master of legerdemain, these are a handful who practice the most exotic form of that art. But what of those who engage in the work of politics, of advertising, of salesmanship?" He laid his finger along his nose in the familiar gesture, and winked. "I am afraid they have all made my art their business."

The doctor smiled. "Since you haven't dragged medicine into it I'm willing to go along with you," he said. "But what I want to know is, exactly how does this knowledge of human nature work in your profession?"

"In this way," Raymond said. "One must judge a person carefully. Then, if he finds in that person certain weaknesses he can state a false premise and it will be accepted without question. Once the false premise is swallowed, the rest is easy. The victim will then see only what the magician wants him to see, or will give his vote to that politician, or will buy merchandise because of that advertising." He shrugged. "And that is all there is to it."

"Is it?" Hugh said. "But what happens when you're with people who have some intelligence and won't swallow your false premise? How do you do your tricks then? Or do you keep them on the same level as selling beads to the savages?"

"Now that's uncalled for, Hugh," the doctor said. "The man's expressing his ideas. No reason to make an issue of them."

"Maybe there is," Hugh said, his eyes fixed on Raymond. "I have found he's full of interesting ideas. I was wondering how far he'd want to go in backing them up."

Raymond touched the napkin to his lips with a precise little flick, and then laid it carefully on the table before him. "In short," he said, addressing himself to Hugh, "you want a small demonstration of my art."

"It depends," Hugh said. "I don't want any trick cigarette cases or rabbits out of hats or any damn nonsense like that. I'd like to see something good."

"Something good," echoed Raymond reflectively. He looked around the room, studied it, and then turned to Hugh, pointing toward the huge oak door which was closed between the dining room and the living room, where we had gathered before dinner.

"That door is not locked, is it?"

"No," Hugh said, "it isn't. It hasn't been locked for years."

"But there is a key to it?"

Hugh pulled out his key chain, and with an effort detached a heavy, old-fashioned key. "Yes, it's the same one we use for the butler's pantry." He was becoming interested despite himself.

"Good. No, do not give it to me. Give it to the doctor. You have faith in the doctor's honor, I am sure?"

"Yes," said Hugh dryly, "I have."

"Very well. Now, doctor, will you please go to that door and lock it."

The doctor marched to the door, with his firm, decisive tread, thrust the key into the lock, and turned it. The click of the bolt snapping into place was loud in the silence of the room. The doctor returned to the table holding the key, but Raymond motioned it away. "It must not leave your hand or everything is lost," he warned.

"Now," Raymond said, "for the finale I approach the door, I flick my handkerchief at it"—the handkerchief barely brushed the keyhole—"and presto, the door is unlocked!"

The doctor went to it. He seized the doorknob, twisted it dubiously, and then watched with genuine astonishment as the door swung silently open.

"Well, I'll be damned," he said.

"Somehow," Elizabeth laughed, "a false premise went down easy as an oyster."

Only Hugh reflected a sense of personal outrage. "All right," he demanded, "how was it done? How did you work it?"

"I?" Raymond said reproachfully, and smiled at all of us with obvious enjoyment. "It was you who did it all. I used only my little knowledge of human nature to help you along the way."

I said, "I can guess part of it. That door was set in advance, and when the doctor thought he was locking it, he wasn't. He was really unlocking it. Isn't that the answer?"

Raymond nodded. "Very much the answer. The door *was* locked in advance. I made sure of that, because with a little fore-thought I suspected there would be such a challenge during the evening, and this was the simplest way of preparing for it. I merely made certain that I was the last one to enter this room, and when I did I used this." He held up his hand so that we could see the sliver of metal in it. "An ordinary skeleton key, of course, but sufficient for an old and primitive lock."

For a moment Raymond looked grave, then he continued brightly, "It was our host himself who stated the false premise when he said the door was unlocked. He was a man so sure of himself that he would not think to test anything so obvious. The doctor is also a man who is sure, and he fell into the same trap. It is, as you now see, a little dangerous always to be so sure."

"I'll go along with that," the doctor said ruefully, "even though it's heresy to admit it in my line of work." He playfully tossed the key he had been holding across the table to Hugh, who let it fall in front of him and made no gesture toward it. "Well, Hugh, like it or not, you must admit the man has proved his point."

"Do I?" said Hugh softly. He sat there smiling a little now, and it was easy to see he was turning some thought over and over in his head.

"Oh, come on, man," the doctor said with some impatience. "You were taken in as much as we were. You know that."

"Of course you were, darling," Elizabeth agreed.

I think that she suddenly saw her opportunity to turn the pro-ceedings into the peace conference she had aimed at, but I could have told her she was choosing her time badly. There was a look in Hugh's eye I didn't like—a veiled look which wasn't natural to him. Ordinarily, when he was really angered, he would blow up a violent storm, and once the thunder and lightning had passed he would be honestly apologetic. But this present mood of his was different. There was a slumbrous quality in it which alarmed me.

He hooked one arm over the back of his chair and rested the other on the table, sitting halfway around to fix his eyes on Ray-mond. "I seem to be a minority of one," he remarked, "but I'm sorry to say I found your little trick disappointing. Not that it wasn't cleverly done—I'll grant that, all right—but because it wasn't any more than you'd expect from a competent locksmith."

"Now there's a large helping of sour grapes," the doctor jeered.

Hugh shook his head. "No, I'm simply saying that where there's a lock on a door and the key to it in your hand, it's no great trick to open it. Considering our friend's reputation, I thought we'd see more from him than that."

Raymond grimaced. "Since I had hoped to entertain," he said, "I must apologize for disappointing."

"Oh, as far as entertainment goes I have no complaints. But for a real test—"

"A real test?"

"Yes, something a little different. Let's say, a door without any locks or keys to tamper with. A closed door which can be opened with a fingertip, but which is nevertheless impossible to open. How does that sound to you?"

Raymond narrowed his eyes thoughtfully, as if he were considering the picture being presented to him. "It sounds most interesting," he said at last. "Tell me more about it."

"No," Hugh said, and from the sudden eagerness in his voice I felt that this was the exact moment he had been looking for. "I'll do better than that. I'll *show* it to you."

He stood up brusquely and the rest of us followed suit—except Elizabeth, who remained in her seat. When I asked her if she wanted to come along, she only shook her head and sat there watching us hopelessly as we left the room.

We were bound for the cellars, I realized, when Hugh picked up a flashlight along the way, but for a part of the cellars I had never seen before. On a few occasions I had gone downstairs to help select a bottle of wine from the racks there, but now we walked past the wine vault and into a long, dimly lit chamber behind it. Our feet scraped loudly on the rough stone, the walls around us showed the stains of seepage, and warm as the night was outside, I could feel the chill of dampness turning my chest to gooseflesh. When the doctor shuddered and said hollowly, "These are the very tombs of Atlantis," I knew I wasn't alone in my feeling, and felt some relief at that.

We stopped at the very end of the chamber, before what I can best describe as a stone closet built from floor to ceiling in the farthest angle of the walls. It was about four feet wide and not quite twice that in length, and its open doorway showed impenetrable blackness inside. Hugh reached into the blackness and pulled a heavy door into place.

"That's it," he said abruptly. "Plain solid wood, four inches thick, fitted flush into the frame so that it's almost airtight. It's a beautiful piece of carpentry, too, the kind they practiced two hundred years ago. And no locks or bolts. Just a ring set into each side to use as a handle." He pushed the door gently and it swung open noiselessly at his touch. "See that? The whole thing is balanced so perfectly on the hinges that it moves like a feather."

"But what is it for?" I asked. "It must have been made for a reason."

Hugh laughed shortly. "It was. Back in the bad old days, when a servant committed a crime—and I don't suppose it had to be more of a crime than talking back to one of the ancient Loziers —he was put in here to repent. And since the air inside was good for only a few hours at the most, he either repented damn soon or not at all."

"And that door?" the doctor said cautiously. "That impressive door of yours which opens at a touch to provide all the air needed —what prevented the servant from opening it?"

"Look," Hugh said. He flashed his light inside the cell and we crowded behind him to peer in. The circle of light reached across the cell to its far wall and picked out a short, heavy chain hanging a little above head level with a U-shaped collar dangling from its bottom link.

"I see," Raymond said, and they were the first words I had heard him speak since we had left the dining room. "It is truly ingenious. The man stands with his back against the wall, facing the door. The collar is placed around his neck, and then—since it is clearly not made for a lock—it is clamped there, hammered around his neck. The door is closed, and the man spends the next few hours like someone on an invisible rack, reaching out with his feet to catch the ring on the door which is just out of reach. If he is lucky he may not strangle himself in his iron collar, but may live until someone chooses to open the door for him."

"My God," the doctor said. "You make me feel as if I were living through it."

Raymond smiled faintly. "I have lived through many such experiences and, believe me, the reality is always a little worse than the worst imaginings. There is always the ultimate moment of terror, of panic, when the heart pounds so madly you think it will burst through your ribs, and the cold sweat soaks clear through you in the space of one breath. That is when you must take yourself in hand, must dispel all weakness, and remember all the lessons you have ever learned. If not—!" He whisked the edge of his hand across his lean throat. "Unfortunately for the usual victim of such a device," he concluded sadly, "since he lacks the essential courage and knowledge to help himself, he succumbs."

"But you wouldn't," Hugh said.

"I have no reason to think so."

"You mean," and the eagerness was creeping back into Hugh's voice, stronger than ever, "that under the very same conditions as someone chained in there two hundred years ago you could get this door open?"

The challenging note was too strong to be brushed aside lightly. Raymond stood silent for a long minute, face strained with concentration, before he answered.

"Yes," he said. "It would not be easy—the problem is made formidable by its very simplicity—but it could be solved."

"How long do you think it would take you?"

"An hour at the most."

Hugh had come a long way around to get to this point. He asked the question slowly, savoring it. "Would you want to bet on that?"

"Now, wait a minute," the doctor said. "I don't like any part of this."

"And I vote we adjourn for a drink," I put in. "Fun's fun, but we'll all wind up with pneumonia, playing games down here."

Neither Hugh nor Raymond appeared to hear a word of this. They stood staring at each other—Hugh waiting on pins and needles, Raymond deliberating—until Raymond said, "What is this bet you offer?"

"This. If you lose, you get out of the Dane house inside of a month, and sell it to me."

"And if I win?"

It was not easy for Hugh to say it, but he finally got it out. "Then I'll be the one to get out. And if you don't want to buy Hilltop I'll arrange to sell it to the first comer."

For anyone who knew Hugh it was so fantastic, so staggering a statement to hear from him, that none of us could find words at first. It was the doctor who recovered most quickly.

"You're not speaking for yourself, Hugh," he warned. "You're a married man. Elizabeth's feelings have to be considered."

"Is it a bet?" Hugh demanded of Raymond. "Do you want to go through with it?"

"I think before I answer that, there is something to be explained." Raymond paused, then went on slowly, "I am afraid I gave the impression—out of pride, perhaps—that when I retired from my work it was because of a boredom, a lack of interest in it. That was not altogether the truth. In reality, I was required to go to a doctor some years ago, the doctor listened to the heart, and suddenly my heart became the most important thing in the world. I tell you this because, while your challenge strikes me as being a most unusual and interesting way of settling differences between neighbors, I must reject it for reasons of health."

"You were healthy enough a minute ago," Hugh said in a hard voice.

"Perhaps not as much as you would want to think, my friend."

"In other words," Hugh said bitterly, "there's no accomplice handy, no keys in your pocket to help out, and no way of tricking anyone into seeing what isn't there! So you have to admit you're beaten."

Raymond stiffened. "I admit no such thing. All the tools I would need even for such a test as this I have with me. Believe me, they would be enough."

Hugh laughed aloud, and the sound of it broke into small echoes all down the corridors behind us. It was that sound, I am sure— the living contempt in it rebounding from wall to wall around us —which sent Raymond into the cell.

Hugh wielded the hammer, a short-handled but heavy sledge, which tightened the collar into a circlet around Raymond's neck, hitting with hard even strokes at the iron which was braced against the wall. When he had finished I saw the pale glow of the radium-painted numbers on a watch as Raymond studied it in his pitch darkness.

"It is now eleven," he said calmly. "The wager is that by midnight this door must be opened, and it does not matter what means are used. Those are the conditions, and you gentlemen are the witnesses to them."

Then the door was closed, and the walking began.

Back and forth we walked—the three of us—as if we were being compelled to trace every possible geometric figure on that stony floor, the doctor with his quick, impatient step, and I matching Hugh's long, nervous strides. A foolish, meaningless march, back and forth across our own shadows, each of us marking the time by counting off the passing seconds, and each ashamed to be the first to look at his watch.

For a while there was a counterpoint to this scraping of feet from inside the cell. It was a barely perceptible clinking of chain coming at brief, regular intervals. Then there would be a long silence, followed by a renewal of the sound. When it stopped again I could not restrain myself any longer. I held up my watch toward the dim yellowish light of the bulb overhead and saw with dismay that barely twenty minutes had passed.

After that there was no hesitancy in the others about looking at the time and, if anything, this made it harder to bear than just wondering. I caught the doctor winding his watch with small, brisk turns, and then a few minutes later he would try to wind it again, and suddenly drop his hand with disgust as he realized he had already done it. Hugh walked with his watch held up near his eyes, as if by concentration on it he could drag that crawling minute hand faster around the dial.

Thirty minutes had passed.

Forty.

Forty-five.

I remember that when I looked at my watch and saw there were less than fifteen minutes to go I wondered if I could last out even that short time. The chill had sunk so deep into me that I ached with it. I was shocked when I saw that Hugh's face was dripping with sweat, and that beads of it gathered and ran off while I watched.

It was while I was looking at him in fascination that it happened. The sound broke through the walls of the cell like a wail of agony heard from far away, and shivered over us as if it were spelling out the words.

"Doctor!" it cried. *"The air!"*

It was Raymond's voice, but the thickness of the wall blocking it off turned it into a high, thin sound. What was clearest in it was the note of pure terror, the plea growing out of that terror.

"Air!" it screamed, the word bubbling and dissolving into a long-drawn sound which made no sense at all.

And then it was silent.

We leaped for the door together, but Hugh was there first, his back against it, barring the way. In his upraised hand was the hammer which had clinched Raymond's collar.

"Keep back!" he cried. "Don't come any nearer, I warn you!"

The fury in him, brought home by the menace of the weapon, stopped us in our tracks.

"Hugh," the doctor pleaded, "I know what you're thinking, but you can forget that now. The bet's off, and I'm opening the door on my own responsibility. You have my word for that."

"Do I? But do you remember the terms of the bet, doctor? This door must be opened within an hour—*and it doesn't matter what means are used!* Do you understand now? He's fooling both of you. He's faking a death scene, so that you'll push open the door and win his bet for him. But it's my bet, not yours, and I have the last word on it!"

I saw from the way he talked, despite the shaking tension in his voice, that he was in perfect command of himself, and it made everything seem that much worse.

"How do you know he's faking?" I demanded. "The man said he had a heart condition. He said there was always a time in a spot like this when he had to fight panic and could feel the strain of it. What right do you have to gamble with his life?"

"Damn it, don't you see he never mentioned any heart condition until he smelled a bet in the wind? Don't you see he set his trap that way, just as he locked the door behind him when he came into dinner! But this time nobody will spring it for him—nobody!"

"Listen to me," the doctor said, and his voice cracked like a whip. "Do you concede that there's one slim possibility of that man being dead in there, or dying?"

"Yes, it is possible—anything is possible."

"I'm not trying to split hairs with you! I'm telling you that if that man is in trouble every second counts, and you're stealing that time from him. And if that's the case, by God, I'll sit in the witness chair at your trial and swear you murdered him! Is that what you want?"

Hugh's head sank forward on his chest, but his hand still tightly gripped the hammer. I could hear the breath drawing heavily in his throat, and when he raised his head, his face was gray and haggard. The torment of indecision was written in every pale sweating line of it.

And then I suddenly understood what Raymond had meant that day when he told Hugh about the revelation he might find in the face of a perfect dilemma. It was the revelation of what a man may learn about himself when he is forced to look into his own depths, and Hugh had found it at last.

In that shadowy cellar, while the relentless seconds thundered louder and louder in our ears, we waited to see what he would do.

THE HAND IS QUICKER THAN THE EYE

Erle Stanley Gardner

A few years ago, Nicaragua decided to commemorate the fiftieth anniversary of the founding of Interpol by issuing a special series of stamps depicting the most famous detectives in literature. Sherlock Holmes was honored, of course, as were Nero Wolfe, Ellery Queen, Dupin, Poirot, and other giants of the genre—twelve in all. One of these immortals was not a detective, however, but a lawyer: Erle Stanley Gardner's invincible Perry Mason. It is the recognizable image of Raymond Burr which appears on the stamp, paying tribute to the popular television series as well as to the more than eighty books in which Mason defends the innocent.

Gardner was himself a lawyer and his most famous literary creations have legal backgrounds: Doug Selby, better known as the D.A., the male half of the Bertha Cool–Donald Lam team, a disbarred lawyer, and two characters who appeared in pulp magazines, lawyers Ken Corning and Peter Wennick, both largely forgotten today.

Lester Leith is a different kettle of herring. He is on the opposite side of the legal coin, a confidence man of the first rank. He appeared in about seventy-five adventures, beginning in 1929 and extending through the vital days of the pulps. He solves crimes merely by reading newspaper accounts of them, then proves to the thieves that crime does not pay by "liberating" their ill-gotten gains. There is little fear of legal retribution because his victims are not likely to press charges. Leith turns the swag over to charity—minus 20 percent for "costs of collection."

This story first appeared in 1939; it has never been published in book form until now.

Lester Leith, sprawled in a chaise longue on the screened balcony of his apartment, read the newspaper account of the theft with considerable interest.

A few paces behind him, Edward H. Beaver, the police undercover man who had insinuated his way into Leith's service as a valet, made a great show of dusting; but his beady eyes were riveted on the slender, well-knit figure of the man whom police considered the most brilliant crime technician of the decade.

The newspaper account was somewhat vague. The theft had taken place at the residence of Charles Sansone, the well-known authority on Asiatic history, who had recently returned from an extended trip in the Orient. The victim of the theft had been one Katiska Shogiro, a Japanese gentleman who owned a pearl necklace of immense value. The clasp of the necklace was of that peculiar bright yellow gold which characterizes Chinese workmanship, and while undoubtedly the necklace bore a resemblance to a priceless museum piece which had vanished from the storeroom of the Forbidden City, Shogiro smilingly explained that the resemblance was purely superficial.

Sansone, it seemed, was interested in the necklace. It had even been intimated that he comtemplated its purchase. In any event, Katiska Shogiro had been invited to the highly cosmopolitan dinner party at which Frank Thoms, the big-game hunter, Peter Grier, the explorer, and Silman Shore, the expert trapshooter, were also present. Because Charles Sansone's secretary, Mah Foy, was Chinese, Sansone had tactfully given her a day and night off, although she usually supervised the details of his dinner parties, and was generally present in the capacity of hostess.

Beaver, the pseudo-valet, becoming more and more absorbed in watching the man upon whom he spied, slowed down his dusting operations until his hands barely moved.

Leith, looking up, said, "Something wrong, Scuttle?"

The valet resumed his duties with alacrity, replying, "No, sir."

It had long been a matter of great irritation to him that Leith refused to address him by the name of Beaver, but habitually referred to him as "Scuttle," a nickname bestowed because of a fancied resemblance in Leith's mind to a reincarnated pirate. Now the valet concealed his irritation by seizing the opportunity to discuss the theft of the necklace. He knew from experience that if he could turn Leith's razor-sharp mind to the problem of the theft, it was quite possible that Leith, with no more information than was given by the newspaper accounts, would spot the thief. Once that had been done, the spy knew that a series of unrelated incidents would then occur which would culminate in Leith urbanely walking off with the loot under such circumstances that the police would be just one jump behind. Later, one of Leith's charities would be enhanced by the exact amount which Leith had received for the sale of the loot, less 20 percent which the police shrewdly suspected was retained by Leith as the costs of collection.

Beaver lived in anticipation of the moment when Leith's smooth-working mind would overlook a bet, and the police would not be that one jump behind. So far that had not happened. At times the police had been almost on Leith's heels, but they had never quite caught up.

"A most baffling crime, sir," the spy said.

"Baffling?" Leith asked.

"Yes, sir. The pearl necklace."

"Oh, that," Leith said. "I fail to see anything baffling about it, Scuttle. It's a run-of-the-mill crime. I suppose it would seem baffling to the untrained mind because of the mystery which seems to surround the manner in which Shogiro acquired the necklace in the first place. However, that's only background. The crime itself is quite simple."

"Simple, sir!" the valet exclaimed.

"Exactly," Leith said.

"Perhaps, then," the spy said, in his best wheedling technique, "you can tell me who committed it."

Leith selected a cigarette and said quite calmly, "That's true, Scuttle."

"What's true, sir?"

"Perhaps I could tell you the identity of the thief."

"Yes, sir?" the spy asked eagerly.

Leith struck a match.

"I'm waiting, sir," the valet said.

"A most commendable habit," Leith said, "that of patience,

Scuttle. I recommend it most highly. At times. I've noticed a tendency on your part to be impatient."

"I beg your pardon, sir, but you said you were going to tell me the identity of the culprit."

Leith said, "Oh, no, Scuttle. There you go, misunderstanding me again. You merely mentioned that *perhaps* I could tell you the identity of the thief, and I admitted that *perhaps* I could."

The spy flushed, but he kept his voice under control. "Yes, sir. I appreciate the distinction. Thank you, sir."

"Don't mention it," Leith said.

The spy tried another approach. "Of course, sir," he said, with a cunning gleam in his eye, "any man of ordinary intelligence could point out the *probable* criminal in five cases out of ten. The police, however, have a different problem. They have to *prove* that a man is guilty."

Leith said, almost musingly, "After all, Scuttle, why not? The crime has everything to challenge the imagination of the investigator: Oriental background, fabulous pearls, a mysterious disappearance, and—yes, Scuttle, I will commission you to do it."

"To do what, sir?"

"To go through the newspapers and note every single fact about the crime."

The spy's eyes lit up. "Yes, sir. When shall I start?"

"Right now," Leith said. "And by the way, Scuttle—"

"Yes, sir."

"I notice that Mr. Sansone has a Chinese secretary."

"Yes, sir."

"Find out about her. Get a full description of the pearls. I think Mr. Shogiro stated they were the duplicate of a string which has been illustrated in some publication on the museum pieces of China. Find out whether Peter Grier speaks Chinese, and whether Frank Thoms, the big-game hunter, intends to go to Alaska this fall for Kodiac grizzly. And, oh, yes, find out if Shogiro has given up his proposed trip to Europe. As I remember it, he intended to sail the middle of the month."

"Yes, sir."

"And get me the address of every manufacturer in the city who handles equipment for amateur magicians."

The spy blinked.

"And," Leith said, "I think that is all—for the moment."

Lester Leith strolled into the newspaper office with a want ad.

"Help Wanted—Female," he said to the young woman behind the counter. "Run this ad in a box so that it will attract considerable attention."

She read it through, then glanced quickly at Leith. "It will cost a lot," she explained.

"Quite all right," he assured her.

She counted the words, made a note of the total, and then looked at the $100-bill which Leith took from his pocket and slipped across the counter. She opened the cash drawer, made change, and handed him a receipt.

"I want the earliest possible publication," he said.

"Yes, sir."

She followed him with her eyes as he left the office, then hastily beckoned to the girl on her left. "Gosh, Mamie," she said, "don't you wish you were Chinese?"

"Shucks, no," the girl said, patting her hair. "Who was the swell, Gert?"

"Read it," Gertrude said, handing Leith's copy over to Mamie. "He wants a Chinese secretary who is young and free to travel. He wants someone who knows Chinese history and who has a college education. He offers to pay $600 a month and all traveling expenses. . . . Think of working for a guy like him and getting six hundred bucks a month for it!"

Meanwhile, Leith took a taxi to one of the largest bookstores. "I want some of your best books," he said, "on legerdemain."

And while this was happening, Beaver sat closeted with Sergeant Ackley at police headquarters. Ackley worried the stump of a cold cigar as he listened, his forehead puckered into a prodigious frown.

When the undercover man had finished, Ackley said, "Listen, Beaver, if we could put this thing across, we could make a cleanup. Shogiro has offered a reward of five thousand bucks and no questions asked."

The undercover man whistled.

Sergeant Ackley said, "I'll get you the file, and you can go over it. Don't let him get away on this, Beaver. This is the biggest thing we've ever tackled. If we could nail him, and at the same time get that necklace, we could kill two birds with one stone. Think of what you could do with twenty-five hundred bucks in cold, hard cash."

The undercover man sighed.

"Don't overlook Charles Sansone in this thing," Sergeant Ackley said. "The facts point to him as the slicker, although he's fired his Chinese secretary—a nice way of diverting suspicion from himself."

"Why?" Beaver asked. "That is, what reason does he give for firing her?"

"Seems she'd violated instructions. Sansone told her to clear out and not come back until after the dinner. He had his eye on that necklace—wanted to buy it from Shogiro. Shogiro wanted to sell it. They were doing a little trading on the price. Apparently, the necklace is a pip, in addition to which it was worn by the empress dowager of China and has a lot of history attached to it. . . . By the way, what's all this stuff about the amateur magic?"

"Hanged if I know," Beaver said. "You know what he does when he starts working on a case. He gets a lot of goofy stuff together. Some of it's important, some of it isn't—but it all fits in some way."

"Well," Sergeant Ackley chuckled, "this is once he'll come a cropper. He hasn't any head start on us this time. We're in on the ground floor."

Lester Leith eyed the Chinese girl thoughtfully. Her skin was smooth as old ivory. The eyes were slightly slanted. She was in her late twenties, and her voice had that delicacy of expression that is indicative of a race which must have vocal chords so finely trained, and an ear so delicately receptive, as to distinguish any one of the eight tones in which a syllable of the Chinese language may be spoken.

She said, very casually, "There are not a great number of Chinese girls in this country who know both the Chinese written and spoken language, have first-hand experience with their native land, and possess a degree from a Western university."

"I daresay that is right."

Her eyes glittered in a swift survey of his face, but her face remained blank. "One might almost have thought," she said, "that the advertisement was intended to single me out."

Leith said, "I hadn't thought of it that way, but anyone who did possess the rather unusual combination of qualifications could be pardoned for thinking so."

"Then you pardon me?"

"Yes."

There was the ghost of a twinkle in her eyes as she said, "Then I think so."

Leith laughed. "All right," he said. "Miss Foy, I acknowledge the guilt. To be perfectly frank with you, I read in the newspaper account of the theft of that necklace that you had been dismissed because of a violation of instructions."

"My dismissal," she said, "was unjust."

"What happened?"

"My employer suggested that because he was desirous of purchasing the necklace, and because Mr. Shogiro would be suspicious if one of my race was a guest at the dinner, that it would be well to absent myself, not only from the dinner, but from the house."

"You failed to do so?"

"I did exactly as he requested. Unfortunately, however, I discovered that I had lost some very valuable jade which my mother had given me. It was a pendant, and evidently the supporting ring had almost worn through. The pendant had caught on something, and all that was left was the chain."

"So you returned to the house?" Lester Leith asked.

"I did. I tried to return in such a way that no one would notice. But I failed."

"Did you find the jade?"

"Yes. It had caught on one of the drapes in my bedroom and had dropped to the floor."

"What sort of chap is Sansone?" Leith asked.

She said, very calmly, "I'm afraid I do not understand. Is it not the purpose to ask the former employer concerning the character of the employee, rather than to ask the employee about the character of her former employer?"

Leith said, "Doubtless that is the custom, but I asked the question for a very particular purpose."

"He is a gentleman," Mah Foy said.

Leith drummed with the tips of his fingers on the table. "If perhaps he had thought that a theft would occur while Shogiro was at his house, and wished to protect you, he might have been shrewd and considerate enough to suggest that you arrange a perfect alibi for yourself."

He saw quick flashing interest in her eyes.

"But how could he have anticipated that a theft would occur while Shogiro was under his roof?"

Lester Leith brushed the question aside. "That, of course, is something for the police to consider. It is just a thought."

"Are you then a detective?"

"Heaven forbid!"

"And do you actually have need for a secretary, Mr. Leith, or did you wish to interrogate me?"

"Both," Leith said. "If you would like the job, you're hired. The salary is six hundred a month. You will have your traveling expenses taken care of and, if necessary, we can consider a reasonable wardrobe a part of your traveling expenses."

"You intend to travel?"

"Yes."

"May I ask where?"

"To the Hawaiian Islands."

She raised her eyebrows. "To Honolulu?"

"Yes."

"That will be delightful," she said. "I am considered an expert typist. I can take rapid dictation in shorthand, and I feel certain that I could do your work. When do you wish me to start?"

"At once."

"You mean now—this instant?"

"Yes."

She said, "Very well. May I see the typewriter please?"

Leith said, "There won't be any typing for the present, Miss Foy."

"What is it you wish me to do?"

"Wait here for my return."

"So I may make appointments?"

"Yes," Leith said, getting to his feet. "I have a valet who should be back at any moment. His name is Beaver. I call him Scuttle. He has been with me for some time, and I have the greatest confidence in his loyalty and integrity."

"But one should expect that of all employees."

"Exactly," Leith said, "but I can double it in the case of Scuttle. I have absolutely no secrets from him."

"That is very nice."

Leith said, "He will probably ask you questions about what you are doing here and what was said in this interview."

She said, "My race considers that it is the province of the servant to work, of the master to ask questions."

"Well, Scuttle has his own ideas," Leith said, "and I would be particularly happy if you would answer all his questions quite truthfully, because, you see, if you didn't, he might think I had cautioned you not to, and I wouldn't want to hurt him for the world."

"Very well," she said.

"And," Leith said, "I really feel, Miss Foy, that you shouldn't hold any grudge against Mr. Sansone. It may well have been that he asked you to leave for your own protection. As I get the story from the newspapers, Mr. Shogiro called on him the day before the dinner at which the necklace was stolen. At that time, Sansone inspected the necklace. The next evening Shogiro came to dinner and brought the necklace with him. It was in a carved ivory jewel case which Shogiro carried in the inside pocket of his coat. After dinner, at the request of Mr. Sansone, he produced the necklace so that Mr. Sansone's guests could see it. At that time, the necklace was found to be an imitation. The assumption, of course, is that a substitution had been made sometime during the evening. But isn't it quite possible that Mr. Sansone had perhaps recognized the necklace as an imitation *when he first saw it?*"

"In that case, why did he not tell Mr. Shogiro?"

"Because," Leith said, "he wasn't certain. You'll note that the dinner was for men only—men who knew something about pearls and about China. In fact, I believe it was one of the guests who observed that the pearls were imitation."

"So I understand," she said.

Leith abruptly got to his feet. "That," he said, "is all, Miss Foy. You are hired. Your salary starts at once. If anyone should appear and ask for me, state that I have gone out and will return in an hour."

Leith opened the door of his apartment and stood to one side. A taxi driver, loaded with parcels, staggered into the room.

"Where do want these put, boss?"

"Any place," Leith said. "My man will put them away. Here, Scuttle, give a hand."

The undercover man, who had been engaged in low-voiced conversation with Mah Foy, jumped forward to help the cabdriver.

Leith said, "There's more in the cab, Scuttle. If you will go back with the driver, you can bring the other parcels up."

When the valet and the cabdriver had gone, Mah Foy said, in her musical voice, "May I assist you in opening the packages and putting them away, Mr. Leith?"

"Not yet," Leith said. "We'll await Scuttle's return. Scuttle will be interested to know what's in the packages. He's very curious, in case you hadn't noticed."

Mah Foy said, "I have noticed."

"Questions?" Leith asked.

"Many questions."

Leith said, "I trust that you remembered to answer them fully."

"Quite fully," she said.

Leith grinned. "We'll stack these bundles to one side," he said. Together they moved the packages so that the doorway was cleared.

Even the Chinese girl showed curiosity as the undercover man and the cabdriver returned with another load of packages.

"That all?" Leith asked.

"That's all, sir," the cabdriver said.

When the cabdriver had left, Leith closed the door and surveyed the array of packages. "Very well, Scuttle," he said, "you may open them."

Eagerly the undercover man produced a knife and started cutting cords.

Leith said, "Be careful, Scuttle. Many of those things are fragile."

"Yes, sir," the undercover man said.

He pulled back the heavy, brown wrapping paper, lifted the lid off a box, and brought out a glass bowl. "What's this?" he said.

"A goldfish bowl, of course, but one that has valuable properties."

"I don't see anything special, sir."

Leith said, "You'll observe, Scuttle, that there's a circular partition in that bowl. When it is filled with water, this circular partition acts as a huge magnifying glass. Place that in front of an audience, and a small section of the bowl directly in back of it is magnified so that it looks as though the whole bowl if filled with water in which goldfish are swimming. As a matter of fact, only a small portion of the bowl contains water or goldfish."

The undercover man straightened. "The audience?"

"Exactly," Lester Leith said calmly.

Scuttle appeared slightly bewildered.

"But I don't see what an audience has to do with it, if you don't mind my saying so, sir?"

Leith said, "We are going in for prestidigitation, legerdemain, sleight of hand, optical illusions, parlor magic, and general hocus-pocus, Scuttle."

"You mean you're going to take that up as an occupation, sir?"

"Tut, tut," Leith said. "You should know me better. I prefer to retain my amateur standing. Well, open the others, Scuttle."

The undercover agent opened a flat, heavy package. "What's this? It looks like an ordinary double slate like those used in school."

"You shouldn't say that, Scuttle," Leith said. "It dates you. However, you are quite right. Observe, Scuttle, how easy it is to communicate with the unseen forces which guard our lives. Ah, there it is—the sponge."

"Yes, sir," the spy said, producing the sponge from a corner of the box.

"Now, Scuttle, if you will just step into the kitchen and dampen this sponge, you can wipe off both sides of the slate. There should be some slate pencils—ah, here they are."

Leith took out a package of slate pencils.

The undercover man, holding the sponge in his hand, stepped into the kitchenette. Leith glanced across at Mah Foy, the Chinese girl, and winked at her.

She watched him with an impassive countenance on which there was not the slightest flicker of expression, but just as the valet returned with the moistened sponge, she lowered her own right lid, although her face remained as calmly placid as though it were carved from old ivory.

"Now then," Leith said, "if you'll just take this slate, Scuttle, and clean it with the wet sponge. Make absolutely certain that there is no writing on it."

"Yes, sir," the valet said, wiping off the surfaces of the slate.

"Now take it into the bathroom, get a towel, and dry it carefully."

Beaver produced a towel and carefully dried the slate.

"Now," Leith said, "I don't want you to let that slate out of your sight, Scuttle. First, we'll put a piece of pencil between the leaves of the slate. Hold it open, Scuttle, just so. That's right. Now we'll close it, and you might take it over and place it on that table in the far corner of the room, being careful not to take your eyes from it for even a moment."

The valet did as he was instructed.

"Now, Scuttle, watch closely. See if you can see the spirits."

"The spirits, sir?"

"Yes, Scuttle, the—*there they are!*"

A faint squeaking noise became distinctly audible.

"Good heavens, sir!" the valet exclaimed. "Is that noise coming from—from the slate?"

"From the slate, Scuttle."

Beaver's eyes widened.

"And now, Scuttle," Leith said, as the noise ceased, "I wouldn't be surprised if we had a message from the unseen world."

"But surely, sir, you're fooling."

"Not at all, Scuttle. Just pick up the slate and bring it to me. Ah, that's right."

Leith took the slate from the valet. Only the Chinese girl noticed the manner in which he fumbled with the catch as he opened the double slate.

A message, written in a distinctly feminine hand, appeared

across the inner surface of the slate. It read: *First warning. Be very careful, Beaver, not to tell any falsehoods after you have started for Honolulu. Ruth.*

The spy was visibly shaken. "Good heavens!" he said.

Leith frowned. "What the devil are they talking about, Scuttle?"

"Who?" the spy asked.

"The spirits. And what is all this about a trip to Honolulu?"

"I assure you, sir, I don't know."

"And who is Ruth? Someone perhaps who has gone to the other shore, Scuttle?"

"The other shore, sir?"

"Yes, Scuttle. I—"

"Good grief!" the valet suddenly exclaimed, staring at Leith with eyes which seemed about to bulge from their sockets.

"What is it, Scuttle?"

"Ruth!" Beaver exclaimed. "My wife!"

"Your wife, Scuttle? I didn't know you were married."

"It was sometime ago, sir. I was married for two years. But she was—she was killed in an auto accident."

Leith said, closing the slate as though that disposed of the matter, "Undoubtedly, Scuttle, the message is from your departed wife who wishes to warn you against the result of any falsehood should you take a trip to Honolulu."

Beaver turned pale. "It's uncanny."

"Oh, quite," Leith said airily, dismissing the subject. "But we can't neglect these other boxes, Scuttle."

The spy took a handkerchief from his pocket and mopped his forehead. "If it's all the same to you, sir," he said, "I'd like to postpone the rest of it for a while. I'm feeling shaky, sir. I—"

Leith said, "That's all right, Scuttle. You'd better have a drink. Perhaps Miss Foy will join us."

The Chinese girl shook her head.

"Well," Leith said, "a couple of Scotches and soda, Scuttle—or perhaps you'd prefer to make yours a double brandy?"

"Yes, sir, I would."

When the valet had filled the glasses, Leith sat on the arm of a chair, casually sipping his Scotch and soda. "Do you know, Scuttle," he said, "there's one other thing I didn't get."

"What's that, sir?"

"A stooge."

"But I don't understand."

"Did you ever see a magician on the stage?"

"Yes, sir, a couple of times."

"Then you've noticed that a magician is invariably accompanied by a young stage assistant, a very beautiful young woman who is easy on the eye and whose skirts are always very short?"

"Yes, sir, I do remember that."

Scuttle was puzzled.

"Exactly, Scuttle," Leith said. "That's the first principle of stage magic—divided attention. The idea is that the hand is quicker than the eye, but the eye can't watch the hand when it's stealing glances at a pair of beautiful legs. So what we need, Scuttle, is a girl with beautiful legs."

"Yes, sir. Do you wish me to get you one, sir?"

"No, Scuttle, I will select my own stooge."

And Lester Leith abruptly left the apartment.

The man who ran the theatrical employment agency was frankly skeptical.

"Do I understand," he said, "that you wish to hire a young woman who has been thrown out of employment by the recent drive against burlesque shows?"

"That's exactly it," Leith said. "I want a young woman who is beautiful, who is accustomed to the public admiration of her curves, and who has just about given up hope."

The agent said, "You might try Ora Sanders. That poor kid certainly has had a tough time. Last Friday her roommate tried to commit suicide. Ora hocked everything she had except the clothes she stood in, and kicked through with every last cent to help the kid out."

"Where," Leith asked, "can I find Miss Sanders?"

"I'll reach her for you. What's the nature of the employment?"

Leith coughed deprecatingly. "I'm an amateur magician," he said. "I want a young woman who can assist me."

"You can't go wrong on Ora," the agent said. "Let me give her a ring."

"If possible," Leith said, "I'd prefer to see her in her room rather than here in the office, and I'd like to see her right away."

The agent dialed a number, said, "Miss Sanders, please," and then, after a moment, "I'm sending a Mr. Leith to discuss employment at $50 a week. Is that satisfactory? . . . Fine. . . . Yes, almost at once."

He hung up, and said to Leith, "She'll be glad to see you. Here's her address."

Leith found Ora Sanders to be a blonde with light blue eyes that were waging a losing battle with the fine wrinkles of worry, a determined chin, and smiling lips. Her small, poorly lighted room was well covered with autographed theatrical pictures.

Leith introduced himself.

"Manna from heaven!" she exclaimed. "Come on in."

"I am in somewhat of a hurry," Leith explained.

"In that event, you can dispense with telling me that times are hard, that there aren't many jobs available, and I'll be fortunate to get work with you; and I'll dispense with telling you that times aren't hard for me, that I've had two offers lately, but that neither is just what I want, so that I *might* consider something good."

Leith smiled. "The salary is $50 a week."

"My agent told me that."

"Your duties," Lester said, "will be highly personal."

"Oh, *oh!*" she remarked.

"I'm an amateur magician," Leith went on. "I have noticed that professional magicians usually have a young woman with beautiful legs appear on the stage to hand them their props."

She stepped back, placed her ankles together, and raised her skirt. "How are my legs?" she asked.

"Perfect," Leith said. "I can't imagine anyone in the audience keeping his mind on the disappearing watch with scenery like that to look at."

She dropped her skirts and with them her manner of easy banter. "Listen," she said, "I simply *have* to get a job. This isn't the sort of work I've been doing. I'm not certain that it's the kind I'd like to do, but if you're willing to take a chance on me, I'm willing to take a chance on you."

Leith opened his wallet and took out $100. "Two weeks' salary," he explained. "And here's an extra hundred."

"An extra hundred," she echoed.

He nodded. "I want you to get some new clothes for your act. Brevity is the soul of wit, and I think you understand what is required."

He reached once more into his wallet and took out three $100-bills. "Here," he said, "is some expense money. Get a wardrobe."

"Now, wait a minute," she said. "I'm not going to pinch myself because I don't want to wake up, but let's not go overboard."

Leith said, "It's quite all right. You're going to take a trip on a boat. You'll need a couple of dinner gowns, a sports outfit, and accessories."

She said again, "Now, wait a minute. What do you want in return for all this?" And her eyes stared at Lester Leith with disconcerting frankness.

"Loyalty," Leith said. "A willingness to follow instructions."

She said, "Listen, I'm no tin angel, but—"

Leith smiled, put his wallet away, and said, "I think we understand each other, Miss Sanders. If you'll get out and do your shopping, I'll telephone instructions later."

The undercover man sat across the table from Sergeant Ackley and said, "Well, sergeant, it's all off."

"What is?" Ackley asked.

"The whole thing," Beaver said. "It's just a runaround. He's either gone nuts, or else he's become suspicious and is taking us for a ride."

"Nonsense," Sergeant Ackley said, "not with a priceless string of matched pearls with a historical value which makes it a collector's item."

"All right, then," Beaver said, "suppose *you* figure it out."

Sergeant Ackley said, "That's what I'm here for, Beaver. You do the leg work. I furnish the brain that directs your energies. You're the contractor. I'm the architect."

"All right, then," the undercover man said, "figure this out. He hires Charles Sansone's Chinese secretary. He hires a girl with the prettiest figure you've ever seen. He gets a thousand dollars' worth of parlor magic stuff, and announces he's taking the whole kit and kaboodle to Honolulu."

"To Honolulu?" Sergeant Ackley exclaimed. Then a look of

smug satisfaction came over Ackley's countenance. "The trouble with you, Beaver, is that you haven't a deductive mind. You're observant and conscientious, but you're dealing with a man who has a chain-lightning brain, and you can't think fast enough to put two and two together."

"Meaning," Beaver said, "that you have a highly trained mind."

"Naturally," Sergeant Ackley said modestly, "or I wouldn't be here."

"All right," Beaver said, "*you* tell *me,* then. What's the answer?"

Sergeant Ackley picked up the morning paper, opened it to an inside page, and said, "Get a load of this. 'The international competition of skeet shooters is scheduled to take place in Honolulu two weeks from today. Silman Shore, a noted trapshooter who has already broken several records, expects to compete. Shore's photo is shown above.'"

Beaver's face showed amazed comprehension. "By gosh," he said, "it *may* make sense at that!"

"Of course it makes sense," Sergeant Ackley said. "Now, tell me exactly what's been going on."

Beaver said, "He wanted to know all about how the crime was committed. I told him. Most of it he could get from the newspapers anyway, and he's a shark at deducing things from what he reads in the papers."

"Exactly what did you tell him?" Sergeant Ackley asked.

"I told him about Shogiro passing the necklace around for examination. Sansone pretended it was a social party. As a matter of fact, every one of the men there knows something about gems— or about Chinese history. Grier had seen the necklace when he was in the Forbidden City five years ago, and remembered it."

"Go on."

"Well, he was interested in finding out how the theft took place. I told him all we knew, that the necklace was shown around, that Grier was the last to look at it. He passed it to Sansone who had already looked at it. Sansone passed it back to Shogiro. Then, after a while, Sansone announced that he was intending to buy the necklace and asked Shore if he had noticed the workmanship of the catch. Shore said he'd paid more attention to the pearls than to the catch, and Shogiro obligingly took the ivory jewel case out of his pocket and handed it to Shore. Shore opened it, picked up the necklace, turned toward the light, and then, said, "By George, this thing is counterfeit!' And then, of course, all hell broke loose.

"Well, Leith asked me to look up all the people who were there. I found out that Grier knows a lot about China. I found out that Charles Sansone is a well-known amateur magician. I found out that Thoms, the big-game hunter, is going to Alaska—"

"Is he?" Sergeant Ackley asked.

"He is," Beaver said.

"Well," Sergeant Ackley said, "as I see the situation, we have three suspects. Grier could very well have substituted necklaces when he handed the necklace to Sansone. Grier had already seen the necklace, knew exactly what it looked like, and could have had an imitation prepared.

"Sansone could have done it. He'd seen the necklace a couple of days before and he could have had an imitation ready. He's pretty good at sleight of hand. We can't leave Silman Shore out— he was the one to discover that it was an imitation."

"And don't overlook the fact that this Shogiro may be pulling a fast one," Beaver said.

"I don't think so," Sergeant Ackley observed. "He had nothing to gain."

"Well," Beaver said, "Leith was very much interested in finding out where Shogiro was going."

"And you found out?"

"Yes. Shogiro's canceling the trip he planned to Europe and is returning to Japan."

Sergeant Ackley's brows furrowed. "By way of Honolulu?" he asked.

"What do you think?" the undercover man replied.

The giant liner *Monterey* sent the long blast of a booming whistle echoing over Los Angeles harbor. On the pier below, thousands of hysterical, waving people shouted farewells to the passengers who lined the decks. Streamers of colored paper, stretching from ship to shore, fluttered in the vagrant, night breeze. The air was filled with shouts and laughter.

Then a dark strip of water appeared between the pier and the white sides of the big ship. A surge of white water churned up from the stern. The big liner, graceful as a yacht, throbbed into motion, and the sleek white sides began to glide along the pier.

Lester Leith said to Ora Sanders, "Well, here we are, on our way —the start of adventure."

She looked up at him with bright eyes. "To think that *I* would ever have an experience like this," she breathed. "Oh, it's wonderful, simply wonderful!"

Leith moved over to rest his elbows on the teakwood rail. He glanced at Mah Foy standing motionless, the breeze swirling her skirts into gentle motion, her face utterly without expression.

Leith caught sight of the huge figure of Beaver towering above the other passengers. He motioned to him, and the valet joined him.

"You've looked over the passenger list, Scuttle?"

"Yes, sir."

"Who's aboard of those at the dinner party when the necklace disappeared?"

"Shogiro," the undercover man said, "Mah Foy, Charles Sansone, and Silman Shore."

"Sansone?" Lester Leith exclaimed in surprise.

"Yes, sir."

"What's *he* doing aboard?"

"Apparently just taking a trip to the islands."

Leith frowned thoughtfully. "Seen anyone else you know, Scuttle?"

"No, sir."

"Who's your cabin mate?"

The undercover man frowned.

"An old gentleman inclined to seasickness, I understand, and something of an invalid, sir. He'll probably be a nuisance. He asked me particularly to entertain my friends outside the cabin. He expects to spend most of the time in bed."

"Most annoying," Leith said. "Too bad you didn't get a more agreeable companion."

"Yes, sir," the valet said. "but I'm quite certain that the trip will be very enjoyable. Is there anything you wish, sir? I've laid your clothes out and—"

"No, Scuttle. That will be all for tonight. Take life easy and enjoy yourself. I'm dog tired and am going to turn in."

Leith waved to Ora Sanders. Her face showed disappointment. She moved swiftly to his side and said, "Aren't you going to watch the mainland out of sight? Have you no romance?"

He whispered, "I'm setting a trap. Meet me on the boat deck in fifteen minutes."

Leith said good night to Mah Foy and started in the direction of his cabin, but detoured to the boat deck where Ora Sanders found him a quarter of an hour later.

Leith said, "I want to be where I can see without being seen. Would you consider the duties of your employment too onerous if you sat over here in the shadow of the lifeboat and went into what is technically known as a huddle?"

She laughed. "I'd have been disappointed to think that I was starting on a trip to the Hawaiian Islands unhuddled," she said.

They sat close together in the shadows, talking in low tones. The couples who promenaded past them grew fewer in number as the ship swung out into the Pacific and the bow began to sway gently to the surge of the incoming swell.

Suddenly Leith exerted pressure on her arm. Ora Sanders followed the direction of his glance.

Beaver, accompanied by a stocky, bull-necked, broad-shouldered man, was promenading past. They heard him say, "It's okay now, Sarge. I told him you were an old invalid and to keep out of our cabin."

They walked past.

"Who was that?" Ora Sanders asked.

Leith smiled. "That," he said, "was Sergeant Arthur Ackley of the metropolitan police force. I don't wish him any bad luck, but I hope he is highly susceptible to seasickness."

On the second day out, Mah Foy said to Lester Leith, "I haven't any definite idea of what you had in mind when you employed me. Certainly it wasn't to work."

Leith, sprawled in a deck chair and watching the intense blue waters of a semitropic ocean, smiled and said, "I am a man of extremes. When I work, I work long hours. When I loaf, I loaf long hours."

"So it would seem. Did you know that Mr. Sansone was going to be on this boat?"

"Frankly," Leith said, "I did not. I'm sorry if his presence causes you any embarrassment."

"It doesn't," she said, "only he was surprised at seeing me here."

"I can understand that."

"Did you know that Katiska Shogiro was going to be a passenger?"

"I suspected that he might go as far as Honolulu."

"On this ship?"

"Yes."

"Did you know that Mr. Shore was going to be a passenger?"

"Yes," Leith said. "I knew that in advance."

She remained silent for several minutes, then she said, "If you have any work for me, please call."

"Wait a minute," Leith said as she arose from the deck chair. "I have one thing to ask of you."

"What is that, Mr. Leith?"

"Don't do anything rash. Promise me that you won't—at least until we are in Honolulu."

"Why?" she asked. "What made you think I contemplated doing anything you might describe as rash?"

"I have my reasons," Leith said.

She laughed. "My race has a proverb. 'Stirring the water does not help it to boil.' "

"A very good proverb," Leith said, "although I don't subscribe to it."

"You don't?"

"No," he said. "Stirring the water may not help it to boil, but it has other advantages."

"What are they?"

"Oh, for one thing," Leith said, "it scrambles the contents of the pot, and makes it difficult for an observer to know that the primary purpose of putting the pot on the stove was to get the water to boil."

"Are you, by any chance, referring to the mysterious cabin mate who takes surreptitious midnight strolls with your valet?"

"Oh," Leith said, "you know about that?"

She said, "In my position, I try to know everything."

"And thought that you should tell me about it?"

"Yes."

"Thanks," Leith said, "for your loyalty."

She met his eyes. "There is one other thing. I was commissioned by my government to recover that necklace, sell it, and bring the proceeds back to China."

"Thanks for telling me," Leith said. "I surmised it."

Leith was reading a book when Ora Sanders, wearing a short-skirted sports outfit, shook off a group of admirers to drop into the empty deck chair beside him.

"When," she asked, "do we do sleight of hand?"

"Tonight," Leith said. "An impromptu entertainment by passengers. I have agreed to do a turn."

"That's fine," she said.

"You will, of course, wear your stage costume."

"I was hoping for that."

"Hoping?" he asked.

"Yes," she laughed. "So many of the male passengers have expressed a desire to see more of me."

"There is always the swimming tank," Leith suggested.

"I thought it might be better not to give them a preview."

"Very wise," he said. "By the way, have you met the captain?"

"Yes," she said.

"Think you could turn loose the battery of your eyes on him and make a suggestion?"

She nodded.

"At two o'clock tomorrow afternoon," Leith said, "I notice a skeet shoot is scheduled. I think it would be an excellent idea to advise the captain that we have aboard in the person of Mr. Silman Shore a trapshooter of nationwide reputation. It would be very appropriate if Mr. Shore should give a little exhibition for the benefit of the passengers. He—" He broke off at the expression on her face. "What is it?"

"How many people do you have making suggestions?" she asked.

"Why?"

"That suggestion," she said, "was communicated to the captain this morning, shortly after the skeet shoot was noticed on the bulletin board."

"Who suggested it to him?"

"A Japanese by the name of Shogiro, a very interesting gentleman who has spent much of his time trying to cultivate my acquaintance."

Leith considered the statement in thoughtful silence. At length, he said, "Proof that great minds run in the same channels."

"Tell me," she said, "did my announcement distress you?"

"Not distress me," Leith said, "but it does give me food for thought—food which must be carefully chewed lest it give me mental indigestion."

She slid out of the chair with her sports skirt sliding up the well-shaped legs. "Okay," she said, "I'll run along before you get a mental tummy ache."

"Don't do that again," Leith said.

"What?"

"Distract my attention," he said. "Remember that your province is to distract the attention of the audience."

"And I can't practice on you a little bit?"

"Well," Leith said judicially, "just a little—a *very* little bit."

Half an hour later, Katiska Shogiro dropped casually into the deck chair next to Lester Leith's. After a moment, he said in his very polite manner, "Excussse, pleassse, but would it be interrupting your honorable meditations unduly if I humbly ask for match?"

"Not in the least," Leith said, and handed over a packet of matches.

Shogiro lit his cigarette. "Passengers," he said conversationally, "have explain that very skillful magician is aboard contained in the person of honorable you. Is possible perhaps that attentive student may look forward to exhibition tonight?"

Leith said, "I would hardly commend my amateurish attempts to the observation of an interested student. You know something of sleight of hand?"

Shogiro laughed. "Only very small ability," he said, "but large interest."

Leith said, "The idea of magic is to furnish entertainment. To a student of the art, the tricks will prove very transparent. I trust that you will remember that explanation destroys the mystery."

"Oh, quite," Shogiro said.

"I trust that I can count upon your silent cooperation?"

"Even clam," Shogiro explained, "is like parrot compared with Japanese contemplation of magic performed by good friend who gives matches to humble and unworthy student."

Lester Leith's face showed relief.

"You are perhaps of long-time proficiency?" Shogiro asked.

"No," Leith said. "My performance makes up in equipment that which it lacks in skill."

"Equipment?" Shogiro asked.

"Equipment for misdirecting attention," Leith said. "As a student, you will realize that the success of all magic lies in misdirecting the attention of the observer."

"Oh, quite," Shogiro said.

"Therefore," Leith said, "I have sought to avail myself of the greatest attention distracter known to science."

"Referring to which?"

"The pulchritude of feminine curves," Leith said. "Miss Sanders has consented to act as my accomplice."

"Very estimable distraction," Shogiro said.

"I trust it will prove quite sufficient."

"Confidence indeed is not misplaced," Shogiro remarked, arising abruptly from the chair. "And now humble student begs permission to retire and leave honorable master in contemplation of mystifying trickery to be performed in evening. Thanking you very much."

"Not at all," Leith said, and Shogiro walked rapidly down the deck, his manner that of a man who is embarking upon a very definite mission.

Entertainment that night was in the hands of the passengers who contributed various forms of diversion. A dance team headed for Australia put on a tap dance, an artistic waltz, and a variation of the rhumba. A poetess whose work had been published in some of the national magazines recited her favorite poem. A pianist played a selection from the classics, followed by some comedy jazz and a ragtime interpretation of one of the more familiar tunes of the Gay Nineties.

Beaver slipped through a rear door and took a seat in the back of the social hall. A moment later he signaled, and Sergeant Ackley, making himself as inconspicuous as possible, slipped into the adjoining chair and slumped down so as to make himself less noticeable. "Watch him, Beaver," he whispered. "He's going to pull something with this sleight-of-hand business."

Up in the front row, Mah Foy was separated only by two chairs from Katiska Shogiro, who sat perfectly still, a smile of fixed politeness frozen on his face.

A couple of stewards started bringing in various pieces of equipment. The purser, who acted as master of ceremonies, said, "We have with us tonight a man who can do tricks that would make masters envious. These are no ordinary sleight-of-hand tricks. These optical illusions represent the latest achievements of science. It gives me great pleasure to introduce Mr. Lester Leith."

Leith came forward and bowed. There was polite applause.

He said, "May I have your indulgence for a moment, please?" and walked down to where Mah Foy was seated.

"Shortly after the performance starts," he whispered in the ear of the Chinese girl, "a man who was at that dinner is going to get up and leave the room. I want you to follow him and later tell me where he goes and what he does."

Mah Foy nodded.

Leith stepped back to the lighted circle and said, "Ladies and gentlemen, let me present my assistant, Miss Ora Sanders."

Ora, attired in a robe which covered her from neck to ankles, came forward and bowed. There was polite applause. She slipped off the robe and stood before the audience, garbed in black and white; a low-cut black blouse with white trimmings, a very short black skirt, a small white lace apron, and high black stockings.

The applause hesitated for a moment, then burst out anew. When the applause had subsided, Lester Leith said, "I'm going to ask your indulgence, ladies and gentlemen. Despite the comments of the purser, I feel that my performance may fall far short of his glowing description. However, I will do my best."

The purser said, "What's the idea of the apology? You told me this afternoon you were the best in the West."

There was a roar of laughter.

Leith said, "A man always exaggerates his qualifications to get the job. No hard feelings."

He advanced and shook hands with the purser. Suddenly he said, "Wait a minute. You don't want this," and took an egg from the purser's side coat pocket. "And what's this? Tut, tut. You shouldn't be carrying a black widow spider around on your sleeve!"

With a startled exclamation the purser jumped back and brushed at his arm. The spider dropped to the floor and lay with its rubber legs quivering.

Leith said, "Tut, tut. Having killed my pet, you should at least give him a decent burial. Here, take this little casket. Put him in that."

He handed the purser a small box. The purser bent forward, and Leith signaled to Ora Sanders, who handed him a loaded slapstick.

Just as the purser picked up the spider, the slapstick connected with that portion of his trousers which stretched tight in the stooping process. The impact set off the blank cartridge which had been imbedded in the slapstick, and the purser's reactions were all that the gleeful audience could have anticipated.

When the discomfited purser had retired, Leith nodded to Ora Sanders. She brought forward a table and, opening a box, took out a goldfish bowl, in which the audience could plainly see goldfish swimming around.

Leith looked at the audience, then singled out Silman Shore. "Mr. Shore," he called.

"What is it?"

"You're an expert hunter, I believe?"

"Yes."

"Can you describe to the audience what you see in this bowl?"

"Goldfish," Shore said.

Leith said, "Tut, tut. You need to have your eyes examined." He reached in the goldfish bowl and pulled out a live, kicking rabbit and, thereafter, while the audience applauded, he took out object after object from a bowl which apparently contained only live goldfish swimming about in water.

"Thank you, Mr. Shore," Leith said, "for your cooperation. After all, you know, it adds to our amusement when we see our fellow travelers taking part. Mr. Shogiro, might I ask you to step forward, please."

"It is pleasure," Shogiro said.

Leith said, "I noticed that you seemed rather hungry in the dining room tonight. Apparently, you're a man with a large appetite. . . . Ah, yes, I thought so. Turn around please."

Shogiro turned around, and Lester Leith reached down the back of his coat to pull out a bunch of celery which he held up to the audience, then tossed to Ora Sanders.

"Now wait a minute," he said as Shogiro, smiling politely, started back toward his seat. "What's that you have in your pocket?"

Shogiro followed the direction of Leith's eyes, and said, "Excusse, pleasse. That is handkerchief for wiping eyes which have tears of laughter caused by amusement at honorable act."

There was just a trace of sarcasm in what he said, although his manner was that of smiling politeness. The audience applauded and waited for Leith's comeback.

Leith reached out to take the corner of the silk handkerchief in his thumb and forefinger. He started pulling it out an inch or two at a time. "Very nice handkerchief," he said, "but what is this?"

Shogiro, smiling broadly, watched Lester Leith pull out yards and yards of silk ribbon and handkerchiefs. When he had finished he tossed the ball of silk to Ora Sanders.

Shogiro, standing very still, said, "Honorable gentleman have removed everything from pocket?"

"I certainly hope so," Leith said.

"Are sure is not more?" Shogiro asked.

The audience, sensing that the Japanese was trying to turn the tables on Leith, leaned forward in their seats.

"Well," Leith said, "if there's anything left in that pocket, Mr. Shogiro, you may keep it."

The audience laughed at the sally, but the laughter changed into roars as Shogiro, reaching into the pocket, pulled out what apparently was a human finger. He held it up and bent it double, showing that it was made of colored rubber. He inserted it between the fingers of his own hand, moved his hand rapidly, and the finger had vanished.

"Excusse, pleasse," Shogiro said, "but in my country when honorable gentleman perform trick with false finger, unwinding yards of silk ribbon stored therein, is always customary to remove empty finger after trick is completed."

Shogiro turned and started toward the front row once more, but Leith again called him back. This time there was an ominous glitter in the eyes of the Japanese, although his lips continued to frame a polite smile.

"Anyone who turns the tables on me that well," Leith said, "is entitled to a reward. Now let me see. What can I give you? I guess food would be the best. How about it, Miss Sanders? Can we cook up a little food for Mr. Shogiro?"

"Oh, I think so," she said.

Leith said, "Well, we might at least fry him an egg."

"We haven't any more eggs," Miss Sanders said.

"That's too bad," Leith said, "but—what's this? Oh, yes, our friend, Shogiro, seems to have something else up his sleeve."

Leith picked up Shogiro's forearm, held his coat by the cuff, and shook it gently. Two eggs rolled out.

Leith, juggling the eggs in his hand, said, "That's fine. Now if we had a frying pan. Has anyone in the audience a frying pan?"

In the silence that followed, one of the stewards, who had been coached in the part, called out, "Why don't you look in the fishbowl?"

"An excellent idea," Leith said.

He walked over to the fishbowl, still holding the eggs, reached down, apparently plunging his hand into the water, and brought out a frying pan without in any way disturbing the fish.

"Now," he said, "we're ready. If you'll hold a match for us, Miss Sanders—"

He broke both eggs into the frying pan, tossed the shells to one side, held the frying pan over a match which Ora Sanders lighted, shook the pan, and then approached the Japanese. "Here you are," he said.

Sergeant Ackley, in the back row, said to Beaver, "Watch him like a hawk, Beaver. He's getting ready to pull something. He's worked the build-up. Now, he's after blood."

Lester Leith, with the frying pan held rather high so that the Japanese could not see its interior, said, "A plate, please, Miss Sanders."

Ora Sanders picked up a plate from a table, started toward Leith, and stumbled. The plate slipped from her hands, fell to the floor, and broke into two pieces.

For a moment there was a gasp from the audience, but it was quickly apparent that Ora Sanders's fall had been far too gracefully done to be accidental. She got to her feet, smiled, then stared ruefully at a run in her stocking.

With the quick instinct which is the natural reaction of a woman, she lifted her abbreviated skirt to see how far up the run had gone, then suddenly, as though realizing her position, laughed and dropped the skirt back into place.

Lester Leith said, "That's too bad. Just pick up the fragments of the plate, Miss Sanders, and I'll see what I can do with them."

She picked up the two segments of the plate and handed them to Leith, who took them in his left hand, still holding the frying pan in his right hand.

"Oh," he said, "this isn't bad."

Ora Sanders stepped forward, swiftly passing between Leith and the audience. A half second later, Leith gave his left hand a deft twist, and there was the plate unbroken and apparently none the worse for having been dropped.

"Now," Lester Leith said, "we'll put the egg into the plate."

He tilted the frying pan and shook it.

"Hello!" he exclaimed. "What's this?"

What came out of the frying pan was not a cooked egg, but a very fine pearl necklace which dangled for a moment on the lip of the frying pan, then dropped with a clatter to the plate which Leith was holding.

Leith dropped the frying pan, picked up the pearl necklace, and said, "What an egg!"

The audience applauded. Leith, as though the trick had been completed, turned back toward the table on which Ora Sanders was rearranging his stage properties.

For a long moment Shogiro stood rigid, the smile frozen on his face. Then he took a quick step toward Leith and said, "Begging honorable pardon, but that is *my* necklace!"

Leith turned to face him, urbanely smiling, holding the necklace in his hand. "Certainly it's your necklace," he said, and handed it to the Japanese.

Shogiro took the necklace, stared at it for a moment, then said ominously, "Begging honorable pardon, but this is not same necklace which came from frying pan."

Leith looked at it and said, "By George, I don't believe it is! It does seem different."

"It is different," Shogiro said. "Begging pardon, this necklace very cheap. Other necklace my property."

Leith said, "Well, there's only one thing for us to do then, and that's put the necklace in the frying pan, and see if we can change it back into the original necklace."

He dropped the necklace into the frying pan, shook it for a moment, then snatched up the plate which Miss Sanders had placed on the table. He tilted the frying pan over the plate—and what came out was not a necklace, but apparently an omelet.

"Tut, tut," Lester Leith said, "I'm afraid we dropped the necklace into those eggs, and we now have a pearl omelet. Here. I'll wrap it up in a handkerchief, and you can take it with you."

He picked up a silk handkerchief, placed it over the plate, apparently wrapped up the omelet, and handed it to Shogiro.

Shogiro took the handkerchief. He shook it out. It was empty. The plate was empty. With quick, purposeful strides, Shogiro walked over to the table, and snatched up the frying pan. It too was empty.

The audience roared.

Leith, smiling broadly, bowed to the right and left, marking the termination of the act.

Shogiro, standing ominously tense, watched him for several seconds, then without a word turned and walked back to his seat.

Leith looked over the audience. Mah Foy was no longer in the front row, and Silman Shore seemed to have vanished as completely as had the omelet in the handkerchief.

Sergeant Ackley and Beaver sat in their stateroom staring moodily at each other.

"Well," Beaver said, "there it is."

Sergeant Ackley said, "It's plain as the nose on your face. Shogiro had the necklace all the time. Leith knew it. He wanted an opportunity to pick his pockets. If he'd tried to do it surreptitiously, there'd have been hell to pay.

"Beaver, do you realize what it means? It means that everyone figures that necklace was as much a part of Leith's magic show as the frying pan and the fake goldfish bowl. Here we've traveled thousands of miles and organized an elaborate spy system to find out when he was going to steal that necklace, and damned if he doesn't do it *right in front of an audience.*"

Beaver said, "Well, he can't get away from us. We know who has the necklace *now.*"

Sergeant Ackley nodded.

There was a moment of silence, then Beaver said, "What pocket did he get the necklace out of, Sergeant? It was done so quick I couldn't see."

"You didn't see?" Ackley said.

"No."

Sergeant Ackley frowned at the undercover man. "I thought so," he said. "The whole thing was staged to happen according to schedule. The girl pretended to fall, and dropped the plate. That distracted the attention of the women in the audience. A broken plate is a domestic tragedy to a woman. The men just don't give a damn about a broken plate, so the girl had her stockings fixed so that when she stumbled, she could pull a run in one of them. She ran her hands up along her leg and that grabbed the men's attention. At any rate, it accounted for yours."

"I only glanced there for half a second," Beaver said. "As soon as I did, I knew I mustn't take my eyes off Leith, so I looked right back."

"That half second was all he needed," Sergeant Ackley said.

"Well," Beaver insisted, "what pocket *did* he take it out of?"

"Well," Sergeant Ackley said, "it was—"

"I thought so," said Beaver. "You were looking at her leg too."

There was a period of uncomfortable silence, then Sergeant Ackley said, "Okay, Beaver, we won't try to do anything here. There are too many places on the ship where he can hide it. He's far too clever to keep it in his stateroom, but he won't dare to *leave* it on the ship. When he gets ashore in Honolulu, he'll have it in his baggage, or on him. Now then, Beaver, it's up to you to go through that baggage the minute he hits shore. I'll see to it that he's detained, and you'll have an opportunity."

"Suppose he has it on him?"

Sergeant Ackley laughed grimly and said, "There's lots of ways of playing that little game. Beaver, send a wireless to the chief of police at Honolulu. Make it read like this: 'MAN WHO WILL DISEMBARK FROM MONTEREY WITH WHITE RIBBON PINNED TO CROWN OF HAT WILL HAVE $10,000 IN DOPE CONCEALED SOMEWHERE IN HIS CLOTHES.'"

Sergeant Ackley beamed.

"That means they'll search his baggage, and find the necklace," Beaver said.

"No, it won't," Sergeant Ackley observed. "You see, they won't know who it is until they see the white ribbon on the hat. As his valet, you can take his hat and brush it just before he starts ashore. Then is when you'll pin on the white ribbon. They'll search him first. You'll get the baggage through before they find out anything about the setup. When they do, I'll explain to them that it was just a joke on the part of Shogiro who was sore because Leith had made a monkey out of him in front of an audience."

Beaver blinked thoughtfully. "It sounds like a good scheme," he said, "only—"

"Only what?" Sergeant Ackley snapped.

"Only I have an idea it won't work," the undercover man blurted.

Leith, lying in a deck chair, enjoyed the tropical ocean breeze. He seemed relaxed, completely at his ease.

Mah Foy slipped into the adjoining deck chair, leaned forward, and spoke in a low voice. "It was Silman Shore who left the social hall," she said.

"Yes, I know," Leith said. "Where did he go, to his stateroom or somewhere else?"

"He went to his stateroom."

"And what did he do? Do you know?"

"Yes," she said. "I could watch him through the window. He

made no attempt to conceal what he was doing. He went to his gun case, picked up his gun, took it out on deck, and started practicing. I strolled by and asked him why he wasn't at the entertainment, and he said that amateurish stuff annoyed him, that he had to put on an exhibition the next day, and he wanted to limber up his muscles."

Leith said, "Most interesting. I think I'll take up skeet shooting . . . And by the way, tomorrow afternoon at two o'clock when Silman Shore is putting on his exhibition, I think it would be an excellent idea for you to be with the purser, and you'll kindly tell Ora Sanders to hunt up the first mate who has been so attentive to her and spend about an hour with him."

Mah Foy thought for a moment, then she said, "How about Scuttle?"

Leith grinned and said, "Let Scuttle be wherever he pleases."

"And you?" she asked.

Leith smiled. "I think," he said, "that I'll have some business with the captain."

Mah Foy said very gently, "That first necklace—as I glimpsed it hanging on the edge of the frying pan—seemed to be the empress dowager's necklace."

"Did it indeed?" Leith said smiling. "An excellent example of optical illusion."

She said, "My first loyalty is to my country. I warn you."

Leith smiled at her. "I wouldn't want it to be otherwise," he said.

It was a calm day with no wind. The sharp prow of the *Monterey* hissed through the water. Passengers, promenading the spotless decks or sprawled lazily in deck chairs, relaxed to the joys of ocean travel.

Katiska Shogiro paced the deck alone. His short, stubby legs propelled his torso with short, vigorous steps. His lips were no longer smiling. When Silman Shore stepped out of the smoking room to lounge against the rail, Shogiro saw him and stopped beside him.

"Excussse, pleassse," he said. "You are recollecting last night?"

"What about it?" Shore asked.

"Pardon intrusion upon your honorable thoughts, but did you notice necklace which came from frying pan?"

Shore snapped his fingers. "Bosh!"

"Not bosh," Shogiro insisted. "I am particularly calling attention to necklace which you saw on night of Sansone dinner. Is not look the same?"

"I didn't even look at it," Shore said impatiently. "I hate all that kindergarten stuff. The minute he started pulling that old hokum, I got up and walked out."

"Thanking you very much," Shogiro said, and resumed pacing the deck, but this time his forehead was creased in a definite frown.

Charles Sansone sought out Leith.

"You'll pardon me," he said, "for intruding. I haven't met you. My name's Sansone. I was a very interested spectator at your performance last night."

Leith shook hands and said, "I'm very glad to know you. I'm afraid my performance was rather crude, but then, when persons are traveling shipboard, any form of spontaneous entertainment is interesting."

"I was particularly interested in one phase of your performance," Sansone said.

"Indeed. What was that?"

"When you made the necklace come out of the frying pan."

Leith laughed deprecatingly. "I'm afraid," he said, "I can't explain how that was done."

"I don't want to know how it was done," Sansone said. "I want to know where you got that necklace."

Leith said, laughing, "You didn't think it was composed of genuine pearls, did you?"

"I didn't know," Sansone said. "It looked very much like a necklace I saw at one time. I don't know whether you've read about it or not."

"Read about it?" Leith asked.

"Yes. A necklace which was stolen from Mr. Shogiro—unfortunately at a dinner where I was the host."

"Oh!" Leith exclaimed.

"I'm rather surprised at your surprise," Sansone told him dryly, "inasmuch as you have engaged the young woman who was formerly my secretary, and have apparently cultivated at least a speaking acquaintance with Shogiro."

"Just what are you getting at?" Leith asked. "As far as the necklace is concerned, it was a part of the stage properties which I use in my act."

"Doesn't it impress you as being a remarkable coincidence," Sansone asked, "that a stage property which you acquired at a house dealing in parlor magic would be almost an exact duplicate of a pearl necklace which was worn by the empress dowager of China?"

"What the devil are you insinuating?"

Sansone got to his feet. "Nothing," he said, and then added significantly, "as yet. I'm something of a magician myself."

He bowed and walked away.

A deck steward made the rounds of the deck, tapping on the ship's xylophone, and calling out, "Trapshooting on the afterdeck, please. An exhibition of trapshooting by a national champion."

Passengers started getting up from chairs, stretching, yawning, and drifting toward the stern. After a while, the popping of a gun could be heard as blue rocks sailed out over the water, only to vanish into puffs of powder as a charge of well-directed shot struck them.

Silman Shore seemed rather bored by what he was doing. His manner was that it was kindergarten stuff.

Bang! Bang!

There wasn't a single miss.

At length Shore finished, acknowledged the applause, placed his gun under his arm, and turned back toward his stateroom.

Charles Sansone, walking along the deck said, "Just a word with you, Shore, if you don't mind."

The two men talked together in low tones for about fifteen minutes. Together they strolled back to the cabin occupied by the trapshooter. Shore's eyes were narrowed in thoughtful consideration.

"By George," he said, with his hand on the knob of the door, "it doesn't seem possible. Of course, I know some of these gem thieves are pretty slick, but—"

He opened the door and stood on the threshold in dismay. His cabin was a complete mess. Trunks had been opened and the contents of the drawers dumped on the floor. Clothes had been jerked from hangers in the closet and thrown to the far end of the stateroom. Some of the leather bags had actually been cut in an attempt to expose false bottoms.

Sansone said, "What's this?"

Shore said, "I've evidently been robbed."

He entered the stateroom, walked rapidly across to one of the open drawers, took out a roll of currency, and a book of travelers' checks. He faced Sansone significantly. "The one who did it," he said, "wasn't looking for money."

Sansone said, "Come on. We're going to see the captain."

The captain received them in his stateroom, said, "Good afternoon, gentlemen. I wonder if you're acquainted with Mr. Leith, our amateur magician."

Leith was sitting in one of the leather-cushioned chairs.

"You're damn right we're acquainted with him," Sansone said. "He broke into Shore's cabin and—well, he stole—"

"Just a minute," the captain interrupted. *"Who* did you say stole what?"

"Mr. Leith—that is—"

"When was this done?" the captain asked.

Shore said, "Some time in the last half hour. It is now two thirty-five. I left my cabin at two o'clock. It was all right then."

The captain looked at his watch and said, "Mr. Leith has been with me for the last forty-five minutes. We chatted until two o'-clock when the skeet shooting started. We walked back along the boat deck, saw some of the blue rocks being broken, then came back here, and sat down. Now then, if you gentlemen have anything to report, report it, but I'll thank you to refrain from making any unfounded accusations."

The men exchanged glances. Shore, somewhat crestfallen, said, "Well, someone broke into my cabin and wrecked it looking for something."

"I'll go with you," the captain said, "at once. You'll pardon me, Mr. Leith?"

"Certainly," Leith said.

The three men walked off. A few moments later Leith strolled down to his own cabin. He opened the door, glanced inside, and then walked back down to where the captain was appraising the damage in Shore's stateroom. "Pardon me," he said. "I don't like to interrupt, but if you gentlemen think *this* cabin is a mess, come take a look at mine. . . ."

The island of Oahu showed as a jagged outline against the sky. The ship, passing Koko Head, swung past Diamond Head and the beach at Waikiki.

A short time later the gangplank had been stretched and the passengers, many of them wearing garlands of fragrant leis made of vividly colored tropical flowers, surged down. Beaver said, "Just a minute, your hat, sir."

He took Leith's hat and brushed off an imaginary speck of dust. Surreptitiously pinning a small bow of white ribbon to the crown, he replaced the hat on Leith's head.

A moment later, Leith was swept down the gangplank. As he paused at the foot, a hand touched his shoulder and an official voice said, "One moment, please."

It was an hour later that Sergeant Ackley, accompanied by a jubilant Beaver, walked into a jewelry store in Honolulu.

"We want this necklace of pearls appraised," Sergeant Ackley said. "In fact, you'd better appraise both of them."

The jeweler examined the necklaces, then he looked up at the two men.

"Well?" Sergeant Ackley asked.

"Worth about five dollars," the jeweler said.

"For which one?" Beaver demanded.

"For both," the jeweler said.

Stunned, the two conspirators looked at each other, then silently took their spoils to another jewelry store. That jeweler studied the pearls under a magnifying glass, and was even less flattering in his appraisal. "About two dollars apiece," he said.

Leith lolled in the reclining chair on the *lanai* of his suite in the Royal Hawaiian Hotel and glanced out over Waikiki Beach where tourists and beach boys were hissing their way into shore on surfboards.

"This," he said, "is the life."

"Yes, sir," the undercover man observed.

Leith said, "By the way, Scuttle, I ordered a gun today."

"A gun, sir?"

"Yes," Leith said, "a shotgun. I think I may run over to one of the other islands and get in a little shooting. It's rather an expensive gun. I think prices went up because of this international trapshooting contest which is being staged tomorrow. By the way, Scuttle, you'll never guess whom I met this afternoon."

"Who?" the undercover man asked.

"Sergeant Ackley."

"What's he doing over here?"

"I'm sure I don't know," Leith said, "but seeing him has made the islands suddenly distasteful to me. I've booked passage on the Clipper tomorrow. I'll fly back to the mainland. Ah, there's a ring at the door. It must be the shotgun."

"You'll hardly be using the shotgun if you're flying back to the mainland," the undercover man said. "Shall I tell them to take it back?"

"No, no," Leith said. "I told them I'd buy it, and I'll buy it. I'm a man of my word, Scuttle."

The undercover man signed a delivery slip and took it to Leith.

"Quite a beauty, isn't it?" Leith said.

"Indeed it is," the undercover man said worriedly. "Did Sergeant Ackley know you had seen him?"

"Oh, yes," Leith said. "I shook hands with him—although he seemed to want to avoid me. He said he'd been over here for two or three weeks, conferring with the local police department on a forgery case."

The valet started to speak, then checked himself.

The Clipper took off for the mainland with roaring motors, the hull dripping globules of water which scintillated like diamonds in the sun. Lester Leith waved good-bye to his valet.

That afternoon Silman Shore met an embarrassing defeat in the international skeet shoot, following which he was seen to inspect the gun he had found in his gun case; but he made no comment.

Katiska Shogiro, watching him with glittering eyes, was heard to break into a sudden string of Japanese expletives.

At five o'clock that night, Mah Foy sailed for China. In her purse was a certified check signed by Lester Leith. It bore the words, "Donation to the Chinese cause—less 20 percent for costs of collection."

It was a week after Beaver's return by passenger ship that Lester Leith, seated in his apartment, heard the sound of authoritative knuckles. The door opened even before Leith could signal his valet. Sergeant Ackley, accompanied by a uniformed officer, Charles Sansone, and Silman Shore, entered the apartment.

"Well, well," Leith said. "Good evening, gentlemen, we seem to be renewing a pleasant shipboard acquaintance. Did you come for—"

Sergeant Ackley said, "We came to make an investigation."

"Of what?" Leith asked.

"You purchased a shotgun while you were in Honolulu?"

"That's right," Leith said.

"Mr. Shore's shotgun was stolen while he was in the hotel in Honolulu. He feels that perhaps, in some unaccountable manner, the thief might have switched shotguns. He wants to see the shotgun which you took away with you on the Clipper."

"Indeed," Leith said, his eyes narrowing. "I think I've had all of Mr. Shore's veiled accusations I care for. If he wishes to make a charge, he can make it in the regular way—and he'd better be prepared to substantiate it."

"I'm not doing this," Shore said sullenly. "It's the sergeant who's responsible."

"Indeed," Leith said, arching his eyebrows. "I'm surprised, sergeant."

"You needn't be," Sergeant Ackley said. "Just bring out that shotgun."

"I'm afraid that's impossible."

"We can get a search warrant," Sergeant Ackley said threateningly.

"I'm afraid that wouldn't do you any good," Leith said.

"Don't stall," Sergeant Ackley accused. "You laid yourself wide open, Leith. The idea of a man carrying a shotgun with him on the Clipper!"

Leith smiled. "It *was* rather a foolish thing to do," he said. "Do you know, sergeant, I became ashamed of myself. I found myself getting enthused when I saw Mr. Shore's performance on the *Monterey,* but after I had a chance to see the wonderful panorama of the islands unfolded beneath the Clipper, as we flew over Oahu, I realized that I didn't want to indulge in any sport which would mean the taking of life. . . . I waited until the ship was about halfway across, and then pitched that shotgun overboard."

"You threw it overboard!" Shore exclaimed.

"Exactly," Leith said, "and that's why a search warrant would do you no good, sergeant."

The men exchanged glances. Shore said, "I guess that's all you want of me, sergeant." He turned and left the apartment. A moment later, Charles Sansone silently followed.

Sergeant Ackley stood staring down at Leith. "Damn you," he said, "you had it all figured out. When you flashed that necklace in your exhibition of magic and Shogiro identified it, Shore got up and dashed to his stateroom. It's significant that he picked up his gun and inspected it. Later on, his stateroom was thoroughly searched by Shogiro, who had tumbled to what happened after he'd searched your stateroom and found nothing. That necklace wasn't concealed *in either place!* There was only one other place it could be, one thing which wasn't in the room when Shogiro searched it—and that was Shore's shotgun. By removing the plate in the end of the butt, there was a hollow where a necklace could easily have been concealed."

Leith blinked. "By George, sergeant," he said, "a man *could* conceal a necklace there."

"Could and did," Sergeant Ackley said.

Leith lit a cigarette, then looked up at Sergeant Ackley with a disarming smile.

"Clever of you, sergeant," he said. "Isn't it a shame you didn't think of it before?" Leith said musingly, "And to think I pitched that gun overboard. Do you *really* think there was any chance the guns could have been substituted, sergeant?"

Sergeant Ackley fumed.

"Tut, tut," Leith said. "You mustn't be that way, sergeant. In your profession, it's easy to make mistakes. You must figure things on a give-and-take basis."

Sergeant Ackley's face was twisted with emotion. "Yes," he said, "and you do all the taking."

Following which, he left, slamming the door behind him with great violence.